"I'm attracted to you,"

Chris told Raylene without hesitation.

"Then, you're saying…?"

"If it's a proposal, I accept…but there are a couple of things I need to clarify. My priorities don't lie solely with work." He bit back a smile when her eyes went round. "And, if we're going to do this right, we're going to live together, correct?"

She fidgeted. "I don't know. I hadn't gotten that far."

"Would it surprise you if I said I had?"

"You?"

"Me," he confirmed, never blinking an eye. "And I'd be proud to be Katie's father, and your husband. But not in name only. If we do this, we do it all the way. My only stipulation is that we have a real marriage—in the bedroom and out."

Dear Reader,

In Arlene James's *Desperately Seeking Daddy*, a harried, single working mom of three feels like Cinderella at the ball when Jack Tyler comes into her life. He wins over her kids, charms her mother and sets straight her grumpy boss. He's the FABULOUS FATHER of her kids' dreams—and the husband of hers!

Although the BUNDLE OF JOY in Amelia Varden's arms is not her natural child, she's loved the baby boy from birth. And now one man has come to claim her son—and her heart—in reader favorite Elizabeth August's *The Rancher and the Baby*.

Won't You Be My Husband? begins Linda Varner's trilogy HOME FOR THE HOLIDAYS, in which a woman ends up engaged to be married after a ten-minute reunion with a bad-boy hunk!

What's a smitten bookkeeper to do when her gorgeous boss asks her to be his bride—even for convenience? Run down the aisle!...in DeAnna Talcott's *The Bachelor and the Bassinet*.

In Pat Montana's *Storybook Bride*, tight-lipped rancher Kody Sanville's been called a half-breed his whole life and doesn't believe in storybook anything. So why can't he stop dreaming of being loved by Becca Covington?

Suzanne McMinn makes her **debut** with *Make Room for Mommy*, in which a single woman with motherhood and marriage on her mind falls for a single dad who isn't at all interested in saying "I do"...or so he thinks!

From classic love stories, to romantic comedies to emotional heart tuggers, Silhouette Romance offers six wonderful new novels each month by six talented authors. I hope you enjoy all six books this month—and every month.

Regards,

Melissa Senate,
Senior Editor

Please address questions and book requests to:
Silhouette Reader Service
U.S.: 3010 Walden Ave., P.O. Box 1325, Buffalo, NY 14269
Canadian: P.O. Box 609, Fort Erie, Ont. L2A 5X3

THE BACHELOR
AND THE BASSINET

DeAnna Talcott

Silhouette®

R O M A N C E™

Published by Silhouette Books

America's Publisher of Contemporary Romance

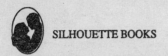

SILHOUETTE BOOKS

ISBN 0-373-19189-8

THE BACHELOR AND THE BASSINET

Books by DeAnna Talcott

Silhouette Romance

The Cowboy and the Christmas Tree #1125
The Bachelor and the Bassinet #1189

DEANNA TALCOTT

lives in Michigan where her three school-age children
fill her outside-writing hours with swimming, diving,
baseball, basketball, wrestling, 4-H and scouting activities. Her husband has a career in law enforcement,
and she fondly dubs him a "professional volunteer"
during his off hours. Together, they enjoy making pil-
grimages to her childhood home near Lincoln,
Nebraska, where DeAnna grew up riding horses and
attending a one-room schoolhouse. As graduates of the
University of Nebraska at Lincoln, both she and her
husband remain avid Big Red fans.

You are cordially invited

to witness the marriage (of convenience) of

Raylene Rafco

(New mother of an adorable baby girl)

and

Christian Jennings

(Staunchly opposed to marriage, but

willing to say "I do" for the baby's sake)

Saturday, May 27 at 9:30 am

The Fireside Room at Bell's Inn

(Bridal—or baby—gifts accepted)

Chapter One

Raylene Rafco let herself into the shop, stoically dismissing her reason for arriving half an hour early for work. She refused to dwell on it. To do so, to think about her baby, would only ignite the pain and make the whole situation more intolerable.

She methodically wiped her feet on the grass mat inside the front door, listening to her boss, Christian Jennings, putter around in the back room. Through puffy eyes, the showroom full of handcrafted furniture blurred and went out of focus. At least the smells were the same. Slipping out of her winter coat, she let the distinctive scent of wood shavings, of pine and walnut and oak, soothe her ragged nerves. Funny how the smells of this old converted warehouse, of fresh-sawed lumber, of paint and stain and varnish, calmed her.

In the six months that she'd worked here, this place, with its wide plank floors and the tin-paneled ceiling, had become more than a business. It had become a refuge. And an important part of that was the comfort of hearing Chris work.

Chris's plane stopped its rhythmical slide. "That you, Raylene?"

"Yes. I'm early, I know." She raised her voice just enough to reach him, before dropping her shoulder bag on the counter. She paused, realizing that, as happy as she was to be among familiar things, her insides recoiled at the thought of another morning hunching over the books, poking keys on the adding machine. She had other, more hideous things on her mind.

She hesitated, listening, wishing he'd come out and talk. He'd done that once. Only once. He'd made a few remarks about the cold weather, then solicited her advice on a tea-cart design. She'd sworn up and down that she didn't know anything about tea carts, but he'd shrugged that off, and taken her advice anyway.

But not before he made some lame remark about her hair being the same color as walnut.

God, she wanted him to come out and talk. It didn't matter what he said. He could compare her to a tree stump, for all she cared. She only wanted to hear another human voice, one that drowned out the thrumming ache in her heart. She had to get the anxiety, the frustration, out of her system.

She had to tell him what she'd done. And then she had to expect the worst.

She cocked her head, listening. Listening. His plane resumed its *whoosh-whoosh* over the wood.

Her shoulders sagged with resignation, and she knew she had to tell him. She had to tell him now, before the uncertainty increased, before the catastrophe became even more complicated. "Chris?"

She detected a lapse in his plane, yet heard nothing else.

The half door between the showroom and workroom was ajar, and she moved to it, stepping inside. The soles of her shoes, on the rubber-matted floor, didn't make a sound. Raking her palms over her wool pants, she reminded herself that she owed him a logical, rational explanation. Nothing more.

"Excuse me, Chris? I need to talk with you."

He looked up, reluctantly dragging his gaze from the length of wood in the vise. He started to unscrew it, not so much looking at her as through her. Even now he was detached, his thumb lovingly stroking the spot he'd most recently worked.

Raylene concentrated on the piece, recognizing it as the cornice for the Andersens' bookcase. "I thought you'd finished that."

"Mmm... I made another. Wasn't satisfied with the fit."

"Oh."

He waited, turning it in his hands, as if getting the feel of it. Then: "Problems?"

He studied her from beneath his brow. Piercing blue eyes, in a sensitive, thoughtful face. Scandinavian features, that was Christian Jennings. Blond hair that was a little too long—it always was—and always fell forward, brushing the tops of his ears, one recalcitrant lock flicking over his forehead. His jaw was taut, and typically hard. He carried an edge about him, one that made it perfectly clear that he didn't want to be bothered, not even by the customers who clamored for his work.

"I... That is..." She hesitated, feeling as if she should be flogged for even intruding into his workroom. "There's a problem. With an order I placed?"

His thumb stopped the rhythmic circles it was making over the wood. "Talk to my sister. She deals with unsatisfied customers." He shifted back onto one hip and returned his attention to the cornice, holding it up to the ceiling to see if it was straight.

"I can't."

He turned his head again, lowering the wood, no longer an artisan practicing his craft. His mouth, typically sensuous and full when working, thinned. The sculptured cheek above his square jaw thumped.

Raylene imagined she'd jump right out of her skin if he looked at her cross-eyed. He was going to go off like a rocket. She knew it. "The thing is, um, this is sort of between us."

"Us?"

She heard his meaning. *Us? There is no us.* "There's a problem."

"And?"

"The order on the balloon crib needs to be canceled. I'm sorry. But something's come up, and I..."

His blue eyes darkened. Raylene had the distinct impression all hell was about to break loose.

"That crib's almost done! I have a no-returns policy. You call them back, and you remind them the contract they signed has a no-refunds-no-returns clause, and you tell them—"

She nodded frantically. But her gaze unwillingly drifted back to the unfinished crib. It was propped up against the far wall. Yesterday he'd stained the balloons routered into the headboard in delicate shades of cranberry and dusky blue.

Last night she'd gotten the news.

Last night she'd known it was all over. Motherhood was an elusive illusion. "I know, I know. I—"

"Then do it."

"But, Chris—"

"Do it."

"I can't!" she practically wailed.

When she heard herself—and when he heard her—they both stopped, staring, as if a gauntlet had been tossed down between employer and employee.

He paused, disbelieving. "What?"

"I said, I can't." The look he gave her was riveting. It also sent shivers over her skin.

"I don't do business on spec. Handmade custom stuff only. On contract. You know that."

"Chris, I'm sorry."

"How about if you quit apologizing, and make the call? Explain the policy."

"That's the problem. I don't need to explain the policy. I already know the policy."

"Okay. Who ordered it?" he demanded, tossing the cornice on the workbench, as if it were suddenly contaminated.

Tell him! Tell him now! a small voice urged.

Raylene wanted to comply, she ached to comply, and her mouth slipped open, but a hot lump of anguish sprouted in her throat, threatening to choke her. Her mind was full of explanations, excuses, pleas. Words quavered indecisively on her tongue.

"I—" Both shoulders lifted apologetically. She nearly strangled on the words. "I—I did. I ordered it."

"You?"

"Yes. I ordered the crib, for me."

He stared at her, briefly. Sure, the shock of her revelation had effectively extinguished the ire in his eyes. Then he dropped his gaze to the flat of her belly. He stood transfixed. When he glanced back up at her, his mouth twisted. "You're pregnant," he said finally, simply.

The assumption floored her. "No!"

"Raylene. Thirty-year-old bookkeepers do not go around getting their jollies by ordering cribs. Most of them go to the Crazy Horse on Friday nights, and the Purple Plum on Saturdays. They—"

"No. Honestly. It's not that, it's that I—" She struggled, between ragged breaths, to organize a plausible explanation. "I already have a baby," she blurted out, blinking back unshed tears.

"You what?" He swiveled toward her and, with his back ramrod-straight, laid the plane aside, on its blade.

He didn't notice. But Raylene did.

"You have a *what?*"

He asked it incredulously, as if she'd just revealed that her baby was a space alien. For the first time since she'd started working for Chris, she knew he saw her. All of her. From the top of her blunt-cut hair to the soles of her everyday work shoes. He peered into her eyes as if he were seeing something other than their mud-brown irises.

It was unnerving, that intense, all-pervading look. A coiling sensation zigzagged through her loins.

She tried to ignore it, tried to pull herself together. But she couldn't quite manage it. Her eyes went watery, and her chin quivered. "I—I have a baby."

"My God. What am I running here? A home for unmarried moms? Between you and Beth and—"

Raylene's face fell. Tears sparked in the corners of her eyes. They came to life slowly, painfully. And they matched the speed with which Chris moved toward her.

"Hey. Hey, I'm sorry. I mean, you and Beth . . ."

She witnessed his hesitant steps through a kind of tunnel vision. When he was a foot away, she picked up the scent of turpentine and wood glue.

Chris. Only Chris could smell like that. The smell evoked soothing impressions she associated only with him.

"Damn, I can't believe this. You have a baby?" His hand, above her elbow, eased her toward him. His touch was warm, prompting a tingle to scamper over her flesh.

She nodded, swallowing hard.

"No. You *had* a baby?"

She avoided his searching look, blinking and biting back the total loss of her composure. "No. Not exactly."

"Not exactly? Then what?"

"I adopted a baby."

His grasp tightened suddenly, as if he'd like to shake her. "You what?"

Raylene stiffened.

The pressure from his fingertips immediately faded, but the spot above her elbow still went numb. He absently circled her flesh with his thumb, as he'd done with the grain on the cornice mere moments before.

A single tear trickled down her cheek. She looked away, but not before he saw it, and not before the salt of it burned into her flesh. "I adopted a baby." She choked the words out, lifting a convulsing shoulder to wipe away the moisture. Her gold chain bit coldly into her chin as a dark, wet spot stained her plaid shirt. "Three weeks ago."

He hesitated, confusion and indecision mottling his blue gaze. "Why didn't you tell me?"

"I'm sorry. I never thought you'd be—" her thoughts went muddy, making her grope for the right word "—interested. I never thought it would matter." He didn't reply, but his hand fell from her arm. "I mean, this is only a part-time job. I'm only here three mornings a week, and I—"

"You had me making that piece, and I didn't even know it."

She heard accusation in his voice, and feebly shrugged it off. "I know. I didn't want it to make a difference."

"Well, it does. Especially now, doesn't it?"

"Look, I said I was sorry. I know it's expensive, I know you put a lot of time into it. But I'll pay for it. Really. Only...I can't have it at the apartment. I can't. And if you don't want to finish it, I'll understand. In fact, I'll—"

"Why'd you do it?"

She looked up, her confusion matching his. "What?"

"Why'd you adopt the baby?"

The old shame suffused her, inexplicably making all rational explanations shrivel up and waste away. She'd thought she was past it, but it was still working its black magic, depleting her, making her feel imperfect, flawed. Rather than face his curiosity, she looked down, at the pile of sawdust beneath the radial-arm saw, at the scuffed toes of his work boots.

He wanted details, intimate details. Details that had successfully ravaged her self-concept for the past three horrific years. Details she wasn't emotionally prepared to share.

"For God's sake, woman, you're young. You've got a life ahead of you. What're you doing adopting a baby?"

She railed inwardly against his premature judgments, shaking herself free from all the pain, from all the loss that was turning her inside out. "Because it's my life, Christian Jennings! And because that's what I want. A family. A—"

He snorted, his attention snapping to the dozens of ceiling-high windowpanes before summarily flicking back to her. "Right. You're what? All of thirty? Big deal. And you're strapping yourself with the responsibility of being a single mother? C'mon... Don't you see how my sister struggles?"

All her pent-up fury and hostility flared. It went off inside her chest, radiating outward like an explosion. Her normally serene features writhed into a contorted mask of rage at the injustice of his reaction. Her arms flailed, and she poked a finger squarely into his chest, forgetting discretion.

"Maybe I want the same thing she's got!"

"Beth was barely eighteen when she had Tyler," he snapped, drawing away. "She juggled part-time jobs, night school, doctor's appointments and finances. And she's still doing it. You don't know what she's given up."

"I know I've got twelve years on her, Chris. I'm financially comfortable, and I made the decision because I thought I was ready."

"You don't know what you're getting into."

"I don't know why you're being so hostile. I only wanted to talk with you about the crib, not about—"

"Just tell me. Why'd you do it?"

"Because I felt like I didn't have a choice."

"What?"

As painful and humiliating as it was, she was determined to sum it all up into one word, and spit it out like poison.

"Infertility."

He stared, then blanched. His mouth eventually worked, but he was at a loss for words.

"The doctor says it's unlikely I'll ever have children of my own."

"I'm sorry, but . . ."

She heard an imminent warning, and it fueled her. "Don't you get it?" she said emphatically, tears welling up again. "I felt like this was my chance. Maybe my only chance. How could I say no? I'm getting older, and the adoption waiting lists are miles long."

"You should've told me," he said gruffly, awkwardly hanging his arm across her shoulders and giving her a slight squeeze. She tensed, aware that up until today they'd never exchanged so much as a handshake. "Heck, maybe I'd have bought a baby gift or something. Maybe knocked a little off the crib."

She relaxed. The horrendous confrontation and admission were over. He'd learned that she wasn't a whole woman, and he'd handled it. No pity. No embarrassment over knowing it. She plastered a grim the-infertility-thing-doesn't-bother-me smile on her face.

He patted her arm, then cautiously withdrew, putting distance between them once again.

"Yeah. Right," she said, doing her best to nail him through blurry eyes. "Knock a little off the crib and have you give me a deal? I do your books. I know the profit margin." He issued one of his rare grins, effectively leveling her. "Who knows?" she went on, fighting to keep her voice even. "Maybe that's why I didn't tell you. You can't afford it."

He squelched the remains of the grin, but his gaze, brooding, lingered. "So?" he said finally, "What is it?"

"What?"

"The baby? What is it? A boy or girl?"

"Oh. A girl. I have a girl. A three-week-old girl."

His lower lip firmed as he resisted emotion. "She got a name?"

"Kate."

"Mmm . . . Nice."

"I named her after my grandmother, even though . . . well, even though she isn't biologically part of my family tree. My brother thought that was a bit crazy. But—" she hesitated "—there's this . . . this other problem. . . ."

He nodded, his gaze casting over to the unfinished crib.

"I'm sorry to do this," she repeated, swallowing back the weariness, the bitterness. "I am. I never should've ordered it, but I'll find a buyer—I promise I will, if you'll give me the time."

"You don't like it—"

"No! It's not that."

"You need it right away. God, she's not sleeping in a dresser drawer, is she? Because I can—"

"No! I borrowed a bassinet."

He scrunched up his unlined face. "God. Not one of those awful things? Beth had one, and the neighbor's dog knocked it over. If Tyler'd been in there—"

"The bassinet's only temporary."

"Forget it. I'm finishing the crib this week." He reached back, picked up the cornice and thoughtfully tapped it against his palm. "Call the Andersens and tell them it'll be another few days on the bookcase, and then—"

"Chris? You don't get it. I can't take the crib. I can't."

A shiver of trepidation skittered up Raylene's spine when he frowned at her. Easy explanations were impossible. If Chris had been a believer in the Fates, she could simply have conceded that they were all in cahoots, determined to strip her of what she wanted most: motherhood and apple pie.

But what could she say to this solitary man, a man whose body housed a wealth of creativity, yet who willingly chose to live within the parameters of distance and cool reserve? There were times when Raylene thought the inside and outside of him were like fire and ice, diametrically opposed.

"I'll have no use for it," she said evenly, vaguely aware that her hands were twisted around the belt buckle at her middle.

"Those silly little bassinets don't have a life span. Why, they—"

She closed her eyes and put her back to him as shudders of anguish racked her. "Don't." She forced herself to look into the showroom, through the huge plate-glass windows and out onto Webster Avenue. Everything was the same. Everything but her life.

The locals were still gossiping at Nikki's Kut 'n' Kurl. The antique dealer was still gluing together bits of her incredible finds and hoping for a nearsighted customer. The waitresses over at Dillon's were crabbing about getting stiffed on their tips because Wednesday was senior citizens' day.

Life in Stronghurst, Michigan was predictable. For everyone but her.

"Believe me on this, Chris. I can't take the crib."

"I told you, if it's the money—"

"No!"

Seconds elapsed. "Then what?"

When she finally replied, her voice was raspy and hoarse. "I won't need it. I just got a phone call. I'm losing my baby, and it looks like there's nothing I can do to stop it from happening."

Chapter Two

"There's something wrong with the baby," Christian said.

"Wrong? No! No, she's perfect. She's happy, she's healthy. I love her. I—" Try as she might, Raylene couldn't stem the grief spiraling through her. She hurt all over; she ached. Sorrow, for what she had and for what she would never know, consumed her.

Strong hands caught her convulsing shoulders, steadying them. That surprised her as much as the fact that she was falling apart again. "Hey. Sit down."

"I'm okay."

"So sit down anyway."

He guided her—or pushed her—to the table and chairs in the back corner of his workshop. No fancy stuff here. Pea-green Formica and chrome, rejects he'd salvaged from the sidewalk café two doors down. Chairs he'd never invited her to sit on, a table he'd never invited her to use.

"You need a cup of coffee."

She awkwardly sank onto the offered seat, all the while protesting. "You don't have to—"

"We're not getting any work done, anyway."

Typical. Only Chris would put work above all else. She'd just shared her most intimate problems with him, and his internal time clock was still ticking to the beat of *work, work, work.*

"I didn't come in here to burden you with this, Chris. You're busy, I know that. But I needed to settle the matter of the crib, that's all."

"Consider it settled," he said, sweeping aside his sketches and pushing them together haphazardly, as if they were fifty-two cards in a loose deck. Raylene watched as the sketches for the whimsical toy chest for the Brannigan children and the display case for Mrs. Jenkins's antique thimbles disappeared into the jumble.

Lives mingled with requests; Chris shoved them all together as if they were nothing.

He moved along the wall of the makeshift kitchen he'd tucked into his workroom. He did his designs here, he took his lunch here, and, by unspoken agreement, this was an area off-limits to anyone else. Raylene never saw him come or go from the apartment he'd fashioned in the northwest corner of the building. To her knowledge, he spent every moment in his shop.

Slipping two mugs off their pegs, he pushed them under the tap, rinsing off the dust before filling them. Then he tore off a couple of paper towels, crunching them against the handles before carrying the whole mess to the table.

Depositing a mug of steaming coffee in front of her, Chris arched a brow. "Better?"

"Yes. Thanks." She flattened the rumpled paper towel with her fingertips, then wiped the corners of her eyes with the back of her wrist. "I'm trying. I'm really trying. I know it doesn't seem like it."

"I thought you were going hysterical on me."

"I felt like it."

He looked at her uncertainly. "Need a tissue?"

"No." But she sniffed involuntarily. "I'll be okay. Really."

"You sure?"

"Yeah."

Uncomfortable silence hovered between them. Chris eventually sank a spoon into his coffee, scraping it across the bottom. "Oh." He looked up, startled. "Maybe cream? Sugar?"

"No. No. Black's fine." She looked down at the shimmering surface, thinking that fresh-sawed wood and coffee complemented each other.

"It probably doesn't matter," he said. "You're not going to drink it anyway."

She didn't look up from the scarred tabletop, but her fingers curled around the mug as she consciously chased away the cold feeling coming straight from her soul. His kindness warmed her as much as the coffee. "No. Probably not. Feels good, though."

He nodded, saying nothing.

He'd refuse to ask or pry. He'd wait it out. She knew that. It was up to her to tell him the facts. Calmly. Without another brilliant display of emotion. She took a deep breath, praying for a new show of strength. "The birth mother wants her baby back."

He stared at her, his blue gaze penetrating, his head slightly tilted. "She changed her mind?"

"No. Not really. Only about me."

Chris lifted a quizzical brow. "You?"

"Yeah. There's not two of me. She wants Kate in a two-parent home." Raylene lifted the coffee, saw the steam whirling away into thin air, and thought of how Kate would drift away from her in exactly the same manner. She'd never know how much she'd been loved; Raylene alone would mourn her loss. "Her mother'll take her away from me and give her to someone else— a couple who can be mom and dad to her. That's why I don't need the crib," she said carefully, slowly. "The birth mother had second thoughts about me being a single parent."

"That's crazy."

"Not if you were raised without a father figure."

The way she phrased it provoked him, reminded him. I should've been, he wanted to say. Instead, he said, "Tyler's—"

"Tyler's got you."

Right. The truth was, he'd been winging it on that score from day one. Sometimes he looked at the kid and actually saw where he'd failed.

Nope, there was no father figure for him, Christian Jennings, to emulate. For him, it was a stab in the dark.

His old man had been a closet drunk. He'd done his forty hours a week on a forklift at the factory. At night and on the weekends, he'd systematically converted his paycheck into an alcoholic haze.

There'd been ranting. There'd been raving. There'd been drunken stupors, and humiliating moments.

His mother had done what she could. But the best she'd ever managed was to keep up the old man's life insurance. And thank God he'd died from an accidental death, rather than cirrhosis of the liver.

"I'm not the best example there is," he finally muttered, avoiding her eyes.

"Still..."

"Still." Remember, he thought, these are her problems, this is her pain.

"Kate's birth mother didn't think it mattered at first, but then her dad heard she had a baby and came back into her life. Ah, yes," she said, sarcasm lacing her voice, "her long-lost dad. Come to turn my life inside out."

"He wants her to keep the baby."

"No. He claims he just wants to get to know his daughter again. It's made her rethink her priorities. Suddenly she sees the value of a two-parent family."

Chris grimaced, remembering how thrilled Beth had been to learn that she was pregnant. And she'd been an eighteen-year-old widow. Hormones and instincts turned a woman's life upside down. Utter the word *baby* and a woman started feathering the nest. "So? Can't she have the family affair from here on out? Why's it have to affect the baby now?"

"I don't know. Maybe seeing her father again made all the old pain come back. She started remembering how much she'd missed him, how much she wanted him around. So she's decided she wants a dad for her baby. A real dad."

A real dad. Sure. The ideal dad, who's sober enough to lever himself off the couch once in a while. With hands steady enough to tie ice skates. One who can take his kid to the dairy store for ice cream, instead of to the liquor store for vodka.

"Havin' a dad shouldn't make the difference," he told her.

"Looks like, in this adoption, it does."

"Forget it, Raylene. The girl ought to know you'd all be better off without one."

She snorted, her shoulders vibrating slightly. Suddenly he was glad she hadn't recognized the bitterness in his voice.

"Convince her."

He shook his head imperceptibly, clearly saying that he wasn't getting involved. "So. How'd you hook up with this crew, anyway? Some adoption-agency screwup?"

"No. Accident. Sheer accident." She took a tranquilizing draw on her coffee, her fingers meshing around the mug. "I met the birth mother at my doctor's office. She was fifteen, pregnant, and scared. We started talking, and pretty soon she was pouring her heart out to me. How her boyfriend had brought her up from Ohio so her mother wouldn't find out, thinking that maybe they were wrong, that maybe she wasn't pregnant. How he'd tried to get her to have an abortion. It was hard to hear, especially since I knew I'd— well, I'd never have..."

Chris nodded when she hesitated. Hell, she didn't need to say it a second time. One thing he understood was hurt, and he'd learned that the best way to deal with it was to keep it under wraps.

He'd been eleven when he first figured out you had to push the hurt out of your life, you had to deny it, and then it became almost inconsequential. It had been the last day of baseball cuts, and his dad had locked him in his room for tipping over a glass of milk. Because of that, he'd lost his place on the team. The coach had brushed him aside afterward, telling him to forget it, that he didn't need a kid with an attitude, a kid too lazy to make tryouts.

He'd never tried out for another team; he'd never talked about it.

No use crying over spilt milk.

"Anyway," Raylene went on, unaware of the memory twisting his gut, "she asked the doctor about me, and I guess, from something he said—or maybe something I said—she guessed about my condition. Maybe the chemistry was right. But right then and there, the birth mother decided she wanted me to have her baby. She wanted the doctor to arrange it."

"And everything was fine until her father came back."

"Everything was fine."

The silence was so profound, he could identify the grinding effort of the second hand of the old clock over the workbench.

"I keep thinking, maybe, if I can hold on long enough, it'll all blow over. I keep thinking maybe the birth mother will change her mind. She's got her father back. Maybe, in the end, that'll make it easier for her to give up the baby."

Not likely. Not with a dad to prod her along, to make her feel guilty every time she tried to please him.

"You think you can hold on long enough to see that happen?"

"I don't know. Right now, my lawyer's advised me to consider myself a temporary caregiver, and that's all. I've stopped calling myself Mommy, and every time I rock Katie, I'm torn between spending every last minute with her and steeling myself against loving her.''

"But you've got custody."

"For as long as it lasts. The birth mother's saying she'll refuse to sign the final adoption papers."

"But the courts would surely—"

"No. No, they wouldn't. Because it was a private adoption—and those are illegal in Michigan—they'll most likely rule against me." The confusion over the legal tangle must have shown on his face. "Since Kate was born in Ohio, all the paperwork has to be done there."

He paused, thoughtfully pulling the spoon from his coffee. It was a little like when his dad had encouraged him to scratch the name off the ball glove he'd found by the bleachers. Of course, doing so had freed up another twenty bucks for liquor, but it had also provided him with a much-needed glove. He distinctly remembered being torn about wanting something— even when that something wasn't his.

"Possession's ninety percent of the law, Raylene."

"So they say. But I don't think I can face losing in court. My lawyer has guaranteed it, so I'd only be prolonging the misery."

Somehow she'd come to hunch over the table, over the coffee, clinging to the cup as if it offered life support. He hated seeing her this way. She was a gem, and she didn't deserve to hurt like this.

"I mean, it'd kill me. It'd—"

"Then give her up now," he said firmly, decisively.

Raylene struggled to sit up, to focus. Her jaw slid off center. "I can't. I—"

"Maybe you think you want this baby, but—"

"I do!"

He ignored her declaration, determined to tell her what he should have told his sister when she was poor and pregnant and in a hopeless situation. "A year of uncertainty, of legal wrangling? The ups, the downs—it'll wipe you out. Physically and financially. I'm telling you. Cut your losses and cut yourself off. Protect yourself now, while you still can."

"God! What are you saying? You don't know anything about me, or... or how I feel... or..."

"I know this isn't the end of the world, Raylene. Other people function quite happily without children. There're other things, other ways to—"

"I don't want to *function!*" she snapped. "I want to feel! I want to keep my baby!"

"Do you?"

His rhetorical question stunned her. "Of course."

"And what if you lose?" He felt like a heel for saying it aloud. "What then? Would it be worth it?"

"Don't. I can't do this. I can't talk about it like this." She slid her chair back, and pushed her mug away.

"Raylene?" His palm covered her wrist, his thumb discovering the mad dashing of her pulse. He blotted out the feelings it evoked in him. "I'm not trying to be an ogre. But you need to think about how much you're willing to sacrifice. Take some time off from work and think about it."

She paused, considering. "I can't," she said, reluctantly letting her eyes drift closed, "I need the money."

"Then take this morning off," he wheedled, unconsciously stroking the inside of her arm. "Consider it a paid holiday. You need the break."

"I don't know...."

"Go ahead. But hey, here's the deal..." He didn't know why he wanted to make her smile, or why he even wanted to make her feel better. Something just seemed right about doing so. He gave her wrist a gentle squeeze before releasing it. "You come back on Friday, and like it or not, the crib'll be done. Bring the baby. We'll see how she fits."

"Oh, Chris—"

"No. I mean it. I've got this strange feeling it's all a moot point, that everything will work out."

He pasted a false smile on his face, and resisted the urge to tell her that this was the stupidest thing he'd ever heard of. To willingly adopt the responsibilities of a baby, and sacrifice yourself for a lifetime punctured with trouble?

What was it his dad always said? Kids were nothing but trouble.

The car was chilly, making Raylene huddle in her coat. She teased her daughter's lips with the baby bottle, then stared out the window at the deserted business district. Overhead, the handpainted sign Chris had once fashioned, now faded to strawberry pinks and folk-art blue, was buffeted by the early-morning breeze. The brass hooks suspending it from a four-by-four creaked beneath its weight.

A few lights were popping on in some of the shops, but the only place with much activity was Bagels 'n' Buns. Shopkeepers were carrying their coffee out in foam cups and their breakfasts in wax-coated white bags.

Stronghurst was a charming, comfortable place to raise a child, no doubt about that. From the outside, it was a fairy-tale existence.

It had recently been promoted as a quaint lakeside town where tourists flocked to buy fudge and steep themselves in ambience and antiques. Because of that, every holiday nurtured another wave of consumerism. The nearby community college provided an endless supply of minimum-wage laborers who tended shops and waitered and waitressed.

The curbs were too high, the brick streets too narrow. Every false-fronted building had been painted and primed, and gift shops and restaurants made a conscious effort to outdo one another. There were mullioned windows, shuttered windows and bay windows. There was gingerbread trim and there were flower boxes. In the summer, inviting sidewalk cafés, with striped canopies and ice-cream-parlour chairs, straddled every street corner. In the winter, the vacant lots were flooded and frozen for ice-skating, and sidewalk vendors with pushcarts popped up, selling brats and hot chocolate.

Oh, the smells were exceptional. The streets were always filled with them. Fresh-cut flowers in the spring, juicy ripe watermelons in summer, apples and spicy mulled cider during the fall, and the fragrance of hot gingerbread when snow dusted the streets. And, always, the scent of roasted peanuts and fudge.

Life in Stronghurst was a repetitive cycle, yet it was always exciting, always anticipated.

Christian Jennings had been raised here. Raylene had not.

In a way, she still saw the town as an outsider would. Maybe that was why she'd intentionally centered her bookkeeping efforts in the downtown area. She liked the pace. There were always dozens of small businesses clamoring for part-time clerical help. Often she'd just take the books and run. It had turned out to be a great way to juggle baby-sitters and jobs.

But Christian Jennings's Handcrafted Furniture Shoppe was different. His was a bigger, more unwieldy business than most. Her duties there ran the gamut from answering phones to helping clients. When she landed the job, she'd thought she'd snared the plum from the pudding. Ha! Little had she known it came with an emotional price tag.

Sure, Christian Jennings's furniture was known throughout mid-Michigan; the man behind the work was an enigma.

He was a hardworking gonna-have-it-all local entrepreneur and craftsman. Yet he went through life with blinders on, effectively shutting out the rest of the world.

His furniture spoke for him . . . and, yes, it said volumes. Cannonball beds and armoires, rolltop desks and sideboards. His expertise was adding flair to a simple little plate rack, or a dash of whimsy to a crib.

Ah, yes. The crib. The damnable crib. The real reason she was here, the real reason she'd brought the baby.

Thinking of it, Raylene saw everything, and yet she saw nothing.

Not the huge display windows beneath the three-foot overhang that Chris had decorated for Easter. Not the glass-and-panel front door, or the leaded-glass fanlight. Not even the brass mail slot that the mail carrier never used but toddlers were fascinated with. Not the dew that dampened the two stories of brick, or the outrageously tall, outrageously expensive double-armed street lamps on the sloped sidewalk outside the warehouse.

She couldn't think straight; she barely knew what she was doing.

Even Lake Syles, and the boat docks, shrouded in mist at the end of the street, reflected her mood: dismal.

She hadn't wanted to bring the baby in today. She'd lain awake half the night, worrying about what Chris might say.

So this is the kid you traded your life in for? Cute. I guess.

But it was more than the hollow words she expected from him. She railed against the torment of placing her baby in that crib. That crib was the epitome of her special, private dream. A bonneted boy and girl had been routered into the oak, their hidden faces gazing up into a cloudless sky, balloons in their hands, a puppy at their feet.

This baby was supposed to bring her motherhood. This baby was supposed to erase all her feelings of inadequacy. This adoption was supposed to make her life complete.

If all she was left with after this adoption thing was over was a crib and some shadowy memory, she'd go crazy.

She couldn't fathom an empty crib, or sheets stripped of the scent of baby powder. Blankets folded to be put away and stored, not rumpled and warm at the end of the mattress.

No matter what she tried to do to prevent it, a hodgepodge of mental souvenirs kept cropping up. Even while she kept chiding herself that this baby might be hers to have and hold, but not to keep.

Oh, God. She was going to lose Katie, she knew it.

Wearily clambering from the car, she put the baby bottle on the dash and lugged the car carrier over the driver's seat.

What the heck! She should just quit her job and put an end to all the uncertainty with Chris. He wasn't going to rally around her, he wasn't going be one of her supporters. She knew that. He'd as much as said she was nuts for even considering adoption.

Trudging past the window displays, she barely saw them. She knew what they contained. An oak bedstead, with the sheets turned back, a rocking chair, and, beyond, a crib. In her rational moments, she'd always thought the coupling of those items amusing.

What was Chris thinking? That one naturally led to the other?

Not in her case, she thought sourly, thoroughly anguished that she'd confided her inability to produce her own, biological child.

She paused long enough to glimpse up, hardheartedly remembering the day Chris had hung the mobile over the crib, the day he'd sent her out to Ye Olde Yarn Shoppe for a baby afghan to loop over the rocker's arm.

He'd puttered around in that display window for a good hour, tossing a velour robe across the foot of the bed and a baby kimono over the crib rail. He'd hung a picture on the side wall, and arranged silk greenery and daffodils in a crock next to the corner post. Raylene had been so mesmerized by his personal touch that she'd instinctively commented on it. Someone who was very happy, very content, must live in these rooms.

He'd glanced at her, sharply. It was just for effect, he'd said shortly. Then he'd angrily plopped a plush bunny at the end of the crib, and closeted himself in his workroom.

Today, Raylene could barely stand to look at the window. But she understood Chris's underlying message: It was an illusion, all of it.

Instead of going straight to her desk, she headed for the workroom, lifting the car seat to the ledge of the half door. Chris had once told her that the door was designed to keep inquisitive children out, yet give their parents a glimpse of where their furniture sprung to life.

Winding her arms securely around the car seat, she brushed her chin over Kate's fuzzy blanket and drank deeply of the mingled scents of baby powder and new lumber. As usual, his workroom was organized chaos.

Before she could look away, the crib loomed before her like an apparition. The oak gleamed, the brass fittings shone. There was a pink-sheeted mattress and a matching comforter, covered in eyelet and white lace.

Raylene had never seen anything more exquisite.

"Chris?"

From the corner of her eye, she saw him look up from his workbench. But she couldn't tear her gaze from the crib. It dominated the room, every other piece paling in comparison.

"Hey. Hello. I didn't hear you come in."

She recognized the smile in his voice. It made her feel good. Right down to the tips of her toes. "You usually don't."

"Okay, I confess. I get immersed." He paused expectantly. "Well? How do you like the crib?"

"It's incredible."

He snorted, as if the opinion had been inflated threefold. "C'mon in," he said easily. "You gonna criticize? Look for scratches, mistakes, flaws in the finish?"

"What?"

"You know. Like everyone else."

"Criticize? What's there to criticize? It's beautiful."

He hesitantly dropped a couple of wood screws in a drawer, then reached around to stick a screwdriver in his back pocket. "Kind of trite, huh?" The question was apologetic, and made her look at him, then hesitate. "The pink, I mean. For girls."

"Why, no. Not at all. It's lovely."

"Beth said you'd ream me out for it." He moved toward her, his eyes on the car carrier. "Sexist, and all that. Said women today are teaching their boys to be soft, and their girls to be hard."

She smiled involuntarily. "Sorry. I haven't gotten into all that yet. Right now, I'm just trying to do the right thing and hold on to her."

His tone changed perceptibly. "It's been two days. Heard anything?"

"The birth mother's petitioned for custody."

Both his brows lifted slightly, but the curious blue light in his eyes was drawn to Kate. It slipped over her pudgy cheeks, before pausing on her almond-shaped eyes and her black lashes. "Got a lot of hair."

"Too much." Raylene pushed back the blanket so that he could see more. "I call it the Mohawk we've tamed with Velcro and sticky bows. I tried putting one of those headband things on her yesterday, and it made her look like she'd fried her hair."

He grinned.

"But, you know, I love her just the same."

The grin disappeared as his gaze slowly drifted back up to her. It was disturbing how intensely he studied her. "Yes," he said finally, "I imagine you do."

Raylene wavered, aware that it felt much safer to continue with the earlier subject of conversation. "Nikki—at the Kut 'n' Kurl, down the street?—she assured me this hair thing's not permanent."

"I see. Probably bigger, more complicated problems later."

Seconds elapsed. "Probably."

She knew what he was getting at: the uncertainty of the adoption. Still, neither of them wanted to actually address that.

"Well. Long as she's here, you gonna try this thing out?" he suddenly asked. Before Raylene could answer, he lifted the carrier to the other side, into the workroom, and unlocked the door for her.

They both faced the crib as if it were an icon.

Wacky thoughts somersaulted through Raylene's head.

This was the crib Kate was supposed to feel secure in, these were the bars she was supposed to teethe upon, this was the mattress she was supposed to kick her feet against.

This was the crib Chris had made.

When she was a foot away from it, Raylene laid a reverent hand on the top rail. "You're a fine craftsman, Chris. I swear, a piece of you is in everything you make."

Chris's head swiveled in her direction, his expression going blank. She had the distinct impression that he was trying to decide whether the compliment was honest.

Then he moved, and did something totally unexpected. Putting the carrier on the floor, he awkwardly lifted the baby from it. Kate didn't even grumble about being disturbed. Chris lifted her against his shoulder, patting her on the back while his free hand turned down the expensive-looking pink-and-white comforter. Supporting the back of her head, he gently laid her on the clean sheets. "We're calling it even on the crib, Raylene."

"But—"

"No," he said firmly. "See? It's a perfect fit."

An unsteady gush of air whooshed from Raylene's lungs, making her light-headed. This was his way of validating the adoption.

"Take it," he said. "From me to you."

Chapter Three

Raylene was vaguely aware of the front door opening, but her mind was on the baby, and on the way Chris had offered her the crib. She'd hurt his feelings if she refused it, she knew that.

Behind her, Raylene heard footsteps and turned to see Chris's bright-eyed sister.

"So! This is the new baby!" Beth, framed within the doorway, beamed expectantly. With her blond hair closely cropped at her ears and flaring out like a crinoline skirt, her anticipation made her dimpled face even wider. "I dropped Tyler off at school, just so I could come by early, hoping I'd catch you."

Chris leaned both elbows on the end of the crib and glanced at his watch. "Thought you had a class."

"I do," Beth said, shrugging, lifting both brows. Her eyes were big and blue. Eyes that were exactly the same shade as her brother's. "So I'll be a little late."

"Beth..."

"Oh, shush. My instructor loves me. He calls me the mature woman of Psych 200." She quickly crossed the threshold into the workshop and started peeling off her coat. "Okay, okay, I'll confess. Having a fifth grader has aged me. But I'll still take anything that professor dishes out as a compliment. And in return, I even sit in the front row and hike my skirt higher than I should."

"Beth!"

"What?" she demanded. "If showing a little leg is going to help me ace that class, I've got no qualms about doing it. These days, a woman's got to take advantage of everything she's got."

"Talk about an example," Chris muttered. "If Tyler heard—"

"Oh, phooey! If Tyler heard," she repeated mimicking him. "Fact is, your nephew's in plenty heap-big trouble." She turned to Raylene while she hung her coat on the hook behind the door. "Know why he's been so preoccupied with recycling lately?"

Raylene shook her head.

"Ulterior motives. Last night I pulled a dozen magazines out from under his bed. And he's trying to tell me it's his duty to preserve this bunch of *Playboy* centerfolds? I don't think so." Raylene bit back the first smidgen of genuine humor she'd experienced in days. "I swear. Like they have to be salvaged like *National Geographic*s or something? Uh-huh. Sure. It was enough to make me go ballistic."

Raylene coughed over her amusement, imagining. Beth strode through life, alleviating the serious side with some snappy retort or wacky, distorted observation. The mother-son face-off had probably been some hullabaloo.

"Good God," she said, straightening her cuffs. "Never thought I'd make the recycling center off limits."

Chris grinned, yet said nothing, as he studied his sister from the corner of his eye.

"Okay. Enough of that," Beth said brusquely. "Let's get down to business here." She wedged herself between them at the crib's rail. "I didn't come here to talk about my kid, I came here to talk about yours." Her gaze passed over the baby, but it was a thorough inspection. "Oh, my God...she's beautiful, Raylene! Beautiful!"

Raylene slipped into her Madonna smile, feeling every inch the new mama.

Beth impulsively leaned over and tucked Kate's frilly collar beneath her chin, pausing before tickling her on the tummy. "And what do you think, huh?" she crooned. "Like your new padded cell, do you?"

In response, Kate merely yawned and stretched.

"Beth!"

"Aw, don't take it personally, Chris," she said, waving away his disbelief. "Psych class has altered my perceptions. From a clinical observation, what we really have here is a self-contained time-out arrangement. Bumpers and bars. To accommodate both mother and child." She nudged Raylene, confiding, "Take it from me, hon, they should have these when your kid's eleven. I mean it. I keep begging Chris to build me a cage."

Raylene grinned. "Tyler's not that difficult."

"Ha!"

"He can't be."

"Right. That kid's in one scrape after another, isn't he, Chris?"

"Well, rumor has it they're renaming the Valentine's Day Massacre after him."

Raylene winced, remembering the most recent debacle. Tyler had filched a piece of Chris's expensive walnut and hacked at it with a band saw to cut twenty-seven wooden hearts from it. One for every member of his class.

"If he'd done to his hand what he did to my blade and my lumber," Chris said dryly, "we'd have had a real mess, and an astronomical hospital bill."

Beth stiffened, and the air in the room suddenly turned icy. "It would have been enough to agree. Besides, I told you, I thought you were here." To Raylene, she said, "I told Tyler to come help Chris while I was studying. I never imagined he'd..." She abruptly flicked her hand, dismissing the matter. "Oh, well. That kid. If he's not getting into trouble, he's scaring off any man I bring home. I keep telling him, if he wants another brother or sister he's going to have to change his act, right?" Beth winked, her effusive energy picking up momentum again. "Hey, I can't stand this. Do you mind, Raylene? Can I pick her up?"

"Oh. Of course. We were just—" Raylene trailed a hand over the top rail "—you know, admiring the crib."

Beth lifted the baby, instinctively snuggling against her neck. "I know. Didn't my brother do a gorgeous job?"

"He did."

"He always does. You've got to give him credit for that, I guess, even if he's fixated on perfection."

"You do," Raylene said absently, staring into the grain of the wood and imagining the crib in her apartment, knowing it would be a daily part of her life, of her baby's life. She was taking a part of Chris home with her. Realizing that sent a ripple through her. "You're a marvelous craftsman, Chris."

He snorted and lifted a shoulder, obviously uncomfortable with the compliment. His forefinger rubbed a spot on one of the spindles, as if there were an invisible flaw.

For some inexplicable reason, Raylene matched his gesture, and ran the pads of her fingers over the top rail. The finish was slick and inviting, making her wonder how much stroking this piece had taken from him before it came to life. She'd never appreciate wood the way Chris did, but she sensed its warmth, its pulse. This piece was guaranteed to endure for generations.

Generations.

And exactly how much time did she have left with Kate?

Would she ever be able to look at the crib afterward, or would it symbolize everything that had been taken from her?

"I thought Chris was going to work himself into a frenzy in order to get it finished for today."

Beth's observation startled her. She lifted her head—just in time to see Chris blanch. "He didn't need—"

"Not according to him."

"I told you," he reminded his sister, frowning as he rearranged the comforter, "she had the baby sleeping in a bassinet."

"Mmm... And that's a no-no, isn't it?" Beth asked, before burrowing her nose beneath Kate's plump cheek. "Mmm... She smells so good, Raylene. Oh, man, I'd give anything for another one of these. God, I want another baby so bad."

"Get a grip," Chris said, his eyes narrowing as he straightened and pushed himself away from the crib. "You can't even take care of the one you've got."

"Oh, for heaven's sake, Chris."

"Well, you can't."

Beth sighed, her arms winding protectively tighter around Kate as she rubbed the round hump of her back. "Ignore this old scrooge, Raylene. And no matter what he says or does, you hang on to this baby."

Raylene swept a surreptitious glance to Chris. Obviously he'd had no qualms about voicing his opinion that she should give the baby up. His eyes, still big and blue, shuttered closed, revealing nothing.

"I plan to hang on to her. At least I'm going to wait it out for the time being. Just to see if the birth mother's having second thoughts or if she's serious."

"Do it," Beth advised, her voice strangely subdued, as she exchanged a glance with Chris. "Two-parent families aren't all they're cracked up to be."

"Even so, it's what the birth mother wants."

"Oh, what does she know? She's just a kid."

"Maybe. But I used to think I knew what I wanted, too. Now, with all this uncertainty, I wonder. Maybe I'm the one who's wrong, maybe I'm the one who's selfish, thinking I needed to be a mother." It was eerie, the way she could feel Chris's eyes on her. Because he said nothing, she figured he was thinking that she was groveling for sympathy, for support. "I know, I know. I should do what's best for her. But—"

"Fight for her, Raylene. Every kid deserves the best."

"Still, there are things a father could give her—"

"Put it out of your mind, Raylene," Chris interjected. "The best things don't always come in pairs."

Raylene stared at him, bewildered, and wondered what, exactly, he was telling her. To go for it? To do anything she had to to keep custody?

"So what if you're single? That shouldn't matter. Don't let that influence your decision."

"What decision? I'm not sure I even have a decision." Raylene reached out, automatically smoothing a wrinkle from Kate's receiving blanket. "I have the strangest feeling that there's something about this that's preordained."

Beth sobered and automatically handed her the baby. Kate curled up against her breast, her limbs coiling into a tight, warm bundle.

"Well, hang in there, girl," Beth offered. "Maybe we'll think of something, and change fate. You know, find you a nice husband or something."

"Oh, gee, thanks."

"Hey, why not? I mean, if it'll fulfill the requirement?"

Raylene's glance collided with Chris's.

He hastily looked away.

In a flash, she knew what he was thinking. He was single; she was single. And the two shall meet as one.

Oh, no. Never in a million years. But the thought was already there.

"So, anyway, I'm going to work on it," Beth went on, oblivious of the awareness ricocheting around her. "Oh, and Chris?"

"Yeah?" he replied, too quickly. His voice was too deep, too garbled, as if he had a frog in his throat.

Raylene fiddled with the baby's pacifier. It was all she could do to look unconcerned.

"I know I said I wouldn't ask you this again...."

"Oh, boy." He yanked a hand over his face, his thumb poking into an eye socket.

"I think Tyler's hanging out with the wrong crowd. Will you talk to him? He always listens to you."

A long, low and very exasperated whistle scuttled between his teeth. "Yeah, sure. I guess."

"Thanks."

"Sure. Just call me the fix-it man. I'm always available."

This was not working out. This was not working out at all. The way things were going, he might as well be running a day-care center, instead of making furniture. Kate squalled, and he winced, the carving knife wobbling between his fingers.

When he glanced up to regain control, he came face-to-face with the article about him in *The Michigan Tradesman*. At least the cameraman had gotten his best side. The photograph made him look knowledgeable, confident. In a smaller photo, with his head bent and his shoulders hunched as he worked over a curio cabinet, he looked intense. He realized now how much the cabinet resembled a coffin.

Katie squalled again.

Yep. Put another nail in my coffin.

The subconscious thought rattled him, and he tossed the knife aside. It clattered on the workbench. Raylene had brought the framed article in for him two days ago, as a thank-you for the crib. She'd said she knew he'd never do it for himself. It was true, he wouldn't.

But he'd hung it over his workbench, both flattered and embarrassed by the hoopla. She said he should display it in the front windows, or behind the front desk as a come-on for potential customers. She was probably right, he should. But he had to get used to the idea.

Aw, hell. He should just take her advice and put the damned article out in the front window. In one of those fancy little easels used to display oil paintings. That'd be classy, wouldn't it? Old man Jennings's kid, passing himself off as one class act, and with his picture plastered smack-dab on page thirty-seven of some highfalutin' magazine.

Aw, she only meant to do the best by him. And he knew it, too, and maybe that was what goaded him. It was probably the sole reason he'd broken down, and said, sure, bring the kid in today, we'll work around the baby-sitter's flu.

But hearing Raylene coo and croon in the other room was just about his undoing. He had this unnatural urge to drop his tools and go in and check on them, to see what the heck was going on. He knew how Raylene could flutter around the car seat. He liked watching her like that, liked seeing a whole different side of her.

It poked at him a little. Like a jab to the heart. And here he'd thought he had no feelings left. Or damn few. Especially in the area of family.

Aw, hell. Why was he fighting it? Scooping the frame up from the bottom, he lifted it off the nail. Country-blue frame, textured cream matting. Expensively done, all of it.

He'd never forget how she'd handed it to him. Reverently, as if she really believed in him.

Hadn't that put a strange, unfamiliar feeling through his flesh?

Striding to the showroom, he walked past the front desk, where a frazzled Raylene was talking on the phone and jangling a set of plastic keys over Kate's head. Tyler, hanging around because of another half day of school, had been bribed with a five-dollar bill to dust the furniture. Chris unlatched the door to the display window, where he had a cannonball bed and crib carefully placed.

Hell, if he was going to lure them, he might as well reel them on in with something in print.

"Uncle Chris?"

"Yeah?"

"Mom said you'd make me a peanut-butter-and-jelly for lunch."

"Yeah. Okay."

"It's okay, then?" Tyler brightened, his mouth widening to expose the new braces Chris had kicked in for. "You aren't going to make a big deal out of the hot-lunch thing, then?"

"Hot-lunch thing?"

"You know."

The old familiar ache ground its way into Chris's belly. The hot lunch thing. The reminders.

Swilling down the paycheck and leaving the kids with withered apples and overripe bananas for their lunches. Filling up on water from the drinking fountain so your stomach wouldn't growl. Feeling it slosh around in your innards, as a testament to how hungry you really were.

He'd never wanted that to happen to Tyler. He'd made Beth promise the kid would always have a hot lunch. Always a hot lunch.

"Yeah, well, I guess peanut-butter-and-jelly's okay every once in a while. If you don't mind."

"I don't. I like lunches I can eat in my hand."

Chris nodded, but his thoughts were on dry bread and Kool-Aid made without sugar. "Okay, then. For today."

"Yeah. For today." Tyler's dust rag polished a little faster. "You gonna check my math?"

Chris reached into the display window and propped the framed article against the leg of the crib, positioning it so that every passerby would notice. "You need me to?"

"I think I got it right this time."

"Sounds like you're on your own, buddy."

Tyler broke into a full-fledged grin. "I need any help, I'll let you know, then."

"Sure."

"Suppose I better get the trash, huh?"

"Sure. Oh, and, Ty? Nothing in there needs to be recycled, all right?"

A guilty flush crept over Tyler's features as he stuck the dust rag in his back pocket. "Yeah, yeah. I know."

Watching his backside disappear into the workroom twisted Chris's sensibilities. The kid was growing up, and away from him. He looked over at Raylene, just as she dropped the receiver into the cradle.

There was a blank look in her eyes, unlike any expression he'd ever seen. "Hey. I took your advice. The article's in the front window."

"The article?" She looked momentarily puzzled. "Oh. Oh, that. Good. It'll be good for business. I promise."

But she didn't look as if she meant it. She looked distracted.

"What's up?"

"I..." She paused, crooking her finger to chuck Kate's cheek. "I may have just made the biggest mistake of my life."

"So what's going on?" he asked.

"I just called the birth mother." She turned round, hopelessly dark eyes on him. "I don't know what made me do it. Maybe it's hearing Kate fuss like this." She hesitated. "I don't know, I keep wondering if her own mother would be able to calm her better than I can."

"Raylene. All babies fuss."

"But, I mean, it's getting to me, her wanting the baby back. The idea of going before a judge, and knowing I'll have to prove myself. Knowing I could lose—"

"Raylene—"

"No, I—I know. I can do this. And I know I can live with the outcome, whatever that may be. But there's this niggling little part of me that says maybe I'm doing the wrong thing. Maybe this baby really does belong with someone else. Maybe even back with the birth mother. That's why I called her. And she wants to meet me this afternoon. To talk."

"What?"

"I don't know why I did it, but I agreed. I thought it might be better without all the lawyers and everybody else around. Just her and me. Like it was at the beginning."

"Aw, dammit! You're asking for trouble! You'll mess up your mind, and—"

"Like it's not already messed up?"

He said nothing. What was there to say?

"I'm shaking so bad, I can hardly think straight."

Her voice quavered, and an overwhelming need to protect her, to make things right with her, burgeoned in him.

"What if she agrees to let me keep the baby? What if I can't make her understand that I'll do everything I can for Kate, and we get in a fight and I alienate her?" Confusion, coupled with fear, rolled through Raylene's eyes. "What if she asks me questions about Kate? Questions only a mother can answer? That'll make me feel like I've got no right to—"

"You'll do the right thing," he said gruffly, refusing to be swayed by her emotions. "You got a good head on your shoulders."

She half laughed, as if the joke were on her. "This head's not thinking too clearly right now."

"You'll do fine. Maybe put this all behind you."

"Maybe."

He looked at the door to the display, closing it woodenly. Seconds elapsed.

"Chris?"

"Yeah?"

"Will you go with me this afternoon? I'm not sure I can do it by myself."

Like a fool, he knew he was going to say yes.

Chapter Four

It looked as if Heather Anne Byrum had decided not to show up. Or maybe her lawyer had warned her against it. Or maybe she just didn't care. But the wait, coupled with her reluctance to leave, was making Raylene edgy.

Chris swirled the ice water in his goblet, nudging aside the lemon floating in it. He tilted it, letting the ice slide to the back before taking a quick sip and abruptly thunking the glass down on the table. "Well?"

Raylene jumped, checking her watch for the umpteenth time. "I'm sorry. She said she'd be here." She craned her neck past the confines of the booth, looking toward the entry. Nothing but empty coat racks. No one but the hostess, who was still yakking on the phone, confirming dinner reservations.

"You think she's coming?"

"I hope so." Raylene looked around, at the salad bar, at the mahogany bar and brass rail, at the fifteen leather-and-brass-tack bar stools, and wondered if Mario's was too imposing for a teenager. "I don't know. Maybe we should've met at Mister Flap Jack, or Burger and the Beast."

He grinned, and the rotating lights from the beer sign over the bar sent scintillating sparks through his blond hair. He looked at ease and unaffected by the restaurant's upscale atmosphere.

"Well, there's noise there." Noise, and ragged vinyl booths and Formica tables. Food in paper bags, and screaming kids running around with ketchup smeared all over their faces. A lot less imposing than a shadowy back booth and the privacy created by a wedge of plastic plants hanging over their heads.

"What's she look like?"

"Brown hair, blue eyes." Raylene leaned over again, her eyes following the dark traffic pattern that ribboned through the red carpet and onto the slate floor. God, her palms were starting to sweat.

"Long? Short?"

"Her hair? Oh, it's long. Frizzy perm." Dropping her hands below the table, she raked them down the front of her pants. "The first day I met her, she was wearing combat boots, a jean jacket and a black lace skirt. I couldn't believe she was pregnant." She laughed, remembering. "But then, hey, look at me." She lifted a shoulder of her raspberry-colored blouse. "Motherhood comes in a variety of disguises, I guess."

Chris's eyes narrowed; his smile was remote, thoughtful. But his gaze trailed over the raspberry-and-pink stripes on her blouse, pausing on the raspberry button cover at the cleft of her breasts.

Raylene suddenly went hot, quivery. She shuddered, stunned by the feelings ricocheting through her. "I...I didn't mean to...to actually, look at me...."

His lips thinned as he bit back a smile. "Of course you didn't," he said, glancing away as if he hadn't been caught looking. "But it fits. Motherhood and you. I've noticed the changes. Anybody would have to be a fool not to."

She cleared her throat, not knowing what to say. She broke another cracker in two. They were supposed to be talking about Kate, and her birth mother, and how they could make this work. *She* wasn't up for discussion. "Heather's a typical teen. She's not sure what she wants to do, or how she wants to do it. But I think she's a good kid. She loves her baby, I'm sure of that."

Chris was about to drain his goblet, but he stopped, holding it in front of him. "Her baby?"

"I meant—" she stopped, flipping the plastic wrap from the cracker onto the decimated antipasto tray as his words echoed through her head. Her baby. Her baby. Dammit! She felt trapped by her own subconscious admission. "I meant it's something I can't take from her. She'll always be the birth mother."

"Raylene—"

"No, it's true. If it wasn't for her..." Her head wobbled from side to side, and seconds elapsed as she stared sightlessly at the water rings on the cherry-red tablecloth. When she spoke again, her voice was thin, and slightly subdued. "I look at it this way—I really should be thanking her for giving me something I can't produce myself."

He snorted. "Forget that. Motherhood's more than being a physiological processing plant."

"Yes? Well, I'd sure like the opportunity to be a participating member. As it is—"

His hand plunked down on the table, covering hers. "You're a whole woman, Raylene. When are you going to accept it?" His grip tightened, making her reluctant to move.

"Chris, you don't have to say…anything. I mean…" Raylene couldn't believe that she and Christian Jennings were sitting together in Mario's. That his hand was over hers, the callused ridge of his palm rubbing against her knuckles. "Chris. I appreciate the fact you're trying to make me feel better, but—"

"I'm not trying to do anything," he told her, squeezing her hand before moving down to lift her wrist.

Her bones had never felt so small, so fragile. Against his thumb, the vein in her wrist pulsed. Could he feel it? "Chris," she finally whispered, "you've been so good about this whole thing. More than I know you're inclined to be," she admitted quietly as someone rounded the corner, hesitating next to their table. "But sometimes I feel like—"

"Excuse me? Raylene?"

Their entwined grasp quickly snapped apart. "Yes! Yes, Heather." Raylene's head popped up, her voice sounding eerily eager. "Sit down, sit down. Please. We were just thinking about getting some breadsticks or something." Breadsticks? Where in heaven's name had that come from?

The background music picked up, pounding out "Baby Love." Dishes in the kitchen clattered, and someone dashed through the revolving door, carrying a sizzling platter that spewed forth the fragrance of garlic and onions.

"Hi," Chris said, sliding out of the booth after the waitress passed. The Supremes belted out a "Whaa-oohh, baby love." He motioned to Heather to take his place across the table while he climbed in next to Raylene.

Heather stood stock-still, eyeing him.

"This is a friend, Heather. Christian Jennings."

"He ain't no lawyer, is he?"

"No, not at all."

The young girl glanced at him, taking in his jeans, his casual pullover. "Well, okay. But I thought this was just between us."

"It is, it is. Chris offered to drive me over. I honestly didn't think you'd mind. If you want him to wait outside, or maybe..." She gestured toward the bar, knowing full well that Chris abhorred drinking.

"No, no, that's okay," she said, reluctantly sitting and scrunching the paper bag she was holding against the zipper of her Pistons jacket. "You didn't bring the baby?" The question was accusing.

"Well, I..." Raylene inclined her head. "No, I'm sorry, I didn't. Chris's sister is watching her. Sometimes she's fussy in the afternoons, and since I knew we wanted to talk—"

"But after I borrowed my girlfriend's car to get here and—" Heather's eyes filled, her childish face crumpling "—and I thought I'd see her, so I brought her presents."

"I'm sorry, I didn't realize." Time passed as they assessed each other. Heather was slight, and she wore an oversize flannel shirt. Gold chains glittered from the neckline. Dangly earrings caught in the tangle of her long permed hair, and were complemented by a heavy swipe of eyeliner and a sweep of blue shadow. She'd never looked more like a kid. A frail, scared kid, one who was trying like hell to grow up. "Thank you for remembering her," Raylene said finally. "It was nice of you to think of something like that."

Heather nodded and ripped into the sack, disturbing the quiet murmurings of the late-afternoon crowd. "When I get a job, I want to get her something special." She yanked free a curly-haired doll that was still encased in a plastic bag and stapled with a pasteboard hang tag. When she offered it to Raylene, the glass eyes rolled up, not quite matching or closing. "I thought it was cute. I thought maybe she'd like it."

"Oh. I'm sure she will." Raylene accepted it, fingering the pink nylon dress, the black Mary Janes, through the plastic bag.

"I wanted to give it to her myself."

"I know..." Raylene trailed off indecisively, torn over how much of herself—and of Katie—she could comfortably share. She lowered the doll, shakily gazing at its blond hair. "I'm sorry. I thought about bringing her. I did. But I was afraid that maybe, if you saw her—" she paused, letting the hard shell of the doll sink into her lap, the stiff, outstretched arms drop against her breast "—that it'd complicate things."

"I just wanted to see her. See how big she's getting."

"Twelve pounds now," Raylene said, her mind on the snapshots in her purse.

"Wow! Twelve pounds! She was only six pounds, three ounces, when—well, you know when."

I know, Raylene thought in silent anguish, arranging her face into a stolid, unaffected mask. When she was born.

When she was delivered of you, by you.

She nodded, as if it didn't matter, but the crushing weight of the natural birthright she could not give Katie snatched away her breath, threatening to suffocate her. "Um, Heather? I have some pictures. Would you like to see them?"

"You do?" Hope suffused Heather's wan features, clearing her watery eyes. "Oh, sure! Yes!"

Raylene blanched, but stalwartly threw back the flap of her purse, rummaging for the small photo album. Finding it, she bent back the cover so that Heather couldn't read the gold embossed script.

Mama's Pride and Joy.

Automatically sliding the precious photos from their plastic slots, she spread them on the table. Katie in her car seat and bundled up in her pink bunny pajamas, the ones with the ears. Katie in her plastic tub, with her rubber duck and a bar of soap on her tummy. Katie in her windup swing, her pacifier pinned and dangling from her terry sleepers. Katie going nose-to-nose with the golden Lab across the street. Katie snuggled against Raylene in her front pack, her chin resting on her bent wrist, her hair standing straight on end.

Heather gasped, her braces gleaming as she smiled widely and she picked them up. "Oh, God, she's gorgeous. Gorgeous." She giggled. "God, look at all that hair. Can you believe it? I remember she had a lot, but— Oh, wow."

"Now that," Raylene advised her, "was a bad hair day. Here. Look at this one." She flicked over another snapshot, of a perfectly coiffed Katie.

"Ohhh... Look. I just love those little headband thingies. They're so cute. I was thinking about getting her one, but..." Her gaze strayed to the next photo.

"Where was this taken?" she asked, interrupting herself.

"At home. In her room."

Heather's eyes slowly lifted from the photo. "She's got her own room?"

"Well, yes."

"I can't believe it," Heather said, her gaze riveted on the photo again. "My little girl's barely eight weeks old, and she has her own room. Here I'm sixteen and still waiting for mine."

Raylene shifted uncomfortably. She didn't want the comparisons to be too great, too pretentious.

"Man! Is this is a cool baby blanket, or what?"

Raylene swallowed her rationalizations. "Thank you. It was a gift. From Chris."

"Really?" Heather closely examined the white eyelet, the lace, before glancing back up at Chris. "From you? No kidding?"

"Is it assassinating my character or something?"

"You just don't look like you'd choose something this—I don't know—this frilly, or whatever."

He lifted a shoulder as his voice dropped melodramatically, teasingly. "Ah... Who knows what lies in the hearts of men."

Heather grinned. "That her crib, then?"

"Yes." Raylene answered, as a funny feeling inched into her heart. "And Christian made it."

"You? You made it?"

"Mmm-hmm... But that's what I do, I work with wood. Raylene was the one who designed it."

Heather picked up another photo of Katie in her crib and stared at it before suddenly going silent, thoughtful. "Looks like you're giving her everything," she said slowly.

A premonition, as deadly as a knife, plunged into Raylene's subconscious. Apologies for all she'd done sprung to the back of her throat. "It probably seems like it, but, to me, I know she'll be my only child. Ever. I mean, I'll never get another chance to do this, or—"

"Don't!" Heather's voice rose hysterically, and she shoved the photos back at Raylene. "Don't try and convince me how wonderful her life is, because she's still my baby! And that's what we're here to talk about. I was the one who had her, I was the one who—"

"I know," Raylene calmly interjected. "You don't have to say it." She sorted through the mess of photos, her hands trembling as she picked them up, one by one, to slot back in the album. She prayed Heather wouldn't notice. "And you know what, Heather? I thank heaven every day you've let me be her mother."

Heather's eyes widened. "Maybe—maybe that was a mistake."

Raylene acted as if she hadn't heard, flipping pages as she put the snapshots back in chronological order. She hesitated over the last one. Katie, on top of the comforter and next to the musical teddy bear they wound up every night before bed. It was the best of the lot. Katie's eyes were as animated as her smile. "Would you like this?" she impulsively offered, extending it between two fingers. "It's my favorite."

Heather stilled, her lips parting slightly. "You'd give it to me?"

"Would it help?"

Heather looked away, swallowing convulsively as she burrowed into the depths of her Pistons jacket. "Nothing will help."

Raylene's throat constricted. Her heart raced, her lungs stung. She forced herself into a calm demeanor, but her insides were raw and burning, and she was torn between empathy and self-preservation. "Heather?"

"Yes?"

"I want you to have this." She placed it faceup, slowly sliding it over the tablecloth, to the other side of the table.

"Thanks."

"It's been really hard, hasn't it?"

Heather's head jerked up and down, her lips grimly compressed. "I told you, my dad's come home."

Beside her, Chris sighed, heavily, as if he were suddenly annoyed that this meeting couldn't just be a pleasant tête-à-tête.

"So it's made a difference?"

"Yeah. It has." Heather angrily picked up the snapshot and stuffed it in her zippered coat pocket before pushing the paper bag onto the table and poking at the toy-store logo. "I feel like he should have been there all along. But this time he says he's going to stay."

"Oh? Really."

"Yeah. And he likes kids, so if he stayed—"

Chris interrupted her, his shoulder brushing Raylene's as he leaned forward. "And what if he doesn't? What then?"

"Well, we'd get along. We've done it before. Besides," she added defiantly, "having him around has made me realize that every kid should have two parents. That's fair, isn't it?"

Raylene's temper flared, and she struggled to control it. Sure, every kid should have that. But that wasn't what she'd first offered, and it wasn't what Heather had bargained for. "Being a single mom doesn't make me any less of a parent, Heather."

"I'm not saying that—"

"It doesn't make the adoption any less legitimate either."

"Yeah? Well, my dad says, technically, she's still my baby. I got rights, and I should be able to choose what I want. If I want her to have a real family, then—"

"We are a family! Katie and me!"

"I'm sorry, Raylene! But my dad says if I'm going to do this, I have to do it now, before it goes any further."

"You mean we can't talk this out?"

"Talking's not going to do any good."

After several painful moments, Chris quietly intervened. "Heather? Remember how Raylene said things aren't always what they seem?"

"Yeah?"

"Well, it's true. Look at us. I mean, really look at us." His arm had somehow wandered around Raylene's shoulders, intimately uniting them in a significant embrace. "There's more to us than meets the eye."

Heather's jaw dropped as she asked, "You two?"

"Yes," Chris replied. "Who's to say Katie's not going to have that father?"

Chapter Five

Heather looked in confusion from Chris to Raylene and back again. "I never figured..."

"We didn't, either. At least not at first." Though Raylene stiffened, Chris's arm tightened possessively around her. "I think we can say we've got a comfortable ongoing relationship. We work at it. We're committed to it."

"But..."

"Raylene didn't want to say anything," he put in easily. "It was enough of a shock for her family to learn she'd adopted a baby."

Heather stared at Raylene, expecting confirmation.

A sick feeling swelled in her stomach. If she went along with this charade, she'd be lying, and Raylene desperately feared that the lie would somehow come back to jeopardize the adoption. "Well, part of that's true," she reluctantly admitted.

"Your family didn't know you were adopting my baby?"

"No."

"You didn't tell anyone?"

"No..."

"She insisted we keep it pretty quiet," Chris explained, nonchalantly massaging her shoulder.

Goose bumps popped out on her flesh. What in the world was he doing?

But Heather, her eyes glued to the affectionate gesture, stayed silent, studying them.

Raylene lurched forward, trying, unsuccessfully, to extricate herself. Chris's arm wound tighter, trapping her. "I—I didn't want to tell anyone, because it happened so fast."

"But if you two got married, then—?" The teenager pointed a finger at them, already weighing the outcome.

Chris plucked at her sleeve, causing tiny air pockets to billow out the fabric and send bursts of cool air jetting over her arm. Raylene jerked backward, crossing her arms over the unresponsive doll. "Even if I got married, I'd still have to adopt."

Chris leaned back, his arm hovering comfortably on the back of the booth. His palm was on her shoulder, his thumb at her nape.

Heather sailed a questioning look to Chris.

"I've told Raylene I want the best for her," he said. "This is her decision, and I'll stand by her. Whatever she wants."

Whatever happened to the "Why saddle yourself with a baby?" argument? Raylene wondered. But she forced herself to look unaffected, to calmly say, "Infertility is not an easy thing to bring into a marriage, Heather."

"Man! Why didn't you tell me this when I called and said how I felt about Katie having a dad and all? I mean, you should've told me that maybe someday you'd get married. It could've made a difference. It still could."

Heather hesitated as if weighing the new information. "But, with the two of you together...even if I changed my mind, you guys could still adopt another baby. It'd be the same thing."

Raylene blanched, her eyelids closing. Sure. Just order another baby like a replacement part. "And you can always have another baby," she finally said. "I can't."

Chris groaned under his breath. His hand splayed over her shoulder, as if he'd like to restrain her—or throttle her.

Heather's eyes flashed, and her mouth flew open as if she were prepared to spawn a dozen damning words. Then, just as the hostess walked past them with extra plates for the salad bar, an illuminating light flickered behind her eyes, dousing the fire. She sat back, her gaze taking in both of them, from the way Chris folded and refolded the shoulder seam of Raylene's blouse to the way Raylene sat perfectly still. "I suppose you've both grown attached to her."

Chris's fingers drummed out a warning. Be careful. Be careful what you say.

"I have," Raylene responded.

"This is probably as hard for you as it is for me. Trying to live with this, and make it work."

"It is!" The urgency in Raylene's voice bordered on desperation. "I swear to you, Heather, I've looked at all the options. Even if I married, an adoption would take—what? Seven, eight years?''

"That long?"

"Yes! And then there's the case study, and the waiting lists, and the red tape. And for me they'll throw in the age factor and tell me I'm too old."

"Come on."

"No, it's true. Really. I'm thirty years old and running out of time. Other people worry about their biological clock, I deal with the red tape of bureaucracy. Most agencies won't even consider placement to anyone over thirty-five. You know I'll be a good mother to Katie," she said imploringly, nearly tearing up over the emotional issue. "You know it. I swear it, and I'd never do anything that—"

"Honey..." Chris said soothingly, patting her on the shoulder.

Honey? Where the hell had that come from? What was going on? Didn't he know how much this meant to her? Was he going to undermine everything she'd worked for?

She batted his hand away, like a lioness intent on protecting her cub. Yet his arm stayed firmly anchored.

Somehow, she was grateful it did.

"Look. Just because you can't have a baby," Heather said, her eyes narrowing, "just because you're getting old—maybe too old—that doesn't mean it's my fault."

"No!"

"Right now, I figure she's better off with you, but..."

"She is!"

"...when I'm with my dad, I think she should have a father."

"She'll always have me," Chris told her, without a second's hesitation.

His quick reply made Heather's features soften, and her smile nearly reached her eyes. It was the first genuine reaction she'd offered since joining them.

"Heather?" Raylene gently prodded her, leaning forward and cradling the doll before putting one elbow on the table. Chris's hand slid to her spine. His comforting touch gave Raylene the courage to reach out to Heather, to cover her hands. "If it helps, I want you to know I love Katie, and that I'll do anything I can to be a good mother to her."

"I know," the teen admitted miserably, "I'm not tryin' to hurt you. Honest."

"I know. But look, I want you to know there's one thing I also believe."

"That is . . . ?" Heather hedged.

"Between the two of us, we can make this adoption repair lives, not destroy them."

Chris had taken a side street away from the restaurant, away from the main drag and its four lanes of traffic.

"How could you do that?" Raylene demanded when they were a good two blocks away. "You intentionally let her think we were involved, that we—"

"Well? Aren't we?"

"We work together," she said emphatically. "That's all."

"Raylene, the way things are going, you're gonna have to do something or lose that baby." His knuckles went white against the steering wheel. "I was only trying to help."

"I work for you," she stated clearly. "Working for you doesn't mean you can interfere in my life, or complicate it. Working for you is not a commitment, nor is it the kind of relationship you tried to misrepresent to Heather."

He thwacked the steering wheel, feeling genuinely peeved. "Hell's bells, Raylene. I told you, I was only trying to help."

"Oh, terrific. Just terrific. Big help you are."

"Well, what did you want? I said we 'worked' at a relationship, didn't I? She's free to interpret it any way she wants. I didn't twist her arm."

"Well, I wish you wouldn't have been twisting mine back there! It made me so nervous I could hardly think."

He paused. "Sorry. I acted on impulse. That's all."

She glared out the side window. A corner fire hydrant whizzed by in a blur. A mailbox, a flash of blue on the next corner, followed.

"She kept harping about having two parents, and a dad, so I figured if—"

"If you intentionally led her to believe we might get married, it would all blow over," she said finishing his thoughts.

"Well? What's wrong with that?"

"You put me in a compromising position, that's what. Here I am, trying to reason with her, and you're hanging your arm around me, offering up this phony illusion of family and two doting parents, and... and..."

"Wait a minute." He peeled his eyes from the road, his head swivelling her direction. "If the birth mother draws the wrong conclusions, I'm not being held responsible.''

"Christian!''

"I'm not. We've all walked away with our own opinions of what just happened back there." He pumped the brake, pulling up along the curb. "She wants to take that kid back to God knows what, and you're yelling at me because I propose to fill in as a father for that baby?''

Raylene silently searched his face, pausing before she glanced away, to the vacant lot beside the car. "It isn't the same, and you know it," she finally muttered.

Raylene rolled her window partway down, to allow the heavy, damp scent of spring to fill the car.

"You want her to take Katie away?" he asked, prodding her.

"Of course not. I never said that."

"Or give her away to someone else?"

"You know better. But I can't influence Heather with something that isn't going to happen. It's not right. If she walked away thinking you were going to be in Katie's life, I'd be deceiving her.''

"Life doesn't offer guarantees, Raylene. Fathers walk in and out of their kids' lives all the time. Heather knows that.''

"I still can't do that to her. I can't let her think that you'll always be around.''

"Okay. Fine. But she's doing you wrong," he snapped. "It's okay for her to go back on her word, and you'll sit still for it?''

"She's a kid! And she's agonizing over this.''

"Like you're not?" He snorted, rolling his eyes. "I thought you said you were going to fight for Katie.''

"I am. But I'm trying to do the right thing, too.''

"It doesn't take a Rhodes scholar to figure out where Katie would be better off. She won't last six months in that environment."

"I know."

"And the way she talked later, it sounds like the old man's a real prize. His solution's terrific. He intends to beat the boyfriend up for doing his daughter."

She half laughed, but then swallowed at the crude reference. "Christian."

"Well? That's what she said. And her boyfriend doesn't want responsibility. He already refused a blood test, he already gave her a choice—either the kid or him. Dammit, Raylene, just knowing that makes me so mad, even I could be reduced to smashing his face in."

"The boy is still Kate's father. He always will be."

"Never in a million years."

"Christian," she said wearily, slanting him a glance, "biologically speaking—"

"Biologically speaking means zero."

"He's the reason she's here."

"The reason she's here is because a sixteen-year-old kid couldn't keep his pants zipped."

"Or maybe," she countered, the darkness of her doe-soft eyes skewering him, "because a fifteen-year-old kid needed her dad, and needed to be loved."

Hooking his wrist over the gearshift, he sighed, then finally threw the car in park. His foot was still on the brake when he lifted her hand. "Raylene, I don't want to argue with you. But the phantom kid's not a dad, and Heather's not a mother."

Raylene watched their hands mesh, and willingly twined her fingers through his. The sensations he caused shot holes clean through their friendship.

He'd touched her today. Really touched her. Not like the time in the workroom, when she'd confided in him and he'd clumsily patted her on the shoulder and said it would all work out. Today was different. Disturbingly different.

"No matter what you say, Chris, Heather's given birth to my daughter, and it looks like she's going to fight to retain custody. So she can give her to someone else. Sure, I'm devastated. But maybe I'm being selfish, too. Maybe I'm the one who can't accept facts. I'm doing this because I can't have a baby, because I can't—"

"Stop it!" he ordered harshly, squeezing her hand. "I don't want to hear about how you can't have kids. It doesn't change you and it doesn't change what you have to offer."

"But I . . ." She splayed her fingers, carefully extricating them from his.

"It doesn't change a thing," he repeated.

She straightened, turning away stiffly. "It changes the way I feel."

"The only thing beating you up and making you half a woman, Raylene, is yourself." She was staring at some climbing thing on a latticework trellis, but he could tell her eyes widened. "Those kids don't know what they want," he repeated gruffly. "Taking Katie away from you to give to another ready-made family is a joke. You're Katie's mother. She belongs with you."

Raylene's jaw tightened. "Will you please stop? You give me this grandiose vote of confidence, and what am I supposed to say?" She sucked in a ragged breath. "I'm not used to this 'rally 'round Raylene' scenario."

"Hey, you've convinced me you're her mother. You and Katie are a family. I believe that."

She shook her head slowly, sadly. "We're still only half of what Heather wants."

"Okay. Then accept me as a surrogate father for Katie."

"Chris."

"Since we put her in the crib that first time, I've felt that way. I never intended for it to happen, I never wanted it to happen. But that's how I feel. Like I have a job to do where she's concerned."

"Katie isn't your responsibility. I'm sorry. I never meant for you to feel like that."

"But I do."

"I shouldn't have asked you to go today. I've intruded on your work, on your time...."

"Forget it." She didn't want his help? Fine. But a weight sank into his belly, and his mind's eye saw a lonely little kid—a rejected kid—skipping stones on Lake Syles. Hell, so what? What did it matter?

"You don't want to get involved and I know it," Raylene said quietly.

He stared at her, hurting, thinking how beautiful she was and reminding himself that he should let her believe whatever she wanted. But, at the same time, he was thinking of the evenings he'd strapped Kate into her car seat because Raylene had her hands full with diaper bags and books. The times Raylene had been busy giving price estimates over the phone and he'd picked Katie up when she was cranky, and he'd crooned, and patted her on the back, and made silly sounds in the back of his throat to keep her quiet.

The way Katie gurgled and laughed had made him feel like a family man. And so did the way Raylene had

cupped her hand over the mouthpiece and rolled her
eyes at him, and scrunched her mouth all up, indicating that she was eager to get off the phone and join
them.

Or the way Katie's little hand would reach up and
touch him, reawakening feelings he hadn't had for a
very, very long time. The way Raylene's hand sliced
between the layers of Katie's blankets and against his
chest when she reached to take her, giving his heart a
fluttery feeling.

Then he'd stand back and watch her fuss over the
blankets and the pacifier and Kate's collar, and he'd
think about how small her hands were, how intent her
brown eyes were.

She had the brownest eyes. Sometimes, after spending time with her, he'd go back and look at the color in
the wood he was staining. The same exquisite color.
Distracting him. Mocking him. Challenging him.

Aw, hell. He'd closed off his feelings a long time ago,
and he knew it. He'd skipped those stones over Lake
Syles and consciously decided to be a solitary man. The
less intrusion in his life, the better.

But something about being with Kate, her baby-
powder smell and the lingering scent of it on Raylene's
clothing, seemed to bind them all together. As if it were
a package he wanted and couldn't help reaching for.

That was why he'd hung his arm around her at Mario's, and that was why he'd tried to shrug the gesture
off as casual. But his subconscious desire had mani-
fested itself. For a few minutes, back in that restaurant, he'd convinced himself that he wanted to father
Katie as much as Raylene wanted to mother her. The
age-old need to take a wife was as instinctual, as strong,
as hers for that baby.

The instinctual need to mate. To reproduce, and be a family. He'd thought it could never happen to him. But it had. And now those feelings were overwhelming him.

He'd sat while they were talking about the photos and remembered the day he'd carried Katie into the workroom, explaining how he was going to use wood screws rather than nails on the Burtons' rocking chair, how he was going to make spindles for the arms, and router grape leaves into the headrest. How, some night, when she'd be sleeping after her last bottle, he'd stain it a dark, rich walnut.

Like her mama's eyes. Like her hair.

He'd felt sheepish when Raylene caught him explaining those same sappy things to Katie.

But Raylene never said a word. She'd simply rocked back on her heels and smiled. Her shoulders against the door frame, her hands behind her hips. Her brows were lifted, her eyes twinkling. She'd finally dismissed it all by accusing him of conditioning her daughter to quality furniture and expensive tastes.

A small joke, nothing more.

But he thought of all that, and the camaraderie between them, and the differences, and wondered what in tarnation they were going to do.

Chapter Six

It had been two weeks since their meeting with Heather, and things were tense.

Raylene was too polite, and Chris knew he was feigning too much interest in work.

But she skirted around him, refraining from asking the most innocent questions, speaking in subdued tones over the phone, and neglecting to mention even the slightest details about Kate.

It grated on him, hearing it all from Beth. Worse, he was doing a slow boil, realizing he wasn't a part of the whole deal.

He should be. Hadn't he been there for her? Hadn't he closed up shop early so that he could accompany her to meet Heather? Hadn't he worked like a dog to get Katie into that crib? Hadn't he tried to put himself in Raylene's shoes, to feel what she was feeling, to take the edge off the pressure when he sensed she needed it?

Sure, he'd said from the first that he wasn't taking any responsibility. But that didn't mean she had to cut him out of her life. She was excluding him, by God.

To hell with it. That was what he told himself as he banged around his workroom. But, God, he felt as if he were being shunned. And it was driving him crazy.

It got so Raylene was all he could think of. He awoke thinking of her, he went to bed at night thinking of her. In between, he'd wake up and look at the clock and wonder whether Katie was squalling and kicking her feet for her midnight bottle and whether Raylene was too tired to hear her. Then he'd wake up in the middle of the night and think about her 5:00 a.m. feeding and go through the whole thing all over again.

Had Katie gotten that cold he'd predicted? She'd sneezed three times in the shop last Friday. Raylene said it was blanket fuzz. He wasn't so sure.

Jeez, that was all Raylene needed right now, a sick kid. And her trying to juggle five bookkeeping jobs. At the same time he was stewing over that, he considered everything else Beth had let slip.

Katie had started taking applesauce with her cereal. She'd spit out the first two bites, then slurped it down, making Raylene affectionately dub her a little "pig-hog." She'd grown out of her newborn diapers, and the higher cost had made Raylene consider using cloth instead. She'd slept through a night feeding, and Raylene hadn't slept a wink. She'd gotten up every five minutes to check on her, worried sick that she'd stopped breathing.

Now, on Sunday night, the night before Raylene was supposed to show up for work, he was puttering around in the shop way longer than he should, his mind trained on every skimpy detail concerning her and Katie. For some reason he couldn't fathom, he'd avoided going up to his apartment. He'd skipped supper, realizing, for the first time in years, how routine it had become to heat up a can of soup and simply be satisfied to go to bed with something warm in his belly.

Thinking crazily, as he vacuumed up a few wood shavings, how he had four good burners on the stove, yet he'd only used one. Only one. Ever.

The realization made him wonder what it would be like to have a kitchen that smelled like real food, the room warmed by roasting meat, the burners filled with steaming pots.

And a woman next to him, a woman with whom he shared the same space. Imagine having to move out of the way for her every once in a while. To have her ask him to get the milk, or slice the meat. One who replied to his questions—and made the silence skitter away.

Of course, there'd be a trade-off.

She'd shuck the make-do cabinets, and probably put place mats on the table. Probably make sure the flatware matched, too.

She'd rearrange the living room, and take the television off the cement-block-and-board arrangement, saying she was scared silly it might tip over on the baby. The hell of it was, she was probably right. He ought to get rid of the setup. And right now, too. Before anything happened to Katie.

Raylene would putter around in his bathroom, mess up his shaving gear. She'd set it aside so that she could have more room, and maybe use his razor without telling him. Oh, he could see it now. Scented soaps by the sink, and matching towels over the bar.

Hell, she'd probably make the bathroom mirror steam over, and he'd have to wipe it down with a towel if he wanted so much as a shot at it! Thinking of that, his right brain got into an out-and-out argument with his left brain.

What a nuisance, the logical side grumbled. Annoying as hell.

The creative side waylaid the argument by conjuring up a few soothing, even comforting, images. Raylene winding that same damp towel around herself, instead of using the robe hanging behind the door. The bottom edges barely coming together, exposing the curve of a thigh. Water droplets freckling the flesh between her shoulder blades, where the towel didn't reach.

His reaction to that image was decidedly masculine. Hard and swift, and purely physical. To counter it, he hurled the awl he'd been using into an opened drawer and stalked off to fix supper.

But he ended up dumping most of the lukewarm tomato soup down the drain, and congratulating himself that, by golly, he'd stood the test of time. There wasn't a woman puttering around in his kitchen. No female arranging canisters on the countertop or magnets on the refrigerator door.

He finally strode into the bedroom and yanked off his T-shirt, damned glad no one else was flitting around, taking over too much drawer space and more than her fair share of the closet. No high heels to trip over, no fancy panties poufing out of a dresser drawer.

But even with all that logical stuff cluttering up his mind, he closed his eyes and thought about dropping into a bed made with clean, sweet-smelling sheets, and a warm body with which to share them.

He actually groaned. Lying there in his empty, undone apartment, with everything the way he wanted it, and groaning.

Groaning, for God's sake!

Even so, he fell asleep dreaming of rising in the morning, and leaving those same clean sheets rumpled. His mind's eye saw percale tangling around slim ankles, ballooning over the lift of a feminine hip.

Okay, okay. So he'd given a lot of thought to having a woman in his bedroom lately. So what?

Would Raylene be spontaneous in bed? Would that nuzzling, gurgling love she shared with Katie stretch to include a man? A man like him? A man who was intentionally cold and unresponsive. A man who felt secure only by keeping people at a distance.

A man who didn't know how to love, and who felt awkward and uncomfortable with intimacy? One who'd had his head messed up by the blooming beauty of a striking adoptive mother and the heart-wrenching flirtatiousness of a two-month-old infant.

God, he didn't know what was happening to him. He only knew he'd wasted one whole day and thrown away a dozen spindles for the Burtons' rocker because he'd made mistakes on every damn one of them. The stupid thing was costing him a fortune.

Raylene was costing him his peace of mind.

At four o'clock Monday afternoon, he strolled out of his workshop, ready to face the torment. "Raylene?"

"Yes?" She pulled the phone down from her ear, her voice a little too high, too pleasantly work-related.

"As long as you're making calls, could you tell the Burtons it's going to be another couple days on the rocker?"

"Of course. I'd be happy to." She automatically flipped open the Rolodex. "Having trouble?"

More than you know. "The spindles. I'm botching them. Must have gotten a bad batch of walnut." Excuses, excuses. Anything instead of confessing his real fears. Raylene Rafco, and commitment, and how much she'd gotten under his skin.

"You having trouble? That's a first."

He thought about turning around, spindle in hand, and leaving her to the office. But he didn't; he loitered, ruefully watching her dial the number, waiting to hear the smooth explanation he expected of her.

She smiled when she talked. He'd always noticed that about her. She smiled and straightened her paperwork, unconsciously cradling the phone against her shoulder. Seeing her like that somehow made him feel that they were a team.

"All done," she suddenly announced.

He nodded, unable to concentrate. For a moment, he felt paralyzed, incapable of moving forward with Raylene and scared half to death of looking back.

"Anything else, Chris?"

"No." Still he stood there, and time skipped by. "But thanks. For the call, I mean."

"You're welcome. No problem."

He stared, mesmerized by how easily kind words tripped off her tongue. *Please* and *thank you* had never been part of his youth. He and Beth had grown up amid orders and grudging replies heavily salted with hateful words. And then, before they knew it, the hitting would begin.

"Chris?"

His head snapped to attention. "Yeah?"

"With the rain, I feel like I should've taken the books home, and gotten out of your hair."

He raised a brow, indicating that she wasn't a bother, that it didn't matter, because there hadn't been any customers. But he couldn't bring himself to say more. He was operating on gut instinct, waging an internal war.

"You want me to close up early?"

He hesitated, rolling the splintered spindle around in his hand. "I don't know. I really don't feel like working today, anyway."

She watched him, and uneasily flipped the top of the Rolodex back and forth. To hell with it. He'd have to just come out and ask. "So. You heard anything from Heather?"

"No... Not exactly... but my lawyer told me to sit tight."

"Mmm..." He nodded. "I suppose the waiting's hard, huh?"

"It is. I can't eat, I don't sleep."

"Shouldn't let yourself get run-down, Raylene." He said it gruffly, cutting off any real show of emotion.

"I know. But there's an upside." She yanked on the waistband of her slacks, pulling away two inches. "Foiled adoptions are more effective than fad diets."

He smiled sadly, thinking that she didn't need to lose one ounce. She was damn near perfect. But the wry grief he saw etched into her features made him move into the room, and sink a hip on her desk. He pitched the wrecked spindle into the Out basket.

"Mmm..." She frowned as she picked it up. "You really did it to this one, didn't you?"

"Yeah. Losing my touch."

"I doubt it."

Seconds passed in silence. She picked at the splinters jutting out from the spindle; he gazed out through the front windows, at the rain sheeting off the overhang.

Bone-chilling cold seeped in beneath the doors, making everything in the old warehouse seem dark, dank. Rubbing the back of his neck, he wearily wondered what the hell he should do.

She was so damned pretty, he couldn't take his eyes off her. She was so damned good, he wanted to grovel at her feet. And because of the adoption, they didn't have much time. Minutes were precious. Days were slipping by.

He glanced at her, guessing that she wanted to get back to Katie. A stab of regret, of jealousy, poked at him, and he reluctantly admitted that he wanted to be a part of her and Katie's life. "You want to take off early?" Her eyes lifted hopefully. "Go on. Nobody's going to venture out this late, not in this downpour."

"You sure?" She glanced over at her purse.

"Yeah. Sure. It's time me and my chicken noodle soup got together, anyway." He chuckled, not meaning it, but wanting to waste a little more time being near her. "Beth claims I should have stock in Campbell's, since we do so much business together."

Raylene tried to smile, but she obviously didn't get the joke.

The tension. The silence. For want of something better to do, he picked up a paper clip, his hand feeling as clumsy as a bear's paw as he let it somersault end over end.

"Well . . ."

82   THE BACHELOR AND THE BASSINET

"Yeah. Well..." He flipped the paper clip like a coin, catching it in his palm before dropping it in the catchall. "Suppose I oughta close up early. Take the night off, too."

Raylene nodded, but neither of them moved. As awkward as it was, they lingered, watching rain pelt the sidewalks and streets in a second, harsher wave.

Outside, a couple shrieked, dashing across the street as they tented a newspaper over their heads. Their jacket backs were pitted with dark, wet spots before they scurried into Bagels 'n' Buns.

With the street deserted, the glow of interior lighting and marquee lights skittered through the moisture whorling over the asphalt. Just then, the twin-armed streetlights sputtered to life, illuminating the street with sickly orange spikes.

"Raylene?" Thunder sounded in the background. The windows rocked in their casings.

"Yes?"

"Have you taken Katie to Barney's Pizza Place yet?" They had climbers there, and a ball pit, and roving characters that worked the crowd, handing out suckers and animals shaped from balloons. He knew all about it because he'd popped for a birthday party there when Tyler was eight.

"Noooo... But she's only two and a half months old."

"Aw, she should go. And I could stand some pizza myself, rather than that cardboard stuff I keep in the freezer." Angling his head, he purposely tried to make the invitation offhand. Another crack of lightning dimmed the streetlights. "What do you say? Lots of pepperoni, extra cheese?"

"Oh, Chris, I...I don't know, it's such a nasty night."

"All the more reason to do it."

"You sure?"

"Of course I'm sure!" Slapping his knee, he rose decisively. "Close 'er up early, Raylene, and let's go get the baby. This'll be a pizza night."

So he liked pepperoni pizza, did he? And soda without ice. And he'd asked the waitress to move them, so that the baby could be propped in her car seat without any danger of being knocked over by the exuberant kids crawling over the booths and running down the aisles. This was family night at Barney's Pizza Place, and all the moms and dads and youngsters were piling into the booths and stacking up tokens to spend at the video arcade, on the minirides and at the candy counter.

To an outside observer, Raylene guessed, she and Christian would fit right in. Like any other couple, they stood in line and put their heads together, deciding what to order. She'd loosened her coat with one hand and trailed the other down the menu, while he held it so that she could see. They'd made sure Katie was carefully nestled in her car seat on the floor, and between their legs. Then he'd hoisted the car seat, carrying it to the table the hostess indicated, and while she peeled the blankets loose and unzipped Katie's blanket sleeper, he'd gotten the drinks.

He sat down and threw back a huge swallow, and she found herself studying the way his Adam's apple bobbed up and down. The way his cheeks briefly hollowed out to make his jawline even more pronounced.

The way his eyes drifted closed as he sucked it down. All in all, he was a handsome man.

But, seeing him that way, honestly relishing something as simple as a soda, put a quavery feeling through her.

She'd been noticing too many things about him lately.

But the discomfiting part was that she was filing them away in the back of her mind, and honoring them, as if they were guidelines, or a how-to manual, or something. She was even starting to gravitate toward them, handing him the lined paper he preferred, the mug that was his favorite.

She was growing to know what he liked, and it was disturbing, that intimate knowledge of another human being, that desire to make him happy.

He liked golden Labs, early-morning talk shows, country music, sharp pencils without erasers, white V-necked T-shirts, homegrown tomatoes, and pine air fresheners in his car. He didn't like Dobermans, red ink, button-down shirts, cucumbers or manual transmissions. And he vehemently groused about the cursing that went on between the teenagers at the basketball court behind the warehouse.

"Sure you don't want a salad?" he asked, setting his soda to one side so that he could wedge a pink balloon in beside Katie. It was a flamingo, and he made every effort to position it so that the beak hung where she could see it. "A few vegetables would do you good."

"No." Katie's gaze veered up to focus on the oversize bird. "You're going to pay for it if that thing scares her," she warned, smiling.

"Nah. It won't. Pink's her favorite color. I had Doo-Hickey make it up special for her."

"Doo-Hickey?"

"Doo-Hickey, the clown. Hey—" the corners of his mouth lifted in a sheepish grin "—that's what the name tag says."

She concentrated on his full mouth. "Doo-Hickey, huh?" It sounded like something right out of adolescence. Hot, steamy kisses and pulsing desire that culminated in purplish, sought-after bruises. "Well, thanks, I know Katie appreciates it."

His lips quirked, almost as if he knew what she was thinking. But he didn't let on. She was grateful for that.

"No problem. I appreciated doing it for her."

She stared at him, weighing his response. Did he really enjoy folding up a soaking-wet umbrella and jamming smelly wool coats to the back of the booth, behind a child carrier? For an infant who wasn't even aware that her future hung in the balance. For an adoptive mother who'd gathered her defenses and refused to share even the slightest tidbit of information.

She felt like a fool. She felt as if she'd betrayed him.

For the past two weeks, she'd come in and done her job, just as she was paid to do. She'd intended to forge ahead and forget the heart-to-heart they'd had in the car after meeting Heather. It hadn't been possible.

Being honest, even for those few moments, had only stirred up a hornet's nest of emotion. She couldn't look at Chris without thinking how earnest, how supportive, he'd become. He'd filled in so well in the surrogate role that, sometimes, she almost forgot that was what it was. A role, without permanence, without responsibilities.

She'd valiantly tried to shed her dependence on him, but in doing so, she'd only become more painfully aware of all he'd done for her. Of every memory he shared with her.

Why, he carried Katie with the ease of a seasoned father, and three weeks ago he'd automatically tucked a cross-stitched bib beneath her chin before giving her a bottle. One afternoon, when he had customers and she was on the phone, he'd cradled Katie with one arm and fished for a disposable diaper—all while negotiating the sale of an expensive armoire with a client. One morning he'd patted Katie's burps away with his wide hand, grinning broadly when she spewed forth, honoring him with a big one.

Every move, every gesture, Chris shared with them was complacent, confident. He went unassumingly about his role, content to fill in when Raylene needed help, content to back off when he sensed she needed it.

She admired his savvy. She coveted it. A wonderful aura hung over him, giving her courage in her uncertainty. His presence, his every nod of approval, sanctioned her fight for Katie.

At the same time she began to feel at ease with Christian, new anxieties, new indecision surfaced. She wondered how convincing he'd been with Heather. Did the girl actually believe they were involved?

She'd probably belabored that point unnecessarily. But had it been enough for Heather? Seeing them sit side by side, his arm around her, holding hands and talking about "their" future? Or would she need something more solid?

Something as clear and concise as a marriage certificate?

She couldn't help thinking about how she could make it work. She lay awake at nights and thought about it, and wondered how much courage it would take to simply blurt it all out and ask him to cement the whole thing.

For Katie's sake, of course. Just for Katie's sake.

She got up in the morning and thought about it, wondering whether he fixed his pot of coffee before he went to bed at night or after he got up. She admitted that she was pretty damn adaptable where those things were concerned, as long as marriage—however long it lasted—saved Katie.

But those thoughts also damaged her perceptions.

Because now, every time she looked at Chris, she imagined him as a father; she imagined him as a husband. She wondered how it would be to be safe inside his arms—and whether it would last a lifetime. Some people did, after all, grow to love one another. Arranged marriages had been around for centuries.

There were advantages, there were disadvantages. She'd be sharing Katie's upbringing with a man who was levelheaded and sure of himself.

A man who stayed silent when she longed to talk.

A man who worked like a dog when she wanted to play.

A man who was often distant and remote when she wanted to spill her guts.

No, it definitely would not be a match made in heaven.

And then the pizza came, and he thoughtfully offered her the first slice.

She glanced at his hand, patiently poised over the pepperoni, and the great debate raged inside her head all over again. Only this time it was colored with appreciation, and with longing.

Chapter Seven

In the two weeks since they'd gone to dinner, Easter had come and gone and Katie had turned three months. She'd gained four pounds, and the floppy-eared rabbit Chris had once tossed into the storefront crib. The fussy period was behind her, and now she smiled all the time, literally grinning whenever she spied Chris.

They were settling into a comfortable routine, with the baby often finding a niche between them. She'd nearly forgotten the volatile meeting with Heather and, although her attraction to Chris was growing, the notion of a "quickie" marriage—or, rather, a false front—to salvage the adoption began to seem preposterous.

Then the letter came.

She'd always remember the event as occurring on a perfect spring day. Sunshine glazed the overhead canopies across the street and winked off the dew still moistening the streets. The air smelled heavy and sweet, fecund with new growth. She impatiently thumped the heels of her new taupe skimmers against the plank flooring as she reviewed Chris's past-due accounts.

When the front door chirred open, she tore her attention from the debacle over the gun cabinet. The one Chris had slaved over and his clients were content to brag about but reluctant to pay for. She was going to do something about that. She refused to see the man work for nothing.

"Hello." The man who strolled through the front door was a tad too burly across the shoulders to be interested in a footstool with a needlepoint cover. "Miss Rafco?"

"Yes?"

"This is for you." He smoothly proffered the envelope, and she saw something sinister in his toothy grin. He turned on his heel to leave, and never looked back.

She stared after him. He'd jaywalked across the street and disappeared around the bend.

Chris stuck his head out the shop door at that particular moment. "Hey, Raylene, it's time to celebrate! I got the stain on the rocker. What d'you say we kill a little time with coffee and doughnuts?"

Raylene's head swiveled, and she frowned, uncomprehending, in the face of his eager mood. She rose from the secretarial chair. "I—I don't know. This just came."

He ambled around the door frame, wiping his hands on a rag. "What? For me?" After poking the rag in his back pocket, he reached for the envelope with stained fingers.

"No. For me. This guy just walked in and delivered it. Looks official, doesn't it?"

"Like?"

"Like something from the court." Turning the envelope upside down, she pried open the flap with a fingernail. Inside, the paper was crisp and flawlessly folded in thirds, the format neat and concise. Her belly instantly roiled. "Chris..."

He moved in closer, sidling around the desk.

"It's a summons." Her breath caught, swelling into a hot lump at the base of her throat. "I'm to appear in court. For a hearing over the adoption. It's been scheduled for July thirtieth."

A soft curse issued from the depths of his lungs. Then his palm tentatively cupped her elbow. But he stayed strangely silent.

"I can't believe it. I'd started thinking it was over. That Heather had second thoughts, that after seeing us, she—"

"Come on, sit down."

"I can't believe this."

"I know," he said. "I thought, too, that maybe, after all this time, it was over." He moved closer, peering over her shoulder to read the summons himself.

"I don't know what I'm going to do."

"Hey. This could take a while. It could take months."

"Months would only make it worse."

"Maybe she's just hedging her bets. Heather probably needs to start the legal stuff to cover herself. She could still back down, and—"

"I don't think so," Raylene said dismally. "Don't be optimistic and upbeat for me. I've been expecting this, no matter how much I've tried to tell myself it couldn't happen." A shudder rippled up her spine like an aftershock. Her shoulder blades quaked, her chin trembled. "Face it," she said, her voice cracking, "the handwriting's on the wall. The most I'll be able to buy is a little time. As long as Heather's dad's there, encouraging her—"

"The bastard."

She silently echoed the obscenity, tempering it with "But Katie's still his grandchild."

"Biologically speaking."

"Everyone says that's what makes the difference. Those good old biological ties. But, dammit—" tears sprang to her eyes "—I love her. I'm still convinced I can do the best for her."

"I know, I know...." He cradled her in his arms, catching them both off balance. They both tried to steady themselves, but they swayed, his chin butting the top of her head. He paused long enough to smooth her hair. "And you are the best for her," he assured her softly, his breath feathering against her ear.

"Sometimes it seems like you're the only one who believes me." She sagged forward, her temple burrowing into the warm spot beneath his jaw. "God, I feel like I'm in emotional purgatory. I can't feel free to enjoy the baby, and I can't bring myself to descend into the hell of letting her go, either."

She was vaguely aware that she moved within his linked arms. Her cheek rode the ridge of his collarbone, her ear now flat against his chest. His flesh vibrated slightly from every rasping breath. Every tic, every burr, was magnified.

"Raylene, I—"

She waited, breathless, listening to indecision sputtering behind his breastbone. "Yes?"

"I want you to know I do believe in you. And I believe in your right to raise Katie."

It wasn't what she'd expected to hear. "Thanks, Chris."

"I've given this a lot of long, hard thought. Whatever happens, whatever you need, I want you to know I'll be there for you. I mean that." He angled his head down, snaring her uplifted gaze and holding it. Time drifted by. "I mean it. Whatever you need."

The significance of what he offered blurred. "Thanks. You've been a great friend, and you've been great to work for. A lot of employers wouldn't have been this—"

"Maybe I didn't make myself clear." His eyes momentarily rolled upwards, to the tin-paneled ceiling, while he cleared his throat. When he looked back down, his blue gaze fastened itself to her dark one. "What I'm trying to say is, if you need anything, or want anything, all you've got to do is ask. Just ask. I'll be there for you, and I won't let you down."

His earnest assurance turned her knees to jelly. Intuition told her the boundaries, the parameters, of their relationship were changing. "Thank you," she finally managed to say, her mouth moving against his soft-flannel work shirt. "But it's too soon for me to ask anything of you. Just knowing that you're here for me..."

"I am." His voice was a tough knot of conviction.

"Thanks." A second slipped by. Then two. "And knowing I don't have to explain myself to you, or even why I'm doing this..."

"You don't."

"Thanks, Chris. I mean it."

His arms tightened, confirming everything he'd said. "Raylene? If there's anything else..."

"No. Honestly. I can handle it."

His hold loosened, his hands pairing over her shoulders. "Even so, a part of me feels like I'm letting you down. Like I should be doing more for you and the baby."

"What more could you do?"

They both hesitated, aware of the answer.

She tried to shrug it off, to act innocently immune and look anywhere but at his perceptive gaze, his thinning mouth. She tried to repulse the thrumming hope and, when he said nothing, tried to stem the quickening stab of urgency.

He looked equally indecisive. As if he wanted to say something and couldn't.

"You've done more than your fair share," she finally managed. "You're my number one confidant." His hands slipped down, pulling the fabric of her blouse slightly. "I trust you, Chris. What more could I ask?"

The hell of it was, they both knew.

And it was getting harder and harder to hide from the truth.

He'd told her to go home, to spend time with the baby, to organize her thoughts and do what she needed to do. She should have done it. But she couldn't bring herself to leave the security of the old warehouse.

There was safety doing the familiar, there was relief in the routine. But being next to Chris was what cemented it.

He must have sensed how much she needed him. Because he kept popping out of the workroom, making small talk, asking her opinion about this or that. Eventually he suggested that they order takeout and share lunch. They settled on Daydreamers' Deli, and splurged on dessert, ordering cherub's delight. It seemed appropriate, making them both think of Katie.

Christian was halfway through his pita-bread sandwich when a call came from Tyler's school. Raylene was pouring him a second cup of coffee when his tone changed.

"Wait a minute. What do you mean, you can't get ahold of her?" He picked up a wood chisel, tapping the butt end against the countertop. "Have you tried the college? Well, sure, but I—" He caught Raylene's inquisitive gaze just then, and dropped the tool, letting it roll aside. Both brows pivoted upward, as if he were saying, *I can't believe this is happening. The kid's in trouble again.* "Now?" His question ended on a high, prolonged note.

Raylene turned the handle of his mug to the center of the pea-green table, acting unaffected, as if she hadn't heard any of the conversation. But when she stole a surreptitious look at Chris, her emotions flip-flopped.

No wonder he was reluctant to shoulder any more responsibility. Beth had burdened him with hers. Every time she was unavailable, he filled in. Every time she needed money, he pitched in. Every time she needed direction, he was there to point the way. The heck of it was, Beth didn't even realize how badly she took advantage of him.

"Okay, okay. I understand. I'll be right down." He wearily dropped the phone in the cradle before sliding her a regretful glance. "Sorry. I've got to cut lunch short. They can't get ahold of my sister, so I've got to go."

"To school?"

"No. Special Services."

"What?"

"He's been remanded to Special Services."

"But...why?"

"Vandalism to school property."

Raylene stared, her jaw going slack.

"He rigged a virus in one of their computer programs, as a joke. Wiped out the school's financial records. Just like that," he said, snapping his fingers. "The budgets for class projects and school-sponsored organizations like the PTO and the Boy Scouts. The principal's livid. Says it'll take months to reconstruct."

"Ah...I...I..."

"I don't know what to say, either," he said simply. "I'd like to kill him. I'd like to throttle him. I'd like to—"

"We both know better than that."

"Not right now, we don't." His lips clenched into a hard, thin line as he neatly wrapped up the remainder of his sandwich and threw it in the trash. "There. So much for lunch."

"Chris, I'm sorry."

He unexpectedly exploded. "Damn that Beth, anyway! I do more taking care of that kid than she does. If she'd just watch him once in a while: She's always gallivanting off, never telling anybody where she's going. I told her from the beginning—from the very beginning—the kid didn't deserve to be raised by a single mother, one who—" He stopped short, aware of what he'd just said.

Raylene stiffened, steeling herself to hear the rest.

"I didn't mean it that way. Not about the single-mother thing. What I meant—"

"Don't even try to apologize," she said, waving away his attempt to make things right. "I understand what you've been through. You've had your hands full."

"But I didn't mean that about you. Or that you..."

"I know."

"Beth was only eighteen. She—"

"Forget it. It's okay. Really."

He grimly wiped a hand over his exasperation. "God, I'm sorry. I'm only making it worse."

She smiled, in spite of the situation. "You are."

"I'm really sorry. But, look, since I've got to go down there, you may as well close up. We've both had rough days, so let's call it quits, and I'll see you on Monday. Okay?" His large, work-worn hand clapped her on the shoulder.

The instant his fingers splayed against her, she saw more than blunt-cut fingernails and wood stain coloring his cuticles. She saw all that those hands had accomplished, accepted and achieved. She saw purpose and independence in the life he'd fashioned. And she knew that she wanted to be an integral part of it.

"We'll see," she said impulsively, her arm flexing crosswise over her breasts, so that she could slide her hand under his. She gently squeezed his fingers. "Just don't worry about it. Okay?"

At the office of Special Services, Christian Jennings felt like a rat trapped in a maze.

One social worker proposed that they stick Ty in a juvenile home for the night. He figured it would do the kid a world of good to have the bejeebers scared out of him and show him what lay on the other side of the straight and narrow.

Protective instincts flared inside of Chris, and after that it was all downhill. During a shouting match, he made it clear—perfectly clear—that nobody used threats like that to teach his nephew a lesson.

He knew that part of the system. He knew how it felt to be terrorized, to constantly watch your backside. He remembered being eight years old, his mind zooming along in a rush as he tried to figure out the mind games—no, the power games—the adults around him played. He knew how it worked, and he wouldn't let that happen to Tyler.

The kid deserved to be a kid, one without mind-boggling fear and apprehension.

But in order to see to that, Chris spent hours going in and out of offices, listening to official rhetoric and professional drivel. Someone hollered about accountability, someone else threatened a lawsuit. Another badgered him about possible probation. One suggested Special Education.

By the time they were done, his mind had turned to jelly, and his thinking was a shade less than logical.

But the kid was in deep doo-doo, and the part that was nagging at him, the part that really goaded him, was that his mother had seemingly disappeared. In the few moments he was given, Chris called every number he could think of, trying to locate her.

Seven hours later, at six-thirty and on the fourth ring, she finally answered at her apartment. She answered the Where-the-hell-have-you-been? question defensively.

What difference did it make? She'd been lunching, and shopping, and getting her nails done.

When she failed to ask where Tyler was, bile rose in his throat, and he turned as livid as the school principal. "What do you mean, you took a day off?" he'd demanded.

"I took a day off, because I deserved it. I got an A in sociology. And I haven't done anything else but study and pick up after Ty since—"

God, she could belch out more excuses... "I don't want to hear it."

"Chris—"

"You better get down here, and pretty quick. I've spent the day keeping him out of Juvenile Hall."

"What?"

They got into their first good fight since they were kids. He accused her of being unreliable; she accused him of not listening. She said she deserved a day off once in a while; he said his understanding of mother-hood was that it was a full-time job. She claimed she was sick and tired of his judgmental, holier-than-thou attitude; he claimed he was sick and tired of the way she shifted Tyler from pillar to post, putting every-thing and everyone before him and his needs.

She screamed and ranted and raved. She felt sorry for herself, and then tried making him feel guilty, say-ing he didn't understand.

He stoically said nothing, let the tantrum subside, and finally pointed out that all the two of them had was each other. He'd be there for her, but either she'd have to pull her weight or the next time he wouldn't inter-vene. He'd let them turn Tyler over to the juvenile courts.

For a full two minutes, she was indignant and spewed forth epithets that their old man would have been proud of. Again he waited her out, clamping his jaws shut until they ached. When finally she was spent, there remained nothing but dead silence over the phone. That, and the hurried way she said she'd meet him downtown in five minutes.

When Beth finally burst through the door, she stared at him, aghast, and obviously ashamed of all the things she'd said.

She begged forgiveness when she finally crumpled into his arms, sobbing. If she weren't his sister, he wouldn't have been able to accept her apologies, her guilt, her remorse.

It all happened so quickly, he comforted her.

The social worker looked away uncomfortably, clearing his throat, apparently affected.

Sure, they resolved the thing, but it took something out of him. He left Special Services depleted. He put Beth and Tyler in her run-down little car, and enviously watched them drive away together. He felt equally relieved and left out.

It was dusk by the time he reached his own car, and he sat in the empty parking lot for a good fifteen minutes, incapable of putting the key in the ignition. It got to him, like a cold sweat, knowing how alone he was. With no one to talk to, no one to run his feelings up against.

The car purred for another five minutes before he threw it in gear, and then he drove around, going down to the lake, chafing at the prospect of returning to an empty apartment. He stared out at the gray water, his feelings magnified. He was forlorn, confused, and hungry.

He passed up a few fast-food places, he knew they'd never ease his starving hunger. His emotions were raw and ragged and hurting. Without purpose or reason, he started mulling over the value of life, convinced that he didn't know how he fit into the scheme of things. It didn't seem fair; nothing seemed fair.

He couldn't change his past, his drunken sot of a father or all the revolting names he'd been called in his youth. He couldn't get the memory of his shop teacher out of his head, either. Or the way he'd taken a skinny kid under his wing, showing him how to make bookends from scrap lumber, teaching him all the little tricks he knew about organizing a shop. Little tricks that had somehow spilled over and organized his life.

The old coot had died six years back, and in his will he'd left Christian Jennings all his tools. Even his workbench. Now, every time he picked up a wood-handled chisel, he thought of how Leroy Jenkins had used it. He could almost see his gnarly, bent-knuckled hands curling around the stem.

Dammit! He missed that gray-haired, wizened old guy.

Driving by the kiddie park, he saw, under the vapor lights, a bonneted baby being pushed in a swing. He immediately thought of Katie, and a bit of hope burgeoned in the vicinity of his heart.

Katie's wild hair tucked beneath a bonnet.

Her almond-shaped eyes glowing as her mother pushed her.

Her mother—Raylene Rafco—and how her love for a child had reawakened feelings he thought he'd long since buried. The pair of them had come into his life, without being invited or welcomed, and he'd come to a crossroads. Looking for them every day, finding ways to keep them near, looking for excuses to couple his life with theirs.

Realizing that, and coming to terms with it, made it easier to turn the car toward home. But his muscles, his bones, felt unstrung. When he turned the corner and saw lights on in the showroom, he went sick with anxiety.

He countered the rush of adrenaline with caution. Maybe she'd forgotten to turn the lights off. She couldn't have stayed this late.

He swallowed, his eyes narrowing, when he saw movement back where the cradle should be. A blur of dark hair dipped and disappeared.

Taking up two diagonal parking spaces, he spun out of the driver's seat, slamming the door so hard the body of his old car shimmied. He jumped the steps up to the curb in double time, all the while telling himself she probably wasn't there, anyway.

Nobody ever waited up for him.

Still, he didn't bother to compose himself when he burst through the door. He wanted to see if she was really there, if he surprised her, if her eyes would widen at his entrance.

She was! They did!

He had this uncanny impulse to scoop her up in his arms. To scoop them both up in his arms, to tell them how grateful he was that they were waiting there. He ached to lose himself in the smells of them, in the cuddly-warm feel of them.

"Oh, good. You're back. I was getting worried," Raylene smiled and half turned, looking back over her shoulder and talking while she tossed a lap pad back in the cradle. "Everything's okay?"

"Yeah. Great." His arms hurt so bad from wanting to reach out to them, to welcome himself back home. Taking deep breaths, he stayed where he was until his feelings went numb. "It'll work out."

"Good."

His cheeks puffed out. He knew he should be making some kind of conversation. But his mind wasn't on Tyler or Beth or what they'd been through; his mind was on Raylene. And how she looked holding the baby. "You waited."

"You don't mind?"

"No." He said it too quickly, aware that she didn't have a clue about the emotions pulsing through him. "No. No, not at all."

"I thought someone should be here." She glanced to the drop-leaf table, to a stack of order forms. "Business was surprisingly good. Three new orders."

He slowly peeled off his jacket, consciously telling himself to be restrained, to feign interest. "No kidding?"

"You'll need to call them back."

He nodded, hooking his jacket over the flat shelf of a plant stand. "She asleep?"

"Yeah. I know, I know. I should let a sleeping baby lie, but..."

He knew. The future was uncertain, and she was hoarding what time she had left with Kate. He nodded, moving toward them as if the magnetism of opposing forces governed his movements. Once he was at her side, the scent of her perfume soothed the turmoil inside him, making him pause long enough to push the receiving blanket back from Katie's shoulder, to touch his fingertip to the dimples in her hands. "Thanks," he said finally, gruffly. "For waiting."

"I didn't know if you'd need to talk."

He barely shrugged, but his eyes were glued to the baby before they slowly lifted to her. "Maybe I do. But not about Tyler, or Beth, or everything that's happened."

"Oh?"

"No, this time I think I want to talk about me."

"You?"

"Yeah. And how I want to change things, but I just don't know how."

"Like?"

"Like my life. And how routine it's become."

"But you love the warehouse, and your work, and—"

"There aren't any people in it. Not any people who care. Only customers who come and go, a nephew I baby-sit, a sister I watch out for."

"But you're well respected, you're admired—"

"Only from a distance. Only for the facade that sells handcrafted furniture outsiders want to buy. Not by the people who remember me growing up, remember a dirty, skinny kid from the wrong side of the tracks. My old man was the town drunk, Raylene. Did you know that? Did you?" He couldn't prevent the challenge riding his voice. If she was going to walk out, she'd better do it now.

A flicker of shock rippled through her dark eyes, but she quickly masked it. "So? You're not him."

"Maybe not, but I've been carrying the ghost of his reputation around with me like dead weight. Since the first-grade Christmas pageant when he came in rip-roaring drunk, singing some bawdy version of "Up on the Housetop." And it seemed like every night he beat my mom, and ridiculed my sister."

Raylene flinched, and her eyes briefly fluttered closed. But she didn't turn away. "Then, if you've been carrying it with you that long, Chris," she said softly as her hand covered his wrist, "it's time to let it go. Maybe what you need—"

"What I need," he said in a guttural voice, interrupting her, "is to be touched. Like this..."

She quizzically lifted her head at the same time he dropped his. Their lips were but inches apart, and their eyes were issuing mutual consent.

"Oh, Chris..." she whispered in protest, when his mouth nuzzled the corner of hers. "Are we doing this for the right reasons? Are we?"

"I am."

With the baby between them, he kissed her. Soundly, provocatively, without fear of recriminations.

Their mouths meshed, and she gave as wholeheartedly as she took. And then the baby, who was wedged tight in the circle of their embrace, squalled, and they knew it was right.

Chapter Eight

That kiss should have confirmed things. It should have made the situation more comfortable, it should have opened up dialogue between them and made them move toward a resolution. It should have proved that they had more between them than a furniture shop and the contested adoption of a baby.

But it didn't. It only made the whole kit and caboodle more intolerable. It threw up unanswered questions. It made Raylene walk a fine line, wondering whether she was Chris's employee, his friend or his casual love interest.

If she became cautious about taking too much for granted, he became expansive, his smile wider and more encouraging.

If she tried to absorb any of the fascinating little details about his past, he cut her off with short answers.

Did you play baseball as a kid, like Ty?

I didn't do anything as a kid.

I'll bet you grew up making wooden candlesticks for your mom and birdhouses for your dad, didn't you?

Actually, my mom never set a table for Sunday dinner, and the only wild life my dad was interested in was his.

She thought about asking Beth about it, then decided not to. She thought about sharing a few stories about her youth, then decided that was too obvious. She wanted to get him to open up, but she simply didn't know how.

Maybe she'd come to accept his stoic silence about the volatile nature of his youth. Perhaps she'd come to accept, as he did, that that part of his life was a closed book.

But the future held another, inevitable problem: If he should ever offer her his heart, Raylene could not give him a family of his own. She couldn't give him a baby. Not his baby. It undermined her self-confidence, making her feel insignificant.

God, infertility had a way of making everything a jumble.

Chris would want a big family. She was sure of it. Hadn't his eyes lit up when the family with two sets of twins and three singles came in to order bunk beds?

But sometimes, she told herself, you settled for things in life. You accepted what was dealt you and you made the best of it.

Maybe Christian Jennings had been the wild card in her hand, and she'd never even recognized it.

The wall between the showroom and workroom separated nothing but their physical bodies. Their thoughts kept floating through the drywall. She was conscious of the way his rubber mallet thwacked the dovetailed joints on Mrs. Melstrom's bureau drawers; he was conscious of the lilting way she answered the phone.

Raylene, who had always kept a compact and a lipstick in her desk drawer, suddenly started using it. Chris began slapping on a little after-shave every morning. Then he started using lip balm.

Just in case.

Raylene's awareness of Katie's bad hair days suddenly refocused on her own. She spent a whopping thirty-five bucks on a guaranteed haircut. In a counterattack, Chris went to a barber to have his hair stylishly trimmed.

Both of them nearly swallowed their tongues when they noticed.

Frequently they were drawn to the connecting doorway with inconsequential questions that simply couldn't wait. Trivialities that called up indebtedness, concern.

I need to turn on the shop vacuum, pick up a little sawdust. It won't bother you, will it?

You're running short on stamps, Chris. Want me to pick some up?

Would it be out of the way to ask you to steady this two-by-eight for me? Just till I get the right angle?

I made a cherry cheesecake last night. Want some?

That was the way it happened, the unimportant, the insignificant, bringing them together. Then, on a Wednesday morning in the middle of May, when the sun was streaming in the windows and dust motes were dancing through the air, he paused in the doorway again. The tour buses hadn't yet crowded the streets, but the smells of fresh-cut flowers, warm pastries and lake water was heavy and thick.

"Raylene?"

"Yes?" She turned, the morning's mail still in her hand.

"Anything important?"

"Nope. Just the regular stuff. No bills."

"Oh. Good." But he looked uninterested, gazing out the front windows before looking back, to the hem of her skirt. "You know, I still can't believe you have legs."

"Jeez." She grinned, her cheeks pinkening. "If I'd known doing something out of the ordinary, like wearing a dress, was going to make that much of an impression on you—"

"You'd have done it sooner, huh?"

"No. Probably not at all." But she was flattered, and he knew it, because his mouth was bunched up into a tight little smile. "So. Want me to call Mrs. Melstrom on the bureau?"

"You can." They parried each other's querulous gazes for a few fleeting seconds.

"Okay, then. Be happy to."

"Well. Okay. Anything else?"

Want to marry me?

She drew a deep, ragged breath, horrified that the question had popped into her head before she could stop it. "Um, no. Not really. Not that I can think of."

Nothing, except how they should sacrifice their pride and take the initiative joining their lives. For Katie's sake, of course. There was nothing left but the uncertainty of who would have the gumption to step up and make the suggestion.

The ultimate proposal.

"Um, look, I'm not bothering you, am I?"

"No, not at all." Her finger rubbed the ends of the business-size envelopes she held.

"Three sets of no-frills bunk beds gets a little mundane. They're making me feel like I'm really working."

She smiled, thinking she'd never heard him complain of being bored with a length of lumber before. A light bulb of an idea simultaneously flashed in her head, making her act on impulse. "You need to do something different." She said it enthusiastically, but her throat went dry and her mouth went watery when she realized where she was heading.

"Any suggestions?"

Her heart tapped out an uneasy warning, but she refused to back down. "Well, I'm not suggesting plant stands or quilt racks."

"No?"

"No." His appearance made her emotions run sappy. He'd leaned a shoulder into the door frame, and one hip rode slightly higher than the other. The toe of his shoe butted up against the heel of the other. The self-made man, in jeans and a plaid work shirt. And she wanted him. All of him. "What I had in mind was your personal life."

He lifted both brows. "My personal life."

She drew in the sweet spring air, swallowing so hard it made her breastbone hurt. "Well, I've been thinking this over. Maybe you were right a few weeks ago. Maybe what Katie needs, and maybe what would make Heather happy, is a live-in daddy."

"Live-in?"

Disappointment rode heavy in his voice, as if he couldn't fathom why she'd even suggested it. As if she'd dropped a notch in his estimation.

"Well, no. I— What I meant was . . . was that . . ."

"Go on." He folded his arms, waiting, a flat-headed screwdriver jutting out from the crease of his elbow.

"Well, it seems to me . . ." Her stomach turned over, and she felt sick. Good grief, did men actually get down on their knees to do this? How did they cushion themselves against the shame of rejection? How did they keep going when they felt stupid? "That we both have a lot in common . . ." What? The only thing they had in common was that they worked in the same building three days a week. "That we have a situation here that could be mutually beneficial . . ."

She implored him with her eyes, begging him to pick up the implication and run with it. He remained impassive.

"Well, look, here's the thing," she said, determined to be brutally frank. "Heather said maybe if she knew Katie had a father she'd feel differently. You said, go ahead, let her think Katie's going to have a whole family, a mom and a dad. And you said you'd be happy to fill in for the charade. And at first I thought it was a little dishonest, but since then I've been thinking maybe you're right, maybe the idea's got merit."

"Thank you."

The way he said it took her breath away. "You're welcome."

"Anything else?"

"Well, yes."

"And that is—?"

She took a deep, cleansing breath. "In order to fix everything, Katie's got to have a daddy, and I've got to have a—" she winced, squaring her shoulders, and threw the obvious solution down like a gauntlet "—a husband."

"Mmm."

"That's all? Mmm?"

"Mm-hmm, I think you're right on target."

"You do?"

"Mm-hmm."

She stared at him, realizing that she'd neglected the little thing about him being the husband. Well, actually, she'd sort of alluded to it. But he must be in wood warp, because he wasn't picking up on it.

"Chris, I know there's a lot I can't give you, like children of your own, or—"

"Doesn't matter."

A quivery feeling rippled through her. "But I've always been good at overcompensating," she said shakily. "If we threw our lot in together, I wouldn't have any regrets about quitting my other jobs to put more time in here at the shop, to free up more time for you." His mouth quirked, but he didn't say anything. "Okay, okay. Maybe I didn't do this right. What I should've said is that I admire you, and that I think you're a...a..." A hunk? God, she couldn't say that out loud, could she? "A dependable, hardworking guy I'd like to introduce as my baby's father. I trust you, and I—"

"You don't have to inflate my ego, Raylene."

"Well, sorry, I guess I don't really know how to do this. I mean, I didn't come to work this morning thinking I was going to . . . to . . ."

"Propose? That's okay. But don't disappoint me. I figured that was what the dress was for."

In spite of the sticky situation, she laughed, dropping her head in embarrassment. What if he shrugged the whole thing off as a joke? Would she be relieved or humiliated?

"Are you attracted to me, Raylene?"

She lifted her head. The unexpected question blew her out of the water, making her jaw slide off center.

"If I wasn't attracted to you," she said slowly, honestly, "I wouldn't have let what happened the other night happen." She couldn't bring herself to say 'kiss' aloud, not when they were standing across the room from each other, discussing this as if it were a business deal.

"I'm attracted to you," he said without hesitation. Unfolding his arms, he moved farther into the room. "And I love Katie. And I certainly could use a little extra help in the shop."

Outside, the clock on the corner chimed the half hour. "Then you're saying—?"

"If it's a proposal, I accept."

Jubilation went winging through her, anticipation made every nerve ending tingle.

"But there are a couple of things I need to clarify."

"Yes?"

"My priorities don't lie solely with work." He bit back a smile when her eyes went round. "And if we're going do to this right, we're going to live together, correct?"

She fidgeted, laying the envelopes on the desk. "I don't know. I hadn't gotten that far."

"Would it surprise you if I said I had?"

"You?"

"Me," he confirmed, never blinking an eye. "And I'd be proud to be Katie's father, and your husband. But not in name only. If we do this, we do it all the way. My only stipulation is that we have a real marriage—in the bedroom and out."

* * *

Flabbergasted would have been an understatement.

But even in her stunned condition, Raylene knew she had to accept. She tried to do so with as much dignity and aplomb as possible.

"Thank you, Chris. I can see where that would be best."

"Really?"

"It makes sense."

It made not a lick of sense, and they both knew it. It was impulse and instinct and lust, pure and simple.

"Well, we don't have to rush things," he amended.

"Maybe not. But we're adults. We can see the long-term benefits, and we can handle this civilly, and without regrets."

Oh, God, what was she saying? She was presenting it all in such a detached manner that she probably looked like a prude.

He cleared his throat and reached around to place the screwdriver in his back pocket. "Well, then. That's that. We're agreed." He took three steps closer and maneuvered around her, to the huge calendar dominating the wall beside her desk. He poked the day's date with his thumb. "I'll clean out a few closets, and you can start moving your things in anytime."

"Into *your* apartment?"

"Well, I just thought..." He looked back over his shoulder.

"Of course. That would be great. My lease is almost up, anyway."

"That's the logical thing to do, then."

"Of course." Right. Logical. They'd just pledged their lives away, and they were making all the right decisions in the guise of self-restraint. No emotion, no enthusiasm. And fear so deep they could both taste it.

His thumbnail scratched at the date, as if he were inclined to permanently banish it from the calendar. "Suppose we should set a date, then, just to make it official?"

"Go ahead. You choose." Good God! She'd made it sound as if they were choosing up sides for a sandlot baseball game.

"I always thought women were partial to June weddings." When she shrugged, he added, "You should have what you want, Raylene. I know this wasn't what you counted on, but it should still be special."

She hesitated, painfully aware of how polite they were being to each other. "All right. The end of May, then. Before the June rush of weddings. I like that."

"Memorial Day weekend would give us an extra day."

"Terrific."

"Okay, great. And Saturday weddings are nice. And it's only two weeks away."

"Will we be able to arrange for a justice of the peace?" she asked.

"Justice of the peace? You sure?"

"Of course." Visions of a white dress, of the once-in-a-lifetime honor of walking down the aisle, fell away from her fantasies. It wasn't important. Katie was important. "Besides, it's a holiday weekend. Everything will be booked."

"Maybe not."

"Most couples plan weddings a year in advance."

"Let's check it out anyway," he chided. "Because you never really struck me as the type to run away and get married. Totally out of character for you."

"This whole thing is totally out of character for both of us."

"Who's going to notice?"

"Your sister. My brother."

"Ah... Well, we'll make it believable for them." An appealing grin tilted the corner of his mouth. "Come on. Let's think about doing this right. We may be getting married under duress, but we don't have to be Spartan about it."

It almost crippled her, the way he was trying so hard to make it better. The way he was trying to humor her, to please her. He looked like an overgrown kid anxiously seeking approval.

"Oh, Christian," she suddenly blurted out, "you're so good to me. What did I do to deserve this?"

"Aw, I dunno," he drawled, obviously affected. "You came in looking for a job, and convinced me you're the best bookkeeper around. Then you turned my life upside down, and had me make a crib without telling me who it was for. And then, when I found out you were using a bassinet, I ended up doing a rush job, so I couldn't possibly charge you full price. I don't know. Things sort of went full steam after that, I guess."

She chuckled, her eyes closing as she remembered how profusely he'd apologized for a few nondescript boo-boos.

"You brought Katie into my life, and made me see there's life outside the four walls of my workshop." He caught her shoulder, his blue gaze penetrating her dark one. "Maybe this is my way of thanking you for that."

"Oh, Chris. You're one in a million."

"So," he said, his voice going suggestively husky. "How about if we seal the deal?"

He moved toward her, and she was in his arms in a heartbeat, thrilling to his touch, and replying to his questioning lips. She had just about convinced herself she'd come out on top of a shameful bargain, and was pretty much ready to take the passion and run, when they were interrupted by the sound of someone chuckling softly.

Chapter Nine

"Excuse me? This something you forgot to mention?" Beth asked, smiling brightly, from just inside the doorway.

Christian and Raylene broke apart guiltily. He recovered first, grinning broadly as Raylene tried to right herself.

"Christian Nathaniel Jennings!" His sister chided lightly. "You, of all people? And during working hours, to boot? Looks like you've got some explaining to do, big brother."

"Yep. Sure do."

"Well?"

He paused for a heartbeat. "We're getting married."

"What?" Beth stared incredulously at them both.

"I said, we're getting married."

"To each other?"

Chris and Raylene exchanged glances, and choked back a pair of nervous giggles.

"An office romance, and I didn't even know about it?"

"We didn't want to give anyone the wrong impression," Chris explained.

"Just in case things didn't work out," Raylene added.

"Are you kidding? This is great! Hallelujah!" Beth raised her fist, then pulled it down, like a trucker pulling an air horn. "Thank you, Raylene, you saved my brother from being a lonely old bachelor." She twirled around, adding a few fancy steps. "I'm going to have a sister-in-law. This is gonna be great!"

"Back off a little, will you?" Chris admonished, drawing Raylene beneath his arm. "Don't scare her away, okay?"

"You know me, I always come on a little strong. So. When's the big day?"

"Your brother picked May twenty-seventh."

"Next year."

"No. This year."

"This year? That's barely two weeks away!"

"I know. We didn't want to wait."

"What do you mean, you didn't want to wait? You're gonna do this up big, aren't you? There's the church, the flowers, the caterer, the dress—"

"We thought we'd do something quiet," Raylene said gently, looking up at Christian for confirmation. He nodded.

"Quiet?" Beth repeated. "God forbid! Not as in justice-of-the-peace quiet?"

"We thought it'd be too much too soon for a big affair, and there's Katie to consider, and—"

"I told Raylene she should have what she wants."

"Get real, Christian. Raylene's just being nice, and maybe a little practical. What she wants is a real wedding. Every woman wants a real wedding!"

"Well, it'll be real. We hereby guarantee authenticity."

Beth ignored Christian's comment and zeroed in on Raylene. "With people like me standing up for you? And matching wedding bands, and a bottle of champagne, and boutonnieres for the guys and stephanotis for the bride?"

"Stephanotis? I don't even know what stephanotis is."

"Sounds like a contagious disease," Chris remarked dryly, winking at Raylene. "I'll pass. How about you?"

"Not funny, Christian," Beth said, annoyed. "Stephanotis is a little flower in the bride's bouquet. And the bride's bouquet should be memorable. Spectacular."

"You're one step ahead of us," Raylene ventured. "I mean, we just decided to get married. We haven't given any thought to details."

"Really? Well, then, holy moly, I can't believe my sense of timing, can you?"

"Not me."

"Me either."

Beth never recognized the undercurrent of sarcasm running between Chris and Raylene. "Okay, so this is how we'll do it—I'll sit down with you this very afternoon, Raylene, and we'll start a to-do list. And you'll want to call your brother, too, won't you? Because he'll want to come."

Raylene, who nodded politely, saw the handwriting on the wall. Life as she knew it was disintegrating.

Beth overwhelmed Raylene with her list-making capabilities. She appeared to know weddings inside and out, everything from how flowers should be attached to the cake server to how high the bride should wear her garter.

It was truly frightening.

By merely mentioning the word *marriage,* they had created a monster. One who thrived on tulle, baby's breath and organ music. One who could debate the validity of writing their own marriage vows as opposed to the traditional ones. One who had a recipe for cream cheese mint molds, and insisted on making twelve dozen as part of her contribution to the festivities.

And she wouldn't back down. On anything.

"I'm telling you, this is really silly," Raylene objected the following afternoon as she automatically punched in a number on the push-button phone, "because he's not home and he's not going to come. Mike works for this hard-nosed advertising firm." The phone started ringing, but she kept talking. "He's going to call me back tonight and tell me he's got a big project in the works. He'll congratulate me and send me a nice check." Two rings and counting. Two more and the answering machine would pop on. "It's the way he does things. My brother, he—"

"Hel-lo."

Hearing the musical shift in her brother's voice, Raylene stood straighter, surprised. "Michael?"

"Yeah?"

"What're you doing home so early?"

"Grabbing a sandwich before trotting off to impress a client."

"Oh. I was positive I'd get your answering machine."

"Didn't want to talk to me, huh? Wanted to put it on my phone bill, huh?"

"No."

"Disposable diapers still eating you alive, are they?"

"No, no. I can still afford long distance."

He chuckled. "So, what's up? And how's the baby?"

"Oh, she's great. Growing. Sleeping through the night."

"No kidding? How about the other?"

She hesitated, knowing what he meant: What was happening in the legal tangle over Katie's adoption? "The same."

"Mmm . . . too bad."

"Yeah, I know. I'm really not calling about that."

"No?"

"Well, it's like this . . ." She took a fortifying breath, and turned her back on Beth so that she could weather the impact of his reaction, "Guess what?" she said with a false note of exuberance. "I'm getting married!"

"You're what?"

"Getting married. And I want you to come." *Please come. Suddenly I know how much I need you.*

"Why?"

She couldn't answer, not without Beth hearing. "I know it's a surprise. It is for us, too." Suspicion hummed over the phone wires. "But it just happened, and we didn't want to wait, and—"

"Who is this guy? I mean, I didn't even know you were dating anyone, and—"

"His name's Christian Jennings. He's the guy I work for, the guy with the furniture store."

"Oh. Uh-huh."

"You know how it is when you're working together. You get to—"

"This is kind of quick, isn't it?"

"In a way. Like I told you, we started spending a lot of time together, and we found out we had a lot in common—"

"This is the same guy you said spent all his time in the back room, brooding over his work, tormented by wood screws and knotty pine."

"Michael. I was being facetious."

"I know you well enough to know you'd—pardon the expression—hit the nail on the head."

"Michael. Stop. You're going to like him. He's terrific. Talented. Hardworking."

He hesitated. "You do sound happy."

"I am. Who'd ever have thought I'd get involved in a whirlwind courtship?"

"Not me. That's for sure." In her mind's eye, she could see him shaking his head, his eyes closed.

"His sister's declaring it an office romance."

"Oh. So I suppose that makes it official. When's the big day?"

"May twenty-seventh."

"A holiday weekend?"

"It just worked out that way," she said apologetically, trying to ease his disbelief. "Because we didn't want to wait."

"Okay. Well, great. I guess a three day weekend will help my vacation schedule."

"You think you'll come?"

"Are you kidding? I wouldn't miss this for the world."

He was coming? He was giving up work to travel halfway across the country to be with her for one of the most misunderstood moments of her life? She felt like a cheat for deceiving him. "Well . . . gee. Thanks."

"Hey. I've only got one sister. The least I can do is be there for you."

An uneasy feeling wormed its way under her skin. Michael was being much too amiable. He was coming to check things out, she knew it. "I was afraid maybe you'd have too much going on."

"Naw, the calendar's pretty clear into June. And if it isn't, I'll clear it."

"You'd do that for me?"

"Of course. Can't wait to meet the guy."

"You'll like him, Mike. Really."

"Gotcha. But right now, Ray, I gotta run. Don't mean to cut you off, but I'm already going to be late. Call you when I make the plane reservations. Oh, and Ray?"

"Yeah?"

"Kiss the baby for me."

"Okay. Sure."

"And, um... Congratulations, I guess. You took me by surprise on this one. I'm real, um...happy for you. I think."

"Thanks. I do appreciate you saying it."

They hadn't addressed his misgivings, but she hung up full of apprehension. She knew Michael would be coming to the wedding prepared to uncover any lies. He'd keep an eye out for any ulterior motives.

If she was going to make this work, she'd have to put on the performance of her life.

"So, tell me!" Beth impatiently demanded, bringing her back to reality. "He's coming, isn't he?"

"He says he is."

"Perfect! Between him and me, I swear, we'll turn this into a family affair!"

But it didn't remain a family affair, not under Beth's guiding hand. Over seventy wedding invitations for an early-morning wedding—9:30—a three-tiered cake—with a fountain tucked between the layers—reservations for brunch at Bell's Inn—in the swanky Fireside Room—an off-the-rack wedding gown—silk and organza—and a single on-sale attendant's dress—Beth's size—coupled with a visit to the Tuxedo Shop, had inflated it into an overblown, overgrown extravaganza.

The candles would be raspberry and white.

The mints raspberry and vanilla.

Trailing silk ivy would flow from two wicker baskets.

The brunch would feature a buffet of ham and a round of beef, eight side dishes, and platters of fruit.

Then, out of the blue, Beth suggested a pianist, in tux and tails, to entertain them while they dined. Either that or a harpist. A harpist, she declared, would really add class. Raylene groped for a reply.

The wedding date loomed, a mere seven days away, and her nerves were frazzled. Nothing was working out except the details. And, to her horror, under Beth's hand, those kept multiplying. Raylene felt as if she didn't even know what was up anymore.

She was incapable of seeing beyond anything other than the facade Beth was weaving around her. She was numb, not even feeling a part of it.

To the suggestion of the harpist, she finally mumbled, "I'll mention it to Chris, and see what he thinks." Chris?

The only contact she had had with him recently were the brief exchanges in which she discussed colors, menus, cakes, printed napkins and blood tests. Beth reminded her to tell him when to mail the invitations, what time to be at the chapel for the rehearsal and when to pick up and return the tuxedos. She couldn't even imagine him wearing a white starched shirt with tucks down the front. And patent-leather shoes? Forget it.

Beth had actually penciled in an appointment for them to go down to the courthouse and get their marriage license. They had both dutifully gone. It remained a blur in her memory.

But she did remember that Christian, bless him, had merely smiled agreeably to whatever was requested of him.

That was the only thing that had gotten her through. That, and the realization that he was doing this for her, and because of that, she couldn't bring herself to let him down.

But the harpist was the absolute last straw.

For the life of her, she couldn't imagine presiding over an elaborate brunch, with Chris trussed up like prime penguin meat in a Pierre Cardin tux, while they were serenaded with deliriously soft, ridiculously expensive music.

They were used to deli sandwiches, flannel shirts and sensible shoes. They were used to the hollow sounds of his old warehouse, to the sounds of his boom box belting out country tunes, with static fracturing the melodies.

Sure, she wanted things nice, but this was beyond the realm of believability. This was no longer the two of them making a commitment to raise Katie together. This was making a silk purse out of a sow's ear.

And it was time to deal with it.

"Hi." Raylene shyly poked her head into the workroom, suddenly awash with trepidation about the man who was to soon become her husband. "Am I bothering you?"

"No. Come on in."

"Sure? I know you've gotten behind these past few days."

He rolled his eyes, his smile going lopsided. God, she was beginning to love that about him. "Doesn't matter. We can play catch-up later."

We? Soon it would not be me and you—but we.

"Be glad to get this rocker out of here," he went on, still balancing on his knees to take one last swipe at the spindles. He seemed unaware that she hadn't answered. "It's been a thorn in my side from the beginning." He paused, laying the brush, still glossy with polyurethane, atop the opened can. "So. What can I do for you? More measurements for tuxedos, more consultations about the white runner or the church music?"

She shook her head, and stepped over the threshold. "No, thank God."

He snorted, his nostrils pinching. Rolling back on his haunches, he lowered himself into a cross-legged position. "I didn't know there was this much involved in the wedding business," she said, sitting opposite him, on the sawhorse. "I thought we'd just get married."

"We will," he stated.

"But...it's getting complicated. This is more than I bargained for."

The expectant light faded from his eyes. "You having second thoughts?" he asked carefully.

"No. No, I—"

"Last-minute jitters?"

She was disappointing him, and knowing that made her want to be completely honest. Wasn't that the ultimate goal of the union they were moving toward? Honesty? Trust? Commitment?

"Only about certain things."

"Like?"

She longed to reach out and touch him and assure him that it wasn't him. But she was scared. How would he react?

"Like the harpist Beth wants to hire for the brunch."

"That's it? A harpist?" Relief flickered in his eyes.

"It doesn't seem right."

"To me either."

"I don't want to hurt her feelings."

"Ha. She's strung with steel." He paused. "Raylene? It's no big deal."

Tears began welling up in her eyes. All this time she'd kept it under control. Now he was being kind to her and dismissing her anxiety, and she felt an inexplicable need to wail.

"Raylene?"

"I—I'm sorry."

"Come here. Sit down with me." He opened his arms to her, and she stared. "Come on."

"I'm being silly."

"No." But he smiled when he said it.

Without realizing how she managed to do so, she slipped down onto the rubber-matted floor, only inches from his extended arms.

"It's okay. Maybe we both need this. There's been a lot of excitement." She nodded. "Maybe we need to talk about it."

"Maybe."

He settled the matter, reaching out to fold one arm around her and tip her against his shoulder. "Feel better?"

"Yes," she lied.

"Then what's going on inside that head of yours?"

Her mouth started curving into a smile, and her body began melting against him. "I don't know. I guess I feel like this wedding's slipping away from me."

"Mmm . . . I understand that."

"I appreciate what Beth's doing, but—"

"But she's taken over." She nodded against his shoulder, and he maneuvered himself around, to pull her across his lap. "I was under the impression this was what you wanted."

"You thought that?"

"I thought, okay, if those things made you happy—"

"Oh, Christian . . ."

"It's okay. It doesn't matter."

"But look what we've done. We lost sight of why we're doing this. We were going to be practical, and—"

"Hey!" He gave her a squeeze. "I'm not sure I want to be one-hundred-percent practical."

She turned and smiled into his chest. God, she'd never realized how sinewy his arms were, how muscled his chest was.

"I know Beth's gone overboard, and I apologize for it," he told her. "I think she wants this wedding so much for herself that she isn't stopping to think about what we want for ourselves."

"I know. I got that feeling, too."

"She always wanted to be a stay-at-home mom. When she was widowed and had to go and get a job, she felt doubly cheated." He stroked her sleeve pensively. "She ended up making Ty too independent. And she's resented it, I think. She's cut herself off from him because of it."

"She doesn't see that?"

"I don't think so."

"Odd. How everything moves in a circle."

"It is. But she's always wanted to get remarried, and she's always wanted more kids. She's real partial to babies."

Raylene stared at the rocker's rungs. "I always wanted a houseful of kids, too," she confided. "That's why, when the doctor told me..." The soothing motion of Chris's hand stilled. He waited, saying nothing, expecting her to continue.

"Well, I was having a lot of pain, and... the doctor told me it was endometriosis. I thought it was something fixable. I never thought it would prevent me from being a mother, or—" she shook her head in frustration "—take away that part of my life. When he said I'd probably never be able to have children, I wasn't the same anymore. I started seeing what I couldn't have, what I couldn't give to someone else."

"That shouldn't stop two people from having a full life together."

"But hasn't it crossed your mind?" she persisted, lifting her head. "Doesn't it bother you to know you're getting married and you'll never have children of your own?"

"You're giving me a daughter."

"But—"

"I never expected more. I consider her a gift."

His reply stunned her. She intuitively knew that the bond they were creating went beyond Katie. What would happen if they lost her? "Why are you doing this for me? I mean, after all these years, you've probably had your share of chances for marriage. You've probably had a dozen girlfriends, and—"

"No."

"I don't believe it."

"I already told you. My father was the town drunk—the guy everybody laughed at."

"And I told you that doesn't bother me."

"Maybe not. But what you don't realize is what it did to me."

She angled her head, considering. Waiting. "Christian?"

"We were his family," he said finally. "We were the ones who had to hold our heads up, knowing everybody was gossiping behind their hands. We tried to act like we didn't care if our pants were getting too short or our hair hadn't been washed or our clothes weren't clean."

"Your mother—"

"Did what she could. But it was a hand-to-mouth existence." He leaned back slightly, pulling her with him. "He used to beat her up pretty bad. Had a hell of a mean streak. Especially on a rum hangover."

"Did he ever hit you and Beth?"

"Sometimes. Not so much." He wondered if the scars across his lower back were still visible. Once they became man and wife and started sharing the bedroom, how long would it take her to notice? "But we used to be pretty damn good at making up stories to explain away the bruises. To hear us tell it, you'd think we spent our childhood falling down steps, out of trees or off our bicycles. The Child Protective Agency came once and scared the hell out of us. Mom panicked and figured they'd take us away. I weighed the guilt of wanting them to take me away against the fear of her being alone. And I knew I couldn't live with that, so I kept on lying, to protect everybody."

She leaned into him harder, hugging him. "I'm sorry. I never knew it was like that."

His arm tightened around her, and he chuckled slightly. "The bicycle excuse was pretty lame—we never had one. I suppose the social worker figured that out pretty quick."

"I'm sorry."

"Don't be." He cleared his throat, rocking her as he would a baby. "But you have to know it's as hard for me to tell you this as it is for you to tell me how it feels not to be able to have kids."

She considered that and, for a moment, slipped into the shoes of his youth. "It wasn't your fault."

"Maybe not. But I've been sitting here sweating it for the last week, wondering when you're going to find out. Wondering how you'll look at me."

"You were worried how I'd feel about the way your dad treated you?"

"No," he said brusquely, raising his head. "About marrying some nobody from the wrong side of the tracks."

"Christian, you're not a nobody."

"Hey. A kid grows up believing certain things."

"That's not the way you live now."

"But it's always going to be there, Ray. And when people talk about me, they're going to talk about my dad, and they're going to wonder if I'll be a screwup, too. You better know that now. You better know you're marrying a reputation you've got to live down."

"It doesn't matter."

"It may."

"If you can overlook my imperfections—"

He cut in gruffly. "There are none."

"And take me as I am, I guess I can accept you for the person you are. I don't need to look over your shoulder and scare up a few black sheep. I refuse to let it shadow what's happening now."

He paused. "You mean you still want to go ahead with this mess of a wedding?"

"Yes."

"This show Beth's putting on?"

"I'm not backing out, no matter how much you try to convince me to."

One of his hands cupped her bent knee. His knuckles were badly scraped, probably from hauling in that new load of oak. She gingerly smoothed the abrasions, her fingertip riding atop the bony rise and dipping into the flesh between the joints.

"We can always call off all the pomp and circumstance, if you want. It's not too late," he told her.

"No. Leave it like it is. I don't want to hurt Beth's feelings. And that way, Michael won't get the impression I'm getting married just for Katie's sake."

"You're sure?" His cheek dropped to rest atop her head.

Contentment welled up inside her. It was as if she wanted to absorb him, all of him, in order to fill up to overflowing on the peace she was feeling. "I'm sure, Christian. More sure about anything than I have been in weeks."

Chapter Ten

The hubbub created an illusion that Raylene found herself falling victim to. She tried on the wedding dress the day before the wedding, and experienced all the anticipation of a bride. She dressed for the rehearsal on Friday night, and realized it was her last night as a single woman. Then, when her brother toasted them during the intimate dinner afterward, she envisioned the beginning of a journey.

With Christian Jennings.

She began to think of Katie as *their* baby, and dismissed the question of the adoption as unimportant. Heather, she was certain, would be content when she learned of Raylene's marriage. The suit would be dropped.

She even began to think of Christian as Katie's daddy.

But through it all, she just couldn't imagine him as her husband.

Though she certainly started appreciating everything about him. The way he grinned whenever she entered a room. The way he frowned at a length of warped wood, as if it should, quite frankly, be ashamed of itself. The way he held Katie in the crook of his elbow, and balanced her bottom atop his forearm. The way, when the baby's eyes were heavy, he gently guided her nodding head onto his shoulder.

She couldn't tag and identify all the component parts—humor, confidence, kindness, direction—but she certainly appreciated them. That was why, when the waitress removed their sorbet glasses after dessert, and Chris shot her a curious look, a funny feeling spiraled right down to her loins.

Tomorrow she would be his wife!

He leaned over and whispered against her ear, "Think we ought to call it a night? I hear there's a big wingding at the Stronghurst Chapel tomorrow morning. I'd hate to miss it."

Pulling herself slightly away, she arched a suggestive brow. "I'd hate to have you."

"Then we better..." Spreading his hand, he indicated the couple seated across from them.

Michael and Beth were in animated conversation. Once she found out he was the advertising director for Tourtelot Cruise and Tour, Beth had plied Raylene's brother with nonstop questions. Michael, with his features that mirrored Raylene's, looked flattered and slightly amused.

"I suppose," Raylene said to Chris. "Hey, you guys?" Both reluctantly looked her way. "We hate to break this up, but we've got an early morning tomorrow."

"All the better to party now," Beth told them. "It'll make for a short night."

"Just what I need," Chris said dryly. "Another short night."

"We've been burning the midnight oil," Raylene explained to Michael, "trying to keep up with the business, and the wedding plans, and get my stuff moved. I have to be out of the apartment in five days."

"That soon?"

"They're being nice and letting me out of the lease a month early if I can vacate by June first. Summer temps are coming in."

"Ah..." The arrival of the tourist season struck Michael's advertising nerve. "Makes sense."

The waitress discreetly slipped the bill for the night's camaraderie next to Christian's elbow in a tasteful leather case. Raylene noted the way he took charge and signed the slip, never flinching at her brother's extravagant filet mignon, or the forty-dollar bottle of wine he'd requested. She suspected Michael had done that on purpose, just to test Christian's mettle, just to see whether he'd balk at supporting his sister in style.

Raylene had compensated by ordering chicken, thinking that between Beth and Michael, they'd soon be in the poorhouse.

"Anyway," Christian went on, slapping the folder shut as if the eye-popping bill were of little significance, "I've got a little rearranging to do, or Raylene's never going to find her way from the bedroom to the bath tomorrow night. Most of her stuff's still in boxes and laundry baskets and—"

"Tomorrow night?" Beth repeated. "Tomorrow night's your wedding night."

"I know, and—"

"You're staying at that god-awful unfinished apartment of yours? In that warehouse? On your wedding night?"

"Well . . ." Chris shifted a guilty look to Raylene. "I . . ."

"We haven't had time to even think anything else," Raylene put in. "We'll do the honeymoon thing later."

"You're celebrating your honeymoon in the warehouse? Why, Christian, you don't even have blinds on those bedroom windows!"

"But they're so high up, it doesn't—"

"Christian."

He snorted.

"It's Raylene's honeymoon," Beth told him emphatically. "God, I can't believe I didn't think of it. After all the other stuff . . ."

"Don't worry," Raylene said reassuringly, leaning over the table toward her. "It's okay. We'll do something later. We've got the baby's room all set up, and really, that's the important thing."

A suspicious light flared in Michael's eyes. Christian must have seen it, too, because his hand immediately settled on her shoulder, pulling her back and against him. "Actually, we thought, when the baby's older—"

"Christian. You only have one wedding night ever," Beth scolded. "Don't try to dismiss it."

Michael's face reflected nothing, but his eyes thoughtfully assessed Chris before moving on to Raylene. A billowing "Harrumph" interrupted his scrutiny. "I've got this great idea," he finally offered. "Since I haven't had time to get you a wedding gift, how about I get you a wedding night? With Beth's help, I'm sure we could scare up something."

"Yes!" Beth nearly jumped out of her chair with enthusiasm. "And we'll even volunteer to take care of Katie for you, so it'll be a real wedding night. Privacy. Hearts and flowers. A night you'll never forget."

"Let your imagination be your guide," Michael quipped.

Apprehension unexpectedly slithered down Raylene's spine. This couldn't be happening, could it? She and Chris spending a night together? Alone? Without the baby?

That wasn't the way she'd pictured it, not for the first few muddling days together.

But if she had him in that particularly compromising position in a bare—oh, dear God, why did she have to think of it like that?—twenty-four hours, what on earth was she going to do with him?

One glance at his ruggedly handsome features, and she knew. That was why her cheeks flushed and her palms went damp. Thinking of him as Katie's daddy was the furthest thing from her mind.

Under Beth's eagle eye and careful administration, everything had gone off without a hitch. She'd impressed Michael so thoroughly that he'd given up trying to impale Chris on carefully constructed questions. Questions that were intended as foils to expose the man and prove that his sister, Raylene Rafco, had no business changing her last name to Jennings.

By the time Beth was done with him, he couldn't have cared less.

He and Beth served as an exemplary host and hostess for the brunch at Bell's. Raylene sat in her scrunched-up wedding dress, with yards of tulle jetting out from the back of her head, and enjoyed herself thoroughly. Sunshine poured in the opened French doors at their back and warmed the terrazzo floor. The banquet and guest tables were strung with swirling raspberry ribbons and white flocked wedding bells. Everything smelled comforting, like blueberry muffins and cranberry-orange sauce.

Sure, there had been that moment, barely an hour before, when the minister asked them to repeat those sacred words *to love, honor and cherish.* Raylene had suffered a temporary loss of composure, and felt a little squeamish and a whole lot less than honest.

But Chris's steady gaze had snagged hers, and he'd silently reassured her. At that crucial moment, she could almost feel him breathing life into her, sustaining her, giving her courage.

Afterward, with his pledge, the one he never once hesitated over, his confidence had filled her. In that fleeting moment, she had yearned to make this thing between them real and genuine.

At the moment he kissed her, in front of seventy-five onlookers and friends, she'd realized she wanted to love him. Honestly and truly love him.

But she wasn't sure that was what she felt.

She was fond of him, certainly. But maybe she'd mixed all that up with gratitude. Because of what he was doing for her—and, ultimately, for Katie.

"So maybe we should have given my sister more credit," Chris suggested, leaning closer, his shoulder coming behind hers. With his opposite arm, he reached over his plate, to his fluted glass, where strawberries floated in champagne. "You know, this stuff's not half-bad."

"It's wonderful."

Christian lifted the flute a fraction of an inch, in a silent toast to her. He'd just raised the glass to his lips when a chorus of flatware pinged against stemware. The guests were growing impatient, laughing, joking. Christian set aside the champagne. "Your eyes are sparkling."

Amusement gurgled from her throat. "This is too much," she confided shyly. "I never thought it would be like this."

"To the beginning," he whispered, simultaneously looping an arm about the back of her chair and against her shoulder blades before he dipped his head towards hers.

The crowd cackled with delight.

The kiss intensified, smothering them both with need. Awareness arose on a level far deeper, and far more profound, than the catalyst of the adoption. Original intentions were flung aside as the longings of two normal, healthy people were recognized and acted upon.

"Whew..." Chris reluctantly broke away. "That was a doozy."

"We want to give them their money's worth," Raylene advised silkily, her eyes riveted to his lips. "Remember all those new sets of towels and bed sheets."

He went white-hot, thinking of her wrapped in a body towel and darting from the bathtub to the sanctuary of their bedroom.

She went quivery, imagining the corner of a sheet wound around his ankle, his knee bent, his leg exposed, as the sheet cascaded and pooled at the juncture of his hips.

"And those new blankets?" he privately prompted, inching closer. "The quilt?"

He silently promised that he'd throw it down in front of the fireplace for a midnight tryst.

She silently promised that they'd cuddle buck naked, drawing it over them, tentlike, after making hot, steamy love.

The crowd howled knowingly, recognizing the private visions and egging them on.

They never heard.

Beth must have pulled some strings, because getting the honeymoon suite at the Windtower over the Memorial Day weekend was unimaginable. Michael slipped them the key in an oversize envelope, winked and clapped Chris on the shoulder, saying, "Have a good time, guys. Don't worry about the baby. Beth and I will get along fine."

"He's right. We'll manage," Beth echoed, giving them each a hug. "So we don't want to see you—or hear from you—till noon tomorrow. Got it?"

Raylene grinned and ducked down to kiss the baby goodbye. Chris kept his hand glued to Raylene's waist, making it clear to everyone that he was eager to snatch her away, and to heck with long-drawn-out farewells.

Tyler, who tilted Katie up like a seasoned pro, feigned boredom during this last brief transaction. He'd been unable to comprehend all the fuss over the wedding, and he hadn't hesitated to make sure everyone knew he resented it. Chris suspected that, although he hadn't voiced it, he was afraid he'd been replaced.

"Thanks," Raylene whispered to Ty as she readjusted Katie's bonnet, making sure the sun wasn't in her eyes. He nodded.

After Raylene pulled back from the baby, looking as if she were going to cry, Chris nudged Tyler's elbow. "Thanks, buddy, for being my number one man today. I couldn't have done it without you."

"S'okay."

"You know, you look pretty good in that monkey suit." The boy's jacket was missing, his tie long gone, his shirtsleeves were rolled up, and the shirttail lapped at the back of his wrinkled pants. Still, Tyler appeared genuinely pleased by the compliment.

"Thanks."

Then, before Raylene could pepper her goodbyes with advice about the baby, he whisked her away. After a cursory look at his car—which had been meticulously decorated with shaving cream, tissue-paper roses, and a ridiculous number of old shoes that hung from the back bumper—he deposited Raylene in the passenger side. He'd jumped in then and, after an ultimatum from Beth, they'd both swiveled toward the center and propped their arms over the front seat to look out the back window and pose for a quick snapshot. The Just Married sign wired to the trunk, complete with cherubs and intertwined hearts, would read like a caption below their smiling faces.

"It'll be the last photo in your wedding album," Beth called after them, waving, the camera in her hand.

Christian pulled away from the warehouse and laid on the horn. Everyone stood on the sidewalk yelling their good wishes and waving. Christian made sure that, for their benefit, he raised a ruckus all up and down Webster Avenue. Tourists waved. Motorists honked. Shopkeepers stood in their doorways.

The boisterous departure made the contrast all the more intense when they turned a corner and rolled onto a quiet side street. The wind, driving in off the water, was warm and gusting. The sun hung bloodred in the sky, while ivory clouds feathered overhead.

Silence seeped in.

"Well, that's over," she remarked tentatively.

"Yeah. Over." But his knuckles went white. The show was over. Now they were getting down to the good stuff.

Your basic intimate bedside-manner sort of stuff.

He suddenly felt inadequate. He was the guy. He was the one who was supposed to have the confidence to know what he was doing. He was supposed to take charge.

With a woman he barely knew.

Why, he'd never even put his hand under her blouse. Not that he hadn't wanted to. But he hadn't wanted to offend her. He hadn't wanted her to think he'd only agreed to this marriage for the sex. He'd made her believe he was doing it for Katie.

Yet hadn't he issued the ultimatum? A marriage, in the bedroom and out.

His words came back to haunt him, and he slanted a glance at Raylene. They were on the highway along Lake Syles, and she had a strange, faraway look in her eyes. The sleeves of her gown billowed against the incoming air, and he noticed that the rise and fall of her breasts seemed tremulous, uncertain.

God, as if it weren't bad enough, the staccato thrum of his libido was making him react to her breasts like a teenager. All he could think of was getting that dress off her.

He cleared his throat. "What're you thinking about? The baby?"

"Oh, no. Beth will be good with her."

"Tired?" He winced the moment he said it, figuring she'd think he'd suggest that they hop in the sack the minute they closed the door to the suite.

"No. Yes." She closed her eyes and leaned back against the headrest. "Emotional strain."

"We can kick back tonight. No pressure, no..."

Her eyes popped open a fraction of an inch and, from the corner of the slit, she studied him, waiting. "No what?"

No clothes. Damn. Where had that come from?

"No...no hurry. Or anything. We can relax, and..." He felt sweat break out on his forehead. "You know."

He was saved from having to explain that suggestive comment, as they conveniently pulled up in front of the hotel. The entrance of the Hightower led onto a circular brick driveway. Adjoining boulevards were magnificently groomed, with long stretches of geraniums and bachelor's buttons. Closer to the lobby's entrance, huge stone urns overflowed with ground cover and were surrounded by carefully manicured beds of marigolds.

Christian slowed near the hotel entrance.

"Just park the car," she said. "We've only got two small bags."

Two small bags. He didn't like the sound of that. As if it weren't official, as if it weren't enough to make it work.

But he pulled into the nearest available parking spot, expecting to open her door. But she was on the driveway before him, her eyes drawn to the adjacent lakeside golf course.

"This is like the Caribbean or something, isn't it?"

He glanced up at the four stories of white stucco. Dozens of balconies cantilevered out, providing every room with a view of the golf course and the boat slips, where Sunfish and pontoon boats were moored. There was a white-sand volleyball court, and hot pink cabanas claimed five hundred feet of beach. "I guess. Not that I'd know."

"Me either."

"Well . . ." Unable to think of anything particularly brilliant to say, he reached for their bags, stuffing one under his arm before flipping the door locks.

"Leave the veil. It'll just get in the way."

He suddenly imagined her clad only in the veil. He slammed the door, one-handed and a little harder than he'd intended, painfully aware that the room key was burning a hole through his inside breast pocket. "Okay. That's it, then."

"Here. Let me—"

"No, I can manage." He took a couple of steps away from the car. "You forget you married a man who hauls lumber from one end of the shop to the other?"

"I didn't forget."

Heads turned when they entered the lobby. Knowing smiles wreathed the faces of murmuring hotel guests.

As Michael had preregistered them, Raylene walked past the reception desk straight to the elevators. She pushed the up button, and the doors yawned wide to receive them. They scurried inside.

"What floor?" she asked Chris.

"I—" he shifted the baggage to both hands and fumbled with it before he realized opportunity knocked in strange ways. "Inside pocket." He hunched one shoulder, making his jacket gap open.

Raylene hesitated, then slipped her hand inside.

Alone in the empty elevator car, the exchange was as intimate as foreplay. The back of her hand brushed his nipple. Chris thought he'd go wild.

She looked at him, her hand still loitering inside his jacket. A secret smile pulled her lips as if she could read his mind. Slyly, she pulled the envelope free.

After that, the ride to the top was fairly uneventful, the hall quiet, the walk short. He put the bags down outside the room and took the key from her.

After he threw the door open, Raylene moved forward, peering inside.

"No. Wait. I think I'm supposed to do this...." Placing his arms beneath her knees and her shoulders, Chris lifted her. "Isn't this traditional?"

"This hasn't been a particularly traditional wedding," she answered, holding herself slightly stiff and away from him.

"So? Every bride should be carried over the threshold." His heart swelled when she smiled up at him, her arms linked around his neck. "Besides, it won't be the same at my place. We'll have an audience—the baby. It'll ruin the effect."

She gave in, nuzzling her mouth—her smile—against the concave warmth of his neck.

They entered the room in one monumental stride, and he paused briefly, kissing her lightly, before passing the bath and the mirrored closets and taking her into the suite. He debated about carrying her to the bed—until he saw it.

She needed to see this standing up. So he gently, reluctantly, lowered her to her feet.

The bed was built on a platform, and to ascend to it, to approach the crown molding on the ceiling and the wispy chiffon side curtains tied with ribbons to each bedpost, bred anticipation. Two long-stemmed roses angled across the chasm of crisp pillows. Both sides of the bed were turned down, exposing shell-pink sheets.

The jacuzzi at the opposite end of the room was filled, and seven lime-green candles were clustered on the tub's rim. Near the balcony, champagne was chilling in a freestanding bucket, next to a table set for two. A folded card on each plate advised them that a seven course prime-rib dinner had been prearranged for their convenience; they merely had to call before nine to confirm it. They both lifted the cards, digesting the luxury.

"Looks like we're eating in," Chris said.

"Looks like it. I swear, Michael and your sister thought of everything."

"I should get the luggage. It's still..." He looked over his shoulder, to the open door, wondering if she had as great an urge to close it as he.

"I know." She set the card aside, next to the plate. "Put mine in the bathroom, will you? I'd like to get out of this dress." Their glances collided and locked. The meaning was clear.

He dragged his gaze away, intent on putting his anxious hands to work.

"It buttons down the back," she murmured quietly. "I never thought of that when I..."

A vision of the sixty-four buttons Beth had told him about flitted through his mind. "It's okay. I can help with that."

"If you don't mind."

He snatched up the bags waiting outside the door, depositing hers inside the bathroom in a split second. He tossed his bag beside the closet and moved to her, trying to look as if her request were routine. "Turn around."

She did as he asked, dropping her head, the column of her neck bending like the stem of a flower. His hands were used to holding nails so tiny most people would smash their fingers with the first whack of the hammer. He'd always handled that effortlessly. Now dozens of small satin-covered buttons taunted him, initiating a whorl of sensation through his loins. "These are pretty little," he said needlessly, conscious of how silky her skin was beneath his fingertips.

"They probably do that on purpose."

"Probably."

Silence ensued. But he felt a tremor skitter over her flesh. The silk fell open, and the weight of the bodice pulled the sleeves off her shoulders, exposing them to his anxious eyes.

He allowed his lips to drift to her neck. "You're so beautiful, Raylene."

She trembled, and he knew that his breath had touched her. He pressed a hot, seductive kiss to her nape, and she arched, her head lolling back, her breasts lifting as her shoulders rose.

Still clutching the gown against her, she half turned, seeking his mouth with her own. He could taste the afternoon's champagne on her tongue. She pulled back slightly, moving her lips against the side of his mouth, his cheek. "My nightgown's in my case. I suppose...if I go get it...it'll interrupt the timing, huh?"

"Most likely."

He kissed her again.

"You could always see it later."

"Mm-hmm..." He reached inside the gown, lifting her buttocks up against him.

"I don't want you to feel deprived."

He chuckled; it was a husky sound, born in the back of his throat. "Trust me. I don't feel deprived." He moved against her, suggestively. "Anything but deprived." He tried to push the gown down farther, but it wouldn't budge. She held it tightly against her.

"You afraid?"

"No." But her words lacked conviction.

"I won't hurt you," he promised. Then it suddenly occurred to him: What if she'd never done it before? Good God, he didn't even know. A man should know that about his bride.

"I know. I just...never thought it would happen this quick. I thought..."

"Of course," he said hoarsely, "I never meant to rush—"

"Christian?"

"Mmm?"

"It isn't that. I was only afraid this would be awkward or embarrassing." Temple-to-temple with her, he nodded against her hair. "But I really want to jump into that bed with you. I mean, I'm thirty years old, Chris. It's not in me to be a reluctant, shy little virgin."

He chuckled, his fingers threading through the hair at the back of her head. "I want you to know I appreciate spontaneity just as much as you do." His mouth moved to the tip of her ear, his tongue tracing the exterior shell before going lower, to nibble at her lobe.

The dress spiraled to the floor, the heavy beadwork falling over his rented shoes.

One impetuous movement took his hands to the elastic holding the crinoline slip at her waist. His lips touched the top of her strapless bra. "I've been wanting to do this since..."

Her hands guided his to the zipper tab. "Since?" The zipper whished down, and she stepped out of the slip, her heel catching on a bit of lace.

"Since that time we were sitting in the car after we met with Heather, and I knew what kind of woman you were."

She kicked off her pump, losing it in the swirl of fabric.

"The other one, too," he urged, supporting her raised thigh, his palm grinding against the elastic top of her thigh-high stockings. "I wanted you clear back then."

A second pump plopped onto taffeta and lace.

His forefinger plied the top of her stocking, peeling it away from the back of her leg. She raised onto the tips of her toes, looping her arms about his neck and making him neglect to finish what he'd started.

Instead, he lifted her and strode to the bed, taking the eight-inch rise and depositing her in the middle of the king-size bed. He shrugged out of his jacket, popping the studs on his tuxedo cuffs and shirtfront. His hand lingered on the closure of his trousers, his mind reminding him how sexy long legs could look when they were encased in silk stockings.

Raylene rolled just then, rising to her knees before him. The remainder of his clothes fell as quickly as hers had.

They tumbled onto the bed in a tangle of arms and legs. She turned onto her back, willing him to lie across her, and lifting her shoulder blades off the comforter to let him forage for the snaps to her bra. When freed, her feminine curves flattened beneath his chest; he never saw them, because his senses were wholly unable to tolerate more. He kissed her long and passionately.

"You feel so good," he groaned, his breathing ragged and labored as he pulled away. "So soft." Yet he moved with restraint, knowing he should take his time.

"Christian, it's okay. Don't wait."

The last barriers—mere scraps of cloth—were stripped away, leaving them flesh-to-flesh. Burrowing a knee between her thighs, he spread her legs, then probed deeper before slipping inside.

The moment her muscles stretched to accommodate him, she gasped, the sharp intake of air rasping against his ear. She struggled, and for an instant he thought she'd changed her mind, that she was trying to escape him.

Not so. Wriggling from the waist up, she juggled him farther into her. Instinctively thrusting into her depths, he found satisfaction so quickly that he was sure she'd be disappointed. Yet waves of pleasure racked him, leaving him a shuddering shell of a man who clung to her. She held him, steadied him, cradled him.

She arched once, her reaction as swift and sure as his own. After that they melded together before sinking back down into the mattress.

"I meant to go slow," he muttered thickly against her shoulder. "I meant to—"

"Christian, no. Don't apologize. This is just the beginning. We've got a lifetime to go slow." A second slipped away. "And it's okay with me if we start tonight."

He sighed into the pillow, his thumb stroking her temple. "It's been a long time for me."

"It's okay. Really."

He raised his head to see that she was smiling contentedly at the ceiling.

"It's been a long time for me, too," she admitted shyly, her eyes sliding over to him, her lashes dipping to cover the color. "Look, would it shock you if I said I felt as right about this as you probably do?"

"Maybe."

"My feelings for you have grown so quickly that I didn't want to wait, either. It just seemed natural."

He lifted himself, bracketing both elbows in the mattress, above her shoulders. "Tell me," he whispered, butting his forehead against hers, "how did I get so damned lucky as to find someone like you?"

He figured, to be honest, he should have said more. But it seemed too soon. Maybe it was best to say nothing, and to prove to her that often making love held another, unspoken meaning.

He could wait till they got back to his apartment to see the nightgown. Right now, he liked her just the way she was.

153

Chapter Eleven

Life in general was terrific.

Michael had left for California convinced that Christian was a real find and that Raylene had done the right thing hurrying the wedding in order for them to be a family. He'd even mentioned coming back for a visit. But his eyes had strayed to Beth, making Raylene wonder just what had gone on during that honeymoon night when they were supposed to be watching Katie.

But she easily dismissed the thought, because for two weeks following the wedding she fairly flew about the apartment, getting everything in order. She found niches for her things, places for theirs. She delighted in using their wedding gifts—from the dish towels to the lead crystal—and, each time she used something, telling Chris who had given what.

He'd just smile and nod and suggest it was time to hang up the towel bars or make a credenza for the fancy stuff. Maybe revinyl the kitchen to match the new place mats or retile the bath to match the towels. Evolution was slow but consistent. They were making plans for their home.

Plans that reached far into the future.

She began to cherish going to sleep in the room that had once been his, the room that she had once decreed was Spartan. She appreciated the small ceiling-high windows spanning the far wall and knew why he wanted to keep them uncovered. At night, stars cast the room in luminescence, and the morning sun served as their alarm clock.

But they'd traded his Hollywood bed in for the oak cannonball one he'd made and so proudly displayed in the front window. The first night together in the apartment, after they made love in it, he'd declared it to be his gift to her.

She never once entered the room after that without smiling when she saw it. She started considering making a quilt for it. Certainly in the wedding-ring pattern—her gift to him.

Like a talisman, that bed—and the time they spent in it—altered their life, their outlook. Even Katie loved being in it. Before bedtime, she'd play peekaboo with Chris or hold her toes and gurgle as Raylene sang nursery rhymes to her. Then, at eleven o'clock, they'd stretch out and put Katie between them and take turns giving her her last bottle. Sometimes Raylene would carry her to her crib. Sometimes Chris would.

All in all, life was perfect.

Raylene silently praised Christian every day for encouraging her to quit her part-time jobs. Doing so allowed her to spend every spare minute with him. In the shop, in the showroom, she was his number one side-kick, sales rep and friend.

It seemed they couldn't get enough of each other. She lived, ate, breathed and slept appreciating the finer points of Christian Jennings. If they were having a slow afternoon, she'd wander over to the connecting door and arch a suggestive eyebrow at him. He'd throw down a two-by-four faster than she could even hint that they should hit the bedroom.

They'd laugh afterward and say they were never going to get the apartment finished doing that. They were never going to get to the desk and bookshelves for the Clements family, or the coffee table for Marge Halvorsen.

But who cared, really? They were a family, and that was all that mattered. If they chose to flip the pasteboard door sign to Closed in the middle of the afternoon, they were adults and that was their choice.

Yes, life was rolling merrily along, and Raylene was enthusiastically embracing her new status as a newlywed. She'd almost forgotten Katie was adopted.

Almost. Until the call came.

Supper was nearly ready, and Christian was slicing the chuck roast, butter was melting over the corn and she was stirring the gravy, one-handed, when she picked up the phone. Without preamble, her lawyer came right to the point.

"She's going ahead with the hearing, Raylene. Your marriage didn't even faze her."

She paused, one hand slowing over the gravy, the other holding the phone a fraction of an inch away from her ear. "Tell me again," she said. "I'm not getting it."

"Heather wants the baby back."

"Oh, God. No." She scrunched her eyes closed, hunching forward as she turned to the wall, the phone cord wrapping around her middle. "What are we going to do?"

"Calm down, Raylene. We're doing nothing. Not yet. We just have to sit tight. Now...here's the way I see it...."

She could actually hear herself breathing and listening and figuring. Figuring how she was going to live with Christian, knowing they might lose custody. Wondering how long they'd last with Kate. Wondering how long they'd last without her.

Fury twisted her into one tight knot. Heather had said all she wanted for Katie was a father. Dammit! They'd provided her with one. Had it all been in vain?

Anguish didn't begin to describe the horrific sense of loss roiling through her. She thought of Katie-the-scene-stealer at the wedding, kicking her black patent-leather shoes against the pew. The new Sesame Street play-gym she batted with her fists. The baby swing Christian had bought exclusively for his workshop.

Her lawyer kept talking. The corn boiled in the butter. The gravy went lumpy. She looked at Christian's kind face and couldn't imagine telling him.

They'd barely had two idyllic weeks together, and now this?

She couldn't begin to predict his reaction.

She vaguely remembered untangling herself from the cord and hanging up the receiver, staring at the rotary dial and irrationally thinking that it needed to be cleaned.

"So what was that about?"

She looked up, aware that Chris had dragged in the high chair, making good on his promise that Kate would join them for dinner. He held her beneath the arms, letting her legs dangle over the tray.

"That was my lawyer."

"Oh?" He paused to look up at her, then maneuvered Katie into the chair before sliding back the tray.

"Heather's changed her mind. She wants Katie back."

"What? But we're married!"

"I know. I guess it didn't matter." Slumping against the wall, Raylene felt as if all the life force, all the energy, had been sucked from her.

"Hell!" He grimly ran a hand over his head, leaving his hair disheveled. He stopped at the back of his neck, his elbow angling up toward the ceiling. "She wanted a dad. Now Katie's got one! What's the deal?"

"He said the marriage didn't faze her."

"What do you mean, didn't faze her?"

"I don't know."

"We did the whole damn thing by the book! We did everything to make it right. Right down to the announcement," he angrily barked, jamming a thumb in the direction of the refrigerator door where a newspaper clipping about their nuptials was held in place by a magnetic bride and groom. "What's it going to take to make her happy, anyway?"

"Don't ask me. I thought it was a given that she'd withdraw the suit. I thought having Katie in a two-parent home was what she wanted, but—"

"But she wants more. She wants to pull our strings. She wants to see how far and how fast we'll dance."

Raylene pulled herself away from the wall. "I never expected this. I feel like I should apologize or something. For dragging you into something that's so unsettled. I mean, I honestly thought things would work out."

Chris didn't address that. "What's the lawyer say?"

"Just that she's still going through with the hearing. I think I went numb after that. I'll have to call him back later."

"So what're we going to do?"

"He said to just sit tight. He once said these cases can take years, and—"

"Years?"

"Yes. Years. Particularly when it's an interstate adoption, like this. She can file in Ohio. We can file in Michigan. The courts could take a lifetime to figure it out. And because Kate's real father never actually signed away his consent, that could complicate things further, and—"

"Oh, terrific!"

"Well, Christian, what do you want me say?"

"We can have this adoption hanging over our heads, be living in limbo, for years?"

Frustration welled in her, making her want to strike out at him, at the way of life he'd offered her, at all the things she'd come to treasure. "Well, you can get out if you want. Nobody's stopping you. We both know you were only doing this as a favor to me. So it didn't work. So what? I won't hold you to it. Not under the circumstances."

The craziest flicker of disbelief shot through his eyes. Hurt pinched his mouth. "I didn't mean that," he muttered, looking away. "I just meant this will be one hell of a way to live."

"I never planned it this way, either."

"I know that." When he lifted his head to look at her again, his features were chiseled into a hard profile, one that revealed nothing. "It's just the uncertainty that has me worried. Never knowing where we're going with this adoption, or what will happen. Or—" he paused, grimacing "—even how long we've got."

Joy faded from their daily routine. Raylene wandered to the connecting door between the shop and the showroom far less often. When she did, it was only because of business, and then she moved around Christian as if she were treading on eggshells.

He had every right to be angry with her, she told herself. They had struck a bargain. He'd expected a wife and a family. Now everything he'd been promised was being jerked out from under him. In its place was now uncertainty and a monumental legal battle. An expensive one. One that would drain them, both financially and emotionally.

Heather's decision had already taken its toll.

With the court date looming ahead of them, their life was slowly, systematically, being undermined. Raylene was devastated, and it showed. She couldn't sleep. She couldn't even taste any of the food she dumped on the table at night. She went through the motions, hoarding memories of Kate, trying to organize plausible arguments, trying to figure a way out. She felt sick to her stomach most of the time.

Sometimes it was so bad, she locked herself in the bathroom and threw up her breakfast. Then, when it was over, she'd hang a forearm across the toilet rim and sob, wondering how God could be so cruel as to give her a child, a marriage, and then snatch it all away.

And since she was down on her knees anyway, she'd pray. Repetitiously begging God to let her keep her baby, to salvage her marriage. Begging him for strength, for understanding.

Christian was no help. He worked in silence, not even bothering to turn on his radio anymore. Not bothering to ask her advice on design or production or advertising anymore. Once, she volunteered her opinion. He waved it away, telling her not to worry, saying he didn't want to bother her with shoptalk. She retreated back to the apartment, feeling left out. He countered by resuming longer hours, claiming he had projects he needed to finish.

Yet Kate, oblivious of all the turmoil surrounding her, grew and thrived and eagerly plastered them both with slobbery kisses. She'd become a daddy's girl, belting out "Da-Da-Da" with such enthusiasm that Raylene's heart withered. Even Christian looked a little sheepish whenever it happened. But he misunderstood Raylene's reaction to Katie's first words.

"I think it's an easier sound for babies to make," he rationalized. "Tyler did the same thing, and he didn't even have a dad around."

"Probably. This is great, isn't it?" Raylene intoned appropriately, without a shred of emotion. "She'll talk early, I'll bet."

But it struck her doubly hard, how her baby's first words were to a father who wouldn't stay, to a man who only hung around in the hope of cementing an already failed adoption.

Chris had been reduced to sorting screws into baby-food jars, and it rattled him. After the news from the lawyer, he'd gone after his projects with a vengeance. Now he was all caught up, and then some. He had a to-do list for the apartment as long as his arm but he didn't want to tackle any of it. It would put an unnecessary burden on Raylene, and he couldn't do that.

The vinyl for the kitchen floor, the tile for the bath, no longer mattered. He'd already done the little stuff. The towel bars, the safety switches to protect the baby.

And that was what it boiled down to, wasn't it? Protecting the baby.

It looked as if they were nothing without the baby between them. He hadn't felt that way, not at first, and he hadn't thought she did, either. But she'd laid it out for him, saying he could leave if he wanted.

That had stung worse than knowing the adoption was in jeopardy. He'd tried to forgive her for it, he'd tried to justify the reasons behind her saying it. She was under pressure, she was shocked, she was scared.

So he tried making things easier for her. He stayed out of her way. He made his requests minimal. He tried to keep busy and look unaffected.

But he still felt guilty as hell. He should have been more understanding after that first phone call. He shouldn't have come at her, demanding explanations, braying out opinions. She'd had enough to deal with, and he'd just compounded it. The sticky part was that he'd been as scared and confused as she. Instead of supporting her, he'd assaulted her with questions. Damn, he had a lot to learn about being a husband.

Pitching the last wood screw into an open jar, he sighed and wearily clambered to his feet. Maybe it was time to make amends. They'd been sidestepping one another for the past few weeks. Maybe it was time to start rebuilding something.

He sighed and moved to the door, leaning a shoulder against the door frame, butting his palm against the opposite side. "Hey!" Her head lifted from the ledger. "You almost done?"

"Almost."

"It's getting late."

"Katie's still sleeping, so..." She trailed off.

"Mmm..."

"Oh." She straightened, focusing in on the clock. "I'll bet you're getting hungry. I'm sorry. It'll only take me a few minutes to get something on the table."

"How about if we go out instead?"

"Tonight?"

"Why not? We could use a break."

"Well...I laid out steaks."

"Lay 'em back."

"Chris. I heard you get up at a quarter of five this morning. You've got to be tired."

"I woke you?"

"Well, no. I was already awake."

"Oh. I..." Couldn't sleep, he thought, remembering. Couldn't stand being in the same bed next to you, with your physical presence driving me mad with want. Hearing your even breathing. Smelling that herbal conditioner on your hair. Feeling pretty damn selfish, feeling pretty damn small, for being aware of that when our problems are bigger and more volatile than a middle-of-the-night tryst. "I had some stuff I needed to get done."

She nodded. "You've gotten up early every morning this week. I was beginning to suspect you didn't like my breakfasts."

I liked what you served before breakfast, he thought. Before this mess with Katie. Before. When we were free to enjoy pleasuring ourselves with each other, to nurturing our bodies and restoring our wholeness. When this burden hadn't blotted out what was left of our lives, our identities. "I'm really not much on breakfasts. A cup of coffee is fine. Old habits die hard, I guess."

She looked at him. Really looked at him. Perception did a slow dance with uncertainty. "I guess."

He was left with the strangest belief that she was telling herself she didn't know him. The realization left him feeling hollow. "So?" He forced himself to sound cheerier. "What about dinner?"

"We could grab something quick, I suppose. Burgers would be fine, if you're tired of staying home."

"Great," he lied.

"That way," Raylene continued, "you could see Tyler afterward. He's got his heart set on making a soapbox car for the Fourth."

"Yeah, we talked about doing it last year."

"It'd probably be good for him, to see that you still want to."

"I suppose."

"He seems a little at loose ends to me. With school out, and Beth going to summer school, and getting that new job, too."

"Maybe."

"He came around today, while you were at the lumberyard. Wanted to know if you had any odd jobs for him. But I—" she rolled her eyes apologetically "—I'd just dusted and taken out the trash. I couldn't think of anything."

"Yeah. Well. I'll look into it, then."

She reluctantly closed the ledger, hesitating. "He probably needs you right now, Chris. Being eleven is tough. And Katie and I, well, we understand you have other things to do. You can't always be waiting for

Katie to get up from her nap, or rearranging your schedule to accommodate us.''

Chris tried to look appreciative of the freedom she was dangling before him. He tried to look as though it all made sense, that, yes, he needed to keep things going with Ty.

He made all the appropriate moves, but one disturbing thought nagged at him.

She was pushing him away.

Chapter Twelve

For the past month, she'd tried to tell herself she was doing the right thing. She was dulling the hurt for Christian. When all was said and done, and Heather had won back custody, and the marriage was kaput, he'd at least be left with his family. He'd have Tyler, he'd have Beth.

It was consoling, really, to be able to tell herself that she hadn't driven a wedge between them. Now, instead of spending most evenings as a family man, he worked on the soapbox-derby car with Tyler.

Tyler often stopped to tell Raylene about the car, dropping words like *aerodynamic styling, comfort suspension,* and *maneuverability.*

Raylene silently, stoically, mourned the loss of Christian's presence.

The stress, the tension, of daily living was becoming increasingly difficult. Raylene found herself constantly in knots. She worked longer hours in an effort to change her focus. She spent as much time as possible with Katie, drawing strength from every milestone of growth. Cheering her on. Loving her. Fretting over how much time they had left.

She coveted Christian from a distance. Painfully aware of how much she'd come to care for him, she idolized every nuance of his character, every mannerism, every pithy statement. She thought it was cute the way he paired his shoes before going to bed each night. She memorized the way he hung his jeans over the top rail of a straight-backed chair, typically slipping his belt from the loops to drape it across the seat.

She loved the way he smelled after a shower. How he came into the bedroom, the curve of his lower back still spotted with water and a towel looped around his neck. She adored the way his hair curled behind his ears when it wasn't quite dry.

She started finding excuses to get into the bathroom whenever she heard him using the blowdryer. She thrilled to see him bare-chested. She surreptitiously watched him thread his fingers through his hair and leave a wind-tossed pattern in his new designer cut.

Then, just when she considered him almost perfect, he'd reach for the bottle of after-shave. He preferred the inexpensive stuff in the big bottles. The stuff that smelled tangy and clean, the stuff that carried generic names like Ocean Breeze or Sport Scent. He'd cup his hand and dribble a generous amount into his palm, letting it run in an irregular pattern in the creases. Then he'd pop his hands together, sluicing it from the heel of his palms to the pads of his fingertips.

She'd go almost dizzy from the fragrance. She was positive that her reaction was a throwback to some long-lost mating ritual. Her nostrils would flare and

curl, and she'd practically want to inhale the man.
Right on the spot.

Then he ran out of the ocean stuff and got something new. Something that shimmered like liquid gold
and had a big black-and-silver banner angling across
the label that declared it to be a "tantalizing scent."

Tantalizing scent? Hah!

It made her gag and go nauseous. It took her stomach two hours to right itself after she got the first whiff.
Every time he passed her desk, every time they passed
in the hall, every time she entered a room he'd left, it
was a pitch-and-roll odyssey.

She battled the discomfort for three days, convinced that the imminent adoption hearing was the real
cause behind the upset.

Then a niggling suspicion struck her. One that sent
her flying, in the middle of the afternoon the day before the hearing, to the local pharmacy.

She locked herself in the bathroom for the umpteenth time that week and turned the faucets on full
force. If Christian had begun to question her recent
preoccupation with the bathroom, she couldn't blame
him. It seemed she spent the majority of her time there.

Only this time it was different. She slipped the re-
ceptacle from the package, experiencing a tremor of
anticipation. Reading the handy-dandy little sheet of
dos and don'ts made her wary. What if she was setting
herself up for disappointment? How would she react if
the result wasn't positive? Or was she merely proving
to herself that she couldn't possibly get pregnant?

Or proving to herself she could?

It was far more likely that stress had knocked a
chunk of time off her regular cycle. Things like that

made a difference. When your emotions were out of whack, everything was out of whack. That was probably the most logical explanation. She'd get her period next week, and feel pretty stupid about the whole thing.

That was the reason she didn't tell Christian about the home pregnancy kit. She refused to look like a fool. She refused to overreact to repressed maternal longing. She'd face reality and deal with it, no matter what the outcome.

She meticulously followed the directions, batting back any surge of hope.

The three-minute wait was the longest she'd ever experienced. During those one hundred and eighty seconds, possibilities seesawed through her head.

What would Christian say? How would he react?

Moments before the test results were achieved, reminders of her wedding vows went winging through her memory.

For better or worse. For richer or poorer. In sickness and in health.

She didn't have time to remember "till death us do part," because she looked down and saw the confirmation of life.

She stopped, staring in disbelief.

Euphoria shot through her. Grief toppled it.

She laughed, she cried. She dropped to her knees and, crossing her arms over the lid of the toilet seat, she wept.

For herself. For Christian.

For the remnants of their broken family.

Raylene spent the afternoon working in a trancelike state. No one suspected the cause. Everyone assumed the upcoming hearing had thrown her into a catatonic state. No one confronted her. No one tried to talk to her about it.

Not Beth, not Tyler, and certainly not Christian.

The end result was that she had ample time to consider the shambles of her life. She was on the eve of losing her first child, a child not born of her, but loved and nurtured by her. A child she had welcomed into her life, to whom she'd voluntarily made a commitment.

Yet her own body was about to yield a second child. An unknown little being was growing inside her, even now pulsing with life. Thoughts of what her hasty marriage had created changed things. Why, it made her giddy with anticipation. The prospect of experiencing the thrill of pregnancy, the ultimate act of fulfillment for her as a woman, was, as Tyler was inclined to say, awesome.

For hours after reading the test results, she waltzed through her duties with an altered self-perception. She felt different, she moved differently. Her senses were sharper, more attuned to her body, to the awareness prickling through her.

So that was why her breasts were tingly, taut, sore. That was why, when Christian reached for her two nights ago, caressing her through her heavy satin nightshirt, she had flinched and instinctively pushed his hand away. He thought she'd rejected him. She'd merely been protecting her sensitive body. At the time, she hadn't understood why she did it. It had unsettled her as much as it had him.

Now the pieces were falling into place.

She thought of the night he'd caught a glimpse of her after her bath towel fell away. How his gaze had unabashedly strayed to her erect nipples, to the full swelling of her breasts.

He'd stared at her, commenting huskily, "It seems your body's changing because of what we do. Like it's becoming harder in the right places, softer in the rest." She'd self-consciously drawn the towel back between her breasts, but he'd shook his head. "Don't, Raylene. We both know what we enjoy together is right. Like it's our gift to each other."

She remembered feeling frozen as he moved to her, stripping the towel from her, and exploring her in all the places the towel had touched. But, more than that, she distinctly remembered how her body had reacted.

He'd suckled at her breasts, making her experience both pleasure and pain. Her belly had felt fuller, rounder, as he settled himself upon it. And she'd never taken him into herself more eagerly than she had that night. Each of them had silently acknowledged that something intangible was growing between them.

Yet neither of them had a clue as to what it was.

With this man, she had conceived a child. He had gifted her with a miracle. But by their own agreement, he remained only a fill-in father and mate. She was certain that they both regarded his status as temporary.

Now, suddenly, the boundaries were changing. They had created life. A second child, who would grow in the shadow of the child they desperately wanted to adopt.

Still, this child, their child, could not possibly replace Katie. Raylene would not want it to. She knew Christian would feel the same.

Yet she was still tormented, because she knew how adamant Christian was about repulsing family responsibilities. What if he'd married her because he thought she couldn't possibly conceive a child. Her doctor had once said it was unlikely. All the odds were against her.

She was in the middle of her mental arguments when Christian stepped out of the workroom at a little after four in the afternoon. Without so much as a glance, he went to the front window and turned over the Open sign.

He turned back, his expression guarded. "I think we ought to call it a day. I can't think. And I don't imagine you can, either. Want to take the baby to the park? We should make the effort to enjoy one nice day with her before the hearing tomorrow. I mean, since we don't know how much longer..." He lifted one shoulder, aware that he didn't need to say the rest.

"You sure?" she asked, her voice a little high, a little unsteady. "I always feel like this deal over Katie is shortchanging your customers."

"They can wait," he said brusquely, locking the door.

Bless him. He meant well. She often got the feeling that he cared about her as much as he did the baby. He'd never say it, though. He'd always remain tight-lipped and silent when it came to emotions.

Tossing the billing envelopes into the side drawer, she paused long enough to switch on the answering machine. "There. I'm ready anytime you are."

She tried not to hear or even imagine the deeper implication. But it was disturbing, that small suggestion of intimacy. Maybe it was because she knew something he didn't know, was privy to a secret that directly involved him.

The knowledge rattled her. This man had made her pregnant. He'd fathered a child she carried inside her.

She might bear him a son. One who might walk like him, talk like him. Wherever she went, whatever she did, she'd witness constant reminders of Christian Jennings.

She'd be both anguished and pleasured by it.

"Raylene?"

"Yes?"

"You with me?"

"Yes. Of course."

"You seem a little distant."

She hesitated. "Sorry. It's not...it's not you, Chris."

He nodded. "Okay. Say...about the hearing tomorrow?"

"Yes?"

"You given much thought to what could happen after this is all over and the decision's made?"

She answered slowly, carefully. "All the time."

"I just...well, I just wanted to suggest we not make any quick decisions. Whatever happens. Okay? Can we do that?"

You don't understand, she wanted to say. We don't have time. It's only a matter of months before you're confronted with the custody of two babies. "Some things can't wait. They need to be taken care of quickly." He stared at her, saying nothing. "Maybe after the initial hearing tomorrow we'll both see things differently."

She silently helped Christian pack the baby, the stroller and the picnic basket in the back of the car. But she was as determined as he to have one good day between them before the hearing—and possibly her news—ripped them apart.

It was dusk when they returned to the apartment. For four hours, they'd managed to put the hearing behind them. It was after nine by the time they'd given Katie her last bottle and slipped her into bed. They'd stood at the crib railing, side by side, and watched her sleep.

"Night, puddin'," Chris whispered.

Raylene covered her with the baby quilt, then patted her bottom. Katie had started sleeping in an endearing manner, with her rear end higher than the rest of her. "Sleep tight, sweetheart," she said, fighting back tears. "We love you."

They stood there for several minutes, just watching her, and listening to the baby-soft rhythm of her breathing. Chris sighed, his arm around her, his thumb gently tracing the side seam at the waist of her nightshirt. Intuition told her that he wanted to make love.

Sudden misgivings turned her inside out. How much longer before a nightshirt wouldn't cover her condition? How much longer before he'd suspect the reason behind her sensitivity? "Chris, I need to check the answering machine."

"Now?"

She heard the edge of desperation in his voice. "Mrs. Dugan may have called after we left. I won't be able to return the call tomorrow."

"Go ahead." He gently swatted her on the backside. "I'll get Katie's diaper bag ready for the baby-sitter tomorrow."

"Would you? Thanks." She turned, fleeing the room in her bare feet, and thinking of how often Chris had warned her against crossing the workroom floor without shoes. But she couldn't wait to find them. Right now, she didn't care if she stepped on splinters or screws. Picking her way through the semidarkness of his workroom, she skirted the table saw, the mingled scents of wood and varnish comforting her.

She needed to get away. To hoard her secret. To have a few minutes to herself to grieve for Katie, to grieve for a marriage whose foundation had been laid on all the wrong reasons.

Slashes of light from the sidewalk street lamps illuminated the showroom. She stood in the middle, where the curious always lingered after they first entered the front doors, identifying all the shadowy pieces her husband had made with his own hands. Every one of them had a history she cherished.

None of it seemed real anymore. None of it seemed true, or honest.

Life had moved beyond her control. Emotions had flared outside the norm. She was on the brink of losing Kate. She was on the brink of losing the man with whom she'd mated, with whom she had created a new, unexpected life.

With whom she'd fallen in love.

God, how could she tell him? How, after living with him for months, could she broach the subject of the baby? Or the fact that she'd fallen hopelessly, heedlessly, in love with him?

Would he simply look at her and remind her that that hadn't been part of the deal? She forced herself to imagine the worst, steeling herself against it.

She eventually moved to the desk, but only because she'd told Chris she'd check the machine. The red light blinked, making her switch it on. She listened without caring. The first call was an inquiry about a computer center. The second was from the lumberyard; they could get the cherry Chris had requested. The third, from her lawyer, stopped her cold.

"Raylene? Where are you? I've been trying all afternoon to track you down. Heather's withdrawing her petition! She came to me today and said her dad left town weeks ago. She's had time to think it over and, well, she wants the baby to stay with you. Said she finally admitted to herself that getting Katie back was just an effort to please her dad." There was a pause, followed by a long sigh. "You know...I honestly believe she never meant to hurt you, she just wanted to keep that part of her family intact. She won't back out now. I guarantee it. Look. Call me, will you? And congratulations, you two! You're newlyweds with a baby. It's going to be over in a wink now. We're going to make honest parents of you yet!"

Her fingers hovered indecisively over the replay button. Her lawyer was going to make honest parents of them yet?

Little did he know....

Her lungs swelled. Everything hurt, the pain of all she knew and all she was keeping secret radiating out from her breastbone. The excruciating sweetness of all they'd won.

Their baby, Katie, right smack-dab in the middle of their lives again.

In that instant, she knew she needed her husband with her. "Chris!" she hollered, looking over her shoulder into the darkness and knowing full well he'd never hear her. "Chris!" She stumbled around the corner of the desk, trying to run to him.

His silhouette loomed like an apparition in the doorway.

He moved toward her, his arms outflung. "I came to find you, Raylene, and I heard."

Chapter Thirteen

He'd been given a reprieve. He'd be able to keep Raylene and Kate in his life until the adoption was final. Somehow, that made everything more manageable.

Maybe, with time on his side, he could win her over. Maybe he could prove to her that he could be a family man. He couldn't imagine playing the part of the bachelor again. Heating up a can of tomato soup and calling it dinner. Yanking a comforter over the bed and calling it made.

He'd grown to like talcum powder speckling the bathroom floor and high heels overturned in front of his side of the closet. He'd adapted to maneuvering around the high chair in the kitchen and the stroller by the back door. He'd gotten used to the way Raylene had rearranged his kitchen. She'd come into his life and done him a world of good.

Inside his head and out.

Raylene had moved into his apartment, and he'd never once been tempted to call his wife a pain as his old man had done. "You lousy bastard" never fell from her lips, either. Instead, it was "Daddy." "Snot-nosed brat" had evolved into "Pudge."

Every phrase, every moniker, was softer and gentler. He had Raylene to thank for that. She'd started making him believe he could raise a kid the right way. She'd made him start hoping she'd stay.

But every indication she offered up proved the opposite. She pushed him away just as gently as she spoke to him. Whether she was encouraging him to spend more time with Tyler or smiling through the late nights he spent in the shop, he recognized the insulation she pulled around herself. Just as he'd done for the first thirty years of his life. Their nights might be wild and passionate, but during the days the emotional barriers snapped into place.

Once the adoption was final, she was prepared to leave. He knew it.

On the morning of the canceled hearing, he intentionally ignored the alarm. Then he stayed in bed a half hour past what was good for him.

Raylene rolled onto her side. "You getting up?"

"No. I'm playing hooky."

"You? Better not tell the boss."

They were facing each other, their heads on adjoining feather pillows. He smiled. She smiled.

Man, she looked great in the morning. Her eyes were heavy-lidded and seductive, and her dark hair was all tousled and unkempt. The middle button on her nightshirt was undone.

"So? What're you playing hooky for?"

"So I can think."

"Think? Think about what?"

He paused. "Think about how much time we've got before the adoption's final."

Her eyes widened, briefly. Then, going solemn, she rolled over on her back, her perfect profile silhouetted against the bedroom wall. Still staring at the ceiling, she pulled the comforter up over her breasts, crossing her arms over it. "Why?"

"I don't know. Thinking about how old Katie will be—"

"A year."

"Thinking about how long we'll have been married—"

"Seven months."

"Seven months," he repeated, watching her, watching for a shred of emotion. Nothing. "A person can get to know another person pretty well in seven months, don't you think?"

"I guess."

But she said it grudgingly, making him reconsider cautiously. After a momentary pause, he plunged ahead. What did he have to lose? His life would be barren without her. "So it looks like we'll have to make the best of these next few months—I mean, make them the best."

"Chris, it may feel like that today, but things change. People change." He waited out the silence until she finally added, "I'm not trying to be negative. Honestly, I'm not. I'm happy about the outcome. Really." He watched her jaw slip forward as she debated how much to reveal. "But I'm trying to come to terms with the fact that I'm going to be a mother again."

"What?" He forced a chuckle. "You've always been a mother to her, Raylene. This little storm over the adoption never took that away. You're going to go right on being the number one person in that little girl's life. I know it.''

Her head swiveled on the pillow, and this time her eyes were troubled and her expression was sobering. ''That's not exactly what I meant.''

''No?''

''No. I—I meant...'' Her mood had inexplicably changed, and she floundered visibly. ''I meant, this balancing act has taken a lot out of me, Chris. The hearing. The marriage. First I can't have a baby, and then I can. Then I can't keep Kate, and then I can. This flip-flopping—''

Without thinking, he reached over to cover her trembling hands. ''What are you trying to say?''

She stared at him, unblinking. ''I'm going to have a baby.''

Numbing euphoria shot through him. Yet, for a split second, he vacillated, wondering suspiciously if he'd been duped. Raylene quivered, waiting for his reaction. Her expression hovered between anxiety and hope. He couldn't stem his most honest, most genuine, response. ''But I thought you said you couldn't get pregnant.''

He hadn't said it.

He hadn't said he loved her. He hadn't said he wanted the baby.

He'd just stared at her, his eyes burning and nearly glazing over, while he tried to make sense of her explanation. She'd fumbled through the explanation. Badly fumbled through the disjointed mess of it. She'd tried to pump a little triumph into her voice, saying they'd beaten the odds. And those, she'd emphasized, had been monumental. He had given her a baby.

A baby.

But he hadn't really replied. He'd only rolled off the bed and away from her, and muttered something about how glad he was that he could help her out, about how it looked like it was time to get serious here. About having to wait and see how things worked out. About not getting her hopes up.

He'd never said he loved her. He'd never said anything about staying. He'd never really said anything about the baby. Or the miracle of it all.

Her morning sickness abated just about the time the doctor jubilantly confirmed her pregnancy and predicted a March birth. He insisted she follow a well-balanced diet, take daily iron supplements and get lots of rest. Then he reassured her that there was no reason she shouldn't carry this baby to term.

She was living her dream. One baby in her arms, another on the way. A good man at her side. She was supposed to feel like one lucky woman.

But she didn't feel like it. She felt like hell.

Then, late one Sunday morning, Christian whapped the flat of his belly. "Look at that, would you?" he groused. "You're feeding me too well, Raylie. All those homecooked meals are wreaking havoc with that lean, muscular build you fell for." He grinned and winked, patting her on the bottom as she struggled with the zipper on her jeans. "Hate to say it, but looks like they're doing the same to you, too, darlin'. Either that or Junior here is putting on a little weight." His hand slid to her abdomen, intimately caressing the spot where their child grew.

She flushed, stopping the zipper tab two inches below the top and leaving the brass button undone.

"You know," he said quizzically, his gaze running unashamedly over her breasts, "you're sure filling that out differently than you used to. I have to admit, I kind of like it."

She tried sucking herself back in. Finding that impossible, she feigned embarrassment and flopped her shirtfront down.

"Um . . . excuse me? Did you get a new bra or something?"

"Christian! You know why I'm getting bigger."

"Mmm . . . So? Hey, you're my wife. Tell me. I got a right to know who to write my testimonials to."

"You're watching too much TV." In the living room, Katie dropped a toy over the rail of her playpen. *Kerplack!*

"Nosiree." He moved behind her, wrapping his forearms under her breasts and above her middle, hunkering down just enough to whisper in her ear. "Dear sirs," he said, "your product—with a little help from me, of course—has changed my life. It's lifted and rounded the two things I cherish most." He stroked the heavy undersides of her breasts with his thumbs for emphasis. "It's separated fact from fiction. Lifting and separating to make a perky little statement in my life."

"Christian! Enough, already!"

He threw back his head and laughed, hugging her. "Okay, okay. But, God, I love—" The telephone jangled, effectively silencing his teasing. They both straightened, glaring at the intrusive phone. It rang again. "I'll get it," he reluctantly offered, moving away.

When his back was to her, it registered. He'd said two of the three magic words. He loved.

He loved what?

The answer had been about to fall from his lips before the interruption snatched it away. Before reality came thundering back, reminding him to keep his guard up. Commanding him to keep his emotional distance.

Her expectancy faltered when he hung up the phone. When he spoke, his voice was strained and unnatural. "I've got to get over to Beth's. Ty's gotten himself into a mess again."

"What?"

"He and some other kids got caught vandalizing a school bus last night. They broke windows and slashed seats. The district's threatening to kick him out of school. Permanently."

"No. How's Beth?"

"A basket case. Damn!" He slammed his fist on the top of the dresser making all her perfume bottles rattle. "I'm so sick of this thing with them. It's always something." He snatched his shirt off the end of the bed and shouldered into it. "And I thought we should go over and tell them about the baby today!"

"You tell them. It's time."

"Forget it," he snapped, angrily clomping out of the room, his unbuttoned shirt flopping beneath his elbows. "And don't wait around for me."

He returned late in the afternoon, his features haggard and drawn. He didn't say a word, he merely came in and slumped into a kitchen chair. Katie, thrilled to see her daddy, banged her spoon on the tray of her high chair. Raylene quickly took it away and offered her a breadstick. She gurgled, happily gnawing at it with her new top teeth.

"I was just fixing myself some iced tea. Want some?"

He lifted his eyes, nailing her with his gaze. "No. But I would like to talk."

"Da! Da!" Katie shrieked between nibbles.

"Let me put her in her playpen first. Then—"

"No. She doesn't bother me. Matter of fact, I think I need you both here. Tell me, Ray, you think it sounds strange for me to say I need my family around me?"

Apprehension skipped through better judgment. Where was he headed with this? "No..."

"Between that damn job of Beth's and that last summer school class, she doesn't have a clue what that kid of hers is up to. I'd like to shake her, but how can I criticize her for trying to better herself?"

"You can't."

"The kid needs more supervision. I know it. She knows it. The probation officer knows it." He raked a hand over the top of his head. "I'm sorry, Raylene. I'm the only one who can make a difference this time. I know I should've talked to you about it, but..."

"But?"

"I've arranged for Ty to come live with us. Until Beth finishes her degree. Until she's got the kind of time she needs to properly raise him, to supervise him. We're down to weeks. But it's still unfair to you, and I know that. I wouldn't be surprised if you're angry, if you're—"

"I'm not angry."

His gaze flickered, and he went on as if he hadn't heard. "When we sat down and talked about alternatives, the only thing I kept thinking about was how bad it was growing up and knowing my dad was never there for me. Maybe that's why I worked on the soapbox car so hard, maybe that's why I help Ty with his homework, and give him odd jobs around the workshop.''

"I understand that."

"No! You don't get it. You just don't get it. I once swore I'd never let that kind of thing happen in my own family. I promised Beth—"

"I understand, Chris."

He stared at her defensively. "Raylene! Just listen. I'm bringing another kid into this house. I'm complicating our life. I know you never bargained for that. You've every right to be mad."

"So? Things change. I'm bringing another child into this house, too."

He feigned exasperation, but a small smile pulled at his lips.

"Okay. You tell me. How can I be mad at you, when I admire you so much for what you're doing? You always say you hate responsibilities, but, Christian—face it—you meet them head-on."

He looked at her significantly. Then his eyes went to the pewter wall clock above the stove. A wedding gift from the owner of Bagels 'n' Buns. He paused as the minute hand made another revolution. "I don't want it to change what's going on between us."

"Tell me," she said softly. "What's going on between us?"

He struggled with the veil that routinely dropped over his eyes whenever she confronted him with something personal. The muscle in his jaw twitched, but he managed to answer. "I like what we've got going. I don't want to complicate it."

"Not until the adoption's final?"

His complexion grew mottled, color creeping up his neck. "No," he said gruffly. "Not ever."

"Funny thing, that. Because I feel the same." Hope flared in his eyes and he gazed at her, searchingly. She picked up his hand, the hand that always chose hammers and awls and sandpaper. The hand that had lifted her. "We can't go on as before, Christian. Because you're changing. I'm changing."

"You?" The light in his eyes faded.

"I've no other choice. If you're bringing another youngster into our home, I'm doing the same. There's no turning back. For either of us."

He stared at her, without a glimpse of comprehension.

"Don't you want this?" she asked.

"I do." Yet his response was garbled, rough.

"Then think about it. There's going to be two babies now. Two."

"Yeah. Damn. But it's great, isn't it?" Though he frowned, a fragile smile eased onto his face. "Don't you think so, Raylene?"

"I do."

"But, before that, we've got an eleven-year-old kid to drive us crazy."

"I don't mind."

"You don't? You really don't?"

"No. I really don't."

Relief erased the remaining worry lines on his face. "Thank you, thank you," he muttered, shaking his head from side to side. "Oh, God, thank you."

Her hand covered his, and she was surprised to find herself blinking back stinging tears. "I've got to admit there were times these past few weeks when I was afraid I might lose you. But now, hey, you've got to keep me around. For Ty, for Katie, and—"

"Don't." He suddenly said, a muscle in his jaw thumping. "Because I was afraid I'd lose you, too."

"Lose me?" she repeated, her heart skipping a beat. "Christian?"

"Yeah?" His answer was hoarse, and his fingers tightened on her abdomen.

"You're not going to lose me."

He pulled her over onto his lap, burying his forehead in the warm spot beneath her jaw. "God, I love you, Raylene. You've given me everything."

The impact of the phrase he'd uttered hit her. Her eyelids fluttered closed, effectively shutting out everything but the black-velvet warmth of him, the distinct touch of him, the unique smells of him. His mouth teased one of the buttons on her shirtfront, and she thought she was going to die from wanting him. "I love you, too."

Something rumbled deep inside him, like unspent emotions that had been freed. It transformed him, gentling him. The edge he always carried relaxed; the guarded expression he always wore evaporated; the brooding quality in his eyes faded.

Everything was the same about him. Yet everything was different. Inexplicably different.

"We're calling the original deal off," he said.

"Excuse me?"

"The deal's off. This time, with the new baby, and Katie—and even Ty—it's a full-time proposition. This time our marriage is forever."

"Forever," she solemnly agreed, dipping her head and rolling her forehead against his.

Behind them, the breadstick went splat against the newly scrubbed floor. The half-empty baby bottle followed. Heels snapped against the footrest. "Da! Ma!" Katie shrieked impatiently.

"Just a minute, Pudge," Chris answered, his hand dipping beneath Raylene's oversized shirt to explore her half-unzipped jeans, "This time Daddy's really got his hands full."

* * * * * *

This holiday season,
Linda Varner brings three very special couples

HOME
FOR THE HOLIDAYS

where they discover the joy of love and family—
and the wonder of wedded bliss.

✽✽✽✽✽✽✽✽✽✽✽✽✽✽✽✽✽✽✽✽✽✽✽✽✽✽✽

WON'T YOU BE MY HUSBAND?—Lauren West and
Nick Gatewood never expected their family and friends to get
word of their temporary engagement and nonintended nuptials. Or
to find themselves falling in love with each other. Is that a *real*
wedding they're planning over Thanksgiving dinner?
(SR#1188, 11/96)

MISTLETOE BRIDE—There was plenty of room at Dani Sellica's
Colorado ranch for stranded holiday guests Ryan Given and his
young son. Until the mistletoe incident! Christmas morning brought
presents from ol' Saint Nick...but would it also bring wedding bells?
(SR#1193, 12/96)

NEW YEAR'S WIFE—Eight years after Tyler Jordan and
Julie McCrae shared a passionate kiss at the stroke of midnight,
Tyler is back and Julie is certain he doesn't fit into her plans for
wedded bliss. But does his plan to prove her wrong include a lifetime
of New Year's kisses? (SR#1200, 1/97)

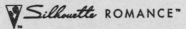

Silhouette ROMANCE™

MILLION DOLLAR SWEEPSTAKES

SWP-M96

Add a double dash of romance to your
festivities this holiday season
with two great stories in

Christmas
Celebration

Featuring full-length stories by bestselling authors

Kasey Michaels
Anne McAllister

These heartwarming stories of love triumphing
against the odds are sure to add some extra
Christmas cheer to your holiday season. And this
distinctive collection features **two full-length novels,**
making it the perfect gift at great value—for
yourself or a friend!

Available this December at your favorite retail outlet.

As seen on TV!
Free Gift Offer

With a Free Gift proof-of-purchase from any Silhouette® book,
you can receive a beautiful cubic zirconia pendant.

This gorgeous marquise-shaped stone is a genuine cubic
zirconia—accented by an 18" gold tone necklace.

(Approximate retail value $19.95)

Send for yours today...
compliments of ▼ *Silhouette*®
™

To receive your free gift, a cubic zirconia pendant, send us one original proof-of-purchase, photocopies not accepted, from the back of any Silhouette Romance™, Silhouette Desire®, Silhouette Special Edition®, Silhouette Intimate Moments® or Silhouette Yours Truly™ title available in August, September, October, November and December at your favorite retail outlet, together with the Free Gift Certificate, plus a check or money order for $1.65 U.S./$2.15 CAN. (do not send cash) to cover postage and handling, payable to Silhouette Free Gift Offer. We will send you the specified gift. Allow 6 to 8 weeks for delivery. Offer good until December 31, 1996 or while quantities last. Offer valid in the U.S. and Canada only.

Free Gift Certificate

Name: _____

Address: _____

City: _____ State/Province: _____ Zip/Postal Code: _____

Mail this certificate, one proof-of-purchase and a check or money order for postage and handling to: SILHOUETTE FREE GIFT OFFER 1996. In the U.S.: 3010 Walden Avenue, P.O. Box 9077, Buffalo NY 14269-9077. In Canada: P.O. Box 613, Fort Erie, Ontario L2Z 5X3.

FREE GIFT OFFER
084-KMD

ONE PROOF-OF-PURCHASE

To collect your fabulous FREE GIFT, a cubic zirconia pendant, you must include this original proof-of-purchase for each gift with the properly completed Free Gift Certificate.

084-KMD-R

You're About to Become a *Privileged Woman*

Reap the rewards of fabulous free gifts and benefits with proofs-of-purchase from Silhouette and Harlequin books

Pages & Privileges™

It's our way of thanking you for buying our books at your favorite retail stores.

PROOF OF PURCHASE
SR-PP19
Offer expires March 31, 1997

Pages & Privileges™

Harlequin and Silhouette—the most privileged readers in the world!

For more information about Harlequin and Silhouette's PAGES & PRIVILEGES program call the Pages & Privileges Benefits Desk: 1-503-794-2499

Silhouette®

SR-PP19

SWEET LITTLE KISSES

Leigh slid down in the chair and closed her eyes. Caesar's strong fingers massaged her scalp as he worked the rinse through her hair. "Don't move." He bent and kissed her. She opened her eyes but he was gone.

He returned with a cap and sat Leigh under the dryer for twenty minutes. Then he rinsed her hair again and she walked to the styling area.

"Not fair," she said, when she noticed he'd covered the mirrors.

"This is my gift to my bride."

He worked quickly but Leigh was anxious. Finally he whispered he was finished. He removed the coverup and turned her toward the mirror. Then, like a magician, he pulled the towel from the mirror.

"You will make a beautiful bride."

Caesar stared at Leigh. She was strong and vulnerable at the same time. He had given her sweet little kisses, when what he wanted to do was make passionate love to her. And he would do just that, but not now. They needed to keep their bargain that this would be a marriage in name only. Together they would bring Cassiopeia back to what it once was. Then they would be lovers. He knew without a doubt that this woman would share his bed.

ALL THAT GLITTERS

VIVECA CARLYSLE

Pinnacle Books
Kensington Publishing Corp.
http://www.pinnaclebooks.com

PINNACLE BOOKS are published by

Kensington Publishing Corp.
850 Third Avenue
New York, NY 10022

First Printing: January, 1999
10 9 8 7 6 5 4 3 2 1

Printed in the United States of America

For my mother, Ruby L. Tanksley
and in memory of my father, Eugene L. Tanksley, Sr.

Acknowledgments

Writing may be a solitary profession but there is always a force that pushes you on as you stare at a blank page.

Thank you to Sylvia Baumgarten (aka Sylvia Halliday) for sharing how a certain salon treated her—she knows the passage in the book.

I'd also like to thank Phoebe Morris, Alicia M. Singleton, Myra Cook, Gayla Slaughter, and Ms. Cyd C. Smith for the cards and letters that kept me going through this book.

ONE

The rain had been falling at a steady pace since late afternoon, and she waited until it slacked off at eight that night. She sat in her car until she saw the lights go out in the living room of the brownstone on Fifth Avenue. She knew the house well since she'd once been a welcome guest there. She knew the occupants—Paul "the Baron of Rock" Lambert and his beautiful wife Stephanie—better than anyone else in the world. It was Paul's fault and someone had to stop him. Once, the Board of Directors of the Cassiopeia Salons had been like a family, but that was before the Salons became a corporation and greed lured them all into a tangled web of thievery. Now they were at each other's throats. Originally there had only been five of them—poor, struggling friends who looked out for each other. Their first venture had been a disaster, but she had convinced the same investors to try again. Only this time they wanted more; they wanted a piece of the action. Now, instead of five with the same goal, there was a committee deciding every move.

It was twenty after eight when she stepped from the car and started down the street toward the brownstone. Her costume did not rate a second glance. New Yorkers would not be surprised to see someone dressed like a clown, even if it hadn't been the night before Halloween.

The plan had fallen into place the week before when Stephanie had announced to the staff that she would be away on a business trip. The board members knew better—it was really a stay at a private resort for alcoholics. Stephanie and Paul had been overheard discussing an end to everything: the salons and their marriage. She'd left three days before and was not expected back for another four. That meant Paul was in the house alone.

The Halloween party at the salon would still be going strong. She had plenty of time to accomplish her mission and get back to the party. Considering how much liquor was flowing when she sneaked out, she wouldn't even be missed.

She'd tested her old key when she made her dry run. Everything had been carefully planned, even down to what she would wear to Paul's funeral. She would look beautifully distraught as she grieved at the loss, knowing that her future with Cassiopeia Salons was secure.

Once inside the house, she crept up the stairs and tiptoed down the hall to Paul's bedroom. She paused a minute as she thought about the reason it had come to this. The fight in the boardroom had gotten ugly. After that, Paul had summoned her to his office. No one had ever spoken to her in that manner—now he would pay. She removed her mask. She wanted him to see her. She wanted him to know she'd won and he'd lost everything.

Paul Lambert sat on the edge of the bed. His wrinkled pink neon shirt lay next to him. The buttons were scattered around the room. In his inebriated state, he'd been unable to unbutton it, so he'd just ripped the buttons off as he pulled the shirt from his body. The Halloween party must be going full strength at the salon, he thought. He'd promised to stop in. He'd lied. He didn't want to be around the peons. He chuckled to himself as he thought about the real Halloween party that would be at his home tomorrow night—the special party that he and Stephanie always gave for the Board and a few select friends. Everyone wanted to attend, but invitations outside the board members were scarce, and that was how the Lamberts wielded their power. It had been that way since the time Helene had suggested it five years before. It fit their lifestyle. Other people celebrated birthdays, holidays, and the like. Only the Baron and his lady would make Halloween the grand event.

There were no clocks in the house. He'd never wanted to know what time it was so it could always be anytime he wanted it to be. He ate when he felt like it, drank when he felt like it and slept when he felt like it. The only time things changed is when Stephanie dragged him off to a Board meeting or some other function associated with Cassiopeia salons.

He yawned and stretched. He and Stephanie had finally come to an understanding. Their marriage had been on the rocks for a while but now they were back on target, no matter what anyone else thought. They had filmed their Living Will in celebration, although only their lawyer knew about it.

Paul was still angry over the remarks made in the boardroom—each member tossing out sarcastic comments about the direction the salons were taking. JoAnn had actually gotten between him and Sarito Valerian. As if he couldn't handle someone much shorter than his own six-foot frame.

After he'd given a few more people a piece of his mind, he and Stephanie had left. He was supposed to drive her to Port Authority to get her bus, but the feelings they'd had from the first time they met were still there. A little extra-marital fling wasn't going to break them up.

He'd downed enough Bacardi's to push that out of his mind. She would never leave him now. He glanced at the empty rum bottle and debated about going down to the bar for another since he'd exhausted his supply. He glanced at the tousled pile of multicolored quilts next to him. Yeah! He'd get another bottle. Not even his loving wife could tell him when to stop drinking just because she was giving it up.

He heard a creaking sound, looked up, and saw the clown. The white-faced make up and white baggy suit trimmed in black surprised him for a moment. He closed his eyes and shook his head. When he opened his eyes, the clown was still there. Jumbled thoughts fought through his brain. Party. Halloween party.

"Idiot," Paul's mouth twisted and his speech slurred. "The party's tomorrow night. Halloween is tomorrow."

It took him a couple of heart beats to focus on the face and to realize she had a gun—a gun equipped with a silencer.

"No!" he screamed. He twisted his body trying to rise, but his drunken condition made him fall back onto the bed. The first two shots missed and sank into the bedcovers. The next three were on target.

She had done it. She watched as he clutched at the stack of quilts on the bed, taking them with him as he slid to the floor. Then it was her turn to scream. Bright, red blood oozed from the two bullet holes in the chest of her other victim. Under the pile of covers, wearing a white, rapidly-turning-red nightgown, was Stephanie Lambert. Dead? No! Her eyes opened and met those of her murderer's. Then they closed. The clown whirled and fled almost falling down the stairs, as her perfect costume became cumbersome. She put her mask back on. She was almost at the front door when she remembered her original mission.

She ran back. Now more than before she needed that will. She ran to the media room, her hands shaking as she struggled in the darkness. She was afraid to turn on any lights. One part of her brain was telling her to move fast, while another part was unsure if she should call for help for Stephanie. In the media room she turned on a small lamp. Just as she was reaching for the tape, she heard something. Someone else was in the house. She grabbed the tape. As she came out of the media room, she saw someone making his way up the stairs. A thief! She fought down a giggle as she stuffed her gun and the tape inside her suit, opened the door, and hurried toward her car. She passed two women and heard one of them ask, "Should we get a clown like that for the kids next year?"

An uncontrollable giggle bubbled inside her. Would they feel the same if they knew she'd just killed two people?

No! She'd only killed one person—Stephanie had been an

accident. The pay phone on the corner gave her an idea. She dialed 911, and in a whisper she told of a robbery in progress, gave the address, and hung up. She walked to her car, got in, and took the mask off. She took a few deep breaths. As she pulled away from the curb, she heard the sirens.

Traffic was still snarled because of the earlier rainstorm. Water had filled most of the potholes and caused several accidents. New York didn't get as much snow as it once did—now it seemed to rain more than snow in the winter. Almost two hours had passed since she had first parked outside the brownstone. She pulled into her apartment complex's garage. There was no way she could return to the party at the salon. She slid into the passenger seat and wriggled out of the costume. She'd worn a black jumpsuit under it. She had a plastic bag in the glove compartment, and she managed to stuff the costume in it after she took the tape out. She got out of the car and put the bag in the trunk. Then she locked her car and headed for the elevator.

Once inside her apartment, she tossed the tape on the table and turned on the TV. She stripped and headed for the shower. After cleansing herself, she'd watch it. She'd be the last one to see it. The lawyer didn't know what he'd caused when he had told her about the will. The reporter on the eleven o'clock news stopped her from walking into the bathroom.

". . . murder on Fifth Avenue," the reporter said, as she stood outside the brownstone. "Tonight between eight-thirty and nine o'clock there was a 911 call from this house. A woman identifying herself as Stephanie Lambert said that both she and her husband had been shot by someone dressed like a clown. The police arrived in minutes. The rest isn't clear, but apparently the man was still in the house when the police arrived. There was a brief shootout and the suspect was killed. Upstairs the police found Paul Lambert, the flamboyant singer known as the Baron of Rock, dead. His wife, Stephanie, was barely clinging to life. She was rushed to the hospital and no one has updated us on her condition."

The anchorman asked, "Stephanie Lambert said she'd been shot by a clown?"

"Yes," the reporter said. "The Lamberts were preparing for their annual Halloween party and there were masks and costumes in the den. The police believe the man put on one of the masks but discarded it during the shootout."

Stephanie was alive? How much would she remember? Sinking down into the chair, she waited. Not paying attention to the rest of the news, she stood up and paced the living room as she ran through scenarios of what could happen if Stephanie survived. It was almost at the end of the program when Stephanie's picture flashed on the screen.

"This just in," the anchorman said. "Stephanie Lambert died shortly after she arrived at the hospital. Now three people are dead, among them Paul Lambert, the Baron of Rock, from what seems to be a robbery gone bad."

She was safe. Breathing a sigh of relief, she changed her mind about the shower and headed for the bar. She poured a shot of Jack Daniel's Green Label Bourbon and tossed it down. She slipped the tape into the VCR. Instead of Stephanie, Paul filled the screen. It was a video from his last concert. The piano hung from the rafters and Paul stood on it, gyrating to the thumping beat of his last hit, "Scream, Baby."

She ejected the tape and looked at the spine. Fear replaced hope. When she had heard the burglar, she must have grabbed the wrong tape. It wasn't over. One more person stood in the way. One more person had to be eliminated. And that was Leigh Barrington.

TWO

Leigh Barrington had discovered the perfect place to put her umbrella, deck chair, and small table. The section in the rear of her borrowed bungalow gave her a better view of the pink sands and turquoise water of the most beautiful beach she'd ever seen. She placed the virgin piña colada on the table and stretched out in the deck chair as she went over the most recent annual report of the Cassiopeia Salon chain.

Her white gossamer shirt covered her multicolored bathing suit and she wore a large pink, gold, and purple hat that she'd purchased the day she'd arrived. The blistering Caribbean sun had been merciless on her skin from the moment she stepped off the company jet. She had spied the hat at an outdoor market—unusually wide, it immediately served its purpose.

The hat was not the only protection for her dark skin. She'd applied a thin layer of sun block. It had been two years since she'd taken a vacation from her administrative assistant position at Westinghouse and Jackson's law firm. The sports attorneys seemed to acquire clients from the first day of baseball's spring training to the last moments of football's pro bowl. The personalities of the players they handled were from flamboyant motor mouths to their closemouthed teammates.

That life was over now for Leigh. Coming to terms with the fact that she'd just inherited 42% of the Cassiopeia Salon chain had been a shock to her system. One day she was keeping track of endorsement offers, and the next she was being pursued by the relentless tabloid press. A murdered rock star and his wife were certainly fodder for the gossip columns. The most extraordinary part had to be that the will had left everything they owned to the wife's estranged sister. The press finally left her alone when a Hollywood blonde bombshell and her groom of ten days had a knock down fight in an exclusive Manhattan restaurant. They found that story more interesting and promptly forgot about Leigh.

As much as she wanted the chance to own the chain, the fact that it had happened because of her sister's death weighed heavily on her mind. She and the Board had agreed to table any decisions and let the day to day operation of the salons remain status quo until they could all sit down and make those decisions without emotion. There were twelve board members. At the time Leigh talked to them, they were still rather dazed by the turn of events. Most were zombie-like about the next step. Her Aunt Helene had introduced them and explained their functions. Helene had taken on the duties of CEO and according to her, that was what Stephanie and Paul would have wanted. Only Helene and three other board members were part of the original team. One recent member of the Board was missing—away on family business, they had explained.

The voice of reason came from the man she worked for, Mark Westinghouse. Mark wouldn't let Leigh allow her emotions to cause her to turn down her inheritance. He outlined a plan to postpone her taking over in order to give herself a chance to learn more about her company.

Mark had handed her the keys to his Caribbean bungalow and she'd used her new corporate jet to take her there. For three days she slept off and on. She hadn't realized how tired she was. Twice a day she spoke to her aunt, who tried to convince Leigh that being a CEO in name only was better than trying to run a business she knew nothing about. Helene hinted that the salon was in a state that needed special handling or all would be lost. Leigh was noncommittal on the phone as she waffled between believing her aunt and standing on the sidelines or jumping into the fray.

* * *

Leigh sipped her drink and began to peruse the annual report. She glanced up as a man jogged by and waved. She absently returned the wave. She'd seen him on the beach a few times, and at first she had thought she knew him. There was something so familiar about him, but she couldn't place it. He didn't try to approach her—he just acknowledged her presence. Her eyes wandered over his powerful form. She judged him to be only one or two inches over her own five-foot-seven-inches. She couldn't take her eyes off him—the coordination between his sinewy arm movements and powerful legs as he moved his whipcord lean body along the sand with as much grace as an Alvin Ailey dancer. A brown Adonis. The only thing she found unusual was that each time she'd seen him he'd been wearing black swim trunks and a black tank top. That was odd on a sun-drenched beach. Most people wanted to show off their tans by contrasting their skin in bright or light colors.

An hour later, Leigh went back in the house to mix herself a second drink; she needed a break from the facts and figures of the salon. She picked up a novel and returned to her deck chair. Soon she was lost in the latest bestseller from her favorite author.

"I think I'll tell you how that book ends," said a deep voice.

Stunned, Leigh dropped the book and bolted from the chair. Her hat tilted with her sudden movement and she grabbed it to keep it from falling. She found herself staring at the jogger she'd waved at earlier. They were almost equal in height, as she'd assessed earlier.

"I'm sorry," the man said. "I didn't mean to startle you."

Leigh could feel the heat rising in her face as she shifted her hat. She knew he was lying. He had meant to unsettle her. This was a deliberate invasion of her privacy. He was probably another reporter looking to breathe life into what was now tabloid old news. She wasn't afraid—just a little leery. "I already know the end."

"Oh, I thought it was a new book, not one you'd already read." His slight accent sounded more Latino than Islander. He now wore a black sweatsuit. His short hair lay in tiny ringlets on his head. Long black lashes framed his black eyes. And she caught the tangy fragrance of aftershave. He'd obviously showered, shaved, and changed clothes since she last saw him. His medium-brown skin was almost flawless. It was broken only by a small jagged scar on his right cheek.

"It is new."

"I don't understand."

"I read the ending before I bought it."

He laughed. "You read the ending and you still bought the book?"

"I like to know if it has a happy ending."

"Doesn't that spoil the book?"

"Not for me."

For three days he'd kept his distance, but now was his chance. This woman was in the way of his fortune. She'd been a surprise. The last time he'd talked to Paul Lambert, the Living Will was on hold and Stephanie was threatening to divorce him. The news of their deaths saddened him but their friendship had already been strained over the direction the salons were taking. Paul favored expansion while he knew it would be disastrous at the time when the salons needed overhauling. He usually controlled his temper, but Paul flaunting his percentage, along with Helene saying, "the Lambert way is the only way," simply was the straw that broke the camel's back. If Gayla hadn't been there . . . . He didn't really want to think about it. So he'd found out where Leigh was staying and promised Helene he'd talk Leigh into being a silent partner while they pulled the salon away from the sharks. He decided to forsake his altar ego of Sarito Valerian and use the name he'd thought was his for the first seventeen years of his life.

He stretched out his hand. "I'm Caesar Montgomery."

She hesitated before lifting her hand to meet his. "Leigh

Barrington." In that brief moment she'd decided not to hide behind an alias. If he was a reporter, she would let him be the only one lying.

"And what brings you to this lovely island?" Caesar asked.

"A need for rest, relaxation, and solitude."

"If that's a hint . . ."

"It wasn't," she said. "Why don't you get the other chair?" She pointed to the folded item next to the house. Leigh was tired of solitude. It hadn't helped her come any closer to a decision about her life. Maybe she needed to mingle with people and forget about her situation. Or as her best friend Stacey had suggested, have an affair. Again the heat crept over her face knowing the man setting up the chair next to her caused that memory spark.

Seconds later he was stretched out beside her, the sleeves to his sweatshirt pulled up to reveal bronze, muscular arms. His monochrome outfit was in direct contrast to the blue, yellow, orange, and green flowery material of the chair. The umbrella was large enough to provide shade for both of them.

"So Leigh Barrington, what do you do when you're not reading the end of novels before you buy them?"

"I make sure my boss gets to all his appointments on time with all the information he needs."

"Secretary?"

"Administrative assistant with a paralegal degree tossed in."

"Sorry. I forgot that 'secretary' was not a politically correct term."

"What do you do when you're not threatening to reveal plot endings?"

"I just finished a stint running a coffee plantation in Colombia."

"Really? How did you get that job?"

"It's my family's business. My brother was hurt in an accident and I had to keep things together until he got better."

"What are your plans now?"

"There's another company that needs my expertise."

"Is that what you do? Act as trouble shooter for ailing businesses?"

"I hope to make this next job permanent."

They watched a roving volleyball group set up a net and recruit players a few feet from where they were sitting. The players ranged from brawny men punching through the ball to nubile women screaming and getting it back over the net. They tried to have a conversation over the screams, but it seemed hopeless. Caesar noticed Leigh was more than a little unnerved by the loud and lively group. Of course, he thought. She needs quiet considering what she's been through with the media. She probably hates crowds as much as anyone. She hadn't craved the limelight. Leigh simply lived her life in anonymous happiness until the will had been read.

Twice the ball came near the bungalow. The third time, it landed near Leigh's feet Caesar got up and retrieved it, but he didn't throw it back. He jogged over to the young man who seemed to be the leader of the group.

"You're a little close. The lady is recuperating from a bad time in her life," Caesar said.

"This is the place to have fun, man."

"Under other circumstances I might even ask if we could join you, but . . ." Caesar let the sentence trail off.

"So what happened to her? She lose her job?" Caesar recognized the New York accent as Bensonhurst, Brooklyn.

"No, her sister." He didn't want to tell them anymore for fear they would know about the crime.

"Sorry. We'll find another spot."

"Thanks."

"No problem."

When he got back to his teammates, he pulled them together, pointed to Caesar, and in moments they had moved the net and the game further down the beach.

The concerned look on Caesar's face as he rejoined Leigh was from his own guilt. He'd used her tragedy to make the volleyball team move away so he could cajole her into giving up her inheritance. He'd done so without one thought about the period of mourning she faced. He'd convinced himself that he was doing it to help her. What did that make him? Could he ever justify the means with the end?

As he turned back to Leigh, she could see his eyes change from a fierce anger to what they looked like when he teased her about reading the ending of a book before buying it. Another shiver of warning oscillated up and down her spine. She saw the man as predator as well as protector. Despite feeling slightly unnerved at his power, she was also fascinated by it. What had brought on the fierce look? Something the young man he spoke with had said, or was it something else that bothered him?

He sat down, stretched out in the lounge chair, and then asked, "Have you seen much of the night life since you've been here?"

Leigh welcomed the change in subject. "No. I've been . . . resting."

"Then have dinner with me?"

"Okay. What time?" She was convinced he wasn't a reporter but sensed there was something he wasn't telling her. Maybe he was hoping she'd be willing to sponsor his business or something to that effect. Anyway, she decided to have a good time and enjoy the remaining two weeks before she told her aunt that she was not going away quietly.

"I'll pick you up at eight."

At seven-thirty, Leigh stood in front of her mirror putting a coat of mascara on her lashes. Her pale brown eyes against her dark skin had been her outstanding feature in what she considered a rather ordinary face. Not ugly. Not pretty. Not a face you would glance at twice except for her eyes. They always made people think she was wearing contacts. She padded around in her bare feet as she dressed. The bungalow had wall to wall burgundy carpeting in every room to highlight the white oak French provincial furniture. She checked her sleeveless royal blue and white silk dress with the plunging neckline, then slipped into her white heels. She paused for a moment as she remembered his height. She had only brought two pairs of evening shoes and both had three-inch heels. That would make her taller than her escort. "Nothing I can do about it," Leigh said aloud.

She brushed her chemically-straightened hair so it formed a short bang over her forehead and the rest of it fell to her cheek-bones. She put on her diamond earrings and took one last look in the mirror as she heard the bell ring. She grabbed a navy crocheted shawl and wrapped it around her shoulders. The breeze off the ocean at night was not welcomed as much as it was in the day on the island of Nassau.

She opened the door and found Caesar standing there in an expertly tailored black linen suit broken only by the black silk tie that shimmered as it lay flat against his black shirt.

"You look exquisite," he said, as he produced a corsage of one white, one red, and one yellow rose twisted together on a stretchable band. "May I?"

She nodded and he slipped the band over her left wrist. They stepped outside and she locked the door. Then he offered his arm. She took it as they walked the short flight of stairs to the beach then took the gravel path that led to the nearby hotel.

Leigh was surprised that he seemed comfortable escorting someone taller than he. She'd reached this height at thirteen and watched her shorter schoolmates have boys flock to their sides. She'd been awkward—all arms and legs until Grandma Gen had enrolled her in a modeling school. Geneva Barrington knew that Leigh didn't have the face to become a model, but she needed confidence. Leigh's shyness faded as she made friends with the young girls who were pretty enough to become models but had the same inferior beliefs because they were tall and gangly. That's where she'd met Stacey. The redhead from Texas was only a year older than Leigh and they became best friends. The lessons she'd learned in modeling school served her well, and as her poise grew, so did her craving for knowledge. By the time she'd reached sixteen, most of the boys in school had caught up with and a few had surpassed her height. She became a popular student as well as a good one.

She wondered if, had she and Caesar gone to the same school, he would have been one of the boys who wasn't afraid to ask her out or one of her tormentors cowed by her stature.

They reached the hotel, which had several restaurants with different themes. He'd made reservations at the Rendevous. It specialized in Caribbean-American food in an intimate setting. The menus were those that had the prices listed in the one presented to the man but not in the one for the woman. The waiter gave them a few minutes, and Leigh selected a salad to begin as she worked her way through an exotic main course menu. Caesar chose the wine.

As she savored the Conch salad, she had time to get to know Caesar a little better. "Where are you going after you finish your vacation?"

"New York."

"Really? Me, too."

Caesar let out an audible breath before his next sentence. "Leigh, I know I told you I'd been living in Colombia for a while, but my home is in New York and I keep up to date on what's happening there."

"So you've known about me all along."

"Yes. I've known that you needed to be left alone with your grief and whatever other decisions you've had to make about your life."

Leigh's silence stretched a full minute before she said anything. "I don't know what to do. One minute I'm elated at being in such a high position, and the next I'm afraid that I'll make mistakes that will cost everything."

"Do you have anyone who can advise you?"

"My boss. Mark's been terrific."

Caesar cringed each time she revealed more of herself and he continued his lie. He just wanted to convince her to delay moving into the CEO's office for a year. Even six months would give him the chance to turn the salons around. The rumors had been overshadowed by the murders, but sooner or later someone was going to point out that Cassiopeia was ripe for a takeover. The only way to prevent it was to convince Leigh Barrington not to use the salons as a training ground.

Still, he admired her courage—to feel afraid and yet be willing to walk away from a secure career and future and try to
grab a star. Maybe this was her last chance and she wanted it
more than he had imagined. But Caesar knew it was his last
chance, and he had to do everything and anything to get control.
He'd fought his way from a small beauty parlor in the Jamaica
section of Queens, New York. He'd reached the highest point
of his career when as Sarito Valerian he'd become the hairstylist
of the stars. Now he wanted something permanent. And if Leigh
Barrington stood in the way, he'd just have to find a way to
move her aside.

He pulled himself back to the present as Leigh touched his
arm. "Caesar, the waiter's trying to get your attention."

"Sorry. I was just thinking about something I have to do."

The waiter was indeed trying to get his attention. He'd
brought the wine and poured the taster portion in the glass next
to Caesar. He lifted the glass, swirled it around, and tasted it
before nodding his approval to the waiter. The man filled both
glasses, set the wine down, and left.

"Were you thinking about your brother?"

"No. I was thinking about my next career move."

"Oh. You looked rather sad. I thought you might be worried
about your older brother."

"Why would you think he's older?"

"Well, I thought the inheritance was always passed to the
eldest son in Spanish-speaking countries."

"Not exactly. It's passed on to the legitimate son."

Leigh gasped then stared into her wine before apologizing.
"I . . . I didn't mean to pry."

"It's all right now. There was a time I hated that I was not
my father's heir, but my mother is an extraordinary woman. She
explained I had two choices. I could bemoan my fate and never
accomplish anything, or I could stop feeling sorry for myself
and get on with my life."

"Tough love school of thought?"

"No. She's a realist. She knew my father would have to choose duty above all. So she prepared herself to accept that. Then she married Trevor Montgomery and he raised me."

"Do you ever use your biological father's name?"

"I haven't for a long time. Have you decided what you want?"

Leigh understood the door was closed to his past. She still wondered why he seemed so familiar, yet she knew they'd never met. She'd thought if she could find out more about him she would remember him, but his short biographical sketch left her more in the dark than before.

THREE

Leigh savored the last spoonful of the restaurant's dessert special of mangoes, papaya, and kiwis topped with a rich creamy sauce. According to Caesar, the recipe for the sauce was so guarded that rumor said the chef wouldn't allow anyone in the kitchen while he prepared each order himself.

"You really should have ordered this, Caesar," Leigh said. Her forehead wrinkled slightly as she stared at the plain chopped pineapples on his dessert plate.

"I think I've sampled enough of that concoction," he laughed. "I've tried it a couple of times this week. By the way, how long do you plan to stay here?"

"I'm not sure. I keep changing my mind."

She knew inside there was a reason she was reluctant to leave the island. One part of her brain urged her to stay and let the others run the salon. Another part told her this was her dream—

to participate in all the decisions and appear in the gossip columns, just like her sister had. Leigh would get the kudos. People would say they admired her the way they had Stephanie. Leigh wanted that. She told herself it was vanity and she should be ashamed. Stephanie was dead, and the only reason Leigh was involved with the salon was because of her sister's will.

Her mind played devil's advocate all the time. She could have the glamour, which she knew meant hard work, or she could have the money and live well. Her nature was not that of someone who could sit at home every day. Despite the pros and cons that bounced around in her head, she knew that she would make one attempt at being an active CEO. She had to try. She had to know if she could do it. Maybe after that she could walk away.

Leigh was grateful that Caesar allowed the silences. Some men would have tried to keep a light patter going all the time. He didn't. He hadn't mentioned contacting her when they returned to New York, and Leigh almost asked for his phone number. But maybe Stacey's idea was the best—to have a vacation fling. She could almost hear her friend's voice urging her to laugh, dance, have an affair, and then walk away. But somehow Leigh wasn't sure she could walk away from Caesar. The man was hypnotic—revealing just enough of himself to keep her interested.

"Hello? Is anyone home?" Caesar's voice broke through her daydream.

"I'm sorry. I guess I got lost in my thoughts for a minute."

"I could forgive that if I thought they were about me," he said. "But something tells me it was about the future."

She felt the heat rising in her face indicating his assumption was on target. She was also a little disturbed at how long she'd let her thoughts wander. But she'd made a decision and she might as well admit it.

"I'll be leaving at the end of the week. Vacation's over."

"I thought you had another week?" Caesar couldn't keep the surprise out of his voice.

"The longer I stay away, the harder it will be to get back to basics."

"So you're leaving Sunday?" He'd hoped for another week—
now he had to change her mind in five days.

"No. Saturday. I'll need some time to unwind."

Four days. His mission wasn't impossible, but on a scale of
one to ten, it ranked a hard eight . "Then let's enjoy the remainder of your stay."

He signaled to the waiter and whispered something in his
ear. The man rushed away and moments later returned with the
check and a large black plastic bag that was too dense to see
the contents. Caesar paid and guided Leigh out of the restaurant
into the hotel lobby.

"Wait here, I'll be right back," he told her.

A few minutes later he appeared with a blanket draped over
his arm.

"I will show you one of the most romantic places on the
island."

Leigh hesitated as they walked out of the hotel and down the
narrow wooden pathway toward the beach. She didn't think her
high-heeled sandals would make the trip. Her dress swished
around her ankles as she walked, and she was positive the Lagerfeld creation was not intended for this activity either. But she
was on vacation. She stopped at the two-step stairway that led
to the beach and stepped out of her sandals. As she bent to pick
them up, she heard the clinking of glass. She raised an eyebrow.

"It's a surprise," he told her as he caught her free hand and
led her down the beach. A narrow sandy path led them to a
small cave-like formation in a huge boulder that had been there
before man. It resembled a room without a ceiling, hidden away
from the rest of the world and open to nature at the same time.

Caesar spread the thick blanket over half of the rock jutting
out from the cave wall. He motioned for Leigh to sit down. He
opened the plastic bag and produced a small red-checked table
cloth, which he spread down so they could sit. Then, like a
magician, he produced a bottle of champagne and two glasses.

"I think this is a good place to toast your success."

"You ran a coffee plantation. What do you think my chances
are?"

"I . . . I wouldn't want to make a guess on that."

"Not very good, huh?"

"I didn't say that."

"No. But you didn't say they were good so that must mean you think they aren't."

Caesar began hating himself for deceiving Leigh. She was so sincere about wanting to run the salons, yet her timing was so wrong.

"My mother insisted I spend summers with my biological father. He taught me everything he knew about the coffee business. He wanted me to be second in command, and if anything happened to his only legitimate heir, he wanted me to take the reins. I had years of learning and still it was difficult to bring in a good crop this year."

"So you don't think I'm ready?"

"Just my opinion."

"Maybe you're right. I don't want to fail, so maybe I should take some time to learn. In fact, I think the next time my aunt calls I'll tell her. But I'm going to sit in on every board meeting."

"Does she call every night?"

"No. More like every other night. She'll be happy about this."

"I hope you won't regret my advice."

She'd thought he was a reporter at first. She told him things that she felt comfortable seeing in print. Even if his family really owned a coffee plantation, she hadn't revealed anything she didn't want to share. "The business has been successful until now, so that shouldn't change in a year."

Caesar grew quiet. He didn't want to tell her that a shark lurked around the shaky waters of Cassiopeia, and that it would take all of his know-how and business acumen to save it. The only sacrifice he would have to make was his relationship with Leigh. She'd never forgive this betrayal. Not even when he saved her inheritance would she overlook his lies. He knew that with a unexplainable certainty.

He opened the champagne and poured it in their glasses. "A toast to your success. I wish you fame and fortune."

Leigh tapped his glass with hers. "I've always felt that I could handle fame and fortune."

"Be careful with fame," he said. He leaned forward, and when she didn't try to push him away, he kissed her.

Like an old and dear friend, she thought. Not like a prospective lover. Maybe he didn't see her in a romantic sense—it was more like a sisterly, girl-next-door attraction.

Just as that thought passed through her head, he kissed her again. Only this time it didn't resemble anything close to a kiss you'd give your sister.

If she wasn't going to run the salon, maybe it was time for romance, for no matter how short, she knew it would be special. She had no doubt spending time in this man's bed would be memorable. She had to leave the island feeling more in control of the situation than when she'd arrived.

Sometimes Caesar hated himself. She was so honest and he was still enveloping her in his duplicity. His mother and late stepfather would have been appalled at his scandalous behavior. His late father, however, would have been pleased, as long as he succeeded and didn't hurt any family members.

He'd charmed women before but never had he lied. Each had known what the game was about. Each had followed the unwritten rules. Each knew when the game was over. Caesar as Sarito Valerian had never been without a woman. Yet when he insisted on a seat on the Board of Cassiopeia, he'd curtailed most of his night roving and concentrated on the salon. He tried to keep everything open and honest, but he'd heard the rumors. The tabloids had linked him with Stephanie and the other two women on the Board. But he'd ignored them and soon they stopped.

Perhaps Paul hadn't believed him. Before the murders, Caesar had noticed a widening between the old board members and the newer ones. Something was going on, but before there was a complete split, Paul and Stephanie were gone.

A week was a considerably short time to romance a woman. From the brief information Helene Adams had provided about her niece, he knew she was accustomed to being surrounded by top sports figures and that she refrained from getting involved with any of them most of the time. The exception had been Marshall Alexander. The basketball player had clawed through her resistance and shortly after announcing their engagement, he'd been traded to a west coast team. The distance look a toll on the relationship. Helene only knew what happened from Alexander's viewpoint and that's what she relayed to Caesar. Leigh's jealousy had led her to believe he was unfaithful and he'd ended the romance. Caesar knew there was more to the story, but he could find out about that later.

Soon their only light was that of the moon. The stars had disappeared into the blue-black sky. The wind from the sea brought a slight chill to the air, and it was time to leave. They made one last toast, then he gathered up the items and tucked them back into the bag. As they walked down the beach toward Leigh's place, Caesar knew he had to convince her in some way that her expectations for the salon were premature. Jameson Miller had begun sniffing around the week after Paul and Stephanie had been murdered. The man had a knack for finding businesses in distress, taking them over, remodeling them, and selling for a higher profit. But Caesar knew that this time it was more. Cassiopeia sat on prime real estate across the street from Trump Tower, and Miller wanted to turn it into his piece of paradise. Caesar had to be with Leigh as much as possible.

When they reached her door, Caesar leaned forward to kiss her. He'd envisioned a light, friendly kiss, but once his lips met hers, he didn't want to let go. He wrapped his arms around her. He held her for a minute and knew that she was as reluctant to say good night as he was. But Caesar would only go so far in breaking his own rules of conduct. He would not sleep with her until she knew his real identity and still said yes to his demands.

"What are you doing for lunch tomorrow?" he asked.

"Absolutely nothing."

"I have some business calls to make and then I'll call you."

" 'Til tomorrow."

FOUR

As she sipped her tea, the next morning, Leigh thought about all that had happened in one month. She'd gone from being an administrative assistant for one of the most powerful corporate lawyers in the city to sitting on the Board of Directors of Cassiopeia Salons. Sometimes she wanted to run away and other times she couldn't wait to walk into that boardroom. Helene had kept her informed but eventually it would be time for her to fish or cut bait, as Mark liked to say. Leigh knew her real problem was accepting the fact that she only had a chance to run the salons because of Stephanie's death. Someone had to do it and she wanted to do it well.

She'd studied the financial statements and knew there were a few shaky areas. Before she'd left for the island, she'd researched newspapers and knew that the Board had been approached by Jameson Miller. The takeover king wanted to add the salons to his burgeoning empire. The main salon's Fifth Avenue location was a prime spot and would put him directly across the street from Trump Tower. Fighting him off would be the first of her tasks as she took over Cassiopeia.

Just as she was outlining her strategy to fight off Miller, the phone rang.

"So, heiress, how's it going?"

"Oh, Mark. I can't thank you enough for lending me your house."

"Nonsense. I may be losing my right hand, but I'm big enough to take it," he teased.

Mark Westinghouse stood an impressive six feet five inches and weighed in the neighborhood of three hundred pounds. His late wife had tried and failed many times to get him to lose weight. It didn't bother him, and soon everyone just accepted it.

"How's Krista working out?"

"She's finding her own way."

"You haven't thrown any books at her, have you?"

"No way. I learned my lesson from you."

When Leigh had first come to work for Mark, he had the habit of throwing a book down on your desk if he discovered you'd made an error. He said it was to make a point of how disgusted he was. The first time he'd done that to Leigh, she'd picked up the book, walked to his office, and dropped it with considerable force on his desk. Then she'd returned to her desk and continued working as if she didn't know he was there. A red-faced Mark had known from that day on that he could criticize her but he couldn't intimidate her.

"I have to tell you that I miss you. It's hard breaking in someone new."

"Krista's not new. She's been there for a year."

"Well she's still new to me."

"What if I want my old job back?"

"Don't even say that. You know if you can handle me, no one on the Board is going to scare you."

"I haven't met them all so I don't know about that."

"I asked you before and you said no, but I think you should let me do a little digging into the pasts of the boardmembers."

"No. I want to see how they respond to me before I play heavy-handed."

"Well you and your aunt together still would control the

Board. It's tightly divided among the board members. If it doesn't work out with your aunt, maybe you need to team up with one of the others."

"I hope we can hold together. That snake Jameson Miller would love to get us to sell."

"I've met the man a few times. He's been known to try anything except murder to get what he wants. I'm not so sure he wouldn't try that, so you watch yourself."

"I know. I seem to be surrounded by strangers I can't trust."

"Yeah. Dangerous ones at that. If you need me you know how to reach me. So, have you met any men trying to sweep you off your feet?"

Leigh was used to Mark's ability to change subjects without a beat. "I've met one."

"What's his name?"

"Caesar Montgomery."

"Sounds familiar."

"Well, he's from New York. His family owns a coffee plantation in Colombia."

"That doesn't ring a bell but I know I've seen that name somewhere. Well, good luck. Call me when you get home."

"Promise. Bye, Mark."

She hung up and grabbed the annual report. "Time to hit the books," she said aloud.

Before she could move, the phone rang again. Mark. Another habit he had was to call right back if he remembered something. It drove a couple of his partners crazy.

"Hi, Mark, what did you forget to tell me?"

"Who's Mark?"

"Caesar! Sorry, I wasn't expecting to hear from you so early."

"I concluded my business and thought I'd take you to lunch."

"Lunch sounds great."

"Let's try one of the other restaurants in the hotel."

"Fine. I'll walk over. It's ten now—what time do you want to have lunch?"

"One."

"Okay. See you at one."

"Leigh? Who's Mark?"

"My former boss. I'm staying in his bungalow. Remember?"

"Oh, sorry. I didn't remember his name. See you at one."

Leigh hung up and couldn't keep the grin from spreading over her face. Caesar sounded a little bit jealous. And she liked that. She'd been pouring her heart out to him about the salons, but she still didn't know a lot about him. It served him right to know that there were still parts of her life she hadn't revealed.

It was twelve-forty when Leigh slipped a salmon-colored dress over her head and slid her feet into matching high-heeled sandals. She was about to leave when the phone rang. She debated answering for a few seconds then picked it up.

"Hello," she said breathlessly.

"Hello, dear. I just wanted to see how you're coming along."

"Aunt Helene, I was just on my way out."

"This will only take a minute dear. I wanted to tell you that the Board is voting to do some renovations on the salon."

"I thought you said there wouldn't be any decisions until I got back," Leigh said.

"I said we wouldn't make any big decisions. I don't think this qualifies."

"But you said it would take about a million dollars to redo the salon. We can't close down yet."

"Of course we aren't going to close down. We've found a wonderful team who will build around us."

" 'When are they going to show us the plans?"

"Monday. Will you be back then?"

Helene's voice was soft and dripping with honey and Leigh knew she wanted to make trouble.

"I don't think so, but you have my proxy," Leigh told her. "I know you'll do the right thing."

"You're right dear. I will do the right thing."

Leigh placed a call to Mark.

"They're going to vote on something and since Helene has my proxy it'll go through. What can I do?"

"Don't do anything."

"What?"

"She's bluffing. The board members are scattered all over—Valerian is out of the country, Bob Hastings is fishing in Canada, and Jimmy Gilbert is hunting in Montana."

Leigh laughed. "I thought I told you not to snoop."

"I didn't do an in-depth thing. I just asked a few questions."

"Thanks, Mark."

"You're welcome. Now go have a good time."

"See you in a week."

"Leigh, think about your reaction to someone holding your proxy and I think you've made your decision."

"Thanks, again."

He was right. She'd gone into a tailspin just imagining decisions that she wasn't part of being made about Cassiopeia. She did want the salon. Badly.

She hadn't fallen for Helene's test. If Leigh jumped on the plane back home they'd know what she was planning—and they'd rush into anything if they thought Leigh was on her way back. She would get the Board prepared for a fight. But she didn't panic the way Helene had wanted her to. She got advice from Mark. Leigh realized she would need help from someone on the Board. Maybe she could find one member of the Board who would be on her side—she only needed someone with 9%, which would give her the leverage she needed. When she got back she'd begin her search for an ally. She fixed her make-up and left to meet her date.

It was one fifteen by the time she got to the hotel. Caesar was waiting at the door.

"What happened? I tried to call but your line was busy."

"My aunt called. She just wanted to know when I was coming home."

Caesar suspected that something had happened during Leigh's conversation with Helene—something that might change his plans. He had to convince her to let the board members run things. They knew how to deal with the problems they were facing. They didn't need a novice interfering.

The waiter showed them to a table by the window that offered a beautiful view of the pink sand and turquoise water.

She chose sautèed soft-shell crabs with leeks and asparagus vinaigrette. Caesar decided on poached shrimp with zucchini cream and basil puree. They talked about their plans for the night. They hadn't been dancing, and according to the locals, the nightclub at the hotel featured the best dance music around.

They ended the meal with a dessert of marinated berries with Mascarpone cream.

"I think I'll have to cut my vacation short," Leigh said.

"Why? What's the matter?"

"If I keep eating desserts like this I won't fit into any of my clothes when I get home."

"Don't worry. If the band is as good as they say, we'll dance away the calories."

Leigh could have sat there enjoying the view and the company for hours, but she noticed the line of people waiting for a table and took pity on them.

"Let's give someone else a chance to get fat," she said.

Caesar nodded in agreement and signaled for the waiter to bring the bill. Then he dashed to his room and returned with a small gym bag. They were going to spend the time until dinner in the deck chairs outside Leigh's bungalow.

Once they stepped out into the hot Caribbean sun they weren't sure if they should have given up their table. In her haste to meet Caesar, Leigh had forgotten her hat.

"You didn't feel the heat when you were walking over?"

"No. I guess I was so worried about being late, I didn't think."

He slipped his hand in hers and it felt so natural. He took off his hat and placed it on her head.

"You should know better than to take a chance and get sun stroke."

"But now you will be the one at risk."

"Not as much. Remember I've just spent several weeks in Colombia. My body is much more adjusted to heat."

"Is that why you wear black? I thought lighter colors were better for this climate."

"I wear black because I like it. Would you believe I was a wild teen and spent my time in fluorescent shoes that matched my jacket?"

"No way."

"Well, maybe not fluorescent, but I did dress rather wild for a time."

"Why?"

"I was a bit of a rebel. But I've changed."

Leigh believed he was a rebel, but that he hadn't changed much. There was something just under the surface that gave her the impression he'd only changed the style of his rebellion.

They reached her bungalow and while he set up the umbrella and chairs, Leigh changed into a silver two-piece bathing suit that had been a bon voyage gift from Stacey. She hadn't had the courage to wear it before.

Caesar emitted a low whistle when she emerged from the house. She picked up her novel and stretched out on her chair.

"I'd better not leave you alone," he told her.

Leigh smiled to herself beneath her hat.

FIVE

The dance floor of the secluded Caribbean hotel was crowded with people enjoying the fast Latin-based beat from a local group, who threw in a little of the old Reggae along with the new rhythms of the islands. Most of the people on the floor were guests at the hotel. Some were locals enjoying an evening out, and some were from the conclave of lavish bungalows nearby. Leigh knew she was getting some envious glances from several of the single women there.

Her dance partner, Caesar Montgomery, was the reason. With so many people twisting and bumping each other for more of a share of the dance space, Leigh had no choice but to allow the man she'd only known for three days to hold her tightly against his body as they swayed to the Reggae version of "I Shot the Sheriff." She smiled as she looked directly into Caesar Montgomery's ebony eyes and watched them narrow into a sensuous stare as he pushed her away from his body as they did an intricate step in the small space allotted to them. She executed a few more twirls and found the space larger than she'd thought. Her strapless deep-yellow dress swirled around her legs as her body moved to the beat of steel drums and guitars. She wondered again why each time she'd met Caesar he'd been dressed in black. It seemed a little eccentric. For the first time in weeks she forgot about the awesome responsibility ahead of her.

Tonight, only the music and being in Caesar's arms mattered. He certainly fit the romantic man-to-have-an-affair-with mold. His devil-may-care ways made him interesting, and the scar on his cheek made him seem like some romantic hero who had fought a battle for his lover and been left with a dueling mark. It felt odd to Leigh to be eye level with a man. Most of the men she dated were more than six feet, since men of lesser stature were usually uncomfortable with her five feet eight inch, one hundred and thirty-pound frame. But not Caesar. He didn't seem to notice that the two-inch heels, which were the lowest heels she'd brought with her, made her slightly taller. She liked that about him. It showed how comfortable he was with himself. Leigh stepped back during the dance and smiled at her companion, and as the band ended the number, he dipped her backwards. He winked at her and people on the floor cheered and applauded. Astonished that the crowd had backed to the outer edges of the dance floor and most were watching her, Leigh looked at Caesar and saw the teasing light in his eyes. She wondered when they had become the main attraction.

She straightened up and was surprised when he didn't move to take her into his arms as the band drifted into a slow ballad. Then reality returned and she remembered why she was here staring into the ebony eyes of a stranger. Caesar Montgomery was still a man she knew little about, despite their long walks and quiet talks. Just as she'd revealed nothing of her true identity, he'd kept what she knew about him to a minuscule amount. Perhaps, she thought to herself, he was in hiding also.

Leigh watched his black eyes narrow into a sensuous stare, then change to a playful "wasn't that fun" look. He slipped his hand to her lower back as he guided them off the dance floor and back to their table.

They'd only been seated for a moment when a husky, linebacker-looking man came over to the table. He flashed strong white teeth as he introduced himself in a West Indian lilt.

"Christopher Franklin. Say, Mon, you mind if your lady and I dance a bit?"

The man reached for Leigh's hand but her response was a little slow, and as she started to take the outstretched hand, Caesar caught the man's wrist before they could make a connection.

"I mind very much." Caesar's voice was low and even on the hot Caribbean night, icicles dripping from every word. Mixed with the cold was something of a threat of bodily harm if the man continued. The man's smile faded and he conceded as he simply threw up his hands. "No harm. No harm," he said as he backed away and looked around until he found someone more susceptible to his solicitations.

Caesar refilled their wine glasses and the inviting, playful look, which had vanished while he dealt with the uninvited guest, returned. "You move as if you've had a lot of practice. Is that what you do in New York? Run around the city, hitting all the clubs? Leading a decadent lifestyle?"

"Actually, I haven't been able to get out much."

"I understand. Your life's been quite hectic lately."

Something was so familiar about him. She couldn't put her

finger on the deja vu feeling she'd had since he approached her on the beach. Then Mark had mentioned that his name sounded familiar. She felt so comfortable with him. And yet afraid because she had those feelings.

"Umm," Leigh shrugged. "Probably just as hectic as the coffee plantation you run." Caesar had explained during their walk on the beach how a few more misfortunes had befallen his family's business.

Leigh and her sister hadn't spoken for several years. She'd had infrequent calls from her aunt, but they'd been short. Aunt Helene wanted her to keep in touch but not to try to be part of the new life her sister and aunt had carved out for themselves. Now she and Aunt Helene would be forced to work together.

Aunt Helene had tried to discourage her from quitting her job and running salon. "Leigh, darling, you haven't been involved in this business. It's not easy. Why don't you give me your proxy? I'll see that your money is just transferred into whatever account you want?"

How dare Aunt Helene think she couldn't handle it. Then came the offer from Sarito Valerian—another board member who thought he could have her proxy and she could sit back and just draw the money without giving a thought to the business. Ten years before, he'd been just another hairstylist trying to develop a following like Jose Eber or Vidal Sassoon. A chance meeting with a glamorous, aging actress created the spark he needed. He started turning up in the celebrity gossip columns as much as the salon. He referred to his relationship with the actress as one of mentor and protégé. The tabloids had a much sleazier definition. Somehow he outlived his bad press and was good enough as a stylist to overcome the remarks and be considered as one of the best in the business. His eclectic style of dress also gave him the gimmick he needed to stand out. His thick black hair worn in a braid that hung over one shoulder and his Armani suits became his uniform.

Leigh was still fuming at the way he assumed that she would be happy to give him her proxy. The phone call requesting it had lasted one second after he made the suggestion. Then she'd summoned the company jet, as Stacey had suggested, and was off to the islands.

She couldn't get over a man she'd never met being so presumptuous about her feelings. That had been the turning point for Leigh—no one would control her business.

"I wonder if he's worth it?" Caesar's question brought her back to the present.

"If who's worth it?"

"The man who brings all those frowns to your lovely face when you think of him?"

"Truthfully," Leigh said, "he's not worth a second of my vacation. I'll deal with him Monday morning."

She wondered how he'd react when she warned him that she'd get the other board members on her side and he might be the persona non grata instead of her.

The clang of steel drums snapped her out of her reverie. She must be really tired to have allowed her attention to wander again and again. She'd be returning to her new life at the end of the week. This was absolutely a vacation fling—one that she now knew couldn't go any farther than it had. When she got on that plane back to New York, none of this would matter. From what she'd seen of Caesar, he wouldn't fit in her new world, nor did she want to fit in his, although she wondered what a coffee plantation would be like.

"Is something wrong?"

"Nothing that a good night's sleep won't cure," she said and flashed a smile she hoped would let him know it wasn't the company that was making her sleepy.

"You may be right. A good night's sleep is very much in order." He signaled the waiter and signed his name and room number.

As they strolled down the beach to her bungalow, Caesar entwined his fingers with hers and closed his hand, preventing her from pulling away.

"So what have you decided about your new business?" he asked.

She'd only revealed that she was trying a new venture and that someone didn't want her to succeed.

"I think I'll play to the cautious side. I don't want to cause friction. I want it to be a smooth change of power."

"If the team has been successful before, why change anything?"

"Because a couple of members of the team want my job."

"Could they handle it?"

"Probably. But I'm the one who decides."

"No room for compromise. What about letting these other people run it and sitting on the sidelines until you learn more about what's going on?"

Leigh's full mouth curved down for a fraction of a moment before she said, "I know what's going on." Her voice took on a harder edge and she stopped suddenly. Caesar had to stop also, release her hand or try to pull her along. He elected to stop. "It's just a suggestion," he whispered.

Leigh smiled and tilted her head. "And a very good one."

"Good enough to try?"

"Maybe. Probably. Yes," she said.

He pulled her into his arms and lightly brushed her lips with his. "You surrendered rather easily," he said. "Is that how you solve all your dilemmas?"

"Only those of the business ilk."

He released her hand so he could hold her at her waist as he kissed her again. This one a little longer. A little deeper. A little bolder. And a lot more frightening for Leigh. Frightening because she found herself liking his kisses and wanting more. Could she really have the runaway fling everyone had encouraged her to try? Everyone who knew about her breakup with Marshall Alexander. They warned her to be careful and to take precautions and to make sure the man did also, but still they had this idea that another man could take the place of her new drive to run Cassiopeia Salons.

She had to admit that Caesar Montgomery had pushed thoughts of the salon to the recesses of her mind. Most men used their large size to dominate situations. Caesar didn't have that as an option but she'd seen the look he'd given to the man who asked her to dance. Lethal. No wonder the man had backed off.

Maybe he was right. Maybe she'd come on too strong with the board members who approached her. Maybe she should re-think . . . As she started to do that, she was amazed at how easily Caesar had gotten her not only to see his point but to adopt it.

They'd reached her door and as he took the keys from her and opened it, she tried to think of a way to say no. She had no time to formulate a plan. He'd pulled her into his arms and kissed her again and she felt the little voice that wanted to say "no" growing smaller and smaller.

Then the telephone rang. She knew who it was. Aunt Helene.

"Don't answer it," Caesar said as he barely raised his lips from hers.

No! Came her little voice. Don't do this. It's not the right time.

"I have to get it," she told him. Aunt Helene would let the phone ring fifty times because she knew that Leigh was on the island to relax.

As she picked up the phone, she realized that Caesar had followed her. He slipped his arms around her, kissing and nib-bling on the back of her neck and murmuring words of love. "Querida", "Darling"; English and Spanish alternated.

"Aunt Helene," she called. She felt Caesar's body shutting down as he was giving up the idea. "Hold one moment, Auntie."

Leigh covered the receiver and Caesar kissed her once more and left. Leigh locked the door before returning to the phone.

"And what can I do for you Aunt Helene?"

"Tell me, did Sarito find you and convince you to be a silent partner?"

"No. Haven't met the man."

"Damn!" came the unladylike reply. "He said he was going down to the island and for the rest of us not to worry."

"Sorry. But I've changed my mind about a few things. I'll talk to you when I get back," she said. "Does Valerian have any distinguishing marks that I might recognize? I hear he's changed his image."

"Well, I guess so. Everything in his wardrobe is black and there's that stupid scar."

Cold chills ran up Leigh's spine. "Scar?"

"Yeah. He was in a car accident and got hit with flying glass. So he has this little scar on his cheek."

"What about his hair?"

"What about it? I just wanted him to talk some sense into you. Make you see the light," her aunt rambled on.

"Does he still have that braid he used as a trademark?"

"Braid?" her aunt paused. "Oh, that. No—not since he had to go to Colombia and play overseer on that coffee plantation. Maybe you'll meet him before you leave. And I want you to listen to him, Leigh. It's for your own good, honey."

"Maybe for mine but not for his."

"What?"

"Nothing. Just get ready for the board meeting on Monday. After that we'll know our next step."

"Still planning to be a hands-on owner?"

"Yes," Leigh said as she mumbled good night and gently placed the receiver down. "What I'd really like to get my 'hands on' is Caesar Montgomery's throat."

SIX

She tossed and turned all that night. The next morning she'd storm over to the hotel and pound on his door until he let her in. Then she'd give him a good piece of her mind. Hadn't she been betrayed enough by her family and her fiancé? When would she ever learn? Maybe this time would be the last. No!

Not maybe. It was time to play hardball. Mentally she ran through ways to repay her knight in tarnished armor. After all, she was now his boss, in a way.

When she heard the knock on the door the next morning, she knew it was Caesar. She opened the door and allowed him to step inside the living room of the bungalow. Clearly visible to him were her packed suitcases.

"I know what you think, but . . ."

"I think that since you became Caesar Montgomery instead of Sarito Valerian, your skills are a little rusty. From what I remember reading of the man, he would have had my signature on an agreement to let the Board run things within a day."

"You of all people should know that the press doesn't always need the truth to make a story."

"Oh, were your charms exaggerated?"

Caesar shrugged his shoulders and laughed. "Maybe. I was as honest with you as I could be."

"Is this kind of 'honesty' prevalent with the people who run the salon?"

Anger seethed through her body. He could have at least been apologetic. There was no sign of remorse in him. He was just a man who would use any method to get what he wanted. Was that how he had connived his way onto the Board in the first place?

"Mr. Valerian, I don't believe we have any more to say to each other."

He pointed at the luggage stacked in the living room. "You don't know what you're getting into. I know you consider my methods underhanded, but in the long run, I was trying to help you . . ."

"How can you do that?" she interrupted. "Make what you did seem like you were helping me!"

"There's a lot more going on at Cassiopeia than you realize. I just hope when you do learn the truth there will still be time to save the business."

"And staunch supporter of the truth as you are, I suppose you'll be the one to save it."

"I might be your only ally on the Board, Leigh. I'll see you in New York."

As soon as he left, she called for the private taxi to take her to the landing strip. She tried to be angry with Caesar. She tried to understand him. She tried to forget she ever met him. But all her ploys vanished every time his face intruded into those thoughts. Then all she could think about was the sly grin that spread across his face when she'd almost accepted his invitation to spend the night with him and the cold look in his eyes when he realized she'd discovered his duplicity. The man hadn't even apologized. He'd had the audacity to say that he was the hero of the moment and she needed him. But she didn't. She didn't need anyone anymore.

As Leigh sat on the plane waiting for the pilot to get clearance, she remembered the advice she'd gotten from her friends and her former boss about having one last romantic fling before she became the CEO of Cassiopeia Salons. Well, she'd had the fling—but Mr. Right hadn't knocked on her door. Mr. Wrong had stolen her heart.

The pilot approached and Leigh lifted her head hoping to hear they were ready for takeoff.

"I'm sorry, Ms. Barrington." He looked contrite as he talked to her. "Your aunt has instructed me to wait for another passenger."

"Thank you."

Leigh had no doubt the other passenger was Caesar—or, rather, Sarito. She mentally told herself that the flight wasn't that long and she could ignore him. Unless he pushed too hard—then she had visions of doing something she hadn't done since the third grade: punch a bully in the face.

* * *

In the perfectly accurate method of hindsight, Leigh had recognized all the signs that Caesar was dangerous, yet she'd allowed
herself to believe they could have a vacation affair. Never in her
life had she been able to sleep with a man unless she believed
she was in love with him. Even with Marshall, when love didn't
last, it still had to be there in the beginning. It was foolish of her
to think otherwise. She wasn't the type and never would be.

Ten minutes after she had settled down to read the annual
report, Caesar walked down the aisle. Today he wore black
slacks and a black T-shirt that was thin enough to show brown
skin and sinewy muscles every time he moved. He nodded then
sat down across from her. He adjusted his seatbelt and looked
up at Leigh.

"Is there any chance we can talk about what's happened?"

"What would you like to say?" She put the report down by
her side. "That you're a snake and not to be trusted?"

"I can explain my actions. Even if you don't forgive me, let
me tell you what's at stake."

"I'm sure you've had all night to think of something witty
to explain how you had my best interest at heart."

"I did . . . I do."

"What did the Board offer you if you could pull this off?"

"I did this for all of us."

"I thought you'd want to spend a few more days relaxing.
Running a coffee plantation must be so taxing."

"That part was true. That's why I wasn't around for your
sister's funeral. My brother was in an accident just after Labor
Day. I stopped in New York to see the board and get my proxy
back."

She remembered his eyes turning soft when he told her about
the accident and that he had to take care of things even though
he would not inherit anything.

"I believe your brother had an accident, but that's no excuse
for . . ."

"For what? Providing a little romance? A distraction for a few days?"

"Sarito Valerian to the rescue. Save Cassiopeia from its dumb little owners."

"Stop it, Leigh. It wasn't like that. I know I tried to soften you up to get you to back off for one year, but there's a very good reason."

"And what's that?"

He pulled the annual report from her side. "On paper we look very good. But the truth is, we're on the verge of bankruptcy."

"I don't believe you."

"It's true. In fact, the last time I saw Paul we were fighting in the boardroom about his spending the profits we made last year."

She stared at him for a moment. Leigh's verbal weapons of warfare were on the tip of her tongue. She understood the business world. She'd seen quite a bit of it at her job and one only had to scan the headlines to see how the rest of the world operated. How dare he think she was so naïve.

"Maybe you should remember that another Caesar was murdered by the very men he once pardoned. A boardroom is no different from a Senate floor."

"Ouch. You go right for the jugular."

"I had a good teacher."

Caesar studied her face, but it was obvious she had her corporate shield up. He'd heard that she could put business before everything. Her aunt had said that was one of the reasons why she and Marshall Alexander had broken up. He was sure she'd learned her tactics from Mark Westinghouse. They didn't call the man a barracuda without reason. He wondered if they had more than a business relationship. Maybe that's why she wanted Cassiopeia. It would make her Westinghouse's equal in a way. Then they could pursue their feelings. Caesar was surprised at the twinges of jealousy that surged inside him when he pictured Leigh and Mark together.

He still held the annual report, so he leaned forward and placed it in her lap.

"You know as well as I do that liars figure and figures lie."

She nodded.

"The problem is some bad advice Paul and Stephanie chose to follow over my warnings. They weren't capable of running an organization this size. It was only luck that they held it together this long."

"So what did they use—stock?"

"Yes. And Jameson Miller bought all of it from the creditors."

"And he wants a hair salon?"

"No, he wants the piece of property on Fifth Avenue that sits across from Trump Tower."

"What does he want from us?"

"He wants a seat on the board or he's going to figure out a way to force a sale. In any case, he'll get what he wants."

She wasn't surprised. Jameson Miller was the newest take-over king. He ate companies up and sold off the parts. She'd met him once at a function she'd attended with Mark.

The man was a walking ad for Armani. Every hair on his blond head was in place. His cold blue eyes had sent chills down her spine. But there was something about him that pulled you in, even though you knew it was a bad move—much like her former fiancé. He was charming as long as he was where he wanted to be. He wanted to be the one to call it quits. If he wasn't, he tried to ruin your reputation. Marshall had tried that. Unfortunately for him, Mark had stepped in and thrown the fear of God into him.

"Why didn't Aunt Helene tell me about this instead of hiding it?"

"She knew you were a fighter. And with Mark Westinghouse behind you, she thought that you'd try to run the salon—and not having all the pieces, we'd lose."

"And I suppose you're the only one capable of changing things? Should I call you Superman instead of Caesar?"

He shrugged his shoulders and ignored her sarcasm. "I know

I sound that way, but if we really want the salon to be what it was at the beginning, you'll help me. I've worked damn hard to give the salon a boost since I got on the board two years ago. Do you know what it's like to create something and have someone destroy it? When Paul and Stephanie approached me after the other salon failed, I couldn't believe it. The plans were terrific. I chose the employee uniforms. I refined the building layout until every man or woman who walked into the salon was made to feel as if they were in their own private spa. Yes, I want it to succeed but I think *we* can do it. I just felt that you would need a learning period, and the salon can't afford to give you that time. I wasn't trying to steal your inheritance. I wouldn't do that. I want this to succeed as much as you do and I think you need my help." He didn't know how to make her believe him, but he felt himself trying to find the words that would make them allies if not friends. He waited for her to make the decision.

She watched the passion in his eyes as he talked about the salon. He loved the business. She couldn't make a decision until she checked on the things he had told her.

She closed her eyes and leaned back. One thing he had said struck a nerve: *do you know what it's like to create something and see other people destroy it?*

SEVEN

Leigh remembered being in an accelerated program at St. John's Prep, a private school that gave students a chance to spend five years in high school and graduate with an Associate of Arts degree. The last year was a combination of senior year in high school and freshman year in college, since it was affiliated with St John's University.

In her senior year, Leigh had chosen business courses and been part of the co-op program that found her a part-time job with Westinghouse and Jackson, one of the most powerful corporate law firms in Manhattan. For Leigh it was the happiest time of her life. She had stopped wishing Aunt Helene would come and take her on the same fabulous trips that Stephanie wrote to her about. Seeing famous sports superstars became common to her. At first she would rush home from work and call Stacey for a five-minute update on which sports star had been in the office. She limited herself to five minutes because she had to do her homework. Leigh knew the only way for her to succeed was to finish college.

On this particular day, Mark Westinghouse had offered her a job and she had turned him down. She had a plan. Mark had a way of finding out your deepest business goals. It helped him with his clients. He'd selected Leigh as his protégée from her first interview. She'd sparkle at what the other temporaries called "grunge" work. She liked details.

When she'd turned down a permanent position, he'd called her into his office and talked to her. She found herself telling him everything—how this idea of a full service beauty salon that catered to people of color but could be used by everyone had been her dream for a long time.

Her parents had set aside a trust fund that she could claim at twenty-one. Until then, she only wanted a part-time job so she could attend school.

Impressed by her mature attitude and forethought, Mark had become her consultant as well as her employer.

Three days later, she arrived home to find Aunt Helene and Stephanie talking to her grandmother. Leigh had only seen her sister intermittently since she was six. Their father had been dead for two years when their mother passed away. Then Aunt

Helene had come to take Stephanie. In the back of her mind Leigh still remembered the pain of going alone for the first time to what had been their bedroom. She'd cried herself to sleep then and for several nights afterwards.

Many times Leigh had wished Stephanie was around. Grannie was good at fixing meals and taking Leigh to church. She even knew that Leigh's height made her self-conscious. But Grannie was not good at "girl talk." Her friends shared certain things with their older sisters, and Leigh had even prayed that her sister would come home and they would do the same thing. Feeling so much like an outsider, Leigh concentrated on her school work. That's why she was surprised when she reached a gangly fourteen that Grannie had insisted she spend the summer at a modeling school.

From time to time, Aunt Helene would bring Stephanie for a visit, but it was usually because another one of her aunt's ventures had failed and she needed a place to stay for a few weeks.

When Leigh was fifteen, Stephanie started dating Paul Lambert, a rock star, known as the "Baron of Rock." If Elvis had been the king, a deejay had pronounced that Paul was the baron.

Suddenly everyone wanted to be her friend. Most people didn't believe that she and Stephanie rarely saw each other.

Aunt Helene and Stephanie looked like the pictures Leigh had seen of her mother. None reached the five foot eight Leigh had grown to by the time she was thirteen. Nor had Leigh become the beauty they were. She wasn't ugly or plain, just rather average. So when Grannie had pushed her into taking the beauty course she was a little apprehensive. If she couldn't be a natural beauty, she could at least make herself glamorous. It gave her something else. The lack of self-esteem that she felt when she compared herself to her beautiful, petite sister faded. The school made her realize her good points. She stopped being ashamed of her height. She wore clothes that enhanced her rounded figure. She met Stacey, who was beautiful, funny, and adventurous, and they became best friends. The two did all the things that sisters would have done. They tried new make-up and hairstyles on each other. They shared their dreams with each other. Stacey was going to model, and Leigh was going to create a beauty salon that provided more than just hair and nail care.

Leigh wasn't half as intimidated at the next visit from Aunt Helene and Stephanie as she'd been in the past. This time they had been to the Orient and returned with beautiful figurines. As she opened her gift, Stephanie told Leigh the news—she was going to marry Paul Lambert. They wanted her to be part of the wedding.

"Stephanie, why can't I come live with you?" It was a question Leigh had asked before and never gotten a satisfactory answer for.

"Leigh," her sister said in a strained voice, "you just can't right now. Right after the wedding, Paul has to go on tour. You'd be in the house alone. Grannie would never agree to that."

Leigh knew she was right this time, but just once she'd like to live the way Stephanie lived. Leigh had only seen the show-place house in California in Ebony Magazine when they did an article on Stephanie and Paul. She wanted to take a swim in the Olympic-size pool. She wanted to play tennis on their courts. But most of all she wanted to know first-hand how being back-stage at a rock concert really felt.

A month later, dressed in a long, lavender chiffon dress, Leigh got her first taste of the paparazzi. Papers from all over the world covered the wedding. Cameras flashed. People pushed her to the side trying to get a look at the smiling couple. It was a life Leigh knew she didn't want for herself. She wanted to be like Helene—always there, but not robbed of her private life. Leigh could go back to her life in the Jamaica Estates section of Queens, New York. Maybe after she finished college she would get to visit them.

While she continued her education, Leigh and Stephanie called each other once a week. Just after her nineteenth birthday, Leigh summoned Aunt Helene and Stephanie home. Grannie was ill and not expected to live.

The aunt and sister who arrived were not the same people who had left. Something was wrong. Grannie tried to tell Leigh something before she passed away but couldn't form the words.

After the funeral, Leigh said that she had enough money to stay in the house she grew up in.

"That's good," Aunt Helene said. "I wouldn't want to uproot you and take you away from this."

How many other nineteen-year-olds were given the chance to live alone? Aunt Helene seemed relieved Leigh didn't ask to come and stay with them. One night before they left, Leigh found Stephanie sitting in the living room, sobbing.

"The last tour was a disaster," she said. "Paul's record sales are slipping. They are even talking about canceling his contract."

"What can he do?" Leigh asked.

"Nothing that makes the kind of money we need to keep living the way we like."

"Are you going to move back to New York? You could live here."

"Maybe," Aunt Helene said. "We need your help."

"How can I help?"

"Sell the house."

Leigh couldn't believe her ears. She didn't want to sell the house. Where would she go? She'd been thinking about living in the city. It was closer to her job, but to sell the house would be like tearing out a piece of her life.

She'd mentioned moving a couple of times to Stephanie. Now Aunt Helene pounced on the idea. Soon after Grannie's will was read (Leigh and Stephanie were the only heirs) Leigh found herself being dragged to real estate agents in the city. She fell in love with the two-bedroom, two-bath apartment with a sunken living room near Central Park. It would be less expensive than one that had the view of the park, and it was a few minutes from work. Once she fell in love with the apartment, she decided to sell the house. Manhattan had a beat of its own and Leigh wanted to live there. She was lucky that once on the market, the house sold quickly.

Stephanie had returned to California for what they were billing as the Baron's Last Tour. He'd planted several articles claiming he was going to retire. The advance sales were tremendous. People who hadn't purchased a CD of his in years were sleeping at the box office to make sure they got tickets.

Leigh was starting a new life in her new apartment. Mark Westinghouse used his influence to expedite the purchase of the condo once Leigh told him about the poor financial condition her sister and aunt were in.

Aunt Helene was helping Leigh pack up the house when she came across a box of school papers.

"Do you want to keep all of these?"

"I don't know. I really enjoyed writing them. I got As for some of my business plans." Leigh wasn't ready to share her dream with anyone but Stacey.

She left her aunt thumbing through the papers as she worked on another room. Most of the items went to storage until they could decide what to do with them. The box of term papers was part of the items Leigh took to her new home.

Helene went back to California, and Leigh began her career full time with Westinghouse and Jackson.

Everything was fine until she picked up the Sunday edition of the *New York Times* and found out her sister and brother-in-law were coming to New York to open a very special beauty salon. It was the name of the salon that sent sparks of anger through her body: Cassiopeia.

She'd done a science paper on the constellations. Her favorite was the Ethiopian princess, named Cassiopeia who had bragged that she and her daughter were more beautiful than the gods and had been punished for that statement. Instead of death, they made her the constellation called "the lady in the chair." For six months of the year she is seen upside down.

When Leigh got to her economics class, she'd created a beauty salon called Cassiopeia. It was upscale and catered to people of color. It had everything that one could want. Besides creative hairstyles, there were facials, manicures, pedicures—everything to make any woman feel pampered.

It was so special that she didn't tell anyone she planned to make it a reality. She'd even asked Mark Westinghouse how to set it up. He told her it was a great idea, but she was so young it would be hard to find backers. Possible, he'd said, but not easy. Wait until you're twenty-one before starting that kind of business venture.

Now Stephanie and Paul were announcing a salon to be opened in New York not far from where Leigh lived.

"How could you?" a tearful Leigh screamed into the phone.

"I'm sorry," Stephanie said. "We needed this. Don't worry, we'll share the wealth."

"I don't want your money. You're not my sister anymore."

For two days Leigh had kept the betrayal to herself. Then finally when Mark noticed her hangdog expression and questioned her, she told him everything.

She had no recourse. If she went after them legally they would just say she borrowed the idea from them.

After her last phone call to Stephanie, the two never spoke again. Nor did Aunt Helene try to contact Leigh and explain why she'd given them Leigh's plan.

She put them to the back of her mind and got on with her life.

Leigh opened her eyes and stared at the sleeping man across from her. *Do you know what it's like to create something and see other people destroy it?* he'd asked her.

"More than you do," she whispered. "More than you do."

EIGHT

They were closing in on New York when Leigh touched Caesar gently to wake him up.

"We're here."

He ran his hand across his face and smiled as he saw that Leigh had changed clothes. Her winter-white suit and her ivory mid-calf boots showed her long legs to their best advantage.

Caesar dashed to the lavatory to wash up and change clothes. When he got back, he saw that Leigh was no longer reading the annual report but had found a magazine that featured Jameson Miller.

"Are you starting to believe me?"

"I met Miller once. I wouldn't be surprised at anything he does."

"I guess this is where we decide if we're partners or enemies."

"I guess this is where I stop calling you Caesar and start calling you Sarito."

"I'd rather you didn't. Everyone calls me Sarito. I'd like you to still call me Caesar."

She thought about it a moment then said, "We'll see. If we can be allies, I'll call you Caesar; if not, I'll call you Sarito."

"Fair enough. When are you going to the salon?"

"Tomorrow. Helene and I are meeting so she can introduce me to the Board."

The winter winds greeted them as they both retrieved their cars from long-term parking.

"I guess we think alike on some things," Caesar said. "Like having a car at the airport rather than taking a cab."

"I love to drive. I didn't even own a car, but when I went looking for a condo I insisted that it had to have or be near a parking lot."

"I don't like driving that much. I live in Connecticut."

"Not near the salon?"

"I usually stay at a hotel or with a friend when I'm needed."

Somehow she didn't think the friend was a man. A pang of jealously went through her. That emotion surprised her. Why should she care? Why did she care? She'd read about women who fell in love with the worst man for them—was this happening to her? Was she falling under the Valerian spell?

"Do you have an 'appointment-only' calendar?"

"I gave up being a hairstylist when I made it to the Board. For you, I might make an exception."

Leigh stopped at her car and took her keys out. "Do you think I need a new look?"

"You might want to try something new after you see what we do there."

"I'll let you know." She started to walk away, only to have him catch her hand and gently pull.

"Leigh," he called softly.

"Yes?" She turned and found herself in his arms. His lips closed on hers in a burning kiss that found no resistance.

"Good night, I'll see you tomorrow."

"G . . . Good night," she stammered.

He waited until she was in her car with the seat belt snugly across her chest before he disappeared into another aisle to retrieve his car.

Home at last, Leigh kicked off her shoes at the door, put her coat in the foyer closet, and walked toward her bedroom. She rarely vacationed because she loved her apartment so much. From the deep coral walls that matched the drapes in the living room to the blue-green and topaz colors of her bedroom, Leigh felt a warmth she could never explain. When she'd bought the apartment at nineteen, she'd been warned that she might tire of it quickly and shouldn't pour so much money into it. But she knew this was made for her the first time the agent gave her a tour. At the time Aunt Helene was her guardian, and she signed for her to get money from her trust fund. It was only later that Leigh realized it was from guilt, not Helene's heart.

In the bedroom she stripped the rest of her clothes from her body and went into the master bath. She turned on the water for the Jacuzzi and returned to the bedroom to go through her dresser drawers to find her white satin nightgown. At the modeling school, she'd been taught to buy beautiful clothes and how to wear them. The wardrobe instructor was a buyer for one of the department stores. The woman said you can sleep just as well in cotton pajamas as you can in a satin gown, but when you wake, up you feel a lot better about yourself if you are in satin. Buy few but find material that makes you feel rich and pampered.

As Leigh emersed herself in a long bubble-bath soak, the phone rang. Another luxury she'd afforded herself was a phone in each room. She shook off the suds from her hand and picked up the receiver.

"Hello."

"Hey girl, didn't you get my messages?"

"No, Stacey, I just got home."

"And the first thing you should do is press that little button on the machine to find out who wants to talk to you."

"No, the first thing I wanted to do was wash away the winter chill. I'm not used to this cold."

"Becoming an island girl?"

"It was tempting."

"Well, enough about you. I got a new commercial."

Stacey had done some modeling, but somehow her red curls that hung almost to her waist called more attention to it than the clothes she modeled. Now she was making commercials.

"What's it about?"

"A limo pulls up to an elegant hotel. The doorman helps me out and I walk up the stairs. I'm wearing a long, tight, backless dress. When I get to the top of the stairs, I turn. I'm wearing cinnamon lipstick and I say, 'Not every woman can wear this color, but I'm not every woman.' "

"All that mystery for a little tube of lipstick. Get out of town."

"Hey, don't knock it."

"How long did it take you to film this one?"

"Three days. I met a fabulous man and we're having dinner tomorrow night. Now enough about me. What happened with you?"

"Mark's beach house is fabulous, and I'm sorry I didn't take him up on his offer before."

"Umm. I would love to go there but I freckle so easily. Did you have that affair I told you to have?"

"No. I didn't. I met a man who turned out to be Sarito Valerian, and he just wanted my proxy."

"Did you figure out what you're going to do with the salon?"

"Yes. I'm going to run it."

"That's a switch. I thought you were leaning toward letting the Board continue."

Stacey was the sister Leigh had always wanted, and they shared so many secrets she knew she could trust her with this information.

"Someone is making takeover moves."

"Jameson Miller."

"How did you know?"

"He's trying to take over everything in New York."

"Well he's in for a rude awakening."

"Good for you."

They chatted a few more minutes and then said good-bye. Leigh leaned back to enjoy the pounding of the jets of water. The phone rang again.

"Yes, Stacey?"

"Who's Stacey?"

"How did you get this number?"

"Relax. I stopped by the salon and got it from your aunt."

"What do you want?"

"To talk. Leigh, you're going to need someone on your side in board meetings. Someone with at least enough power to make a majority."

"My aunt owns 10% just like you."

"She's not on your side. She could align herself with the others and you wouldn't stand a chance."

"I don't think so."

"I know you. We want the same thing. Let me give you my number?"

"Sorry, I'm taking a bath."

His low sensuous laugh just made her angry. "It's okay. I'm staying at the Plaza. I'll put your name on the list and they'll ring me."

"I don't see myself making that call."

"You never know. Good night, Leigh."

"I'll see you tomorrow."

The next morning Leigh decided to walk the few blocks from her condo to the salon. She arrived just as the first customer did. As they got to the door, Leigh found the heel of her shoe caught in the mesh of the door mat that spelled Cassiopeia.

"That's a hazard we'll have to get rid of," she mumbled.

She looked around. It was the first time she'd been in the salon. She couldn't bring herself to even peek in while her sister was alive, and she had refused to meet the Board there after the funeral. That was when she gave her aunt the proxy and went off to decide if this was what she really wanted.

Now she scanned the lower floor with its circles of light. Each circle had a special feature. She noticed the employees wore pink and pale-blue dresses with short skirts and white coats styled like a doctors. She remembered Caesar had selected the uniforms. The manicurists wore pink and the shampoo-people wore blue; each category was designated to a circle of light.

As she started toward the winding staircase, Gayla Evans intercepted her. She'd met Gayla at the funeral. The woman had served as Paul's secretary and was also a stylist.

"Ms. Barrington," she caught Leigh's arm. "Your aunt would like you to meet the other board members before your tour."

She followed Gayla up two flights of stairs and down a long hall to the clearly designated boardroom. "If you like I'll take notes for you until you get your own secretary."

"Thanks, but I thought this was just an informal session."

"Your aunt prefers everything to be recorded."

Gayla pulled open the door and stepped back for Leigh to enter.

She came face to face with the people who would be her enemies or allies. Helene stood up from the CEO chair. "We decided that I should chair the meeting just to give you an idea of how we run things. We took a vote. It was almost unanimous.

Caesar Montgomery sat at the far end of the table. From the look Aunt Helene gave him, Leigh knew he was the dissenter.

Quickly, Helene went around the table and introduced the people. While she supplied the names, Leigh mentally filled in what she knew about them.

JoAnn Desmond was one of the few black runway models who had given Naomi Campbell the closest competition.

Rick Adams was an original member of Paul's band.

Bob Hastings had inherited wealth that was still considered a fortune after four marriages. The fifth Mrs. Hastings was a former Miss Canada, twenty years his junior.

Jimmy Gilbert was a sixth-generation Texan with one of the biggest cattle ranches around.

Dean Roman was a man whose knowledge of chemistry kept Cassiopeia on top.

Kevin Parker, a former actor, parlayed the money he had earned from being second lead in a series that lasted six years into a fortune and switched to business when roles for Black actors waned.

Angela Betencourt was another model who only did print ads.

And of course, dressed in his signature black, Caesar Montgomery, who, for this crowd, was better known as Sarito Valerian.

Helene directed Leigh to the chair next to hers and called the meeting to begin. Gayla sat at a table on the side and took notes.

After a few inconsequential mailers, Helene turned to Leigh. "Is there anything you noticed, dear? Someone new might notice something we've overlooked."

"Well, I did notice we need a new welcome mat. I caught my heel . . ." Leigh looked around and saw JoAnn put her fingers over her mouth trying to hide a smile. The other members seemed to be doing the same—except for Caesar. His face gave nothing away. But when Leigh turned to her aunt, she could see the anger in the woman's face.

"No one moves that mat," she said between clenched teeth. "Stephanie selected it and it stays."

"I . . . I'm sorry, I didn't realize . . ."

"Of course you didn't realize, dear," Helene's mouth smiled, but her eyes didn't. "There are so many things for you to learn. And we're here to help you. Does anyone else have a complaint about the mat?"

No one said a word. Leigh tried not to deliberately look at anyone but her eyes met Caesar's. His smile was not one of joy that she'd committed her first faux pas, but one of a comrade in arms.

NINE

The rest of the day, Leigh managed to just nod and not step on any more toes. While she waited for Helene to finish a telephone call, Leigh walked over to the receptionist and asked to see the profile cards of the customers. She thumbed through them quickly and from the information she could tell the salon was what she wanted it to be—people of all shades. She slipped them back into the drawer.

Helene joined her and they began their tour. "Let's start with our special services."

In one room, an attractive Asian woman taught a class in Tai Chi. In another, children played games while waiting for their mothers, and in another room men read the Wall Street Journal, played chess, or just took a nap in one of the recliners while they waited.

Leigh regretted for a moment that she had been too bitter to come into the salon in the nine years it had been open. But she didn't know how she would react if she'd known for sure how much of her dream they'd stolen.

The restaurant on the lower level served good food but would not get a four star rating. Helene took her in for a quick look but suggested they go out for lunch, then they would rejoin the board members for a few more items that had to be discussed. Helene was called to the phone and suggested Leigh eat lunch alone.

"You can even run home from here if you'd like. We'll resume at three."

Leigh walked out onto crowded Fifth Avenue and was debating about whether she would go home or stop in one of the many places on 57th Street when she heard her name.

She turned and saw JoAnn Desmond striding toward her. "I thought you and Helene were having lunch together."

"She got an important call and had to cancel."

"Well, come on with me."

Leigh fell into step with the woman. "I have to confess, Leigh, I'm glad you're going to be around. I feel like such a giraffe around most people."

"I know. I used to feel like that in school."

They slipped into a diner, picked out sandwiches, soup, and drinks, and found a table in the back.

"Leigh, I don't want you to think we were laughing at you this morning. But you're not the first to suggest they get rid of that mat."

"I couldn't tell. No one said anything."

"Because we've all had our head handed to us for making that suggestion. First it was Paul who said no. Then . . . well, while you were away and Helene was running things, someone else said to get rid of it. Helene's like a bear about it now."

"I just hope no one falls and sues us."

"It's the chance they have to take to be beautiful."

They ate and continued to talk about everything but the salon. Then they walked back and entered the boardroom a couple of minutes after three.

Before she knew it, her first day at the salon was over. As they left, Leigh started to walk home. This time she recognized the voice that called her.

Caesar fell into step beside her. "Are you going to walk home?"

"It's not that far."

"And what are you doing for dinner?"

"Nothing."

"We need to talk."

"Why?"

"Do you really think that you got overruled because of a welcome mat?"

No. She didn't think that. She knew it was a power play and she'd lost.

"Let's go to your place and talk."

As much as she wanted to say she could take care of herself, she knew she needed help. She hated to admit he was right.

"Okay. But we'll have to go shopping if you're hungry."

"I guess we'll have to go shopping."

Forty-five minutes later they arrived at Leigh's apartment loaded down with plastic shopping bags.

"I knew we should have had them deliver," Leigh told him.

"No way. I'm hungry enough as it is."

"But it doesn't take that long."

"I plan to be in the kitchen two minutes after you open the door. Unless they were coming over with us, it wouldn't be fast enough."

Leigh turned on the light, showed him where to hang his coat and wash his hands, and pointed him in the direction of the kitchen. Caesar walked ahead of her but couldn't help notice the elegant, comfortable living room. He was a bit surprised to see the big screen television covering most of a wall. Leigh hadn't impressed him as the TV type.

The living room, dining room, and kitchen were in an open floor plan. They were putting the items away when she noticed the clock. "Goodness, I'm going to miss her finest hour."

She grabbed the remote and pointed it at the television. That morning Stacey had called to tell her when the commercial would be on. Larger than life, she saw the limousine pull up. After Stacey's line, the screen went to black and Leigh turned it off.

"That's it? You just wanted to watch a commercial?"

"Uh-huh." She waited while he tried to find a reasonable answer, then laughed. "She's my best friend."

Caesar smiled. "For a moment I thought you'd slipped off the deep end."

He assembled the ingredients he'd tossed into her shopping

cart and rambled through the cabinets for the equipment, shushing Leigh when she tried to help.

"Can you put some music on? I do my best work by music."

Leigh found a Kenny G. CD and put it on. She sat at the table while she watched him slice and dice and chop. Before she knew it, she had a plate of grilled chicken, a side dish of mixed greens salad, and a steaming cup of tea in front of her.

He fixed himself an identical plate and they sat down in the dining area. She tasted it tentatively at first, then admitted, "It's good."

"Did you doubt it?"

"Yes. I thought you were kidding when you offered to cook."

As they lingered over a second cup of tea, he brought up the subject she'd been dreading.

"You realize you need an ally on the Board?"

"Yes. I see Aunt Helene isn't going to let the reins go easily."

"She's not going to let them go at all. I guarantee you that right now she's canvasing the others to see if she can get enough votes to force you out."

"And how do you feel about that?"

"I want to make some changes and I know I can't do that without you. But think about it. If I'm on your side, you have a majority vote."

"And if you're not?"

"You're in trouble."

He made it seem so simple. She needed him and he needed her. But she really didn't know how the rest of the Board felt and she didn't want to rush into an uneasy alliance.

"How much time do I have to decide?"

"That depends on how fast Jameson Miller wants to move."

Leigh had read that if Miller just stood outside a building, employees started checking their 401K plans.

"Give me until the end of the week."

"Deal."

Caesar didn't object when Leigh said she'd do the clean up since he had cooked. She walked him to the door. He put on his coat and for a moment she thought he was going to kiss her, then he turned and walked toward the elevator.

The next morning, Leigh looked through her closet and chose a navy pinstripe suit. The jacket had a wide white shawl collar and Leigh decided not to wear a blouse but to button the form-fitting jacket to the top. It gave her a soft, feminine look that was quite different from her usual business attire of severe suits with starchy Brooks Brothers shirts.

Despite the brisk November day, Leigh again chose to walk from her condo on 57th Street and Ninth Avenue to the flagship salon on 56th and Fifth.

In fifteen minutes, she was standing in front of the smoky glass complex that housed Cassiopeia Salons. It was an homage to Trump Tower, the towering glass building across the street.

She waved to Gayla, who was manning the reception desk. No meetings were planned for the morning so she didn't expect to find any of the board members around. Leigh just wanted to take her own private tour. She had just introduced herself to a few employees in the body massage section when she heard screams coming from the stylist zone.

She and Gayla rushed over to find a woman staring into the mirror and screaming at her purple and pink strands of hair with the dye dripping onto the towel around her neck.

"Look at this! I'm a mess," she screamed.

"I'm sorry, ma'am. I must have added too much of the brown."

"Well can you fix it or not?" the woman yelled.

Suddenly a man stepped up to the woman. Leigh then remembered that he was the manager of the area. He'd been hired shortly after arriving from an international styling school.

"Yes, we can fix it. But we're not going to."

To Leigh's dismay, the man ripped the plastic bib from around the woman's neck, signaled for someone to bring the woman's coat and hat, then shoved them into her arms.

"You are never satisfied with anything. I suggest you find another salon. Cassiopeia is not for you."

Leigh started toward the fracas but was pulled back by Gayla.

"Don't get involved in this," she warned. "It's going to be a lot of trouble you don't need right now."

The woman, angry and upset at her treatment, put on her hat making sure it covered her wet hair. Then she put on her coat and stormed out.

When the Board convened that afternoon, Leigh couldn't hold back.

"The man should be fired, immediately."

"Dear, you don't understand the nature of creative people," Helene offered.

"I know when someone treats a customer badly for no reason."

"I understand that the woman is never satisfied with her colorist. We've tried three and she's complained about every one of them," Angela said.

"I don't care," Leigh's fury remained. "That isn't how any member of our staff should treat a client."

"The problem is," Kevin explained, "he's a very popular stylist. Women wait for months to have him color their hair."

Leigh looked around the room for an ally and didn't find one. Caesar wasn't around and since he hadn't given anyone the right to vote for him, Leigh was voted down.

She couldn't believe it. She stormed out of the boardroom and into her office. She'd been using Paul's old office while Helene was arranging for her to move into Stephanie's.

That's where Caesar found her when he stopped by later. They sat on the sofa in the office as she told him what happened. She'd sent Gayla home early.

"The man should be packing his things and the Board is just going to let him stay a manager."

"I'm sorry. I got tied up in a family matter and I had to go to the airport."

"You're right—all they have to do is move you out of the way and I'm helpless."

"You don't have to be. We can work together. We'll talk about it later."

"Are you going to come over for dinner?"

"I'll try, it's just . . ."

Before he could answer, there was a knock on the door and a woman entered. She was tiny, barely more than five feet. She wore a wide black hat and a black sequined dress that fell about two inches above her knees. Stunningly beautiful, she impatiently tapped her foot.

"Where are your manners?" she demanded of Caesar.

He breathed an audible sigh. "This is Leigh Barrington, the new CEO of Cassiopeia. Leigh, may I introduce Juliette Montgomery, my mother."

TEN

"As you can see, my mother loves to make an entrance."

Leigh was too startled by the woman to say anything. She didn't know what she expected Caesar's mother to look like, but this had never entered her head.

The woman stepped forward. "Call me Juliette," she said, as she held her hand out and waited for Leigh to acknowledge her.

Leigh stood up and shook the woman's hand. "I'm pleased to meet you."

"I suspect my son was supposed to be somewhere with you and I dragged him to the airport. I apologize, but I needed him."

"Mother, if you wouldn't travel with fifteen pieces of luggage, you wouldn't need me."

"But I don't know where I'm going to go or what I'm going to do. I have to be prepared for anything."

"You have a loft downtown. Why don't you leave some clothes there?"

She shook her head and turned to Leigh. "Men. You'd think that being my son he'd understand how quickly fashion changes. I need to be able to give away my old clothes and replenish my wardrobe at a moment's notice."

Leigh had always thought Aunt Helene was a clothes horse, but she seemed dull compared to Caesar's mother.

"Mother, I was about to ask Leigh to have dinner with us."

"Sorry, I am not having dinner with you. I met a charming man on the plane and . . ."

"What's his name?"

"Don't tell him," Leigh said. She couldn't resist winking at Juliette and watching Caesar lose control.

It was more a demand rather than a question. Usually the man was so calm Leigh wanted to shake him, but not today—he was bordering on rage.

Leigh covered her mouth but could not keep down the giggle. She loved seeing Caesar so worried.

"Stay out of this. You don't know my mother."

"He's afraid I'll get married again. He still calls me Montgomery and I have had three husbands since Caesar's stepfather died."

"That's nothing to brag about, Mother."

"I wasn't bragging. It is simply a statement of fact."

Leigh was beginning to like Juliette more and more. "It's too bad we can't get your mother on the Board. She'd make a formidable ally."

"Or enemy," Caesar countered.

"I'll be at the loft," she told him. "I just wanted to meet Leigh and change our dinner plans, Sarito. I'll be around for a while and we can have dinner another time." To Leigh she waved, "Don't let him bully you. We must have lunch." Ignoring her petulant son, Juliette swept out of the office.

Leigh forgot about her trouble with the Board. She wanted to know more about Juliette Montgomery.

"Where do you want to go for dinner?"

"I'll cook tonight," Leigh volunteered. "If you promise to tell me all about that woman."

"If it's the only way I can get a free meal, let's go."

He took her hand and they were both shocked at the easy camaraderie that came over them.

At the lobby level, Leigh looked around to see if she could point out the man she wanted fired. She had given up, when suddenly she heard her aunt's voice.

"How dare you put your hands on a client?" Helene's anger was clear. "If it happens again, you'll be back in England so fast you'll think you took the Concorde."

They were standing just under the staircase. Caesar and Leigh stood listening for a moment, then he took her hand and they left the salon. As they walked to the store, Caesar noticed her mood had changed.

"What's the matter?"

"My aunt. Acting as if I don't know what I'm doing and then acting on my suggestion as if she thought of it."

After picking up fresh vegetables, they made their way to Leigh's apartment.

"So where do we go from here?" Leigh asked as she slammed another package from the refrigerator on the counter.

"Hopefully we can make a decision before you wreck your house."

"I'm so angry. I can't fire him, but she can. I can't even reprimand him but she can threaten him anytime. What good is 42% if I can't have a voice in what happens?"

He realized she wasn't really talking to him nor was she listening. Caesar waited in the living room. Leigh had begun slamming utensils and food from the moment they'd walked in the door. She'd thrown her coat on the sofa and headed straight for the kitchen.

He'd simply hung his coat in the closet and tried to ignore Leigh's way of controlling stress.

"Do you mind if I look around?"

"No, go ahead," she said, as she continued to bang pots and pans.

He'd never gotten a chance to explore her condo. While she muttered expletives and fought with something that started out as a chicken but wouldn't be recognizable after she finished hacking away at it, Caesar walked around the condo. He wasn't snooping, as much as he was keeping out of her way. The two-bedroom condo wasn't that old. Leigh must have been one of the first tenants. He remembered the battered, red brick building that had stood on the corner. It had fallen into such disarray in the upscale neighborhood that the people who lived there started to protest. Finally a construction team showed up one morning and leveled it. The vacant lot was only a little better than the old building. Caesar remembered even he'd felt good when the sign went up that condos were being built—not that he was fond of condos. That's why he preferred his house in Connecticut to apartments in the city.

Leigh had decorated the place sparsely but elegantly. Her bedroom was painted a rich blue-green that complemented the huge brass bed and the hunter green and gold comforter. He didn't stay long in that room. He didn't want to appear voyeuristic. He moved down the hall to the guest room that Leigh must have used as an office. He knew the bath was at the end of the hall. He walked back to the living-dining-kitchen area where Leigh was still cooking in a frantic kind of manner.

"Is this how you get ideas?" he asked. "Butchering poor defenseless chickens?"

She looked up as if she were surprised to see him. "I'm not butchering the chicken. Who says you have to cut the bird only in a certain way? I'm just being . . . creative."

He thought she was serious until a smile cracked her icy demeanor. They both burst into laughter.

She waved the knife in the air. "You should see me when I'm really angry."

"I don't think so." He went into the living room, sat down in the brown suede lounge chair, and turned on the television.

Her anger dissipated, Leigh tossed the chicken pieces in a pot, added broth, and began chopping vegetables. From time to time she glanced over at him. He must think she was a complete lunatic. But she was not about to apologize. Once all the ingredients were in the pot and simmering slowly, she joined him.

"Find anything interesting?"

"No, just surfing. Have you calmed down enough for us to talk?"

"I think so . . ."

She was interrupted by the sound of the doorbell.

"Don't they call you from downstairs?"

"I have a few friends they know."

As she went to the door, Caesar wondered if her boss was one of those friends. He chastised himself—it was none of his business.

The woman who came bursting through the door was definitely not Mark Westinghouse. She stood at least six feet and her curly red hair hung from under her white fur hat, which matched her white fur jacket. The rest of her slender frame seemed to be encased in black stretch pants. Her black boots came up to her knees.

"Hi, I'm Stacey. Sorry, Leigh, didn't know you were entertaining."

"I'm Caesar Montgomery. We watched your commercial last night."

"Thanks, I just came by to say I'm off to Miami."

"I thought you were going to California?"

"First Miami, then California. I'll call you."

"Well, before you buzz away, come in and sit down for a while."

"I don't want to interrupt anything . . ."

"You're not," Caesar assured her.

"Darn. I was hoping things had progressed. You must be slowing down, Valerian." She grinned at him and shrugged her shoulders.

"Stacey," came Leigh's warning.

The woman was not offended. She took off her coat and threw her body on the brown suede sofa.

"What do you think I should do with my hair?" She stared at Caesar waiting for an answer.

"Stacey, he doesn't consult anymore."

"That's true, but since she's a friend of yours I'll make an exception."

He walked behind the sofa and gently ran his hands through Stacey's hair. "You need to use a conditioner more. Your hair has a nice texture."

"Your hands are very gentle. Smooth. Will you give me a Valerian hairstyle one day?"

Caesar laughed and walked down the hall to the bathroom. He washed his hands and returned. "May I give you some advice, Stacey?"

"Of course, Mr. Valerian."

"Call me Caesar. If you want to do runway you'll need a new style that tames that mop of curls. Designers don't want a model's hair taking away from the clothes she's wearing. None of the top models are redheads. But I think that the hair is too much a part of you. Go for print ads and commercials."

"Thanks for nothing," Stacey grinned. "That's what Leigh says and she's not the best hairstylist in the world."

"Are you saying I am?"

"Well, do I hear the famous Sarito Valerian fishing for compliments?" Leigh called from the kitchen.

"Maybe. You've shaken my confidence."

"How did she do that?" Stacey's eyes widened.

"By not falling madly in love with me and asking me to do her hair."

"Shame on you, Leigh Barrington."

"Well, he's just not my type," Leigh said. Her eyes met Caesar's, held for a moment, then she turned away.

Her eyes said she was lying, Caesar thought. She's as attracted to me as I am to her.

"I'm starved. What are you cooking?"

"Chicken and vegetables. And it's ready."

Caesar and Stacey sat at the table and waited as Leigh pulled the dish from the microwave. Caesar would have volunteered to set the table or get the silverware, but Leigh still seemed as if she didn't want anyone to help her while she worked off her anger.

"Stacey, tell Caesar about that last commercial you filmed."

For an hour, she told them stories of her adventures in the modeling world as they ate.

"This is good," Stacey said. "Why did Caesar turn a little green when I asked you what you were cooking earlier?"

"It wasn't her cooking. She wasn't in a good frame of mind to be around knives."

"Oh, this is her kamikaze meal. I've watched her fix it a couple of times."

"I'm not sure what she did," Caesar explained. "I tried to stay out of her way when she started wielding that cleaver."

"What did you butcher?"

"Nothing," Leigh said.

"A chicken, the vegetables, everything," Caesar said at the same time.

Leigh shooed them out of the kitchen while she cleaned up and then joined them for more of Stacey's stories.

After Stacey left, Leigh picked up one of the throw pillows and hit Caesar lightly on the shoulder.

"You scared my friend a little when you started analyzing her hair."

"Is she always like that?"

"Always. We met at modeling school when we were teens."

"You wanted to be a model?"

"No. My grandmother thought I was too shy."

"Did your grandmother ever see you cook?"

She hit him with another pillow. "She also thought I was too self-conscious about my height. The women in my family run to the petite side. I took after my father."

"I took after my mother."

"Since my parents had passed away and Stephanie was with Aunt Helene, Stacey filled that void."

"It's good to have a close friend."

"Where does your mother live?"

"She lives in Paris."

"Were your mother and stepfather, the one you acknowledge, married for a long time?"

"Twelve years. She divorced him right after I got out of high school."

"Do you see him?"

"He passed away a few years ago, but until then we kept in touch."

Caesar didn't know how to explain his mother's sometimes bizarre behavior. She had been the mainstay in his life, yet at times she was like a butterfly. She was the most beautiful woman he had ever seen. Her dark skin was flawless and her oval face with its large black eyes brought her suitors from all walks of life. But she'd fallen in love with Carlos Valerian. They'd met in college and become inseparable. But he was pulled by tradition while she was willing to defy it.

"She doesn't seem 'motherly.' "

"She's not. We sort of grew up together, but she's wise about a lot of things. I hope she's not planning to stay long."

"That's awful."

"You don't know my mother."

"I think we should talk about what Cassiopeia needs."

In some way Leigh had been putting that off. She didn't want to think what he'd ask for to be on her side. She knew he wanted more control, but what would he do with it?

"No one on the Board cares about the true mundane things that make the salon run. They are just happy that it makes a profit and they get paid."

"I did notice that some things need to be repaired. But I'm really worried about the customer service aspect of the salon. Now that woman may decide just never to come back again but she could also decide to sue. And what about the other custom ers who witnessed it?"

"I agree. Something has to be done."

"So how do we make it happen?"

"It's simple. You need my 10% to make it happen."

"That's an offer I'd like to take. What's the catch?"
"You have to marry me."

ELEVEN

Leigh could not believe the arrogance of the man. "Marriage? Why?"

"We need to show that we are a united force," he explained.

"Can't we do that without being married?"

"Of course. But look at the power Paul and Stephanie wielded. They were quite formidable."

"I could do the same with Aunt Helene's vote."

Caesar laughed. "You saw what happened today. When would you be able to trust her? How long will it take for her to convince the others that you can be controlled?"

Leigh stood up and began to clear the table. "So you're saying I can't count on your vote to keep the wolf away."

"I'm saying that my vote is too important for both of us not to use it well."

"I don't think that's a good idea."

"We'll see. Think about it."

Long after Caesar left, Leigh pondered the 'proposal.' Marriage was a serious consideration. She didn't see it as a means to an end. But she wasn't in love with anyone and apparently neither was Caesar.

Still, when she cuddled under the covers, she wondered how 'real' he wanted this marriage to be.

* * *

The next day, Leigh didn't go to the salon. They weren't having meetings, so she decided to catch up on correspondence, put her house in order, and make a stop at the library. She needed to know more about the Board and about Caesar Montgomery.

Leigh decided to stop wondering what her options were. She decided to find out. She picked up the phone and dialed, but the recording came on.

Just as she began to leave a message, her aunt picked up the phone.

"Leigh, what's the matter?"

"I thought I'd buy you dinner and we could talk."

"Fine. Let's go to Wine and Apples."

Wine and Apples was near the salon, walking distance from Leigh's place. The small restaurant was just the place to find out where she stood with Helene.

Although the restaurant was closer to the salon, Leigh got there first. She had them seat her and waited. Helene got there ten minutes later.

"I thought we needed to talk away from the office," Leigh said.

Helene perused the menu, selected quickly, and ordered. "Leigh, there's just too much going on for you to try to learn on the job. I wish you'd taken Sarito seriously when he approached you on the island. We're not trying to take your power."

"What if we worked together? Just as you did with Paul and Stephanie."

Helene's brows knitted together. "I don't think that's possible."

"Why not?"

"Dear, you don't listen the way they did."

"Are you saying they were just puppets?"

"Don't you call your sister a puppet. She was smart enough to marry someone with money."

"And I was smart enough to come up with the idea."

Helene was silent until the waiter put her food down and moved away from the table.

"She didn't know it was your idea."

"What? You took the paper when you helped me move."

"I mean, I didn't tell her right away."

Leigh's eyes widened. "When did you tell her?"

"Three months ago. We were having dinner at my house and she found the papers. I don't know why I kept them."

"So you had to tell her the truth."

"I wish I hadn't."

"That's why she and Paul made the living will."

Helene bent over and whispered, "They changed the will twice this year. We thought they were getting a divorce."

"Stephanie never would have left Paul. She really loved him."

From time to time Leigh heard what was happening in Stephanie and Paul's life. Something had been in the papers, but Leigh couldn't remember what.

"Who would have benefitted under the old will?"

"The Board."

"How?"

"The shares would have been divided among the Board. If it didn't work out evenly, I would get the odd share. Cassiopeia would have been run by a team. If you don't let us handle Jameson Miller, we won't be having any conversations as owners of the salon."

"Did the Board know?"

"Paul didn't keep anything secret. He bragged about the fact he was changing it. JoAnn got all excited and started calling him a liar and a cheat."

"You've had some interesting board meetings."

"I'll say."

Leigh sat back and let her aunt tell her about the fighting that had gone on at the salon.

"Why did JoAnn get so upset?"

"Paul wasn't the best husband in the world. There were always rumors he was having an affair with JoAnn, until Sarito showed up."

"Caesar and JoAnn?"

* * *

Her aunt was pleased to tell her that from the moment Sarito walked in the door JoAnn set her sights on him. Helene explained that as soon as people saw what was happening they shifted their finances around. According to Helene, all were prepared to let Cassiopeia go down the drain and use it for a tax write-off. Everyone except Leigh would benefit from the salon's failure.

Leigh knew she was not going to give up her vote and that Helene would not help her. No wonder JoAnn had been so quick to befriend her, while the rest of the Board just tolerated her. Somehow she was going to hold onto her company. Somehow she was going to get through the quagmire that held Cassiopeia down. With plans to open three other salons Leigh knew that she was the one who had to pull things together and that she couldn't trust anyone on the Board to help her. Every member was ready to use it as a tax write off.

Caesar lay across the bed in the hotel. He'd played a trump card and lost. The look on Leigh's face when he suggested marriage told him all he wanted to know. He should have waited. He should have let her get friendly with a couple of the other members—like Rick Adams. He'd bet Leigh would find out about Rick's proclivities for fast cars and faster women. But it was too late. He'd made a bad move and couldn't recoup. He loved the salon. He could only hope that Leigh would learn that before it was too late.

When Helene went to the ladies' room, Leigh made a quick call. When she returned, Leigh paid the bill and they walked out. Before they parted, Helene hugged Leigh.

"I know you mean well, dear, but give up trying to play with the big boys before we lose everything."

* * *

Mark Westinghouse lived in Gramercy Park. He'd inherited the house from his father, who'd been smart enough to know it would be prime real estate one day.

He belonged to the Players Club, an organization for people connected with the theater. It was founded by Edwin Boothe, brother of the man who assassinated President Lincoln. Boothe had amassed a small fortune and since 'actors' were not permitted in the uptown clubs, Booth formed one for them. Mark had done some theater in college and still qualified to be a member.

It was a great place to shoot a game of billiards, meet friends, and have dinner. Although Leigh told him she'd already eaten, he said he'd buy her a drink and she could watch him eat.

He remembered the first time he'd seen Leigh. The firm where he was then a junior partner had been besieged with requests from schools to provide after school or weekend jobs for the youth. Sixteen-year-old Leigh Barrington applied.

She seemed more mature for her age. He found out later that her grandmother had sent her to a kind of finishing school for models. It had given her poise and confidence.

One day after she'd been working there for a month, he'd come in on a Saturday to find Leigh hard at work. At lunchtime he saw her taking notes from one of the law books on forming a business.

When he'd asked her about it, she produced a paper she'd written for her economics class. She had created a business that was simple and viable.

A year later she'd come to him in tears. Her sister and brother-in-law were using her papers to form the exact type of business she had created. He was the one who had to explain she couldn't do anything. She was devastated. After that she worked even harder and when she graduated from St. John's University with a degree in business, they hired her.

* * *

Leigh arrived at the Players Club just after Mark finished eating. He sat at a table in the corner and acknowledged a few people as they entered or left.

He called her over, stood up, and enveloped her in a bear hug.

"So how is my favorite protégée?"

"Mark, you better give up all this rich food. It'll kill you."

"How do you know it was 'rich food'? I may be on a diet."

"When did you ever eat anything that wasn't under a thousand calories? I saw a few people playing billiards downstairs. I bet you can't even get to the table."

When she became his administrative assistant, she'd badgered him about losing weight until she realized it wasn't going to do any good. Mark loved food.

Leigh sat down and began relaying the facts. She needed to stop a takeover.

"Mark," she said, "I don't think I have any help on this one. The only one who acts as if he wants to save Cassiopeia is Caesar."

"I know you told me not to snoop, but it's just my nature," Mark said. He pulled a notebook out and started flipping pages. "You're right about Caesar. Sarito Valerian wants something of his own. He started out fixing hair in a little salon uptown, then he got a lucky break. Believe me, honey, he's a man who knows when to make a move."

"But can I trust him?"

"That's something you have to decide. I never heard anything bad about him, but these are high stakes and it's anyone's game."

For the next hour, Leigh listened as Mark gave her little biographies of her Board. It all came back to Caesar.

Mark also gave her some valuable information on the man who wanted her property. He'd only backed down once before, when a company found a white knight. When a company was faced with a hostile takeover, they could merge with another, creating a friendly takeover. The second company was called a white knight for saving the company from the hostile one. For Leigh, that wasn't an option. She considered any takeover a hostile one.

"Do you have anyone in mind?"

"There might be. You want to get someone who has money and is willing to take a chance. You don't want to pick an enemy of Miller's."

"Why not?"

"You pick an enemy and he's going to have to prove himself by fighting you. You pick someone considered a nice, rich person and Miller might not want to look like the bad guy this time."

By the time she got home she was exhausted. The Board had decided to meet again in a week with a strategy against Jameson Miller.

Leigh decided what she needed now was a hot bath. She drew the water and poured in two capfuls of her favorite scented bubble bath. While the bath was running, she undressed, piled her hair under a shower cap, and sank into the water. She turned on the jets and let the powerful spray pound against her body.

Leigh racked her brains over Mark's suggestion. A nice person who was willing to take a chance? She'd find one.

She had to find a way to push back against Miller She could put up a good front and hint that there was white knight lurking about. Tomorrow she'd ask for a meeting with the elusive Mr. Miller. Tonight she'd just forget everything.

TWELVE

Just after six the next morning, the first thing Leigh did was pick up her phone and call the hotel. A sleepy Caesar answered.

"It's Leigh. We need to talk."

"I'll pick you up for breakfast in an hour."

She agreed but wondered what all these breakfast, lunch, and dinner conferences were going to do to her waistline. She'd eaten more since coming back from the islands than when she was on vacation. Somewhere along the line she was going to have to give that up or she was going to give Mark some competition in the weight department.

Caesar arrived at Leigh's condo at five minutes to seven. She was waiting in the lobby. For him that was a good sign. She was going to accept his proposal and they were going to make the salon work. They walked around for a few minutes and decided on a restaurant. As they waited for their food, Caesar was anxious to confirm his theory.

"You didn't come to the salon yesterday." When she nodded, he continued. "What did you do last night?"

"I had dinner with Helene."

His heart lurched. If she and Helene got together, he was out. "What did she tell you?"

"A little bit about you and JoAnn."

"Leigh, I'm not going to lie about my life. What JoAnn and I had was brief and fun. We both knew what we wanted. We had no reason to think that it was forever. It was before I was on the Board."

"You seem to have a lot of 'brief and fun' relationships."

"I did most of that when I got my first taste of fame. I grew up quickly. I'm not about to risk my life with that sort of nonsense any longer."

Satisfied with his answers, she continued. "She also hinted that there was a problem with my sister's marriage."

"Whatever Stephanie and Paul did outside, neither brought it to the office."

She didn't say anything else about the salon until after they had eaten and were back in Leigh's condo. They were standing in her living room when she turned to him and said, "I've decided to marry you."

Caesar pulled her around to face him. "Do you mean it?"

"There's a small catch."

"What is it?"

"You have to find us a white knight."

He couldn't believe she would do this. She wanted him to find someone to buy Cassiopeia.

"And then what?" There was a cold, sharp edge to his voice.

"We make Miller think we have someone we would rather merge with and he goes away."

"If he doesn't?"

"Then we're going to need that white knight to hold onto as much of Cassiopeia as we can."

"You'd settle for less than controlling interest?"

She lifted her chin. "I'm ready to make a deal with anyone who helps me keep my salon."

He'd never heard so much determination from Leigh. He felt the same way. The salon meant as much to him as it did to her.

"Then why get married?"

"Because if you fail, we're in for the fight of our lives against Miller. I don't want him to think you can be bought."

Caesar thought about it for a minute. "Maybe we should let him think that."

"No. I've been to the library and read quite a bit about the man. He's not someone we want to antagonize."

"We just want him to go away."

"Right, but, Caesar, I want a prenuptial agreement. One that says your 10 percent converts to me immediately."

"Now just a minute . . ."

Leigh had thought of all the angles. "I'll agree to 15 percent being part of the divorce settlement."

"So it's your decision on whether or not I keep shares of Cassiopeia?"

"That's it. New York is not a community property state."

"You've thought about this quite a bit. But let me warn you, I want my 15 percent back the day we get a divorce."

"I stand by my word. But I'll feel safer with a prenuptial agreement. I want control for as long as we're married."

Caesar strolled over to where Leigh stood. "We have to convince the Board that we're in love."

"I can play that game." She managed a nervous grin. She stretched out her hand.

"If we're going to get married, I can think of something better to seal the deal."

He swept her into his arms and kissed her. She suddenly felt as if she were back in the Caribbean. Heat seemed to be rising in her apartment. She could smell his aftershave—the same fresh scent he had worn then. Leigh was lost in the kiss, until she remembered what this was supposed to be. This wasn't the real thing—it was a game. She pulled away.

Caesar caught his breath. He hadn't meant for the kiss to be anything but friendly. Something about Leigh Barrington made him want her. Here she was, no make-up, just a freshly scrubbed face that made her look sixteen. She was dressed in gray sweats and his heart was pounding like a jackhammer. He wanted her. And while she thought this was a marriage in name only, he started to think maybe it could be more. They were adults. So what if he seduced his wife?

Leigh pushed him away. "I think we'd better establish some ground rules."

"I think we should let nature take its course." He stepped toward her.

"No!"

"Leigh, we're not kids."

"I'm not a woman who sleeps with a man just because he's attractive. If that's what you're thinking, we'd better stop now."

"I'll agree to this. I believe in seduction, not rape. You can always say no but I'm not going to pretend I'm not going to try to change your mind."

"I've been told that I can be quite stubborn about things. I think we'll be too busy trying to save Cassiopeia."

"You're right. That comes first for both of us. Now how do we break the news to the Board?"

That night was a benefit ball at Tavern on the Green. Invitations had arrived at Cassiopeia weeks before. Gayla had accepted for all the members, then Paul and Stephanie had been murdered. Leigh knew about it before she went on vacation but she hadn't planned to attend until she needed a way to show that she and Caesar were an item.

Leigh hadn't had a chance to wear something fancy for a long time. She pulled her favorite Lagerfeld from the closet. The silver dress with one sleeve fell just above her knees. Her high-heeled silver sandals would make her slightly taller than Caesar, but she felt she needed any advantage she could get. A matching jacket with padded shoulders and chiffon sleeves completed the outfit. She slipped into her pale blue evening coat and did one last make-up check before going downstairs to meet Caesar for the short ride through Central Park.

Downstairs, Caesar waited nervously in the limousine he'd hired for the night. He glanced at his watch; they had plenty of time, but how would the people react to them as a couple?

He saw a woman emerge from the building but had to take a second look to realize it was Leigh. He'd thought she looked sexy on the island but tonight it was something unbelievable. He got out and stood by the door. He held her hand as she sat down then in one swift movement swung her legs into the car.

Caesar had laughed when Leigh insisted on meeting him in the lobby rather than letting him come up to her apartment. He thought that she was taken aback by his promise to seduce her. Now he realized she was throwing down the gauntlet. They arrived, gave their invitations, and joined the other members of the Board at their table.

Leigh was just as impressed. Caesar's tux was obviously not something off the rack. It hugged his frame and managed to hide the muscular frame she'd seen jogging on the beach.

Only Rick, JoAnn, and Helene were representing Cassiopeia. Caesar was not pleased at Rick's perusal of Leigh nor the low wolf-whistle he emitted when she took off the coat to reveal the sexy one-sleeved dress. He slipped his arm around her shoulders in a possessive manner as they listened to the speeches.

Caesar wasn't the only one annoyed. JoAnn lost no time in nudging Rick in his ribcage to bring his attention back to her.

Leigh leaned back in his arms knowing the others at the table were taking in every move. Then the band started and Caesar led her to the dance floor. It was an old classic that was popular when people danced close and easy. She knew Caesar had mastered the fast beats, but she was surprised at how easily he danced to this music. The only problem was his hands—her dress was so sheer that she could count his fingers against her back. It set her on fire. It reminded her that it had been a long time since anyone had held her this way.

It had been more than a year since Marshall Alexander had cheated on her and then expected her to forgive him. He didn't believe that she wouldn't until she removed his name from the list of people who could bypass the concierge.

She remembered the angry words he'd hurled at her. Saying she was cold and unfeeling and that's why he sought the company of another. He may have been correct in his assessment of her then but the sensuous heat she felt in Caesar's arms told her she wasn't unfeeling.

As the song ended, she started to step back, only to find she couldn't move from Caesar's grip. Their eyes met and he winked at her. Then they walked from the dance floor. Three pairs of eyes glared at them as they returned to their table. The band swung into a fast-paced tune and Rick grabbed JoAnn's hand.

"Come on, baby, Let's dance."

Caesar whispered in Leigh's ear that he'd spotted an old friend and would be right back. As soon as he left, Helene slid over next to Leigh.

"What was that all about?"

"What?"

"Your little spectacle with Sarito Valerian."

"We only danced. What's wrong with that?"

"Is that what you call it these days? You didn't even know when the music stopped."

Leigh shrugged her shoulders. "He's quite a man."

"I thought you were smarter." Helene moved back to her seat.

Caesar returned right before Rick and JoAnn. Another slow tune began and Rick looked at Leigh.

"Absolutely not," Caesar said.

Rick wasn't about to pretend that he didn't understand. He just bowed his head admitting he understood that Leigh was not available.

Several people stopped by to greet them. Leigh was having a wonderful time until the last visitor.

"Can you imagine getting dressed up and dancing in the name of a charity?" Jameson Miller asked. "I like the way rich people help others, don't you?"

And then he was gone.

"Miller's always throwing out the fact that he was poor," Rick hissed. "We better do something, because if he takes over Cassiopeia, he can buy me out. I don't want to be in the same room with the man."

"That's not going to happen," Leigh said.

"Yeah, from your mouth to God's ear," replied JoAnn.

Caesar hadn't even looked up when Miller stood by their table. He said nothing to indicate he was even willing to fight. Leigh thought it must be a self-defense reaction. Don't let the enemy see you sweat.

Later, when the host declared the evening a success, they prepared to leave. As they started for their cars, JoAnn pulled Leigh to the side.

"So what's happening with you two? Decide to continue what you started in the Caribbean?"

"Maybe," Leigh smiled.

"Well, don't get too cozy. The man is not one for the long haul."

"I guess that depends on the woman."

THIRTEEN

Caesar felt a surge of pride as they stood in line waiting for their limousine. Rick wasn't the only man looking at Leigh. The weatherman had predicted heavy rains were on the way, but the night had turned out beautiful and his plan was on target. The only thing to accomplish was his part of the bargain. Finding a white knight. Someone with enough money to bail them out. Someone willing to take a chance. Someone who owed him a favor. The temperature had dropped a little and when Leigh shivered he put his arm around her. He was about to offer her his top coat when their driver pulled up.

He was more amazed that Leigh didn't acknowledge any of the stares. He wanted to ask her about her conversation with JoAnn but decided against it. What he should be concerned about was Miller's appearance. Why would the man go to such pains to flaunt his wealth and at the same time show such disdain for others who did the same thing?

They were pulling out of the park when Caesar pointed to her shoes.

"Why do women do such things to their feet?"

"For the same reason they pay to have you style their hair. To impress other women."

"Not for men?"

"Most men wouldn't notice what we wear on our feet. It's just a select few that understand and appreciate our efforts. I think we made quite a splash tonight."

"I agree."

"Aunt Helene is furious. She thinks I've lost my mind."

Caesar laughed then fell silent. How was he going to broach the next subject? He had "accidently" bumped into one of the most powerful gossip columnists in the city. She pried the information from him that he and Leigh had spent some time together in the Caribbean. He knew that the next day the woman's column would begin to drop little hints about a budding romance at the salon.

Leigh was surprised when Caesar dismissed the driver after he retrieved a gym bag from the trunk. He caught her hand as he escorted her into the building. They were alone in the elevator when her curiosity got the better of her.

"Why do you need the bag?"

"Because I plan to spend the night here."

"Wait a minute . . ."

"We only have to give the appearance of an affair. I'll leave early, but I'm sure someone will see me and the next thing you know, we'll be considered a couple."

Leigh understood his reasoning and her home office also served as a guest bedroom. "You're right. People would expect us to practically live together. How long do we have to do this until we announce our engagement?"

"I think next week. It'll be Thanksgiving."

They got out of the elevator and as she put her key in the door, Caesar wrapped his arms around her and murmured in Spanish and English. Leigh was shocked, but as she turned to face him she caught a glimpse of her neighbor bringing his dog out for a walk. She relaxed and allowed the caress until the elevator doors closed.

"Now that you've scandalized me," she teased, "you'll have to make an honest woman out of me."

"Let's go in and plan this whirlwind courtship."

They hung their coats in the closet.

"I don't want a large ring. Just something tasteful. And I don't want a big wedding. It would take too long to plan."

Caesar agreed to her demands as he tried to smother a yawn.

It had been a long day and he was beginning to like the idea of being engaged to the most beautiful CEO in New York.

Leigh tossed and turned and fell into a restless sleep at about two in the morning. The sound of something tapping against her window woke her just three hours later. Normally she would not have been bothered by a little rain, but tonight, despite her brave front about letting people know that Caesar was spending the night, she was really a little nervous about having a man around. Marshall Alexander had left his mark on her.

She threw the covers back and tipped over to the window. The weatherman had been wrong again. It wasn't rain. It was snow. Tiny flakes that were sure to stick. How was she going to shop for an engagement ring? How was she going to find a dress for the wedding? Maybe this was an omen that they should call the whole thing off.

She crawled back into bed and snuggled under the comforter. Four hours later she was awake again. Leigh staggered into the master bath attached to her room and splashed cold water on her face. Her feet hurt and her mouth felt like she'd eaten dry sand. She couldn't shake her lethargic mood.

Leigh felt better after a brief shower. She slipped into her jeans, and the fact that she could just barely snap them told her that all the lunches and dinners had slipped a few pounds on her frame. She didn't even want to get on the scale. It would be a liquid diet for the next week to get rid of the excess.

She remembered that Caesar was still there and she hoped that he was feeling some of the same symptoms of the morning after that she was feeling.

Leigh stepped from her bedroom and heard the low sounds of Latin music coming from the living room. She padded down the hall in her bare feet and decided there was no justice. Caesar was dressed in jeans just as she was, but he was doing some intricate steps as he raided her refrigerator and cabinets to prepare breakfast. She looked at the light fluffy pancakes piled on a serving platter and decided that she'd start her diet the next day.

"I guess you slept well," she told him. "Have you looked outside?"

He laughed. "Can you believe that? Snow."

Leigh picked up the phone and dialed the salon. She just liked to keep in touch. Even when she had no plans to stop in. Gayla assured her that most of the staff had gotten in and there hadn't been any cancellations. Leigh relayed that information to Caesar.

"Let's just get to know each other a little better. We should at least sound as if we've talked," she said.

"Sounds good."

They played twenty questions. At first it was just learning where they went to school and how they got started. Then when it was Caesar's turn he asked, "Why do you want Cassiopeia?"

Leigh couldn't control her tears. She wanted to share her whole story with Caesar but she couldn't. She could only share a small part of herself.

"My sister and I had drifted apart. We fought and never got a chance to make up. We held a grudge too long. The will was Stephanie's way of healing past wounds."

Instinctively Caesar knew not to try to hold her as she talked, but when she finished he pulled her into his lap and just held her for five or six minutes. Then he felt he should share a little more of himself as she had done with him.

"I told you my brother was in a car accident. When I reached Bogata, I learned that his mother had been a little hysterical when she called me."

Caesar shifted Leigh to a more comfortable position for both of them. One that maintained body contact comfortably with her head resting against his chest.

"Esteban hadn't been hurt too badly but the car was totaled. I stayed to help make sense of some of his business deals. He's really good about who he wants to be. Still, his wild ways were embarrassing his mother. One night we went out to a club and he got drunk. We had a fight and I wouldn't let him drive. We were arguing, so I didn't see debris in the road. By the time I did, it was too late. My brother had refused to put on his seatbelt and was thrown against the windshield. I got this little scar. He almost died."

"So you stayed until he recovered."

"That's why I wasn't here when Stephanie and Paul were . . ."

"Why did you come to look for me?"

Caesar grimaced. "That was Helene's idea. She wanted me to charm you into backing off for a year. I got off the plane from Bogota and she was waiting for me. She laughed at my scar and said I was too pretty before."

"Do you still think I should?"

Several beats passed before he answered. "Helene ordered me to find you. She said I should turn on the charm and get

"And so are you."

He leaned forward, but just as his lips brushed hers, the phone rang and jarred them apart. Leigh picked it up and listened. "It's my aunt. She's on her way up."

Helene rang the bell and when Leigh opened the door she breezed in. "I thought we should have a little girl talk . . ." She stopped mid-sentence when she saw Caesar. "Well, I guess it's too late for girl talk."

"I made a batch of pancakes. Would you like some?"

"No, I've already had breakfast. I stopped by the salon and when Gayla said you weren't coming in, I decided to visit you. But since you already have company I'll just leave."

"You don't have to go, Aunt Helene."

"Yes, I do. I have a few errands to run. But let me just check my make-up."

Helene was halfway down the hall when Leigh realized her true mission—she wanted to look in the guest room. She turned into the guest room and came right out. "Wrong turn," she called, then proceeded to the correct room.

Caesar seemed unmoved. Helene came out of the bathroom, said a quick good-bye, and was gone.

"You know why she deliberately took that wrong turn?"

"Sure. She wanted to see if I was sleeping in the guest room."

"And that doesn't bother you?"

Caesar rolled his eyes in the air and said, "Come on."

Leigh followed him down the hall and was amazed. The room

was back to her office, the love seat had been folded up, and it didn't look as if anyone had spent the night there.

"You women have this idea that bachelors live in a hovel. My mother was a tyrant about an unmade bed."

"I knew I liked your mother."

The phone rang. It was the concierge telling Leigh she had another visitor, It was Juliette.

"Caesar, we'll have to play the loving couple again. Your mother's on her way up."

"I'm going to the gym."

"But what about your mother?"

"You entertain her."

"You coward. You're afraid that Juliette will zoom in on our little pretense."

"My mother likes you. She'll start planning a large wedding and we'll be in trouble."

"I don't want a large wedding. I want to elope."

"You explain that to Mother." He put on his jacket and started for the door. The bell rang. "That's Mother. Have fun and I'll call you later."

"You can't run . . ."

He pulled the door open and smiled at his mother. "I've got to go to the gym. Leigh will entertain you, Mother."

Leigh could not believe this. On the island, he had backed down a man more than 200 pounds but today he was afraid to deal with a 95–pound woman.

"Come on in, Juliette. It's so nice to see you again."

"Sarito, why did you keep it a secret from me that you were romantically involved with Leigh?"

"How did you find out, Juliette? Did you meet my aunt?"

"No. But several of my friends were talking and they showed me this."

She held up the gossip page of the paper. Leigh crossed over and took it from her hand. She read the article in silence first then turned to Caesar.

"There's a column that says we're having an affair. That it started on the island and is continuing."

"Sarito, what do you know of this column?"

"Nothing. The woman was at the ball last night and probably saw us together."

"If I find out who started this, I'm going to kill him or her, as the case may be."

"You mean it is not true?" Juliette was clearly disappointed.

"It's true, Mother, we just don't want to announce it now."

"Sarito, why do you persist in lying to me? Something else is going on. I demand to know."

"Mother, please. You can't know everything all the time." He stepped into the hall.

"Aren't you going to follow him?"

"No. I understand my son better than he understands himself sometimes. But it's time we had a talk."

"Juliette, we're not really having an affair. We just want it to look like we're having one."

"So you and Sarito can save your company."

"That's right. Why do you call him Sarito?"

"I named him Sarito. I don't care what he calls himself now."

"I don't want you to think it's real."

"That's what you tell yourselves and others. The truth is you're both crazy about each other and you don't even know it."

FOURTEEN

"Juliette, I think you've lived in Paris too long," Leigh told her. "Caesar and I have an . . . arrangement."

Even as she said it, she knew it wasn't believable. Nor could she make it any more believable. She was attracted to the man, but he only wanted to use her to get to the salons. So she found a way to use him first.

"Ah! Call it whatever you will. But I don't think either of you are unwilling for it to progress from what you think it is to what I know it is."

"It's just better for business right now."

Juliette shook her head, walked over to the sofa, and sat down. "I knew when I met Carlos that he was bad for me. At first I thought that he would give everything up for love. When I realized he wouldn't, it was too late. I was already expecting Sarito."

"What did he do?"

"What his father wanted him to do. I then did what I had to do. I saw to it that my son knew his father. But I also taught my son that the coffee plantation would never be his."

"Have you ever regretted what you've done?"

"You always have regrets, but you do not let them color the rest of your life."

The concierge called to say that Caesar was in the lobby. Juliette decided not to stay any longer.

"I'm sorry to have to rush off, but I'm meeting someone. I just want to say this before I leave—I knew the value of my beauty; know the value of your brain."

The bell rang and Caesar came in. "Hello, Mother."

"I have a date. I was just leaving." The tiny woman swept from the room like the diva she was. Leigh understood the reason for the short visit. Juliette wanted her to know she had an ally.

"What did you and my mother talk about?"

Leigh was about to answer when Helene called to speak with Sarito. When he put down the phone, he turned to her and said, "We'd better put the war on hold. Helene wants to throw an engagement party for us."

"Terrific," she said, as she tossed the paper on the table.

"Do you have other plans?"

"No"

"Leigh, don't worry. We can make it work. It isn't as if we're in love."

"You're right. It doesn't matter," she lied. Leigh couldn't help but compare herself to Stephanie. Both married for the same reason: they'd found someone who could make their dreams come true. And no matter how much they wanted to be independent women of the '90s, they married to get what they wanted.

Helene opened her home for the party. She'd purchased two apartments when the building first opened and gotten permission to combine them, so there was plenty of space.

She hired a caterer and personally called two hundred people, hoping that one hundred of them would show up. The crowded room attested to the fact that almost everyone who had been invited came; they all who wanted to get a glimpse of the couple.

"Who's the man in the gray suit?"

For twenty minutes, Leigh had avoided part of the room and hoped that Caesar wouldn't notice. But it seemed that he noticed everything.

"What man?"

"The one you've been taking surreptitious glances at since we got here. Are you going to tell me or should I go over and introduce myself?"

Leigh caught his arm, "Don't start anything."

"Then tell me his name."

"Marshall Alexander."

"Your ex-fiancé?"

"The one and, fortunately for the women in America, the only."

Leigh decided the best thing to do would be to brazen it out. Obviously Helene meant to cause trouble and Leigh was determined that she wouldn't succeed. It had only been two years ago that Leigh had worn another engagement ring, one that she thought she'd never remove until her wedding day—until the man made a fool of her and wanted her to accept his wandering eye.

"I think I should have a little talk with him. He seems to think you're still on the market."

"Does it matter? This is only temporary. Besides, he married one of my classmates last year."

"Yes, it matters. I don't care what we've decided—I won't be cuckolded by someone from your past. Is she here?"

"Cuckolded? Do you think this is regency England? And no, I don't see his wife. Do you want me to formally introduce you? Are you jealous?"

"That won't be necessary right now. Let me get you a refill."

He set her half-empty glass down on the table and looked around for a waiter.

"Would you like to see what could happen when I'm expressing jealousy?"

Leigh shrugged at this point. She didn't care. She knew that Marshall was trying to get her attention, though she couldn't imagine why. She guessed that he was one of those men who didn't want a woman unless she belonged to someone else.

"While you're expressing your jealousy, just remember that there are several reporters here."

"Okay. All I know of the man is what I learned when we were playing twenty questions."

"I thought you were getting me another drink?"

Caesar spotted a waiter and decided to walk over to him to cool down a bit. He was congratulated by several men as he tried to weave through the crowd. Rick caught his arm and Caesar turned.

"I wanted to introduce you to Lissa," Rick told him.

"I don't think I've seen her before. How do you do, Lissa?"

"Just fine, Sarito."

Caesar cringed inwardly whenever a stranger used that name. It usually meant they wanted to pretend to be a close friend. Lissa appeared to be beautifully made up but there was a lack of intelligence around her eyes. They seemed to be roving the room for celebrities rather than paying attention.

"Lissa wants to know if you ever use your stylist skills now that you've become so corporate."

"No, sorry, Lissa. I don't do that anymore."

Leigh was getting tired of waiting for Caesar to pry himself away from his conversation long enough to get her that drink he promised. Fortunately a waiter passed right by her and she grabbed a ginger ale. She also needed some fresh air, so she stepped out onto the terrace.

No one was around and she didn't mind the cold night. She'd been claustrophobic inside. The view wasn't much to brag about, but she welcomed the solitude. She sipped her drink and thought about Caesar's betrayal. How could he have alerted the press like that? She wanted the engagement and the wedding to be low key because they didn't really count. Leigh was also annoyed at Marshall Alexander. Even if her aunt did invite him, he didn't have to show up.

"How are you doing, Leigh?" Marshall's voice shattered her calm, but wasn't unexpected. She knew he might follow her and she wanted a chance to talk to him before Caesar leveled him.

"I'm fine, Marshall."

His gray suit caught the light from the other balcony. He came closer and she could see the aquiline nose and thin moustache that she once had loved.

"Life's been good to you lately. I like your new dress. You've changed since we were together."

The dress was nothing special. Leigh had worn the forest green satin dress to a wedding when she was dating Marshall and he didn't even remember it.

"Thank you," she said, preferring not to comment on their past relationship. "I didn't see your wife. Is she here?"

"I don't know where she is. Barbara and I broke up a couple of months ago."

"Sorry to hear that."

"Yeah, it was a big mistake. Of course, not as big as the one I made when I let you get away. I tried to reach you right after I heard about your sister."

"I went away for a few days."

"With your fiancé?"

"No I met him on the island." She wanted to stay as close to the truth as possible.

"He's kinda possessive. I didn't think you liked that type of guy."

"People change."

"Right. Like me for example. I'm nothing like the guy you left."

Two years ago she would have been ecstatic to hear him say that. A year ago she might even have given him another chance, but now his lines just sounded tired.

"When I met you, Leigh, I was all confused about what I wanted in a relationship. My marriage taught me how I went after the wrong woman."

"Right."

"That doesn't sound like the Leigh I knew."

"As you said, people change."

"I would hate to think that I caused you to lose that sweetness."

"Don't flatter yourself."

"Now I know that's not like you."

Leigh wanted to scream out that she was finally over him. He looked the same. He talked the same. But it just didn't have the same effect on her. She'd been so passive in the relationship that she probably did sound different now.

"Don't feel bad or think you changed me. I'm not bitter."

"I know I hurt you. But we can start over."

"Marshall, do you know how pathetic you sound? This is my engagement party. I'm marrying someone else."

She didn't understand how she could have shed tears over this arrogant man before her. He left her for a woman he knew had more money, and now that Leigh was perceived as wealthy, he wanted to start again. When she compared him to Caesar, he just didn't measure up.

"You may still be on the rebound."

The arrogance of the man was astonishing. He thought he

could just talk his way back. "I am not on the rebound. It's been two years."

"That doesn't matter. You know you belong with me."

"I belong with the man I came with. Do I have to spell it out for you? L-O-V-E. He makes me feel like I'm the only woman in the world—not part of some harem. His kisses make yours seem like dishwater."

"Yeah. Well suppose we try a little experiment?" Marshall reached for her, but she stepped away. He came toward her and she threw the remainder of her glass in his face. It stopped him long enough.

"I think the lady's made it clear she doesn't want you," Caesar said, in that cold manner she'd heard him use on the island.

She was surprised to see him because Marshall's body had blocked her view of the sliding glass doorway.

"Well, don't blame me," Marshall said. He wiped his face with his handkerchief. "She came onto me."

"From what I heard, the lady told you several times to leave her alone."

"I'm telling you—she wanted me to kiss her."

"And I'm telling you she's never backed away when I wanted to kiss her. Now why don't you go find someone who's available. Leigh Barrington—soon to be Montgomery—is not available."

Without a word, Marshall left the terrace. Leigh started to laugh nervously.

"He just wouldn't take no for an answer."

"Well, what do you expect? You come out here alone after he's been flashing that phony smile at you all night."

"I came out here to get away from the heat, the smoke, and the crowd. I didn't ask anyone to follow me."

"If you don't start behaving, I'm going to have to get you a chaperone."

"Like who?"

"How about Stacey?"

The thought of Stacey as a chaperone had them both laughing. As they stepped off the terrace, someone took their picture.

Two days later it was plastered all over a tabloid newspaper. It was accompanied by a story from Marshall Alexander about how Leigh dumped him for a wealthier man.

FIFTEEN

Revenge was not so sweet now, Leigh thought, as she tossed the paper on the table. Caesar had called her to say she'd better get a copy. She'd rushed to the corner newsstand and groaned when she saw the headlines. Why did everything that happened to her have to end up on the front page?

She thought Marshall must be congratulating himself on getting back at her. He was furious that she wasn't thrilled at the idea of getting back together with him.

She didn't care anymore today; she was going to select her wedding gown. It was three weeks before Christmas and most of the stores would not be carrying wedding gowns as they would in March for those June brides.

She found the perfect dress at Bergdorf's. It was ivory with a bodice of chiffon. The padded shoulders made her waist appear smaller. She loved the satin strips that fell from its waist to her ankles. She selected an ivory hat with a large bow on the back that looked perfect for the dress. A trip to the shoe department and she was ready.

The night before the wedding, Caesar had insisted she meet him at the salon. He wouldn't tell her why. She met him at the door and he was dressed in the blue jacket of the stylists. He led her to the area where Gayla was waiting.

"She's going to wash your hair and I'm going to style it."

"I'll have to sleep sitting up to keep it," Leigh protested.

"I've told you before, women do strange things to be beautiful."

"Gayla, I'm so sorry about this . . ."

"Don't think about it. I've done it before. Once Helene dragged me out of bed to come down here and fix her hair."

"When was that?"

"The night after Stephanie . . ."

She didn't continue. Leigh knew she was talking about the night of the murders.

"Why did she need a fresh hairstyle?"

"JoAnn said she got so upset when she heard about Stephanie that she forgot to put on her shower cap. Then when she looked in the mirror she started yelling and the next thing I knew they were calling me to come down and do something with that mop of hair."

Caesar came in just as Gayla wrapped the towel around Leigh's wet hair.

"Thanks, Gayla. I can take it from here."

"See you tomorrow for the big day. I just can't tell you how excited I am."

Gayla rushed off to clean up and Caesar took over. He removed the towel and held up a bottle. "I think just a hint of color tomorrow."

Leigh slid down in the chair and closed her eyes. Caesar's strong fingers massaged her scalp as he worked the rinse through her hair. "Don't move, I need to get a plastic cap." He bent and kissed her. She opened her eyes but he was gone.

Deep inside Leigh wished it was real that they had fallen in love and now were about to really become man and wife. She thought about his smooth, strong fingers as they massaged her scalp.

He returned with the cap, put it on, and sat Leigh under the dryer for twenty minutes. Then he rinsed her hair again and she walked to the styling area.

"Not fair," she said, when she noticed he'd covered the mirrors.

"This is my gift to my bride. A Sarito Valerian special."

He worked quickly but Leigh was anxious. She fidgeted in the chair as he tried to blow dry her hair until he threatened to stop in the middle of the creation.

Finally he whispered that he was finished. He removed the coverup and turned her toward the mirror. Then, like a magician, he pulled the towel from the mirror. Leigh was shocked. Her normally black hair now had a hint of red. Just enough to show when the light caught it. Tendrils hung down from her upswept hairstyle.

"You will make a beautiful bride."

Caesar stared at the woman rather than the creation. She was strong and vulnerable at the same time. He'd given her sweet little kisses, when what he wanted to do was make passionate love to her. And he would do just that. Not now. They needed to keep their bargain, that this would be a marriage in name only. Together they would bring Cassiopeia back to what it once was and get Jameson Miller out of their lives. Then they would be lovers. He knew without a doubt that this woman would share his bed, but not just yet.

Leigh preened in front of the mirror. "Thank you. Now I understand why women would fight to get an appointment with you."

He kissed her and produced a thin scarf to tie over her head. "You're right about having to sleep sitting up tonight. I have a car waiting outside. I will see you in the morning." He kissed her again.

Leigh absolutely refused to marry in a church. They opted instead for Mark's apartment. It would limit the guests. He had agreed to give her away. Reporters were all around but she managed to battle through. In Mark's bedroom she stared at her reflection.

Caesar came into the room. Leigh gasped.

"You're not supposed to see the bride before the wedding."

"We have such a nontraditional marriage, I didn't think it

would be bad luck." He wore a cutaway jacket with dark gray trousers. "Have you worked out the something old, something new bit?" he asked.

"Uh-huh. The something old—my earrings. They were my grandmother's. The something new—my hairstyle, courtesy of my future husband. We are borrowing Mark's apartment, and there's a blue ribbon around my bouquet."

"Seems we have everything covered. I wanted to tell you that my brother got in last night and he's going to be my best man."

"That's great. I don't think Rick will be too disappointed."

"I think he was relieved when I told him. I know you think of your hairstyle as a gift but this is really from me to you." He pulled out a long, thin box and opened it. He stepped behind her and looped the three gold strands around her neck. Each strand had a different stone attached. The top was a deep red ruby, the second was a blue topaz, and the third a marquis-cut diamond.

"Oh, Caesar, it's beautiful. Thank you."

"You are very welcome."

"This is my gift to you."

"I didn't expect anything. . . ." He fumbled with the neatly wrapped box. Inside he found a silver Mark Cross pen with "Sarito Valerian" engraved on one side and "Caesar Montgomery" on the other. The note read, "To the perfect man for the perfect signature."

He laughed and kissed her. "I think it's time for me to join my brother."

Leigh held onto Mark's arm as they walked from the bedroom to the living room. Stacey had managed to tame her cascade of red hair and looked stunning in her deep blue dress.

Caesar stood beside a tall, handsome man who could only be Esteban Valerian. There were certain features, like their eyes, that said they were related, but at the same time their height and body build said they were so different.

They had chosen "cherish" rather than "obey" and "husband

and wife" rather than "man and wife" but other than that, it was a traditional wedding.

As Leigh said her vows, she knew that she meant them. She wished she wasn't in love with her husband. How would she ever handle it when they ended it? Leigh didn't care. She was completely in love with the man.

When the wedding was over, Leigh was surprised to find tears in her eyes as well as several of her friends and guests. What seemed real was just an illusion. One that Leigh was determined to make so much more than when Stephanie and Paul had the salon. She could do it. She could have the same glamorous life as her sister. The life that had escaped her for so long.

Helene was there in a gold and beige creation in a failed attempt to overshadow the bride. She pulled Leigh to the side and apologized profusely about the scandalous way Marshall Alexander had behaved.

Juliette was the surprise. Leigh's mother-in-law was sedately dressed in a navy beaded dress that fell just below her knees.

"Where's this new man in your life?" Leigh whispered as they posed for a family picture.

"He, like most men, chose business over me," Juliette sighed. She didn't seem particularly disturbed by it.

The photographer warned them that talking would spoil his pictures and they stopped.

Besides being her only attendant, Stacey took care of the reception. A friend had let them use his restaurant.

As they led the first dance as husband and wife, Leigh saw the burning desire in Caesar's eyes and knew she couldn't resist him. There was no doubt in her mind that the marriage would be consummated.

Caesar hoped the glow in his wife's eyes meant she would forgive him for breaking his promise, but he knew there was no way they could share a house and not share a bed.

All of his plans to become her hero as he saved what she wanted most were no longer feasible. He liked holding her against his body, and if only a dance could make him feel his clothes were suddenly too small, what would the dance of love do to him? No matter how he tried to justify his feelings, he wanted Leigh the way a man should want a woman. After all, it was their wedding day.

Esteban seemed to be enjoying himself. Caesar watched his brother as he moved around the room impressing the women but not offending the men. Younger by five years, Esteban's life had been more sheltered since he was being groomed to take over the family business. Then his brother headed toward Caesar and Leigh.

"I have not had the pleasure of even meeting my new sister-in-law," he said. "I am, I believe the English saying is, cutting in."

In a split second, Leigh was being whirled around the floor. Esteban was a terrific dancer. She suspected his English was a lot better than he led people to believe. He asked a few questions about the haste in which Caesar and Leigh married, and she knew that Caesar had not shared the true reason with him.

They decided to spend the first night in Leigh's apartment then drive to Connecticut in the morning. Caesar stood in the hallway in front of her bedroom.

"I know I said we would be married in name only, and if that is what you want, I will keep my word. But I want you to know it's not what I want."

"It's not what I want either."

"I'll change in the guest room and then join you."

Leigh quickly stripped off her wedding gown. She slipped into the gift from Caesar's mother—a satin and lace white gown that hugged her figure—and slipped into bed. She turned on only one of the lamps that were on either side of her bed. She waited.

He walked into her bedroom and sat by her feet. His gaze never left her face as he slid into bed beside her. The gown she'd only worn for ten minutes was swept from her body by his strong hands. He traced her body with his hands.

Leigh closed her eyes as pleasure racked her body. Then she opened her eyes so she could enjoy her husband's body as much as he enjoyed hers.

"I'm afraid you were right, my darling. This hairstyle could only last one day." He ran his fingers alongside her face, then down her body across her breasts and further down to her thighs. He repeated the action, each time coming closer to where she wanted him to be.

He pulled back the bed covers, leaned over, and turned on the other lamp. He moved over her, and though he was gentle, she gasped when he entered her. It had been a long time since she had been with a man and she had never been with anyone the size of Caesar.

Leigh held onto her husband—for now that's what he truly was. Somehow they would learn to fight for everything that belonged to them.

They were almost at Caesar's Connecticut house, when he looked over at her and frowned. "Stop looking at me like that," Caesar told her.

"Like what?"

"Like you're remembering last night."

"It was a night I will always remember. And I expect a return engagement often."

"If I had known that making love to you would create a brazen hussy . . ."

"Yes?"

"I would have done so on the island."

She laughed and turned to look out at the countryside.

"I get the impression that your mind just switched to something else."

"We just got married. You're not supposed to read my mind for another fifty years."

He didn't have to ask. He knew. Cassiopeia was never far from her mind. Now was the time to tell her—Cassiopeia was theirs.

"I was saving this for later, but I like your other mood better."

"I'm sorry. I didn't mean to start thinking about the salon."

"Don't apologize. It's never completely out of my mind either. But we don't have to worry."

"I'll try not to."

"Jameson Miller wants to address the Board next week."

"What?"

"Don't worry. He'll make his offer and we'll turn it down."

SIXTEEN

As they turned onto a dirt road driveway, Leigh was not prepared for the palatial estate that seemed right for Caesar and at the same time different from her expectations. The Colonial-style house sat on at least an acre of land. Sarito pulled up to the front door rather than the garage. They got out and he quickly unloaded their luggage.

Leigh grabbed her overnight bag and waited for Caesar to open the door. He did and showed her the panel on the inside that controlled all the lights in the house. The two-story cathedral-ceiling foyer just off the livingroom was painted a rich cream that matched the welcome mat. Under Caesar's directions, Leigh turned left and she placed her bag down next to the ivory sofa. There were two straight-back chairs that faced the sofa, giving the room a warm conversation-oriented section. The windows behind the sofa were open with the beautiful trees, lightly dusted with snow in the background. Despite the cold there had been no snow in Manhattan.

"What do you want first?" Caesar asked. "A tour or food?"

Leigh hesitated for a split second and then said, "Food."

Caesar showed her to the powder room and while she washed her hands he strolled into the kitchen. He washed his hands in the sink and then started pulling open the cabinets, grabbing cans, and rifling through the refrigerator. When Leigh joined him in the kitchen, he'd assembled the makings for a hearty soup.

"Can I help?"

"Sure. Grab a cutting board. The knives are in that drawer." He indicated a long drawer under the sink.

Seconds later they were sitting side by side at the yellow pinewood table tossing vegetables into a huge pot. Then Caesar opened some cans of broth, poured them into the pot, and set it on the restaurant-style stove.

"Do you entertain a lot?" Leigh asked.

"I used to. When I first came on board, Cassiopeia was losing money. I gave a few women free hairstyles and then gave a party. Paul didn't think my idea would work."

"I get it. The women who had been to the salon let it be known where they got their hair done, and the next day you had thousands trying to beat down the salon door."

"Not quite thousands, but it was a start."

Leigh realized how little they knew about each other outside of the passion that was always just beneath the surface. Could she really trust him or would he use the revival of the salon as part of his resume to go elsewhere? He said he wanted to stay, but Leigh had seen too many sports stars swear allegiance only to be offered a bigger contract elsewhere. With the change of a few numbers on the contract, the stars were soon swearing loyalty to another team.

If they couldn't save the salon, would it mean their marriage could also be a casualty of the takeover?

"I hate when you do that," Caesar said abruptly.

"Do what?"

"Go off into another world."

"Sorry. I just . . . never mind."

Caesar slammed his fist on the table. "That's what I mean.

You have this little walkabout and you start sending these mixed messages."

"Mixed messages? Why, because I have a private thought?"

"No, because your private thoughts always have to do with the salon."

"Oh, so now you're a mind reader."

"I don't have to be. Tell me I'm wrong. Tell me you weren't thinking about losing the salon."

Leigh ignored him. He was only half right. She was thinking that without the salon she wouldn't have a marriage.

"I'm waiting for an answer."

"Okay. You were right, I was thinking about the salon, but what do you expect? I gave up a very good career to go for this brass ring." There was no way she'd give him any more hold on her heart than he already had. She didn't just want to have the best salon in New York. She wanted to have the best marriage. She wanted that marriage to be more than Stephanie and Paul's. Even Helene had admitted that during the last Board meeting Stephanie had threatened to leave Paul.

"A career you can always go back to. Not much of a loss."

"Thomas Wolfe said it best: 'You can't go home again.' "

"Mark would take you back in a second."

"And I'd be the little admin assistant who thought she could run an empire. Stephanie ran it and so can I."

"Stephanie had Paul . . ."

"No, she had Paul's money. She and Helene only needed money."

"And you need me in the same way."

Leigh's jaw dropped. She hadn't meant it to sound that way. She just wanted to show she could run what she created. But if she said that that was her idea, Caesar wouldn't believe her at this point. He'd just think she wanted her sister's life.

"Damn!" Caesar leaped from the table and rescued their dinner that had started to burn.

They ate in silence. Toward the end of the meal, Caesar looked up and said, "We need to back off a little. We can't seem to find a common ground except . . ."

She knew what he wanted to say: except in bed. "So what do you want to do?"

"Try separate bedrooms for a while."

"Fine."

He put the dishes in the dishwasher and led Leigh out of the kitchen back into the living room, where he picked up her suitcase. She took her overnight bag and followed him up the wide, winding staircase. The door to the master bedroom was open, and Leigh caught a quick glance of the large four-poster bed. She passed two other bedrooms before Caesar turned into a room with a chair, a half chaise, and a queen-size bed occupying most of the space. He quickly showed her the bath that was attached, and also a terrace that could be a great private space in the summer. Now it was completely closed off against the December winds.

That night, after she showered and slipped into the big, lonely bed, Leigh remembered, she hadn't opened her wedding gift from Aunt Helene. It was obviously a book of some kind but Leigh was almost afraid to unwrap it. Something told her that unlike Juliette, her aunt was not happy about the marriage.

Leigh dozed but awakened when her dreams were of the night spent in Caesar's arms. Could they live in the same house and not sleep in the same bed? Leigh didn't think so. Tomorrow she would have to confront him. Tomorrow she would tell him the truth about why she wanted the salon and maybe then she'd be free.

She opened the drawer on her night table and tossed the book in. Christmas was about two weeks away. She'd wait until then. How could she and Caesar be so close one moment and so far apart the next? Why shouldn't she think about the salon? It was still the common denominator in this marriage.

Caesar fared no better at getting a good night's sleep. He berated himself over and over for allowing his feelings to over-rule his quest. He took his frustration out on his pillows as he pounded them and rearranged them several times. Leigh was right. Why shouldn't she think of Cassiopeia? He did the same thing most of the time. It was the other times that bothered him even more. He wanted his wife to be in love with him. How ridiculous. He'd blackmailed her into the marriage. What did he expect? Even as the question formed in his mind, the answer was right behind it. He wanted her to love him as much as he loved her. But it was not the tide to tell her. When he saved the salon and she was secure in the CEO position, then he could ask for her love, because then and only then would she be free to give it. She wouldn't need him for anything else. Until then they'd have to find a way to coexist. They couldn't let anyone know that they were not sleeping in the same bed. Tomorrow he and Leigh would have to talk. There had to be a better way than this.

Back in New York another couple faced the problems of the salon and the marriage of the two people who could topple everything.

JoAnn Desmond sat in her penthouse apartment overlooking Central Park. Her climb had started on the runways of Paris when she was barely seventeen years old and now if anyone learned the truth all of this could be lost. She lifted the glass of champagne to her lips and sipped as she stared into the darkness.

Rick Adams sat across from her strumming his guitar. "They don't know about the money. Why are you so scared?"

They'd been together since the first failed venture with Stephanie and Paul. But Rick and JoAnn wanted more. Never did they suspect the will would be changed. Originally the shares were to be divided evenly between the original partners, Rick, JoAnn, and Helene. When Stephanie and Paul appeared to be splitting up, she'd come up with this living will.

"Because if they dig deep enough, they're going to find out."

"Who's going to dig that deep? The 'newlyweds' only care about getting the salon back on its feet."

"What about Jameson Miller?"

Rick stopped strumming his guitar. "What about him?"

"He wants the salon. He's like a pit bull. He's not just going to go away."

JoAnn was right. Miller had become a thorn in the Board's side ever since he announced his intentions of going after the salon. He didn't even have enough stock, but that fool Hastings had allowed some of his shares to get tied up in his last messy divorce. Not much, but still, it gave Jameson Miller the opening he needed. He could hold onto those few shares and pounce when the salon took a turn for the worse. They might all have to take the money and bail out.

"Well, maybe he needs to be taken care of?"

"Don't even go there. We can't afford another murder that ties too closely to the salon."

She rose from her seat, crossed the floor, and stood by Rick. He moved over enough for her to squeeze into the chair with him. He wrapped his arms around her so he could hold her and play the guitar at the same time. The guitar had been a gift from Paul, when their first album went platinum. "Well, we'd better think of something to distract the man."

"He already has something that's distracting him. A woman."

"Really?"

"I had a little talk with one of the underlings in his office. She says her boss is quite smitten with a new woman and that he's been neglecting business lately."

Rick smiled. This was what they needed. "So if he's got someone, why are you worried about him?"

JoAnn shook her head. Trying to get Rick to read between the lines had always been difficult. Unless it was lit up like a neon sign, he wouldn't have a clue of the problems that any liaison could have on the salon. Whether it was Jameson or the newlyweds. "He's kept her under wraps. No one, not even his closest associates, know who she is. What if they break up? He'd come tearing after Cassiopeia and we wouldn't even know he was back in the game."

"The woman must be very special if she's distracted him

from business. So I guess we'd better find out who she is and see how she fits into our little puzzle."

Rick turned JoAnn's face around and kissed her. The kiss deepened and he put his guitar down as she turned to stretch out her body tightly against his.

"Don't worry, baby," he crooned. "We still have a chance to get rid of all of our excess baggage."

SEVENTEEN

The morning brought no more confidence to Leigh than the night before. She still didn't know how to approach Caesar. She showered, slipped into a comfortable denim dress, and put on her favorite jogging shoes. Before going downstairs, she unpacked.

As she walked down the hall, she took the opportunity to examine the house more thoroughly than she had the night before. Across the hall from her bedroom was another bedroom just as well appointed. There was another bedroom at the opposite end of the hall. Then she came to the glass wall that overlooked the family room below. She saw Caesar reading the paper and sipping coffee. This gave her the courage to look at the master bedroom. The four-poster bed had been made up and Leigh remembered Caesar saying that his mother had insisted on him making the bed every morning. The colors were bold—burgundy, navy, masculine colors that Leigh thought needed a little softening. She left the room and headed downstairs, where she prepared a breakfast of scrambled eggs and bacon in the kitchen then joined Caesar in the family room.

"Good morning."

"Good morning," he replied.

Leigh took the place across from him. He seemed calm. She was calm. It was a now or never situation.

"Caesar, I . . ."

"Leigh, I . . ."

They spoke at the same time.

"Ladies first."

"No. I think the man should get a chance to be first sometimes. You start." She settled in at the table and stared at him as if she didn't want to miss a single word.

"Very well. I think we are under a lot of pressure. We both want Cassiopeia and we want each other also. We just don't know the priority rank."

"You are so right. I don't know why we were fighting."

Caesar smiled and rocked back in his chair. "This is the first time we've been in my territory. In New York you felt safe. There were your friends you could depend on. But now, you're stranded in Connecticut and you have only me to depend on."

"So Dr. Valerian-Montgomery, where did you get your degree?"

"I'm serious. The light didn't go on in my dense brain until about three o'clock this morning."

Leigh nodded. She too remembered staring at the digital clock by her bed as it registered that same time. Perhaps her mind had linked with his. There wasn't anyone she could contact. Stacey flew back to Miami as soon as the reception was over. Aunt Helene did not inspire confidence. And Mark was a friend and former employer but she couldn't tell him that she was failing. He'd have insisted she come back to work for him, and if she'd been scared enough at the time she would have done so.

"What's the remedy for my fear?"

"You need to meet the neighbors and this." He handed her a cell phone. "Now, as for the neighbors, that is a little difficult. They have homes in warm climates and spend the winters away. You'll have to wait until spring."

The wait until spring was the answer Leigh was looking for. Caesar expected this marriage to still be going strong. It was an olive branch that Leigh wanted to grab and hold onto for life. But she'd felt that same way with Marshall Alexander and he'd betrayed her. Though she told herself Caesar was different, she was still frightened of the consequences of being vulnerable.

"I'm going to get another pot of coffee. We have to talk."

She returned with the steaming brew and Caesar indicated the rack at the table that could hold it.

After they each poured a cup, Leigh began.

"When I was in high school I came up with a very special business plan . . ."

An hour later she'd revealed her dream and the nightmare that followed her after that dream was stolen. Leigh felt relieved that she didn't have to hold back anymore.

"My God! The entire salon was your idea?"

Until now, Caesar had considered her obsession with the salon as envy of her sister but now he understood a lot more about Leigh Barrington Valerian Montgomery.

"With very few changes. I thought of hiring a designer to do the uniforms. But that's where you came in."

Caesar remembered that Stephanie had suggested a designer but he wouldn't have it. This was their dream they were putting together. The fewer people involved the better. So he had designed their staff's uniforms.

"All this time, I thought you were jealous of Stephanie and wanted to live her life."

"I admit I was a little jealous. She was petite and beautiful and married to a rock star. I felt like a klutz next to her. Thank God for my grandmother."

"It's good, but you had other skills."

"It's good I couldn't get my hands on my relatives. I would have punched them both out."

"While we're sharing secrets—I was driving the car when my brother was hurt but I've never told anyone about the woman we were fighting over. She was from France. I'd met her when I was visiting my mother and I fell in love. When she learned that I was not the legal heir to the coffee plantation, she began to find excuses why we should not be together."

"She was trying to let you down easy."

"No, she was trying to marry wealth. Once she found out I wasn't it, she moved on to my brother. When I tried to explain, he became belligerent and I turned to him to demand that he stop seeing her. When I looked up, a truck was bearing down on us. I turned the wheel and we slid down an embankment."

"You got a minor cut and he broke several limbs. What happened to the woman?"

"Once she thought that she might be marrying a cripple, she found someone else to pursue."

"How did Esteban handle that?"

"Badly. He felt I'd interfered with his happiness. That I was like our father and did not believe anyone was good enough to be in the Valerian family."

"Oh."

"Yes, he was referring to my mother."

"Who was his mother?"

"It was an arranged marriage." Seeing the look on Leigh's face, he added, "Yes, they still exist. She came from a good family. Unfortunately they did not believe in educating a woman. After Father died, she could not hold onto the land or any of the other businesses. That's where I came in."

"I see we both have skeletons in our closet that we don't want to reveal."

"I was glad I could help, but it is not my life. My life is here."

"I'm curious—you said you bought the house so you could entertain. But why not a pied-à-terre in New York?"

"I didn't want to entertain too often. If I lived in New York, I'd have a never-ending stream of people dropping by."

Caesar stood and stretched. "Let's take a walk around the house and then I think I'm going to take a nap."

A nap sounded so good to Leigh that she could not believe

she'd only been up for a few hours and her eyelids were already getting heavy. She almost dozed off at the table. She stood and yawned but when she closed her eyes she almost toppled over.

"Come on, sleepyhead," Caesar said. "We can do the grand tour later."

He took her hand and led her upstairs to the master suite. She balked at the door but he coaxed her in. "I think we both need sleep and I doubt very seriously that I could l fill any overtures I might make."

"I think I might fall asleep in the middle of one of those overtures and that might give you reason to worry about your . . . talents. But my nightclothes are in the other bedroom."

"Why don't we leave them there for now?"

Leigh turned and faced him. She caught the twinkle in his eye. He didn't want to do anything now but climb into that big bed with her.

He walked to his side of the bed and began to undress. She went to the other side and followed suit. She felt slightly wicked as she climbed into bed nude. She'd never done that before. The sheets were cool but their bodies were hot. They wiggled around until they found a comfortable position, then Caesar took the little key pad from the night table and pressed a few buttons. The room darkened as the drapes closed and the lights went out. Moments later they were asleep.

JoAnn and Rick were not letting a little snow keep them down. They had to prepare a cushion that would keep them above water if Miller got his way. Rick picked up his phone and dialed.

He waited. The phone rang several times before a gravelly voice said 'hello.'

"I've got a proposition for you, Miller."

"I'm listening."

"If you make a run for Cassiopeia and JoAnn and I throw our votes your way, what's in it for us?"

"I don't like to discuss those details over an open line. Perhaps we should meet for lunch."

"I agree. But I need some kind of a good faith gesture."

"I'm not making any guarantees. But I've always taken care of the people who help me along the way."

"When can we meet?"

"My . . . friend is visiting me right now. Let me get back to you."

Rick agreed and hung up, then turned to JoAnn. "This new lady is making Miller forget the rules of a takeover. But that's to our advantage."

"Good. Now if we keep him pointed in the right direction and away from digging up everything on us, we'll be in great shape."

JoAnn rubbed her arms as if she was trying to get warm. "I hope he doesn't tell our partners."

"We'll just deny it. And if he tapes his calls we'll still deny it. JoAnn, we have to look out for ourselves." He noticed that JoAnn was getting little bursts of chills. Probably just nerves.

"I know. I just don't want to be in the line of fire if Leigh and Valerian find out about this."

Rick wrapped his arms around her and pulled her close. "Don't quit on me now. We're almost there."

He also began to make sure that she could never attend any meetings he set up with Miller. If she was getting cold feet now, he'd better make arrangements to secure his position and let her worry about hers.

Helene stood on her terrace and looked at the night sky. It was clear but there were rumors of a snowstorm making its way toward New York. She wondered if Leigh and Caesar would be back by then. She wondered if Leigh had opened her gift. She'd only recently come across the diary. Somehow it had been left in the property room and only recently had an apologetic policeman called her and sent the diary to her.

How could Stephanie allow herself to be lured by so many

men? She'd bought items she didn't need because the salesman was cute. She got involved with projects that someone else had to finish. Her diary told the story. Stephanie had come to hate the salon. She felt it gave Paul access to a class of women he'd never have met as a rock singer. The diary also revealed his infidelities. So many that Stephanie felt she had to have an affair to get back at him. Helene knew it was one of the Board members. She suspected it was Sarito Valerian. Stephanie had done these things because she wanted to be free—free from the salon, free from responsibilities, and free from Paul. During the review of the diary, Helene had seen Sarito's name mentioned but not in conjunction with a liaison. Still, he was such a ladies' man, it could have been him.

Once Leigh saw the description of the affair in Stephanie's own handwriting, then she'd know not to trust men. Then they could run the salon together.

EIGHTEEN

The honeymoon was over the minute the newspaper was delivered. Leigh read the article twice.

> *Ms. Erica Parkson has filed a ten million-dollar lawsuit against the Cassiopeia salon. Ms. Parkson alleges that she was assaulted by one of the stylists and thrown out of the salon while her hair was still wet. She said the assault took place when she questioned an employee about dye that Ms. Parkson alleges was turning her hair shades of pink and purple. No one at the salon could be reached for comment.*

Leigh shook her head and looked up at her new husband.

"So what does this mean?" she asked.

"As it relates to the salon or to Miller?"

"Both."

Sarito sipped the last of his coffee and then poured himself another cup before answering. His voice didn't tremble but his need to think before saying anything spoke volumes. Leigh could tell he was worried.

"It gives us another battle to fight, which will take away from our preparations for Miller."

Leigh slammed the paper down. "I knew we should have fired him. Then at least it would give the appearance of us being in control rather than the staff."

"We'd better get back and do some clever damage control."

"What good would that do? I don't know if the woman saw me but if she did I'm sure her lawyers have a game plan for me." Her voice had taken a slight edge to it and she wasn't trying to hide her anger.

"Don't panic . . ."

"I'm not! But this could have been a closed issue. You just sat there and let Aunt Helene have her way."

Leigh decided not to hide her frustration. She'd been on target and the rest had missed the mark. It was time to stop deferring to her aunt just because she had been the mainstay of the salon during a crisis period. It was Leigh's legacy. It was her dream and was now becoming a nightmare because she needed someone else to complete her power as CEO. She sat back in her chair, folded her arms across her chest, and stared out of the window. Did Stephanie have to put up with this? Did she have to fight or because she was Stephanie Lambert did the Board listen to her without threats or bribes? And yes, she admitted to herself, she had bribed Caesar Montgomery. She knew how badly they both wanted the salon, but rather than give him her proxy she'd been determined to run the organization. Her plans for expansion were slowly disintegrating as each problem turned into a chink in her armor. She didn't know how much more she could take.

* * *

Caesar knew Leigh blamed him for this new fiasco. She had been outvoted on an issue that had come back to haunt them. Still, he felt he was right in not being so quick to fire the stylist. He didn't condone the man's actions but he couldn't prove the customer hadn't pushed the right buttons. The customer wasn't always right but needed to be handled that way.

"What time do you want to leave for the city?" he asked.

She noticed that like most New Yorkers, Caesar called Manhattan 'the city' no matter where they were. "I guess as soon as possible."

"How's thirty minutes?"

"I'll be ready."

Leigh stepped into the shower and let the hot beads of water give her a slight massage, soothing the knotted muscles in her back and neck. The tension was becoming unbearable. She pulled the neatly wrapped package her aunt had given her from the drawer and slipped it into her handbag. Maybe she'd have time to read it on the drive back to New York.

Caesar had come into the bedroom, gathered his clothes, and walked down the hall to the guest room to shower and change.

Thirty minutes later they were pulling the car out of the driveway and heading back to New York. The air had a slight chill, rather frosty, as they pulled onto the expressway. Leigh made a quick call to her aunt and scheduled a board meeting for later that day. Somehow they managed to find things to talk about other than the salon. She thought about the book and decided to read it later, realizing silence only meant they both would get lost in their thoughts and make assumptions about their future. While neither wanted to apologize, both felt that marriage hadn't been the answer to all their problems.

* * *

By the time they put the car in Leigh's apartment's garage and walked over to the salon, the other members of the Board were waiting.

"I think you should know that Jameson Miller's been all over TV saying that the salon is too unique to be run so badly," Jimmy said, his Texas accent more pronounced by his anger.

"And what is the rest of the city saying?" Caesar asked.

"You're not going to believe this," JoAnn said. "We've had twenty cancellations, women protesting the treatment of Ms. Parkson. And we've had fifty requests for appointments with Nigel."

"Some women like dangerous men," Rick said and began to laugh. He made a motion as if he was strumming his guitar. Unlike other members of Paul's band, Rick had never tried for another band. He occasionally practiced to keep from losing his touch but the guitar was mostly history for him.

"It's not funny," Angela yelled. "This Nigel person humiliated someone and you dare think that's funny?"

"Don't get upset . . ."

"She's right to get upset," Leigh interrupted. "I don't care if a hundred women think he's terrific. We're involved with a ten million-dollar lawsuit because of him."

"Calm down, Leigh," Helene said. "No court is going to give her that kind of money over a bad hair dye."

The others found that amusing and bursts of deep, loud, hearty laughter scattered across the room. It lasted a minute before Caesar brought them back to the center of the problem.

"What are we going to do about Nigel?"

"Fire him." Leigh's answer was quick and firm.

"Suspend him for a month without pay," Helene suggested.

"What's our contract with him look like?" Angela asked.

"It's very tight. We can fire him with cause. If his actions mean we can lose business . . ."

"But we have more people wanting to be his client than before," Leigh said.

"True, but he still offended a client and the result of the lawsuit could show cause."

* * *

"Our real issue is whether or not this woman wants the money or something else," Caesar told them in a calm voice.

"Why wouldn't she want ten million dollars?" Leigh asked.

"Because her lawyer had already told her she can't get it. And think about the case. Do you really think a group of average citizens is going to give her the money when all that's involved is a dye job that went wrong?"

"I think if anything sways them it'll be the fact that Nigel pushed the woman out of the salon," Leigh said.

Caesar and Leigh had begun to talk to each other as if the rest of the Board wasn't there. Since they were raising pertinent issues the members fell silent and just listened.

"Did she go to a doctor? Are there pictures of her injuries somewhere?"

"I understand you, Caesar, but what if she's claiming mental anguish?"

"Did she see a psychiatrist or psychologist?"

"You're right. We need to know just what we're fighting before we go into court."

"So let's call our lawyers, and let them talk to her lawyers, and then . . ." Leigh shrugged.

They seemed to have eyes only for each other as they silently apologized for their earlier disagreement. They could work together. They needed each other and Leigh knew that whether or not the marriage worked, the partnership certainly did.

Helene looked around the room. The board members weren't focused on the problem but at the way Leigh and Caesar talked to each other. The way they found a common ground and worked together to find a solution. Not what she expected after Leigh read Stephanie's diary. Or maybe she hadn't read it.

"Are you two going to solve the whole matter or share with the rest of us?"

* * *

Her aunt was not the only one unhappy about Caesar and Leigh's connection. JoAnn had been trying to catch Caesar's eye from the time he had walked into the room and was amazed that he hadn't even noticed her. Despite her relationship with Rick, she couldn't let go of the nagging feeling that Caesar had been the one man she couldn't lure into her circle of men. He had walked away from their brief affair and never looked back. If only she had more power. If only a few of the others would sell out to her. If only Stephanie hadn't changed the will.

The rest of the Board just took their money and ran. They were content with letting the most vocal members like JoAnn, Rick, Jimmy, and Bob make the decisions. They could be easily swayed on a vote, but once she'd approached Kevin about selling his interest and he'd laughed in her face. She listened while the others congratulated Leigh and Caesar. Tomorrow their lawyers would hack away at the figures and soon they would be yesterday's news.

"So I guess that's all the business we have to conduct today," JoAnn announced.

"Not quite," said Angela and she glanced over at Kevin.

Helene saw the furtive looks. "Do we have another romance brewing among the Board?"

"Uh . . . yes and no," Kevin answered.

"What does that mean?" Jimmy asked.

"I know it's not the time to bring this up, but Angela and I are getting married. I've been offered a chance to direct a new series and we're moving back to California. We don't want this anymore. We've received a substantial offer for our stock . . ."

"But the sale has to be approved by the Board," Leigh said.

"Or purchased by another board member," Caesar added.

"Are you asking us to buy you out, man?" Jimmy asked.

Angela and Kevin looked at each other then at the board members.

"We're asking you to approve a sale."

"I don't think this is the time," Helene said. "Can't you wait until this lawsuit thing is settled?"

"No. we can't," Kevin explained. "We have a lot to do before we leave and I have to be there by the first week in March."

"So, it's only December," JoAnn protested. But her mind ran through her assets—could she pull off buying them out to have a whopping 16% of the salon?

"Yeah, you sure handed us a nice Christmas present," Jimmy said.

"Well, it could be a nice present for someone," Angela said, as she looked at Leigh.

She was right. If Leigh acquired their shares she would have enough to run the salon alone. She would be able to make decisions and not have to depend on anyone else.

"That's only if we approve the sale," Caesar reminded them.

Leigh felt it was a reminder to her, that the people in this room could block the sale just to prevent her from having too much power. How far would they go to hold her back?

"I know you want this to be over with as quickly as possible," Caesar told them, "but we have to meet with the lawyers tomorrow, and that takes precedence over everything else. Why don't you wait until Wednesday or Thursday?"

"I don't mind a few days, but I want it settled by the end of the week," Kevin said. Angela nodded, showing they were in agreement.

They adjourned the meeting and went their separate ways. None of the problems seemed insurmountable and Caesar was relieved as he waited by the glass double doors.

Leigh spent some time with Helene. Her aunt's warning about how things worked when there were fewer people involved wasn't new. It was the desperation in her voice that made Leigh listen. She heard that same desperation when JoAnn spoke about the salon. It made her wonder if Helene and JoAnn knew something the rest of them should.

NINETEEN

It was Helene's last comment that disturbed Leigh the most. "So after my little gift, do you know as much as you should about your husband?" She couldn't admit she hadn't read it. Something in it gave Helene a reason to believe that Leigh was in danger, or so her aunt told her. Leigh took the escalator, and as she got halfway down she could see Caesar and JoAnn. The woman was standing much too close to him for Leigh's taste. She watched them as she rode down and just as she reached the last step she saw them embrace. Then she saw Caesar try to slip away from her but the woman was persistent. The shoulder strap bag slipped down her arm. Even from the distance Leigh could tell that Caesar wasn't responding. Once Mark had told her about that. If a man could allow a woman to kiss him and plaster herself against him and not respond at all, it meant he really didn't want her.

Rather than allow her heels to click on the marble floor, Leigh walked on her toes until she was a foot away. Then she let the sound of her heels come down with that familiar sound.

Caesar and JoAnn jumped apart and when JoAnn realized how close Leigh was, it was too late.

"It's not what you think," Caesar told Leigh.

"I . . ." JoAnn started.

"Don't bother trying to apologize or explain, JoAnn." Leigh walked around until she was facing both Caesar and JoAnn. "He's my husband. And I don't like you kissing him. . . ."

"What makes you think that I initiated the kiss?"

"Because it wouldn't have happened if you hadn't. I'm not going to go into hysterics and threaten you. I'm just going to say that if it happens again I'll punch your lights out."

"That's a threat."

"No, that's a promise."

JoAnn stormed off back upstairs. Then Leigh turned to Caesar. "Did I sound wifely enough?"

"Why?"

"Because I don't want you distracted by anything or anyone."

"I want you to know that I'm not attracted to JoAnn."

"Just remember. We have to keep up the appearance of a happy couple."

"Leigh, I thought it was you."

"Me?"

"I heard her coming and I thought it was you. Then when she stepped in front of me, I was surprised. That's the only reason I let her kiss me."

"Right!" She believed him but she wasn't prepared to let him know that.

As Leigh started for the door, Caesar caught her hand and pulled her into his arms. "If I had been kissing her, it would have looked like this."

He wrapped his arms around her and pinned her tightly against his body. His lips teased hers and then became hungry and more demanding.

Why was it like this? Leigh waffled between wanting him desperately and wishing they didn't have the salon always there between them. She was afraid to let herself believe this could become a real marriage. Afraid that no matter how much she loved him, and she admitted to herself that she did, his reason was still the salon not her.

He broke off the kiss. "I think we'd better head for a nice comfortable bed."

"I think you're right."

JoAnn leaned over the railing and watched them. She was too far up to hear what was being said on the lower level. She had her suspicions that the marriage was in name only and that

Caesar would be looking for fun and games on the side. But watching them made her change her mind. This would not be easy to break up. She couldn't wait to tell Rick her suspicions. Caesar Montgomery was in love with his wife. How ironic. She'd bet money that Leigh only wanted the salon. It might be fun to flirt with Caesar—to see their faces when they discovered that Jameson Miller was only days away from getting a piece of Cassiopeia.

"So what do you think of the newlyweds?" Helene asked.

Helene's voice startled JoAnn and she dropped her shoulder bag. The items spilled across the floor. JoAnn quickly grabbed for Jameson Miller's business card. Then she concentrated on her wallet, make-up kit, and a guitar pick.

"I'm sorry. I didn't mean to scare you." Helene waited until JoAnn had scooped up everything and dumped it back into her bag.

"Be honest, Helene. You know they only married so they could control the salon."

"Sometimes a business marriage is better than that foolishness of marrying for love."

"It's great if you can have both."

"If you say so. Why were you spying on them?"

"I wasn't spying. I was waiting for Rick and I just happened to see them." The lie rolled off her tongue easily. Since they'd met with Miller, she'd become accustomed to lying. She just hoped that this would be over soon. She wondered what would happen to Helene when Miller owned the salon. He might keep her. Then again, she thought it might be nice to see that haughty face when she had to clean out her desk and leave the salon forever.

"Do you think this marriage thing will help the salon?"

Helene refused to allow JoAnn to see how worried she was. "If it doesn't, I guess I'll take that world cruise I've been thinking about."

Rick came out of his office, and he and JoAnn kissed. "Ready, hon?"

"Yes, Rick, I'm ready."

They said their good-byes to Helene and left. Outside, JoAnn told him about her attempt to see if Caesar was open to any other proposition. She admitted her failure.

"I think she's in love with him. She was serious about attacking me if she caught me kissing him again."

"Do you think he's in love with her?"

"No," JoAnn lied. Caesar's response had ended the moment he realized that it was JoAnn not Leigh. But she wouldn't tell Rick that part.

"So he can't be pulled over to Miller's side."

"I don't know. I don't care. I think there's only room for you and me in this deal."

They reached Miller's hotel and went in. The desk clerk called the room and gave the phone to JoAnn. She spoke for a few seconds then hung up.

"That's his mistress. She says we can come upstairs."

The suite was a recent make over, from its coffered ceilings to the well-stocked bar to the king-size bed.

Jameson wore a black and red silk dressing gown over pale blue pajamas. He walked over to a chair, motioned for them to sit down, and then explained.

"I've had a long day, so forgive me for being abrupt. What's the boardroom climate?"

"Well, they don't seem to be fighting about whether or not to entertain your offer. Now it's something about the other arenas of their world. Two board members want to sell and that's what we'll be discussing tomorrow."

"There's no way they'll let me pick up those shares," Miller said.

"No, but if we could convince the Board to let us to buy them out, we could be in good shape," Rick told him.

"Ah, now I understand. The more shares you own when I take over, the more chance you have of staying with the new Board I create."

"But with the way things are now, do you really think you could take over?"

Miller laughed. "If enough things go wrong, the faster my offer will become attractive."

When they left Miller, both JoAnn and Rick were thinking about the things that could go wrong at the salon. Things that the Board couldn't control. Things they would have to create.

"You're over him, aren't you?" Rick asked. They were in the cab on the way to JoAnn's apartment.

"Over who?"

"Paul."

"What are you talking about?"

"I've known for some time that you were sneaking off with Paul every chance you got. I didn't mind playing the beard for a while but it was getting a bit old."

"Paul told me he was going back to Stephanie. That was the reason he made the living will the way she wanted."

"And you thought you could change his mind if the will was missing."

"I'd forgotten about the man you hired."

"And then you left the party at the salon early."

"I was so angry, I had to get away. Thanks for saying I was with you."

"We're partners now. We have to stick together this time."

"I know, Rick. I'm going to see this through."

"Right. No breakups until we have the money."

By the time Leigh and Caesar got to her apartment, the events of the day had caught up with them. They started yawning in the elevator and then burst into giggles.

"I am so tired. I can't believe it."

"Well, you did all the driving. No wonder you're starting to feel it."

"I would have let you drive part of the way."

"Sure, and have you bouncing around in the car watching every move I make. No, thank you."

"I wouldn't do that. I'm basically very calm."

Leigh laughed. She remembered the island. How easily he

handled the fact that she knew who he really was. But she'd also seen the way he 'babied' his car.

They parted at Leigh's door and Caesar gently kissed her. She showered and slipped into her robe. She was tired but sleep wouldn't come easily. She picked up a magazine and began thumbing through it. She felt restless. It was not a feeling that she had often. Most of the time she was just too tired to think about anything and fell asleep as soon as her head hit the pillow. Why was tonight so different? There were no answers forthcoming as she shifted, trying to get a better position. The knock on the door was light, almost as if he didn't want her to hear it.

"Come in," she called.

Caesar opened the door and stood there for a moment. He wore a burgundy robe over his black silk pajamas. He glanced at her magazine and smiled. "I felt so sleepy but I found myself just lying there and staring at the ceiling."

"I know. Same thing happened to me. I was hoping to find something to read—that used to make me drift right off. I see you have other colors in your wardrobe besides black."

He laughed. "Gift from my mother."

"Did you want to talk to me about something?"

"No, I was hoping you were in the same dilemma as I am."

"Dilemma?"

"I think I know what's wrong." He came over and pulled back the covers. "I know why we can't sleep." He slid into bed next to her. The comforter on top of them created a cocoon-like feeling. Warm. Restful. Homey.

She let him take the magazine from her and toss it on the night table. Then he pulled her into his arms and laid down. Instinctively she wrapped her body around his and let her head rest on his chest. Her eyelids felt heavy.

"I think we just need to be there for each other sometimes. Like now. No frantic lovemaking. Just a comfortable way to sleep."

Soon Caesar was listening to the rhythmic sound of Leigh's breathing. He could only imagine one thing being more perfect than this. That they were laying here after they had fought off all threats and Cassiopeia was truly theirs forever.

The salon was no longer the issue. Getting rid of Leigh and Caesar had become more important. She was tired of taking a backseat. First Stephanie flaunting her tiny figure and bragging about her rock star husband. She wanted to run the salon to call the shots and to be considered powerful. Those shares should have been divided among the Board. The way they had originally planned it. But Stephanie's will had destroyed that chance. Only their deaths could have done this. If only she'd selected the correct tape, the old will would still be in place. If they hadn't died, she would have convinced Stephanie to change the will back. Now Leigh felt it was her right to take her turn at the helm and Sarito wanted to help. How could he do this? It was better when there were only the five of them.

TWENTY

"May I offer a suggestion?" Juliette had listened to her son and daughter-in-law bounce ideas around about the things that were going wrong and why. They'd forgotten she was there until she spoke.

"What do you suggest. Mother?"

"That you stop wondering what's happening. Obviously someone, or perhaps more than one person wants Cassiopeia, the building, or maybe just money."

"Jameson wants the building, but I think he's started looking at how profitable it could be. So who wants money?"

"How about someone on the Board?" Juliette offered.

"Your mother may have a point."

"Who on the Board might need money?"

"Probably everyone," Caesar said. "I've heard rumblings before about taking the money Miller's offering. I think Helene wants the salon to stay as it is. But she'd like the rest of the Board to disappear."

"My aunt hasn't gotten over Stephanie's death. I think she sees it as some sort of legacy."

"No matter," Juliette waved her hand. "You and Sarito must work together as a team. If you show any signs of problems then you are lost. So what you must do is see if money is more important to some of the other board members and buy them out," she suggested.

"We'd like to Mother, but we can't afford to do that. If we make the offer I know what the others will do."

"Try to get more money than the next. I think Rick would hold out for a long time, let you try to buy him out, and then just simply say he doesn't want to sell. Of course JoAnn might sell her shares to you, darling."

"Don't start."

"Start what?" Juliette refilled her coffee cup and returned to the living room.

"Leigh . . ." Caesar warned.

"He sounds ominous, tell me quickly."

"I just happened to surprise them. She was plastered against him like a wet rain coat."

"And what were you doing?" Juliette turned to her son.

"Trying to discourage the lady gently."

"Too gently. I warned her that kissing him again wasn't in her best interest."

"She wasn't even jealous. She just did it for a little show."

"Why weren't you jealous?"

"She's not his type," Leigh began.

"And what type am I interested in?"

Stephanie, Leigh thought. She couldn't explain it. It just popped into her head. She never realized how much Juliette was like Helene and Stephanie. Tiny. Beautiful. That was his type.

"You haven't answered me." Caesar's voice broke through her trance.

"You like to pursue, to be the aggressor."

"Umm, I think she's right, Sarito."

"Well, there's always that one woman who makes a man forget . . ."

He didn't get to finish his sentence as Leigh threw a tiny pillow from the sofa at him.

"Now, children, let's get back to our mission. Who is the most likely target for you to buy out."

"Bob Hastings."

"Why?"

"I hear rumors that he and his wife are having difficulties living in New York. She wants to go back to California."

"Where did you hear that?" Leigh asked.

"Darling, women tell their hairdressers more than they think. One of the stylists says that she constantly complains about New York and how much she misses California."

"Ah ha!" Juliette whooped. "You should try to get his shares right away."

"Mother, they're just rumors. Bob still likes New York. She's his fifth wife anyway."

"What's that supposed to mean?"

"That he might change wives before he gives up his business holdings."

"Well, that's for you two to find out. I must rush off. I have a dinner engagement."

"With?"

"Never mind. You are too choosy where I'm concerned. I may never find another husband with your interference."

"Good for you. Don't tell him anything." Leigh winked at Juliette.

Nothing Caesar could do or say could convince her to reveal her companion. After she left, Leigh and Caesar talked about

Juliette's idea. Suppose they could buy someone out. It would give them more power and less people to fight on the Board. After all, the original group had only five members.

"There's only one thing I absolutely have to know," Caesar said.

"What's that?"

"Do you have anything under that jacket and is that single button all that's holding it together?"

"That's two questions."

He sat next to her on the sofa and put one arm around her shoulders. He stretched his other arm across her waist and laid his hand on the button.

"Answer either question?"

"The answer is no."

"Interesting to find out which question you answered." He opened the button and found there were three hidden snaps that held the jacket closed. "Ah, it's no, the button isn't the only thing holding the jacket together. So that must mean you have nothing on under it." He gently peeled back the jacket and found she was ensconced in a lycra body suit.

"Now you really didn't believe that I didn't have on anything under this jacket, did you?"

"Why not?"

"I'm too curvy to go without support."

"Maybe." He helped her out of the jacket and slid the body suit off her shoulders.

The phone rang. "Don't answer it," he said.

"I hadn't planned to," she responded.

They let the phone ring until the answering machine picked it up. By that time they were already in their bedroom oblivious to the urgent call from Helene.

Hours later, they decided to raid the refrigerator. They were munching on toasted almond ice cream when Leigh played her messages back and realized she hadn't done so all day.

The first was a message from Stacey about a charity event and that she expected to see both of them.

The last was Helene.

"Leigh. Where are you? Bob Hastings's wife filed for divorce. He says he has to sell his stock to bail out."

"I wonder what this is going to cost us?"

The Board assembled quickly and waited for Bob. He was locked up with his lawyers trying to figure out a way out of the situation.

"Can't believe the man got married in California and didn't have a prenuptial agreement," Jimmy slammed his fist on the table.

"Well he thought he'd found true love," Angela offered.

"The man had four other chances." Jimmy found Bob's actions irresponsible.

After they tossed around the possibilities for a short time, Bob came in.

Leigh couldn't stop the barrage of questions that were leveled at the man. Finally she banged on the desk.

"Let the man talk and then we'll kill him."

"Thanks, Leigh," Bob said and laughed. "Although I don't know why you'd want to kill me."

"What's this we hear about you not having a prenuptial agreement?"

"Jimmy, where did you get that? I've been married too many times not to know how to secure my fortune. What there is left of it anyway."

"So you do have a prenup?"

"Ironclad."

"And the Cassiopeia stock?"

"I've been thinking about selling it. Look guys, I can't go rounds with Jameson Miller. I wanted something that would be simple to control. I thought the salon would be a breeze."

Leigh nodded. She understood what he meant. When she had conceived the idea and again when she became CEO, she thought it would be easy. But one problem had led to another and one solution had created another problem. If she wasn't so determined to make it work, she, like Bob, would be throwing in the towel. How did Stephanie take it?

"I'm telling you now I'll take the best offer."

Leigh left the room for a few minutes, then returned, and they continued to question Bob. The report of no prenuptial agreement had come from somewhere. Bob assumed it was because only his stocks and land outside of California was covered.

"Are you sure you can do this? What about the divorce?"

"The prenup covers it. The lady wants cash like the others and the house in Malibu. Stock doesn't interest her."

Relieved they wouldn't have to worry about an outsider getting his hands on Cassiopeia stock, they made their offers. The Board was shocked when Leigh's bid turned out to be the highest.

The rest of the Board approved the sale. Now Leigh and Caesar owned 57% of Cassiopeia. Leigh was delighted. The more control, the easier it would be to make decisions.

"Where did you get the money?" Caesar asked as soon as the room cleared.

"From two very reliable sources."

"Same question. Or maybe I should just guess. You called Mark."

"Yes, Mark was one of the people I called."

"Just what is your relationship?"

"You aren't jealous, are you?"

"I want to know where I stand. He seems to always be there when you need help."

"Mark is a friend. And if you must know, I made a second call. To your mother."

"My mother is giving you money?"

"Only if Mark doesn't come up with the full amount."

"I can't believe you called my mother."

"She happens to be a very wise woman and you should listen to her more."

On one hand he was glad that Leigh and his mother were getting along so well. On the other, he sometimes felt that Leigh would do anything to keep Cassiopeia.

Rick and JoAnn were in her office since it was the furthest from Leigh's.

"What the hell happened?" Rick asked.

"I didn't expect anyone to be able to come up with the money so quickly."

"We should have made a bid."

"Right, and they would know we got the money from Jameson Miller."

"How?"

"Miller isn't about to kick away a measly 5 percent. I thought I'd get money from another source."

"Maybe not Rick, but I think he'd look at it as five percent that he had."

"Let me worry about Jameson." He turned and loped down the hall to the elevator.

It had not worked out for the better. Jameson was furious when they told him about the clause and what had transpired.

"And neither of you thought to give me a call? I would have helped you buy another five percent. This isn't just business. This is a war. The next time, I fully expect you to get in touch with me. So what's in store for the Board?"

"There's some charity event. Everyone's who is anyone is going to be there."

"Make sure I get invited. Then maybe I can convince another Board member to sell me his or her shares?"

Rick and JoAnn left Miller to his musings. They were glad they escaped with just a lecture and they were still part of the

deal. When Jameson took over, he would know they could provide a lot of insider information.

They wanted to be as discreet as possible. If the venture failed
then they could still be part of the organization and no one
would know that they had ever schemed against the Board.

Somehow they had to get the ball rolling. JoAnn said she'd
talk to Gayla. The woman knew a lot about the people who
came to the salon and probably just as much as the people who
owned it.

TWENTY-ONE

Leigh sat next to a Park Avenue matron who told her over
and over how very upset she was that the Real Estate Board
had chosen a cold month to have their annual networking affair.
She still remembered when only the commercial agents traded
information. Now they were into the affordable housing kick
and gave these dinners to help the homeless.

Their proposal was to fix abandoned houses for the homeless
to live in while they got back on their feet. Leigh wondered if
it would be better to find a way to give the money to the homeless instead of having these benefits to raise mostly to give to
the homeless. Somehow she didn't think buying a new dress
was the way to help. She was relieved when Caesar stood up
and held out his hand as he silently asked her to dance.

Tonight she wore a Vera Wang dress. The simple lines were
always flattering to her figure, even though it was a little more
curvy than the actresses who wore the designer's clothes.

Caesar was one of those men who looked good in jeans and

elegant in a tux. Cameras flashed as they danced. Leigh found the music too restraining. She wished they were back on the island and she could do a wild, hip-shaking rhumba instead of this pseudo waltz.

"What's the matter?"

Leigh shook her head. "Nothing."

"Nothing? I think you are not telling the truth."

She laughed. He sounded so much like his mother, using long sentences instead of the Americanized short cuts.

"Why are we suddenly on the A-List? I got another bushel of invitations from the high society types."

"I guess they want to rub shoulders with the front page set. After all, everything we do seems to end up there."

"I've turned down half of them but a few seemed interesting."

"Well let me look them over. They may be people we don't want to be around no matter how 'interesting' they sound."

By the time they got back to the table the rest of their party had joined them. The matron was now telling the same story to them as she'd told to Leigh.

Stacey wore tuxedo pants topped with a cream-colored satin blouse that came down to her knees. Her date was working on the movie with her. He was taller than Stacey and must have weighed two hundred pounds. Leigh made a note to ask her friend about the man. He seemed quite attentive.

Juliette had joined them and surprised everyone by showing up with Mark Westinghouse. They'd met at the wedding but neither had given the impression they were interested in each other. As always, Juliette stood out in a crowd. She wore a white pullover dress with a lace bodice that made her look waif-like. The matching jacket was long and hung well below her hips. She looked as stunning as always.

Leigh gave her mother-in-law and Mark a kiss and sat next to Juliette so that the Park Avenue matron could bend Caesar's ear for a while. The women talked for a few minutes before Mark swept Juliette out on the dance floor.

"They make a nice looking couple," the matron said. Leigh

agreed. When the matron left to shmoose with acquaintances, Caesar leaned over and whispered, "Don't get your hopes up."

"Why not?"

"My mother lives too much on the edge of trouble to fit into Mark's world."

"You don't know for sure that she hasn't decided to settle down."

"I've been through enough stepfathers to know that she isn't happy if she isn't on the edge of danger."

"But she waited until you were an adult before she left the man who raised you."

"I know. I don't think she wants to be tied to that kind of life. If she can't decide tomorrow to fly off to Paris and then go to Cannes the next day, she will become more and more miserable."

"She's so sweet. I was hoping to get to know her better."

"We'll see."

The things he said about Juliette made Leigh wonder what kind of childhood he had. Her grandmother had been her anchor and then Mark had taken over that role. His stepfather had held them together. What made Juliette the way she was?

Leigh found herself greeting people she'd met at the last charity function. Was that all they did? She felt as if someone was watching her. Her eyes darted around the room but people seemed involved in their own little groups. No one seemed out of place and yet the feeling returned again and again.

She watched from the shadows. Leigh and Caesar. Juliette and Mark. Laughing and dancing. Having fun while the salon went downhill. Business had picked up, but they were mostly tourists and others who wanted to get a glimpse of the celebrities the board members had become. That wouldn't last long. Like most scandals, it would be replaced with whatever the media found more interesting. Then where would they be? Still struggling. Jameson Miller was the way out of all of this. The man had enough money to float the salon for years. And besides, when he took over, he'd need knowledgeable people to help him run it. She wasn't worried about that. She just didn't want Leigh and Caesar to bankrupt them before the takeover. Not even their 57% would be able to save them if a few more little problems cropped up. They'd be gone and she'd still be on the Board. That would be sweet revenge since Leigh and Caesar wanted Cassiopeia so badly.

The lights flickered, indicating it was time to start the fashion show. For the next hour they watched men and women strut down a makeshift runway. Halfway through, Juliette asked Leigh if JoAnn and Angela were modeling.

"I expect to see Angela in the next group. She modeled sportswear for most of her career. JoAnn was supposed to be here but she begged off at the last minute. Something about a personal crisis."

"So where is the rest of the Board?"

"Probably scattered around the room. Everyone got an invitation but I don't think we wanted to make this a team effort."

"I understand."

They watched the rest of the show and applauded their favorite designers, but all were relieved when it was over. Angela had modeled three outfits. She still held her own with the new faces that were destined to be just as famous, if not more so.

During the next dance session Leigh was shocked to see Jameson Miller approach Mark and ask if he could dance with Juliette. To Leigh's dismay, Mark nodded his consent.

"Why did you say it was okay?"

Mark patted her hand. "You have to understand a woman like Juliette. She's still of the old school. Use one man to make another jealous."

"And you don't mind that my mother's using you?"

"Caesar, she's a fine woman. Not my type, though. At least not long term. I think she's met her match in Miller."

"I hope not," Caesar said.

Leigh watched Jameson whirl Juliette around on the floor.

As much as she liked Mark and hoped that he and Juliette would fall in love, she could tell that it was not to be.

After a few songs, Jameson Miller returned Juliette to Mark and went back to his table. Leigh could tell that Juliette was more than attracted to him. She tried to pretend that everything was all right, but her hand was shaking as she picked up the champagne glass and made a toast.

Stacey tapped Leigh and they made their escape to the ladies' room.

"I can't believe it," Leigh said. "Something's going on with Juliette and Miller."

"Don't get yourself upset until you find out the truth."

The door opened and Juliette Montgomery entered.

"Before you say anything, Leigh," Juliette began. "Let me try to make you understand."

"Understand what? That you're sleeping with the enemy." Leigh knew she was right when she saw Juliette's face.

"I didn't mean for it to happen."

"Caesar and I have been killing ourselves and you're giving out trade secrets."

Juliette shook her head. "Jameson says he won't actively try to take the company but if you don't know how to hold onto it he will step in. I'm . . . what is the saying, between a rock and a hard place."

"It's obvious you believe Miller. I don't and Caesar and I will not let him have Cassiopeia."

"I knew he wouldn't understand. I thought I'd join you and give Sarito time to talk to Mark."

"What do you think he'll say to Mark?" Stacey queried.

" 'What's wrong with my mother? She wants a boy instead of a man.' "

"What would your answer to that be?" Leigh asked.

"I know Sarito thinks Jameson's too young for me. But for the first time in years a man is listening to my opinions. He's interested in what's inside my brain. And he's fun. The only thing we don't talk about is his business with Cassiopeia."

Leigh understood. "You got caught in your own trap. You

went to him hoping to find a way out for Caesar and me. But you found something you wanted even more."

"I feel stupid, but at the same time I know it's right." Tears filled her eyes. "I don't want to hurt Sarito but I need to be happy also."

"He's not that much younger."

"Fifteen years is a lot. I may give my official age as fifty-one, but I'm fifty-three."

"He's thirty-eight. Old enough to know what he's doing."

Other women entered the ladies' room and Leigh and Stacey left Juliette there to pull herself together.

"Where's Juliette?" Mark asked.

"She'll be along," Stacey answered as she tapped her date on the shoulder. "I think we'd better be going. I have a go-see tomorrow."

After they left, Mark leaned over and asked, "What's a go-see?"

"It's like an interview for a job. Stacey will meet with some people who will decide if she's right for the ad or commercial."

"She'd be great in a shampoo commercial," Mark said.

"Or an ad," Leigh sounded surprised at her own voice.

"What kind of ad?" Caesar asked cautiously.

"For Cassiopeia."

"You're kidding?"

"No. You always said that she couldn't get many jobs because of her hair color and texture."

"It's too noticeable."

"For anything but a hair commercial."

Juliette had returned to the table but only heard the last sentence.

"What about a hair commercial?"

"I think we should put something together at the salon and Stacey should be one of the models."

"I'm not sure if this is a good idea, darling. Let's think about it."

Even as he said it, he knew it was too late. Leigh had made up her mind.

"We'll call it 'Cassiopeia's Answer to a Bad Hair Day.' "

"That sounds marvelous," Juliette chimed in.

"Ladies, we'll talk about it tomorrow." Caesar told them.

They said goodnight at the curb and walked to their respective limos. Leigh pulled out a pen and pad from her evening bag and began writing. There was no sense in trying to talk to her. She'd made her decision and there was nothing he could do but go along with it.

He refused to admit the idea sounded good. He'd been around long enough to know that it might not work, but if it did, it would be the best publicity they could hope for now.

When they got home, Leigh was still writing. She put her pad down and replaced it with a tape recorder as she performed her nightly ritual. She talked as she cleaned the make-up from her face and patted on the astringent. She was so excited about it she carried the recorder into the bedroom.

Caesar gently pulled it from her hand mid-sentence. He snapped it off and put it on his side of the bed.

"I guess that means I'm through planning for the night."

They were startled by the buzz from the concierge. Caesar muttered a few expletives before he picked up the phone.

"Yes. Let her come up." he said. He dropped the phone back into the cradle. "My mother."

From the time they'd left the party it had been an unspoken agreement not to talk about his mother and Jameson Miller. They pulled on robes and went into the living room to wait.

Juliette was much more subdued than usual as she entered their apartment. "I need to explain about Jameson."

"No, Mother you don't have to explain," Caesar's voice was low pitched but the anger crept in. "We could lose everything but that shouldn't interfere with your fun."

"It's not like that. I went to see him on your behalf . . ."

"I don't need you begging for me."

Leigh watched Caesar as the anger left his body and was

replaced by pain. He adored the woman and now her intervention may have been just the thing Miller needed to succeed.

"Maybe this is not the time to talk about it," Leigh suggested.

"Oh no. Let's be fair and hear her side of the story." Caesar sat on the sofa and crossed his arms across his chest. Leigh sat next to him. Juliette remained standing.

"I know you think that I don't know what I'm doing. I didn't get this far in life and not know how to read people. I went to see Jameson about Cassiopeia. We found we had mutual acquaintances and we liked each other. Sarito, you of all people should know that what is in the newspapers is not always true."

Caesar nodded as he remembered how many times he'd been linked with starlets, actresses and socialites.

"Are you saying that Miller doesn't want Cassiopeia?" Leigh asked.

"No. He wants the location. He just isn't actively going after it."

"What's he doing then?" Caesar asked.

"He's waiting until the board self-destructs. He says you are not a cohesive group and that you will not be able to pay off the debts to hold onto the salon."

"Juliette, he could tell you anything."

"That's true but he holds several of the loans the board made to renovate and he could call them in any time. He could have owned Cassiopeia when Stephanie and Paul were . . . died."

"Is that something we could verify, Caesar?"

Juliette opened her small beaded handbag and pulled out a folded envelope. She handed it to Caesar. He opened it and read it.

"What does it say?" Leigh asked.

"It says that my mother is telling the truth. Miller could call in the loans at anytime."

"So what is he doing, playing cat and mouse with us. Juliette what makes you think he won't just lead you on and still take everything we own?"

Juliette's chin came up as she looked directly at Leigh. "I am not a foolish woman. I would not have just believed anything a man told me. I have this." She pulled another paper from her bag and handed it to Leigh.

Leigh perused the document and then handed it to Caesar who did the same. "So Miller gave you a notarized letter saying he would not call in the loans for another ninety days. This gives us enough time to find someone to lend us the money. How does he know we won't go to another venture capitalist who will just take a piece of the salons for his fee?"

"He doesn't. You . . . we should worry about what he does know. Someone on the board wants him to buy it. There is a traitor among us. That's what is most important."

"Miller knows who it is, why didn't he tell you?"

"He will let you have a fighting chance to find out for yourself and save your business. He's not going to just give you the salons on a silver platter. I'm leaving but I just wanted you to know that I am not aiding the enemy."

Juliette left and Leigh and Caesar went back to bed.

"Do you believe her?" Leigh whispered.

"Yes, but I still think that Miller is the enemy. Now I think he has help from someone on the board. We'll have to be very careful. Don't tell anyone about this extension, not even Helene."

"I wasn't planning to."

"Let's just take things in a normal routine. We need to get out of debt and I think I'll talk to my brother. If I can't save the salon, I'll give you my ten percent and let you make the best deal you can with Miller."

Leigh lay in the darkness long after Caesar fell asleep. If he couldn't save it he was going to give up any profit from it. She knew how much it took for him to even think of asking his brother for money. He'd never done that before. He'd protected his father's heir and held the plantation together. He'd never taken a penny from them, but he was willing to do this for Cassiopeia. She snuggled against his sleeping form. No, he was doing this for her.

TWENTY-TWO

Leigh ran her plans by the Board and they were ready for any good publicity. Everyone got involved in some way. Stacey screamed when Leigh called her.

"Great. A show that will not make me wear wigs or try to tone down my hair."

They planned it for February 14th so it would be a Valentine's wish. They hired Jennifer Chalmers, a well-known image consultant to work with them. Leigh wanted it fast and good and Jennifer was the best. Her flawless make-up and her business suits did not disguise her sense of fun. She loved what she did. She worked hard at it. In fact, she warned them that she was a hard task master and she proved that comment right as she started ordering the staff around. Jennifer had been in the business for fifteen years. She knew what looked good on her clients. A few designers came to Leigh with ruffled feathers when she eschewed their clothes for lesser-known designers.

Caesar became Sarito Valerian again, combing the most troublesome hair into sleek, manageable styles. The newspapers picked up on the event and reservations came in so fast that in three days they were sold out. In one short month they had created an event people would be talking about for a long time.

The big day arrived and the stage was set. Leigh was so nervous, she needed Caesar to help pull her together. She chose a velvet hunter-green dress with tiny diamond chips as buttons and a white lace collar. Caesar presented her with a small bouquet that she carried on stage as she acted as mistress of ceremonies.

The minute she walked into the room, there were soft whispers since she'd had Caesar style her hair the same way as he had for the wedding.

"Ladies, have you ever had a bad hair day? Have you ever said, 'Why don't I cut it all off and wear a wig?' Have you ever thought just once that men were lucky because they didn't have the problems with their hair that you have with yours? Then this is where you should be."

As the people gathered, they had been asked to fill out profile cards much like the ones used by the salon. While Leigh made the introduction speech, Caesar quickly ran through the cards and selected three candidates.

One by one, models came on stage and on a projection screen they showed how they had looked when they came into Cassiopeia. Then pictures took them step by step through their transformation.

In the middle of the show, Caesar coaxed the people he selected to participate in a makeover. He selected the first woman because her hair was pulled back in a bun and she had the graying hair called salt and pepper—more salt than pepper. He also picked a high school student whose mother was there and allowed her to participate, and an average working woman.

While Stacey pranced around the stage showing off her coppery curls that had been pulled into a manageable french twist, Caesar was off stage working frantically getting the women from the audience ready. Then when he was finished, Jennifer took over. She slipped over to Bergdorf's and picked up a dress, shoes, and jewelry for each of them.

Leigh was grateful when Gayla signaled to her that the women were ready.

"We've shown you many different styles today, but I know you're saying, 'That's fine for models but what about the average working woman' or 'I go to school—what's in it for me' or

'I just don't have the time.' Remember our three people from the audience? What do you think now?"

Gayla led the women on stage to tremendous applause from the audience. The show was a rousing success according to the survey cards the people filled out. The next day the newspapers confirmed their success. Although one reporter mentioned the pending lawsuit, the reviews were great.

"The Cassiopeia Salon opened its doors today to the world of makeovers. Showing before and after shots, models danced along the makeshift ramp as if they were on high fashion European stages. The highlight was when three unsuspecting women got a Jennifer Chalmers clothing makeover and a Sarito Valerian hairstyle. Valerian, as you know, retired several years ago and recently wed the CEO of Cassiopeia, Leigh Barrington."

The phones started ringing the minute people read their morning papers. At last Cassiopeia seemed back on track. They would try to settle the lawsuit out of court and that way they could concentrate on making the salon better. Leigh had a lot of ideas on that.

There were calls for interviews with Leigh and more calls for Caesar to become a stylist again. Leigh accepted her calls while Caesar declined his.

The mood of the salon changed. Leigh hadn't realized how low spirited the staff had become, not knowing from one day to the next if they had a career or if it was time to hit the unemployment line.

Leigh was practically dancing in her office as she read still another review about their presentation. Helene had joined her but was not as sure about the turnaround.

"The public is too fickle at this point. They still might turn on us."

"I know. But I just feel so good that we did something they liked," Leigh said, as she recalled

Leigh knew Aunt Helene was right. It was a small success. There were still a few hills to climb before they could feel safe from people like Jameson Miller.

* * *

Across town, Jameson Miller threw the paper across the breakfast table. Fortunately he was dining alone and no one saw his disgust, except for his butler who would never reveal the secrets of the Miller household. By the time he appeared in public, he would be the calm, takeover king the papers said he was.

He couldn't cry on Juliette's shoulder either. He knew how torn she was to have her lover and her son fighting over the same company. Why hadn't the two 'inside' people called to tell him what was going on? The doorbell rang. A few minutes later his butler escorted JoAnn and Rick in.

"I've seen the papers so there's little you can tell me. Who came up with the idea?"

"Leigh. But she still has that lawsuit, and there are so many other things that could happen."

"No matter. I'm not going after the salon anymore."

"What? You can't be serious that after all the fighting for that scrap of space, you're just going to walk away from it." Rick couldn't believe his ears.

"The one thing I've learned is that when you go after something you get it or you try until you realize it's hopeless."

"Mr. Miller, we've put ourselves on the line for you," JoAnn told him.

"I know. But the little lady has luck on her side and I'm going to walk away from this one."

"So when's the announcement?"

"Oh, I don't plan to tell them."

"I get it," Rick said and laughed. "You want them to always be looking over their shoulders."

Miller shrugged. He didn't care what they believed. He wasn't going after the salon again. When someone bounces back as quickly as Leigh Barrington, it may mean to move on. She holds all the cards this time. But he intended to let them think that he was still after them.

They left his penthouse and strolled down Fifth Avenue toward the salon.

"I can't believe that twit came up with this idea," JoAnn fumed.

"It doesn't matter. Look at the bright side. If the salon's a success then we'll be in good shape anyway."

"I didn't plan to live in New York after the takeover."

"What are you trying to pull?"

"Nothing. I just wanted to use the money to buy a little house away from the city."

"And you didn't think about letting me know?" He grabbed her arm and then realized his loud voice had alerted passersby. He cast a furtive glance around him and then released her.

"There's got to be a way."

"Let's go back to the salon."

They saw a white limo, the kind that Miller had, and waited. Unaware she was being watched, Juliette Montgomery waited untill the chauffeur opened the door and let her out. Then she walked up to the building and was greeted by the doorman.

"Now it makes sense. Sarito's mother has convinced Miller to back off," said JoAnn.

"But how?"

"It doesn't matter. She did. I just know it. I've been hearing rumors about them having a little rendevous but I never believed it. Since Miller could have his choice of women there's probably a very good reason he picked her."

Rick nodded. "She could inadvertently provide information that would help him in the takeover and he wouldn't need us."

"The snake. He's still interested in the salon and we'd better get ready for him."

Upstairs, Juliette was being shown in by the butler, who left after inquiring if she wanted breakfast and hearing her refusal.

Jameson walked over to her and removed the wrap-around sunglasses she was wearing.

"I don't think it's sunny enough for these." He studied her swollen eyes. "What's the matter?"

"I can't continue seeing you. It's hurting my family."

"Not much, in case you haven't seen the papers."

"I've seen them. That's why we have to end our relationship. Leigh and Sarito are working themselves into the ground trying to hold onto the salon."

"And they're doing an excellent job. I just finished reading about their latest success."

"But if you keep going after them, then sooner or later you'll wear them down. Because that's how you are when you want something."

He ushered her to a seat at the table, even though she had said she didn't want to stay. He poured her a cup of coffee. All the time she was telling him good-bye he was keeping her there.

"True. I go after what I want. I drop what I don't want."

"Then we have to stop this."

"No, we don't. I've decided that I want something else instead of the salon."

"Really?" She was so relieved. "What are you setting your sights on now?"

"You."

TWENTY-THREE

The feeling was one of victory all over the salon. They had met the challenge of a takeover and they were in good shape to find a white knight. They could fight back and that sent a wave of relief throughout the Board.

It gave Caesar another idea. Perhaps his marriage wasn't such a bad idea. Maybe they needed to get away—go back to the island. Mark was involved in a big negotiation with the NBA and a sophomore at St. John's University. He wouldn't be using the beach house, and if no one was using the company jet, now was the time. In fact, it would show how much confidence they had in running the salon. Before he found a reason to stay in New York, he called Mark.

Late that evening as he and Leigh were eating dinner at her place he told her his plans.

"We can't just leave."

"Sure we can."

"But what if something happens?"

"For example?"

"If Miller makes a move on the Salon."

"We can be back within hours. I think we need this time together."

Leigh had wondered every now and then if she would still have a marriage after the takeover threat was gone. She felt this was Caesar's way of saying yes. And she wanted this marriage to work. She had fallen in love with her husband.

Caesar alerted the pilot and then the Board. Almost everyone encouraged it except for Helene and JoAnn. Both felt that it was too soon to celebrate. But the majority always ruled and they were headed for paradise.

The jet landed on the same private runway as before, and since they had opted for just a few clothes, they found it easy to unload their own baggage and jump into the hired car they had waiting. The last time Leigh had been here she was unsure of her life; this time she was positive that everything would work out. They whisked though customs and Leigh didn't have the old feelings of being treated a certain way because she had money. That was always going to exist—she might as well enjoy it when it came but try not to abuse it.

As they left the airport Leigh relaxed even more. It was going to be great not to think about the salon for the whole week.

"How did your mother feel about us leaving the States?"

"She was ecstatic. I'm not sure that's a good thing."

"Oh, you aren't going to spend this week wondering what she's up to."

"No. My mother is going to do whatever she decides and it's time I faced that. I may not like it but I don't have a say in the woman's life. Especially not her love life."

Leigh smiled. She was so glad to hear that. She had liked Juliette from the start and there was nothing flighty about her. She'd been very honest when she said that she knew the value of her beauty. She told Leigh to know the value of her brain. Leigh hadn't deliberately done so, but somehow she'd managed to use her brain and get Cassiopeia some good publicity.

It was obvious that they needed this trip when she turned to show Caesar something that struck her fancy and heard his light snore. She hoped he wasn't going to sleep the whole week. She remembered vacations where she'd done just that. She'd worked so hard the week before she went on vacation making sure that everything was in order and that they'd be able to find any forms or reports they needed, that she was exhausted when she got home. She had planned to catch up on movies, plays, and buying some things for the apartment, and all she did was sleep.

When she saw the pink sands of the beach, she wanted to jump out and run along the edge of the ocean. She resolved to do that as soon as they put their clothing away. Caesar woke up when the car stopped at its destination.

Leigh was surprised to see a woman on the steps of the beach house. She was medium height with her salt-and-pepper hair in dreadlocks. As Leigh approached, she realized the woman seemed so familiar.

"Welcome back to our island," she said. "I'm Cynthia. Mark asked me to make sure everything is in order for you."

Caesar helped Leigh from the car, and as she got closer, she realized why the woman seemed so familiar. There was a picture on Mark's desk—he was standing next to a huge fish he'd caught and she was standing next to him. When Leigh asked him about the woman, he'd been evasive. So maybe Mark hadn't been spending time in the beach house alone. But she wasn't here to dig into Mark's life. She was here to enjoy her own.

Leigh followed the woman into the house while Caesar followed with their two dufflebags. It was then she realized that her clothes were sticking to her body. She'd been so wrapped up in the beauty of the island that she hadn't felt the sun beating down on her.

Cynthia pointed out some new amenities that were added shortly after Leigh left the island and then, pleading other work, she left Caesar and Leigh alone.

"So what do you want to do first?"

Leigh giggled.

"What's so funny?"

"I thought of this joke about these two men returning from war and deciding to ski across the mountains home. One asked the other what he planned to do first. The second man said he was pulled away from his wedding and put on a plane to fight. He didn't spend one night with his bride. The first man said he understood. 'What's the second thing you're going to do?' The man said, 'Take off these skis.' "

"I like the way that man thinks."

They closed the shutters to block off the sun, showered, and crawled into bed. This was going to be a real honeymoon.

When they woke up they showered again and dressed in the only evening wear items they'd brought along.

Caesar hadn't given up his black and it still gave him an air of mystery. Leigh chose a pink sun dress and hot pink sandals. They walked over to the restaurant where they'd dined before she found out who he was.

"Ever wonder what would have happened if your aunt hadn't called you that night?"

"I know what would have happened."

"Really?"

"Yes. I would have made a fool of myself."

"Letting your heart tell you something is not always bad. I

thought we'd have an easier time if we'd gotten to know each
other before you found out."

"Not for me. Caesar, I can't tell you how angry I was when
Aunt Helene called. I felt I was being betrayed and I didn't even
know why."

"It was meant to be a seduction, not a betrayal."

"Maybe. But we still see some things differently."

"That will always be. A man and woman don't always think
alike."

"So you understand that your mother will never think of it
as a betrayal that she's seeing a man you consider an enemy."

"That's another story. My mother has lived by her own rules
too long. She needs someone who's strong enough to stand up
to her."

"Someone with his own money, so she can't intimidate him."

"Right."

"Someone not afraid to confront power because he has so
much himself."

"Right again."

It took a beat for him to realize all the attributes he considered
important to stand up to his mother were the ones that Jameson
Miller had.

"He's too young."

"You're just a little jealous."

"It's not jealousy. It's . . . concern. For all my mother's living
in Europe, she's still naive about some things."

"I think you're the one who's naive. Your mother knows exactly what she's doing."

She let the subject drop because she knew that Caesar thought
Jameson was taking advantage of his mother. But Leigh knew
better. Juliette would end the relationship if she thought it would
hurt Caesar too much.

In New York, two couples gazed at the Manhattan skyline.
Rick and JoAnn sat in his apartment as he strummed his guitar.
With Leigh and Caesar out of the way for a whole week, they

had brainstormed on what would get Jameson Miller back on their side.

"He wants that building. I think if the salon went bankrupt he'd scoop it up in a minute," Rick said.

"I don't know. I think he's given up."

"That's what he wants you to think. He hasn't. He's not the type."

"I think the saying you'd better remember is, 'Never under-estimate the power of a woman.' "

"You think Juliette can manipulate him so that he forgets about the salon. I think he's anxious to prove he could do it without anyone."

"She reminds me of Stephanie."

"Ahhh. Now I know why you're so afraid. You think if Juliette controls Jameson the way Stephanie controlled Paul . . ."

"Stephanie didn't control Paul."

"Oh, yes, she did. In her own way she got him to do every-thing she wanted him to do. Look at that will. That had to be Stephanie's idea."

"And he was probably drunk. She couldn't force him to do anything if he wasn't drunk."

"But she got what she wanted. Every time."

The other couple stared at the sky and wondered if they had a future together. What if, Juliette thought, we only have this passion and there is nothing else to hold him?

"Stop it," Jameson ordered. He tugged at the chain around her neck.

"Stop what?"

"Don't try to fool me. I know when you get quiet you're wondering if we should be together."

"You know me too well. I don't like that."

"Actually you love it. It's what you've been looking for all along."

"It can't last."

"There are no guarantees. But if you don't give us a chance then it's an automatic failure."

"Once, I would have resorted to simplifications to get things to work out my way. But now I know that isn't going to happen all the time. And the one time it doesn't, it will be the most important."

"Juliette, I think you have been reading too much into situations instead of letting them happen. You might be right. This might not work. But I'm not going to think about the end, just about the present."

"Only the young say those things."

"I'm also not going to get into a fight about age. We can't change it. So live with it."

"But you will want children . . ."

"I will want a lot of things I can't have. But we will live with it."

They were shown to a table and Leigh studied the menu wanting to find something she hadn't tried before. But the conch salad still made her think of something exotic and she ordered it again.

It was a different band, but Leigh nudged Caesar when she spotted the man who had tried to dance with her. He was still flirting with the American women whether they were with anyone or not. By the time she finished her salad, he was in front of her table.

"I'm Christopher . . ." He stopped mid-sentence and scurried away.

"I think he remembered you."

"It wasn't that long ago."

"I think he will remember you for years."

"I'm sure I'm not the first or the last man who wouldn't let his wife dance with him."

Leigh smiled. Caesar didn't know the murderous gaze he'd fixed on the man. Other men may have denied Christopher the privilege of dancing with their wives but not too many of them had threatened the man with a look like that.

They left early, sleep getting in the way of their fun. They needed to rest, so they walked back. Caesar opted for a quick shower and was in bed while Leigh decided on a bath. She sprinkled the pink bath salts into the water and climbed in. Most people would think she was crazy for making the water so hot on an island but it was the only way she could take a bath. She lounged until the water grew tepid and then wrapped herself in one of the bath sheets. After softly patting her body dry, she slipped into a short cotton nightshirt.

She smelled of roses. Caesar drifted into wakefulness. He opened his eyes but knew that his mind was making suggestions his body couldn't complete. Instead he wrapped his arms around her, murmured something about her smelling like roses, and drifted into a deep sleep.

TWENTY-FOUR

Leigh woke up before Caesar. She showered, threw on a muu-muu, and tiptoed to the kitchen. She was suddenly famished. After a brief check, she affirmed that Cynthia had stocked the refrigerator and the mini bar. They had everything they needed. She quietly assembled the food and the equipment, then started the coffee. The rich aroma filled the kitchen and she made a bet with herself that Caesar would wake up as soon as it filled his nostrils.

Minutes later he staggered into the kitchen. "How can I be hungry and sleepy at the same time?"

"I feel the same. But we need food for fuel, so that later this week we can do something besides eat and sleep."

"I'd like to go swimming later."

"I might join you."

He set the table, and as she finished, put the eggs in one dish, the bacon in another, and retrieved some bottled juices from the refrigerator. He thought she'd cooked enough for a small army, but was surprised that they left only crumbs.

They slept another three hours and woke up just as the sun was setting. Instead of a swim they opted for a long walk.

The night breeze swirled around her ankles as she padded down the beach. Every now and then she would dip her feet in the ocean and then run back to Caesar's side. There was something about being near an ocean that was still warm at night.

They got back to the house and spent a little time preparing and eating a light meal. Tomorrow they would be fully recovered from the tiredness.

The next day Caesar pulled her from the bed. He told her to get her suit because they were going swimming. She muttered something about eating, but he said they needed to build an appetite.

Somehow she forced herself into a shower and slipped into a black swimsuit that clung to her frame.

Caesar wanted to protect her and love her and have fun with her. They were starting to have a real vacation.

They walked over to their hidden cove and were surprised and elated that no one was using it. Leigh sat on the rock, dangled her feet in the water, and let the breeze cover her warm body.

Caesar dived right in and swam around for a while, then joined Leigh on the rock.

"Mark sure has a great place. I think we should shop around for one," Caesar said. If this trip didn't convince her that Caesar was thinking long term, then the idea of buying property certainly did.

"I have to tell you something about Cynthia. Mark has a picture of the two of them on his desk."

"What kind of picture?"

"I never paid any attention to it. It's Mark holding up a huge fish he's just caught and a woman standing near him. Until I met her the other day I didn't know she was the woman."

"So, Mark has a life we don't know about."

"And to think we tried to hook him up with your mother."

"But my mother prefers . . ."

"Don't start."

They sat listening to the water slapping against the rocks. In a matter of hours the cave would be filled with water. But now it was so peaceful.

She took off her bathing cap and shook her hair so it fell around her shoulders.

"I guess that means you're not going to swim."

"I don't feel like it. I just want to sit and enjoy this peace."

He shifted his body so he was sitting parallel to her. She was right. This was their own private little world. The rock wasn't large enough for them to make love but on but that's what he wanted to do. He felt that if somehow they shared something so special it would make her his forever.

For the first time in his life, Caesar Montgomery was thinking about forever. He'd never allowed a woman inside his soul. Leigh had gotten there without even trying. He pulled her closer and kissed her just below the ear.

He studied her face. She was one of those women that each feature wasn't quite right but together they created a beauty unlike anyone else. Without make-up her flawless skin glowed. He wished he could bottle it. They would both become millionaires in a few short months. She was sexy without even trying. He was in love with everything about her.

They still didn't know how they were going to live. It was comfortable now but that was because most of Caesar's clothes and books were still in his suite at the St. Regis.

How would they combine their lives—or would they?

He knew a few couples who kept two places, but what about children? He felt his body grow warm as he thought about her carrying his child.

He put his arms around her. "I never thought that I would

marry. I used to tell myself that I would leave the marrying to my mother."

"I know. After Marshall I just threw myself into my work. I read somewhere that single women use work as a substitute for sex. I guess that was what I was doing."

"I've got an idea. I'm going back to get the champagne. Let's toast to a successful and happy life together."

She turned and kissed him. "I'll wait here."

She was dangling her feet above the water and staring down at the turquoise water filling the cove when she heard a noise. Just as she turned, it was if someone threw a bright light into her eyes and then she was falling.

Caesar returned with the champagne and called out to her. She didn't answer.

"I hope you haven't fallen asleep on that rock."

He was surprised not to find her still sitting on the rock. He looked down into the water and saw her floating. "I thought you said you didn't want to swim . . ."

He broke off when he saw the bathing cap on the side of the rock. "Oh God! No!" He dropped the bottle, dived in, and swam toward Leigh.

Just as he reached her, she turned over and was face down in the water. Caesar pulled her face out of the water and half-carried, half-dragged her to shore. Fortunately she hadn't swallowed a lot of water and didn't even need mouth to mouth.

"Come on, honey. Try to walk."

She staggered a few steps and fell, unconscious. Caesar picked her up in a fireman's carry and made his way down the beach until some swimmers realized they weren't playing around and rushed to help them. Leigh was still unconscious when they reached the doctor.

A few minutes after the doctor examined her, she opened her eyes. "You are a very lucky young woman," the man standing over her said.

She was still disoriented, not sure of where she was, but the fear was still there and she flailed out at the doctor.

"Calm down. Calm down. You're safe."

Caesar must have heard the commotion because he was suddenly by her side. "Leigh! Leigh! Darling, you're safe. We're at the doctor's."

His voice penetrated the darkness and she stopped fighting. Caesar left while the doctor continued his examination.

When he came out, he was most concerned by the bruise on the side of Leigh's head. "I would recommend a hospital but I think the young lady will fight me on that. She has a mild concussion. Take her home. Wake her every hour to see if she's coherent. If not, get her to the hospital."

"What happened? Did she fall asleep and tumble into the water?"

"I don't know. She has a nasty bruise on the side of her head—as if someone struck her. But she was alone. I believe you may be right. She fell asleep, tumbled into the water, and hit her face. Whatever she hit turned her body face up. That's why she didn't drown. It's good you found her when you did."

Caesar felt his blood run cold. "When can I take her home?"

"Let her rest another hour. We'll test her reflexes and then I'll know if she should be in the hospital."

A freak accident—something neither of them could have counted on. He could have lost her. Caesar paced the tiny beach house, checking the clock. Another twenty minutes and he could wake her again. The last time she'd snarled at him about disturbing her sleep. He took that for a good sign. What worried him was the first time he woke her up she fought him and babbled about being hit with a bright light. He hadn't seen anyone in the cave. Maybe it was just a nightmare. But their idyllic paradise had become just that. Caesar wasn't sure if he should buy into his paranoia and take her someplace else, like his mother's house in France. He could, but that would just make her feel that someone had attacked her deliberately. He would just have to watch over her more carefully. Without proof there was nothing he could do. But deep in his heart he didn't believe it was an accident. He believed that someone had tried to kill her. Maybe Cassiopeia wasn't out of the woods. Maybe a man like Jameson Miller had talons that reached as far as an island paradise.

TWENTY-FIVE

Caesar spent a restless night watching over Leigh, and he was glad to see the smile on her face when he woke her for the last time. She seemed to be in good spirits despite her lack of sleep. The crisis was over, he thought. Maybe they could enjoy a few days before heading back to their real-world problems. He mulled over Leigh's suggestion that they walk over to the restaurant for breakfast.

"Maybe you should rest today and we'll just eat here."

"I don't think so. I feel cooped up. Let's try breakfast and see what happens."

Caesar reluctantly agreed. It was only a few minutes before they were on their way.

Once at the restaurant, Leigh ordered light even though she felt as if she could eat a lumberjack's breakfast. Caesar hadn't asked and she didn't know how to open the discussion of her mishap, but she did want to talk about it. She waited until the fresh fruit dish she'd ordered and the eggs, juice, toast, and cereal Caesar had ordered was served. She didn't want to be interrupted once she started. The only way is to plunge right in, she told herself, then took a deep breath.

"The doctor says I fell asleep in the cave," she said. "I don't understand how it happened. I mean I know it did . . ."

"You've been on a roller coaster ride since your sister's death. You probably only thought you were getting enough sleep but you were really fighting off your body clock. You know there are some people who buy tapes of sounds of the ocean, the wind, whatever calms them down enough to sleep."

"That's always been a little too 'New Age' for me."

"I've had clients who swear by it. I was once the stylist for an actress who used to tell me that when she was in bed she played ocean sounds because they relaxed her enough so she fell asleep without pills."

"So you think it's possible that I was lulled to sleep by the waves bouncing off the cave walls?"

"Yes, I think that's what happened."

They finished their meal and by the time they left the restaurant both were satisfied with the doctor's decision that she'd merely fallen asleep.

It was the possibility of her death that made Leigh realize that she needed a will. Something Mark had been suggesting all along but Leigh had put off. She wouldn't put it off any longer. Once she was back in New York she and Caesar would see a lawyer.

JoAnn paced back and forth in Helene's office. As soon as she had arrived at the salon, she received the message that Helene wanted to see her. As she waited, she glanced at her surroundings. This was an office she normally avoided. It was almost like a shrine to Stephanie, and, it gave JoAnn eerie feelings of being watched by the departed. Helene had decorated her office walls in muted pastels that JoAnn felt cried out for a little color. The cream walls that ended with a slightly darker beige carpet were perfect for the chrome and glass table that Helene used as a desk, and the tan sofa and chairs were supposed to make visitors to the office feel comfortable. JoAnn didn't.

To the rear of the office was a little door, which most people didn't notice, that led to the bathroom. JoAnn remembered when they were renovating the building how emphatic Helene had been about the design. It was a miniature version of Stephanie's.

JoAnn and Stephanie had never been the best of friends but JoAnn had known she was aligning herself to a rising star when they met. Later she would see that most of the innovative ideas came from Helene not Stephanie.

JoAnn walked over to the shelves of knickknacks from Helene's travels. The shelf was the place she'd gotten her best idea about what to wear at the Halloween party. The woman was obsessed with clowns. They were in every shape and form. But the ones that struck her the most were the harlequins. Especially the white-faced one with the white baggy suit trimmed in black that sat on the top shelf and the colorful patchwork quilted one that sat on one of the lower shelves.

JoAnn stifled a giggle remembering how she'd been summoned three days before Halloween. She saw the large box on the sofa with the label from a costume store. She couldn't resist peeking inside. It contained the white harlequin costume and JoAnn deliberately called a costume store and ordered one just like it. She planned to wear it the night of the party and, since she was several inches taller than Helene, she knew she'd stand out in the crowd. JoAnn knew it would irk Helene and there would be nothing the woman could do about it. But Paul, Stephanie, and Caesar had had that fight in the boardroom and made those threats about changing their wills. That would have been a disaster. It had to be stopped.

"They died for nothing," she said.

"Well, we agree on something," Helene said from the doorway.

JoAnn hadn't realized she'd spoken aloud until Helene replied. "I . . . I . . . didn't know you were here . . ."

"I'm sure you didn't. Let's get down to business." JoAnn watched as Helene strolled over to the chair and sat down. This forced JoAnn to sit on the sofa facing the older woman. Inside she groaned. Helene had been reading one of those be-a-better-executive books—the kind that told you if you sat behind your

desk it was a show of power, but if you sat next to the person
in front of the desk it was a talk between equals.

She had to admit the woman was always the epitome of style.
Today she wore a black tailored suit with a red blouse and a
red cloche hat. JoAnn never liked the tailored looks she modeled
but her pink and gray designer dress felt inadequate against
Helene's bold colors.

Unfortunately for JoAnn, sitting on the sofa put her directly
across the wall of Paul's and Stephanie's pictures. She shivered.

"What did you want to talk about, Helene?" JoAnn wanted
to cut to the chase and get out of this office.

"I thought we might brainstorm a bit before the honeymooners' return."

"Brainstorm about what? How we can get control of Cassiopeia and toss them out? It will never happen."

"They have the upper hand now, but what if we could convince them we had their best interest at heart but at the same
time turn them against each other?"

"Helene, they may not have married for love but they are
determined to make this work."

"Until they suspect that one of them isn't completely truthful."

"Don't do the riddle thing with me, Helene. What are you
suggesting?"

"You young people know nothing of subtlety. Make Leigh
think that you and Caesar are still seeing each other."

"And should I tell Rick about this little deception?"

"That's up to you."

"So how do I go about this?" Helen talked and JoAnn felt
more confident about the idea of moving Leigh and Caesar out.
For three months, she'd been the love of Caesar's life but he'd
ended the relationship. He'd been the first man to leave her. Paul
had been the next, but he'd paid for that when Stephanie made
him change his will. All the other times, she'd been the one to
say when a romance ended. It might be fun to see Leigh walk
away from him. Let him experience a period of inadequacy as
she had done when he left her. Only this would be a better way
of getting revenge. He wanted Cassiopeia and if Leigh took that

away from him, it would be a better revenge than anything she could wish for at this time.

"I'll think about it," JoAnn, said as she stood up and walked toward the door.

"Very well, dear, but I think you could help greatly in getting rid of these two obstacles."

Helene waited until JoAnn had closed the door and her heels tapping on the marble-floored hallway had faded before giving a triumphant yell. She walked over to the wall that held the pictures of Paul and Stephanie. She selected her favorite and let her hand run across Stephanie's face. "You weren't supposed to die. Paul was the one having the affair with JoAnn. You were always true to him."

JoAnn reveled in the idea of getting back at Caesar the way Helene suggested but she had an added joy that she would also get Helene out of her life at the same time.

She sat in her office laughing about the way her deal with Jameson Miller would be even sweeter. What she really needed was to get a tape of Helene giving her more than just little hints on how to get rid of Leigh and Caesar. Then Miller would have a way to neutralize Helene. Jameson Miller would have it all.

TWENTY SIX

Jameson Miller poured another drink for his guest and carried it to the glass—enclosed terrace. They stared out at the dazzling lights of the city. New York was beautiful at night. So was his guest, Juliette Montgomery.

"The wedding was beautiful, from what I got to see in the papers," he said.

"Don't pout. I couldn't possibly have arrived at the wedding with my son's biggest nemesis."

"True. But are we ever going to go public with the fact that we're seeing each other or will I be hidden away forever?"

"Eventually everyone will know but for now I think it's best to keep things the way they are."

Jameson took her hand and gently led her back to the living room. The soft white walls made the black furniture stand out. The extra large cocktail table sat between two black leather sofas and held the remains of the dinner they had shared.

"No matter how long you wait, your son is not going to like it."

"I know. I want him to achieve a measure of success in his new venture before I shock his sensibilities."

"He could think you're the enemy?"

"Not as long as we keep to the rules of this relationship."

"They're your rules not mine."

"But you will follow them?"

"Of course. However, I don't think he'll believe you when you tell him that we never discuss Cassiopeia business."

"Perhaps. But I would know the truth and he will see that in my eyes."

Juliette Montgomery had been raised by an unconventional aunt who dragged her across three continents by the time Juliette was fifteen. They never had a great deal of money, but they survived, and the education of travel was not lost on Juliette. When she met Caesar's father, she fell in love for the first time. Juliette and her aunt were living in New York at the time. As a lark she took some art courses with another young woman who was a diplomat's daughter. That's when she was introduced to the glamorous world of wealth combined with careers. She even entertained the idea that he would defy his father and marry her instead of the handpicked bride waiting at home. By the time she found out she was pregnant with Caesar, she knew that love did not conquer all. He returned to Colombia and Juliette became a single mother. Caesar's step-father came into her life and, although she was supported in style by Caesar's father, she thought they had a better chance if she married. For a while she was happy and they were a family. Still the wanderlust of her childhood was stronger than that love and the marriage ended. So did her other short-lived relationships and marriages. The moment a man tried to tie her down or restrict her in any way, she bolted.

"I can't believe I'm that boring." Jameson Miller's deep voice snapped her back to the present.

"I apologize," she said, and truly meant it. She hadn't meant to drift into the past and there was nothing boring about her companion.

"I'd offer a penny for your thoughts but I don't believe you're willing to share them."

"Most of them happened before you were out of diapers."

"Don't go there tonight."

He was right. There was no sense in bringing up his age. It was a fact that neither could change. He wasn't the first younger man, in her life but he touched part of her that she wanted to push away on one hand and welcome into her life on the other.

If Jameson and Caesar ever had a nonadversarial meeting, she knew they would be friends. What made them successful also made them brothers under the skin.

Juliette wanted to enjoy their time together and then walk away as she'd done before. Her feelings for Jameson Miller went deeper than she wanted. He didn't even know her real age Like some women do, she'd lied about it. She'd only removed two years, but she knew it was her vanity at trying to stay the younger side of the 50's.

She took a healthy swallow of the champagne and banished all thoughts of why she should not be with a man who made her feel wonderful. Even if it couldn't last.

* * *

Leigh had decided she needed a nap as soon as they'd returned from breakfast. She hated that she felt so weak. She wished she could stay on the island and forget the conundrum that waited for them at home. Today she'd awoken from her nap with only one thought. Why?

Why was she forcing herself onto a board that did not want her? Why was she forcing herself into a marriage that neither party wanted? That wasn't true. They wanted the marriage, but for the wrong reason. Despite her attraction to Caesar, she knew it wasn't love, at least not on his part. Sometimes she wanted it to be a real marriage but other times she knew it couldn't happen because Caesar Montgomery was too career—minded to worry about matters of the heart.

Almost as if he could read her mind, he appeared in the doorway. "Think you're strong enough to sit on the beach?"

"I know I am," Leigh replied. "If you would just stop treating me like an invalid."

"Getting testy? Now I know you're improving."

Being testy was a mechanism that worked for Leigh. She'd married a handsome, dynamic man. She didn't want to be as foolish as the other women in his life. She didn't want to be in love with her husband.

Leigh forced a smile. "Give me a minute."

Maybe if they didn't spend so much time together she wouldn't grow close to him. How long could she fill this honeymoon up with other people?

Caesar waited while his bride found something suitable to wear. His biggest fear was that while they were away, the Board would find some underhanded trick to steal the salon. He couldn't let that happen. Even with controlling interest, he still felt the need to be able to watch what was going on.

Leigh was becoming the most important part of his life, but if he didn't hold onto Cassiopeia, how could he hold onto his wife? Once they had things under control he could declare his love. Once they pushed Jameson Miller out of their lives, he would have a chance. Saving the salon would prove his love, unless Miller or the Board had a secret weapon.

* * *

Leigh and Caesar developed a silent agreement not to talk about the salon but to enjoy the freedom and the beauty of their tropical paradise. The last night they were going to be there they went to a nightclub, much like the one they had been to on their first date. She wanted to go some place quiet where they could talk.

Once they were led to their table, Leigh noticed that the restaurant was filled to capacity. The mode of dress seemed to be everything from sport jacket casual seated at tables in the middle of the room to those in formal attire at tables stretching along the wall of the tiny establishment.

The waiter explained the tux and gown-attired crowd were celebrating a wedding that had taken place earlier in the day. It was a spur of the moment type of wedding of a singer and actor from America.

Leigh tried to get a glimpse of the bride and groom but couldn't and finally turned to concentrate on her meal. The thumping beat of the band allowed no room for conversation. She glanced at Caesar a few times and saw his eyes twinkling with amusement. Talking to each other was obviously not going to happen until after they left.

Halfway through her meal, Leigh noticed a petite figure coming toward their table. Leigh had noticed the woman staring at them earlier but ignored her. She seemed to be part of the wedding party. Caesar's back was to the woman and Leigh couldn't say anything over the steel drums. The band chose that moment to take a break, but before Leigh could say anything, the woman walked over and draped herself around Caesar.

Leigh watched as her startled husband turned to put a face to the arms that encircled him. The woman then planted a searing kiss on his lips.

"Sarito, darling. Haven't seen you in ages," she drawled.

She looked at Leigh. "We're old friends," she said, as if that explained the kiss. The green silk dress she wore slipped from one shoulder revealing dark gold skin that seemed flawless.

"Who's your friend?" Leigh asked between clenched teeth.

"She . . . she's," Caesar stammered then recovered. "Leigh, may I introduce you to Rita Holliday. She's on a soap opera. Rita, this is my wife, Leigh Barrington Montgomery."

Leigh nodded in the woman's direction. The woman nodded back but did not take her arms from Caesar's shoulders until he rose from the table and stepped back.

Uninvited, the woman slithered into the chair between Leigh and Caesar.

"I heard you got married. I was disappointed about not getting an invitation."

"It was a small, family-and-close-friends-only kind of wedding," Leigh said and smiled.

"I heard you were on the West Coast now, " Caesar said as he sat down.

"Yes, I just finished a pilot for a new series. I play some kind of diva." She waved her fingers in the air as if she couldn't imagine why she was chosen for the role. She turned to Leigh. "If the series is picked up, may I steal your husband?"

"Sorry, he's going to have to stay in New York for a very long time."

"I never asked before but how did your sister come up with the name, Cassiopeia?"

"Do you know what a constellation is?" Leigh asked.

"Yeah, but I could never see them in the sky myself."

"Well, one of the constellations is an Ethiopian queen who was too smart for her own good. She's the one that's upside down for six months of the year."

"Oh." Leigh knew the woman didn't get the connection she was making when Rita again suggested that Caesar come to the coast for the show. "But think of the publicity it would mean for your salon. He could simply fly out for a few days a month. You could style my hair and maybe a few other cast members'."

Of course, I would have the most creative Sarito Valerian style, since I'm the star."

"No, he couldn't."

"Ah, don't tell me you're henpecked already, Sarito. You used to be so much fun."

"There's a big difference between being henpecked and devoted, Rita," Caesar said. He spoke to Rita but his eyes never left Leigh's face. Leigh smiled at him.

Rita glanced at the two for a moment. "Well, I must get back to my friends." She waited a beat and Leigh assumed she wanted an invitation to stay. That was not going to happen and Rita sashayed away from the table.

"Who is she?"

"Don't start."

"What's that supposed to mean?"

"Nothing. She's an actress who used to come into the salon when she was doing a prime time show set in New York."

"Was that so hard to say or did you need time to formulate a simple sentence?"

"I'm not going to pretend I didn't enjoy a full life before I met you. I just know that you'll read something into it that no longer exists."

"Darling, you aren't the only one who had a 'full life' before we met. I just wonder why you find it so difficult to just say she's an old friend."

"I don't want to discuss it."

"Of course you don't want to discuss it, and why should you? As soon as Cassiopeia has a healthy bottom line, we can end this sham."

TWENTY-SEVEN

As they left the restaurant, Caesar didn't know whether he should bring up the subject of Rita again. He hadn't meant to sound so defensive about the woman. He just wasn't accustomed to having to explain anything. Now, with Leigh, he seemed to waffle between wanting to assure her that she had nothing to worry about and telling her not to pry into his former lifestyle. He knew he was sending mixed messages but he couldn't help himself. What if he lay his soul bare only to find out that the feeling wasn't reciprocated?

He remembered how he'd pitied women who did not believe him in the past when he said he did not want any entanglements. He discovered that no matter how straightforward he was with them, those same women had thoughts of wedding rings and matching monogrammed towels. Hadn't Leigh said that as soon as Cassiopeia was sound she wanted a divorce? He'd just have to wait until after the crisis and see if she still felt that way. If she did, he wasn't going to beg her to stay.

I sounded like a shrew, Leigh thought. Of course she was going to run into women who Caesar had been involved with in business and socially. What had she read in the newspaper files in the library? The man was a magnet for women. That was why the salon had been so successful. And wasn't that what this marriage was all about? It was a way to put the salon back on the map. She was the one who was wrong and she should be the one to try to make amends. He'd only reacted as any caged animal would. He was defensive because he didn't want to be married.

Caesar opened the bungalow door and held it as Leigh entered and turned on the light.

"I . . . uh . . . I've been thinking," she said, "maybe Rita was right. Maybe if you flew out to California and styled her hair for the show it would be good publicity."

"So what? You want me to call Rita and tell her I've changed my mind."

"No. I want you to call Rita's agent and say you'd be interested in an offer."

"I'll think about it. I don't want to leave the Board or Miller room to move in on us."

That was easy thought Leigh. If he's in California enough, I can get used to not having him in my life.

Caesar stared in the mirror as he shaved. Maybe Leigh had a point. If he was out of town a few days a month, that might give her a chance to miss him.

Leigh's hearty appetite at breakfast the next morning was a sign she had come to terms with their situation and how they would handle it. By the time Caesar joined her, she had devoured her fruit and was making her way through the eggs and bacon.

The tray had been delivered from the restaurant while Caesar was still in the shower.

"Good morning," he said. He sat down lifted the lid of one of the trays in front of him, and he saw a sumptuous mixture of fresh coconut, mangoes, and kiwi fruit. The second tray contained the eggs, kept warm by a burner underneath the tray and the third and fourth trays contained an assortment of thin slices of meat. He put huge helpings on his plate that made Leigh wonder why he didn't weigh a lot more than he did. He skewered pieces of fruit on a fork and tasted them before speaking again.

"I think you're right about doing Rita's series," he said, as if only a second instead of a night had passed since they'd discussed it. "I don't have to do anything at the salon. I mean I wouldn't want people to think I was completely back in the styling business."

"I know. I just feel that each thing we do right to bring in revenue will be everything wrong for Jameson Miller's takeover plans."

"What would you like to do today?"

"I don't know. I feel as if I could do something daring. I might try parasailing."

"I don't think so," he said and laughed at the idea that she'd even want to see water after the cave.

The phone rang while they were still trying to decide. Caesar answered and heard Mark's voice

"I wouldn't have called if I didn't think it was important."

"I know that. What happened?"

"Nothing yet. I'm sending you a fax and you can tell if it's trouble. Say hello to Leigh for me."

Caesar said goodbye, told Leigh what Mark had said, and they both waited for the dedicated fax machine to spit out the information.

It was a blind article from a gossip column. The woman who wrote it had been around New York long enough to know when trouble was brewing.

"Who was that woman leaving Jameson Miller's apartment last night? Doesn't she have a very close link with a certain board member of the Cassiopeia salon? Isn't that the piece of property Miller wants badly enough to rip out his eye teeth for? Could the woman be helping him negotiate the deal of his life?"

Caesar read it twice before handing it to Leigh. After waiting for her to finish reading it, he then asked, "Do we have a traitor in our midst?"

"It sounds like a problem we can handle. All we need to do

is give the Board some information and see if it gets back to Miller."

"That would only tell us if it's a board member sneaking in and out of Miller's place. What if it's someone's wife or girl-friend?"

"We still wouldn't know. What if we don't tell anyone about the offer Rita made?"

"Will her people keep it quiet?"

"I just stipulate if it leaks to the press there's no deal."

"Do you think we should go home?"

"No way. We cut the honeymoon short and they'll know something's up."

Caesar watched a smile creep across Leigh's face. "Okay, what do you have in mind?"

"When we first met, I had come here to do a little catching up on the salon business. After all, I hadn't paid any attention to it since Stephanie and I stopped speaking to each other."

"I always wondered how you could live so close and never let your curious mind force you to walk past it. You know, just to see what it was like."

"The Barringtons have a trait stronger than curiosity. It's stubbornness. As I was saying, when we met I was here to hide from the paparazzi and learn the business, so that's what I'm going to do."

She saw the crestfallen look on Caesar's face. "I was hoping for something . . . different," he told her.

Leigh shrugged and went to the guest bedroom's closet. There was a box she'd brought along with her on her first trip that was still sealed. She'd met Caesar and completely forgotten about her study plan. Then she'd found out how he'd tricked her and she'd rushed back to the States.

In New York, JoAnn and Rick were doing their own study of the salon business in Rick's living room. Most of the time he insisted they go to her place so this should have been an enjoyable evening. Instead it had been a constant go around on how to keep the salon in the red, but not so much that it was worthless once Miller bought it. Despite his promise of positions both Rick and JoAnn knew that having cold, hard cash was the best thing all around.

"Do you realize that appointments are off this week again?" JoAnn turned the receptionist's book around and Rick scanned the pages. They would take it back in the morning before the salon opened.

"That's great. We'll be so cash poor by the time the honeymooners get back they'll be ready to throw in the towel."

"Caesar, maybe. He knows when to give up. It's Leigh who will try to hold on until any offer will be a good offer."

"JoAnn, haven't you noticed how Leigh and Caesar tiptoe around each other?"

"Yes, I've noticed. What does that mean to you?"

"That they don't trust each other. We know they just got married so they could control the salon," Rick snorted. "The public can eat up that whirlwind courtship nonsense all they want."

JoAnn nodded. "Knowing that it's not a love match and proving that it's not are two different things."

Rick folded his arms across his chest. "Sometimes I wonder if you'll ever see the forest for the trees."

He stood over JoAnn, who was sprawled on the sofa. "We plant little seeds of doubt and let their imaginations do the rest. I'll talk to Leigh and you talk to Caesar. We'll hint that each wants the other out."

"If that doesn't work?"

"We'll find a plan B. In two months I want the gates to be pulled down on Cassiopeia salon and a sold sign on the front door. Then maybe we'll take a little pre-wedding honeymoon."

JoAnn glowed at the thought. Things would work out for all concerned as soon as they got rid of the salon.

Hours later Leigh sat on the bed with books and papers scattered around her.

Caesar had been banished to the living-room while she

worked. Now she was ready to ask him some questions about the clientele. She was beginning to develop a germ of an idea that might make a difference in the appointments.

She hadn't felt this excited about the salon since she'd first created it on paper all those years ago.

Caesar looked up from the book that he was reading. "I get the feeling you've discovered a lost treasure. Or maybe you've found the secret of the Sphinx?"

"Or maybe it's a way to bring more people to the salon."

Caesar thought about the many ads they'd run, TV shows they'd done, and fundraisers they'd attended since opening. He thought they'd gone as far as possible. He didn't want to hurt her feelings but he didn't think they could do any more.

"What's your angle?"

"A spokesperson."

"What?"

"Well, actually several people. We could use the store window. A display like Saks does for Christmas, but with real people."

"And what would these real people be doing?"

"Everything. From going to work, to church, to a night on the town, all the things a busy New York couple would do."

"Would we use models?"

"No, that's the other part. We'd use real people. We'd put an ad in the paper that says: Cassiopeia is looking for people to represent the New York Life style. Come by the salon and pick up an application." She stopped talking when she looked at the frown on Caesar's face. "You hate the idea."

"No, not exactly. It's different, but can you imagine the people who just want to see what it looks like inside? We'll be mobbed."

"So what? It may be the first and last time they come into Cassiopeia but they'll tell their friends, and maybe their friends, will have wanted to come to a salon but were a little nervous about the size or that it's located on Fifth Avenue."

Leigh's enthusiasm began to rub off on Caesar. He could see the possibilities.

"We'd use an Anglo, African-American, Latino, and Asian

group. Hairstyles and hair cuts for the age range in each group. Hey, we could start with the youngest group. We could put them in a nursery school setting."

"Right! We could have them get older each week. The nursery school, the elementary school, high school, college, work force, marriage, and retirement."

Caesar threw his head back and laughed. "This is a great idea. Now we have to convince the Board."

"I don't think it will be easy. They'll think we're crazy."

"I don't care. We'll find a way to do this."

Through the night they worked on the plan. They tossed ideas around. They played devil's advocate with each other. Finally, as the sun began to rise they felt sleep coming and reluctantly put down their pens and paper and padded off to the master bedroom.

Leigh took her shower first and put on a filmy black nightgown. "It doesn't really matter," she told her reflection. "We're both too tired for anything but sleep."

Caesar had used the shower in the guest bathroom and was in bed. Leigh climbed in and didn't fight as he pulled her into his arms. She was right. They were too tired for anything but sleep, and Leigh's last thought before she drifted off was that it was too bad. They were closer now than they had ever been.

TWENTY-EIGHT

Leigh and Caesar slept well past noon the following day. He awoke first. He didn't want to move because he was enjoying the idea of having his wife snuggled against him spoon-style.

Unfortunately, he'd never been one who could stay in bed once fully awake and reluctantly he released her and slipped out of bed.

He'd developed the pattern early in his career of shaving every morning whether he needed to or not. After he shaved, he dressed quietly and went into the kitchen. Rather than call the restaurant and have a meal delivered, Caesar felt like cooking for them today. They would have breakfast in bed. At least Leigh would. He assembled, the equipment but when he got back to the bedroom he heard the shower and knew that Leigh must have awakened as soon as he left the bed. He put the tray with the plates, utensils, napkins, and glasses on the dresser and returned to the kitchen. His second trip he took the juice and glasses with ice back to the bedroom and put them on the tray.

He hummed an old tune as he searched for the whisk for the eggs he'd cracked and put into a bowl. He remembered to add cheese to the egg mixture. It was high cholesterol but since he didn't do it often, he couldn't see the harm. He found the whisk and proceeded to heat oil in a pan while he whipped the eggs until they were light and fluffy. Once the oil was hot, he poured the egg and cheese mixture in. Moments later he was spooning the omelet onto a large platter, and he added toast and a large bowl of fruit.

This time when he returned Leigh had finished her shower and dressed in a simple blue and white striped sun dress. She was about to pour herself a glass of juice.

"Pour one for me," Caesar said as he sat the second tray down. "I'll go get the coffee."

"Don't bother. I'm awake now, so why don't we just eat on the porch?"

"Good idea." He picked up the tray and carried it to the screened-in porch. Leigh brought the other tray and put it on the table. Caesar hurried back to the kitchen and got the coffee. He was still humming when they sat down to eat. Others were probably ordering lunch, but this was their first meal of the day.

"I know I shouldn't look a gift horse in the mouth," Leigh said, "but why are you so happy this morning?"

"Because, Mrs. Montgomery, you may have just come up with an idea to make us different. Being different attracts newspaper columnists, and newspaper columnists attract clients for us."

"I know it will work. I just hope the Board thinks so."

"Don't worry about the Board. I'll convince them that we aren't taking any wild chances. We're just being innovative."

After they'd finished eating and gone for a walk on the beach they returned to the cabin to refine the ideas from the previous night.

By honeymoon's end, they couldn't wait to get started. For Leigh this would be a chance to really get to know the business the way Caesar did.

New York's unpredictable weather had decided on heavy rain when they arrived at Kennedy Airport. They'd spent more time working on their plan on the company jet.

Leigh settled in the back of the limousine while Caesar picked up several newspapers. He got in and gave a couple to Leigh. They read as the driver delivered them to Leigh's apartment.

Once home, Caesar called his mother but only got her machine. He told her they were back and left the number in case Juliette couldn't remember it.

"Where could she be in this weather?"

"Your mother is perfectly capable of taking care of herself. A little rain won't keep her from her plans, whatever they were."

"I know, but I think she's keeping something from me."

"What makes you say that?"

"She always stays in touch the entire time she's here, but this trip she's so secretive."

Leigh had wondered about the short trips Juliette made to the salon and the apartment. It was as if she were on her way to something else and just touched base with them before going to her original destination. She hadn't wanted to mention it to Caesar. He was so protective, he'd probably hire a private detective to follow her. Leigh suspected it was a man—someone Caesar wouldn't like.

"Do you think we should call the board members?"

"And tell them what?"

"That we're back and ready to go to work."

"Leigh, darling, believe me, the moment we got on that plane everyone on the Board knew we were heading home."

"So what do we do?"

"Just show up at the salon tomorrow and see how quickly an impromptu board meeting is suggested."

"So when do we spring the idea on them?"

"After we do a little more research. I was thinking of calling a couple of designer friends who might want to get in on this deal."

"What are we going to call it?"

"I was thinking 'Cassiopeia City' since we want the salon to be mentioned in any newspaper write-ups."

"I like it."

"Let's go down to Strand's tomorrow before we go to the salon."

Strand's was the popular bookstore, in the Greenwich Village section of New York, that boasted having eight miles of books. They specialized in used books but also had a huge supply of new books that were sent to critics by publishers. The books were read, reviewed, and somehow ended up at Strand's, where they could be purchased for half price. It didn't take long for the books on the *New York Times* Bestseller List to end up at the bookstore. It was something that Leigh hadn't had a chance to do for some time and she looked forward to it.

The next day, Leigh roamed her favorite section of the store while Caesar was in the lower level of the store checking out new books on New York. She spent her time at the tables where a conglomeration of paperbacks were lined up. Leigh thumbed through them remembering when she'd come here after looking all over for an out of print book. At that time there was no internet to help with a book search. Thumbing through the books on the very table she was searching, she'd found it. Today she wasn't looking for that special book. She flinched as she touched a book with Paul and Stephanie on the cover. It was one of those quick, gossip riddled books but Leigh was drawn to it. She picked it up and decided she would buy it. She went to pay for it, put it in her bag, then looked at a few more paperbacks before wandering off to another aisle. She was looking through a book on fashion at the rear of the store when Caesar found her.

"Find anything?" he asked.

"Nothing important," she lied. "Unlike you," she added when she saw the pile of books in the basket provided by the store.

"Come on, let's go," he said. "I've got a whole bunch of ideas to run by the Board. Cassiopeia City is going to be fabulous."

When they reached the salon, Gayla shook her finger at them.

"Do you know how many times board members called me to find out if you were here yet? Don't you answer your beepers?"

Caesar and Leigh had deliberately left their beepers home, but they pretended they'd just gotten so used to island life they'd forgotten them.

They barely had time to put their packages down before they were summoned by the Board.

Helene rushed over and hugged them as they entered the room. "You terrible children. How can you stay out of touch when we need you so?"

"I'm sorry, Aunt Helene," Leigh started.

"We just got back from our honeymoon, Helene. Work isn't the first thing on our minds."

"I hope not," said Jimmy.

Several others agreed, but Rick and JoAnn sided with Helene.

"That's all well and good but we've got a serious problem," Rick said.

"We could lose all this," JoAnn added.

"But we won't. Tell them, honey," he said to Leigh. Then he turned to the Board. "I think Leigh has saved the game."

Leigh was a bit startled. All along Caesar had said he'd handle the Board and now he was giving her the ball and saying run.

The members took their seats and waited.

"I'll make this quick. Cassiopeia is going to build a city in the window. Something to draw attention to the salon. Something that will make the people come back to look at it week after week."

"You're not going to do anything crazy are you?" Helene asked.

"No. We're going to take the people of New York through all phases of their lives. But our emphasis will of course be on hairstyles."

"We are not going to do one of those hairstyles-through-the-ages, are we?" JoAnn asked as she wrinkled her nose.

"No. We are going to have real people. We're going to start with pregnant mothers, take them through having the baby, watching the baby go off to school, and then college, getting a job, getting married and having a family of their own."

"That's a big undertaking," Bob said thoughtfully.

"Don't worry, we'll go slow."

The board members mulled it over for a while and then nodded in agreement that they should try it.

The only warning came when Jim pointed out that if it didn't work they might as well hand the keys to Jameson Miller and get out of town. Leigh knew what they weren't saying out loud but everyone felt. This was her idea. If it worked, everyone won. If it failed, she would be responsible for making them a laughing stock and losing the business. It was like anything else—they would only love a winner. For a brief moment, she wondered if that was why Caesar had stayed in the background. Did he really want her to take all the credit—or get all the blame?

Leigh went back to her office and asked Gayla to hold all calls. She took the book out of the bag and began reading. She'd always felt that there was a grain of truth in all rumors.

The book wasn't large. It was noon; she'd just have her lunch brought in and learn a little about her sister. She looked down the table of contents and read a little about how and where Stephanie grew up. Leigh was mentioned as a younger sister who had her own career. They didn't say what kind of career. Leigh was ready to bet that they didn't even know. She flipped back to the table of contents. There was a listing for "The opposite sex." She opened it to and read about all the girlfriends Paul had had before he met Stephanie. They mentioned a few men Stephanie had dated and then in the last paragraph they dropped the bombshell. *"Rumors of trouble with the marriage may stem from Stephanie's constant escort, hair stylist Sarito Valerian."*

TWENTY-NINE

Helene paid one of her rare visits to Leigh's office. "I have to admit your idea is a good one." She sat on the sofa facing Leigh.

"Did you think I'd lost my touch?"

"I thought you might want to stay where you belong. I thought Mark Westinghouse paid you enough. I guess I was wrong."

"Sometimes it isn't the money that makes people do things."

"That's what people would like you to believe. The truth is, it's always the money."

"If it's the money, then you should be happy that I have an idea that might get us over that last hurdle. Don't you want to get Jameson Miller out of our lives?"

"I want to get you out of my life."

Leigh was startled into silence. She'd known that Aunt Helene wanted the salon to hold onto something of Stephanie's. Leigh hadn't told anyone who would use the fact that she created Cassiopeia. She'd just wanted a chance to run it to prove to herself that she could.

"I would never say anything to hurt Stephanie," Leigh told her aunt.

"Just see that you don't. Her memory is all I have left."

"I know that. Why can't we find some peaceful ground and work from there."

"You didn't read Stephanie's diary or you would know that Caesar Montgomery used her to get where he is today, then he just ignored her."

"We both know that I married Caesar to hold onto the salon."

"No! We could have held on to the salon. You married him so you could be in control. You got this place because of the way Stephanie's will was worded. You could lose it the same way."

The older woman stood up and walked toward the door. She turned and smiled at Leigh. "You're not like Stephanie. She knew what Caesar Montgomery was. He tried to lure her away from the business. He tried to talk her into letting him have her proxy. But she was too smart. She knew that if he got it, he would force her out. She wasn't silly enough to fall in love. She used him before he could use her and then she walked away."

"What are you talking about?"

"People thought they were having an affair."

"Aunt Helene, no one would believe that."

"One day you will. One day you'll find that Stephanie's diary chronicled their affair. Stephanie stumbled once. But she came to me for advice, and most of the time she took it. Men are playthings—never take them seriously."

After Helene left, Leigh thought about the book she'd purchased from Strand's. She picked it up and thumbed a few pages. Her hands grew clammy and she dropped the book back in her tote bag. She hadn't wanted to know about the women in Caesar's life when he tried to tell her. Maybe that's what he wanted to say.

She looked in the index and saw Sarito Valerian's name. She turned to the page he was mentioned and started reading.

The book insinuated that he and Stephanie had been an item—that they'd been lovers. Did Leigh really want to know if Caesar had married her not just for the salon but because it was as close as he could get to the woman he loved?

* * *

That night Leigh made a decision to confront Caesar. She just needed to know the truth. If she was a substitute she would end the marriage after they found out if Cassiopeia City would work.

Caesar was in the living room pouring over books on New York. He'd found some terrific pictures and couldn't wait to tell Leigh his idea. When she came into the room he knew something was wrong. She handed him the book and asked him to read page 100. In less than thirty seconds he read the passage and she watched his eyes go cold.

"What do you want me to do? Explain what they're talking about or confess that your sister and I had an affair?"

"I want the truth."

"No, you don't. You want to run some old rumors by me and see which ones make me afraid."

Caesar tossed the book across the room. "Your sister was lonely and scared. She wanted to leave Paul because he was having an affair."

"With whom?"

"Doesn't matter. There was always some woman in Paul's life. Your sister wanted someone to talk to. She wanted a man's point of view. So we talked. We became friends. If you're asking me if I escorted her to parties and premieres the answer is yes. If you're asking me if I was her lover, the answer is no. But I don't think you want answers. You want to know if I can feel so much passion for one woman that I would accept her sister if I couldn't have her. Isn't that what you're really asking?"

"I guess I am."

"The answer is no. I could never do that and call myself a man."

Leigh breathed a sigh of relief. She'd watched his face and she believed every word.

"But Leigh, you are right about something you once said,"

he told her. "This marriage is a sham. The sooner it's over, the better for both of us."

Leigh stood in the same spot long after Caesar picked up a few of the books on the coffee table and headed for the guest room. She couldn't believe she'd ruined everything. All she wanted was the truth. Wasn't she entitled to that?

She went to bed, but tossed and turned wondering how she could have rephrased her question. How could she have let him know that she wanted him to love her? She just didn't want to be a stand-in.

Caesar tried to concentrate and take notes on his project but his mind kept coming back to Leigh's question. He'd never told anyone how many nights Stephanie had spent crying at his house while Paul was out making conquests. He'd found a vulnerable woman under all the make-up, fancy clothes and wild hairstyles he'd designed for her. He had been her confidante, her friend, but he had never been her lover. Somehow he just couldn't tell Leigh that. He had never told anyone that Stephanie had come to him the night she died—that she had begged him to make love to her and he had sent her home to her husband. How could he tell Leigh that if he'd been Stephanie's lover she'd still be alive?

THIRTY

Somehow they made it through the next few days. They talked only about business and only in the presence of others. At the apartment he retreated to the guest room and she to her bedroom.

But as much as their personal life fell apart, the salon idea took wings. Caesar got a theatre set designer and a clothing designer to be a part of the event. They had sworn key personnel to secrecy and so far it was working. When they covered up the window, speculation began that they were going out of business. But when Ken Harrow, the set designer, and Reggi Winteres, the clothing designer, were seen going in and out of Cassiopeia, a rumor of remodeling began.

They asked a modeling agency to assist in the search of the first group the public would see: the under five set. The Board let Leigh work out the arrangements. She selected three each of Anglo, African-American, Latino and Asian babies from one year old to five years old.

There was no announcement when Ken Harrow's window nursery was completed. And they had enough designer diapers, dresses, slacks and formal attire. One morning it was a covered window the next there were babies playing. The sign read: this is the future, let's take care of it. Their success is our success.

Success was not the word, Leigh was looking for. She had put Cassiopeia in the forefront of everyone' mind. She'd hinted to the press that there was more to come and the response was when can we see it.

Leigh had just come from doing a morning talk-show and was on her way up the spiral staircase when she heard something. Coins were falling onto the staircase, but there was no sound of anything else. When Leigh went to check on things, she stepped up on the top steps. Something slippery was on the carpet. Her foot got stuck on it and as she tried to remove it, she felt a heavy weight alongside her head. She fell backwards and tried to grab a rail, the carpet—something to stop her fall.

Leigh woke up with a frantic Caesar bending over her. His voice cleared the heavy fog.

"Leigh, darling. Wake up. Talk to me."

She could say nothing but at least she was alive. Leigh rolled into Caesar's arms and let him hold her.

Caesar's mind was going a mile a minute. He couldn't lose her—Not before he told her the truth. Despite her protests, everyone insisted she go to the hospital. Caesar rode with her in the ambulance. She tried to speak but no words formed. By, the time she regained her faculties, she was ensconced in a private room in the hospital. Caesar was sitting by her bedside.

"All this for me?" She waved at the phone next to her bedside and her TV on a mechanical arm so she could turn it to suit her.

"Why not? Why shouldn't you have the comforts of home?" He smiled halfheartedly. "You deserve whatever we can give you."

Somewhere in the back of her mind she remembered an article that said if only one side of your face showed an emotion it was a lie.

"I'm going to be fine," she said.

"I know. I just don't want you to spend a night here but the Doctor insists. Get some sleep and I'll be back in the morning."

"You get some sleep also. If you have to go to the salon first, it's all right."

"I don't think the salon is as important as you are. I'll see you in the morning."

He stood up and leaned over her. She thought he was going to kiss her forehead and was surprised to feel his warm lips on hers. He was gone in seconds but that warmth spread through her body even before the medication that made her drift off to sleep.

THIRTY ONE

Two days later, Jameson Miller was still not amused that Leigh had ended up in the hospital. Rick and JoAnn said nothing as he raged at them. "I want the salon but I don't want anyone hurt. How could you do that?"

"Do what?" Rick didn't know what to say other than the truth. "You wanted her to lose the business, didn't you?"

"I didn't want her injured in the process. Whose bright idea was that?"

"No one's; she fell."

"All by herself?"

"Look, Miller," Rick told him. "I want the business to die and I want to make a lot of money. But pushing women down a staircase is not my style."

"I thought the paper said she may have been pushed?"

"I'm sure the papers would love a scandal, but no way did I push her."

"Neither did I." JoAnn's voice quivered as she defended herself.

"Then who?"

"We don't know," Rick said. "Let's do this job and not have anymore talk about hurting Leigh. We wouldn't do that."

"And you can speak for your girlfriend?"

"What's that suppose to mean?" yelled JoAnn.

"I think that Mrs. Leigh Montgomery is too much for you to handle. She came up with a plan to save the salon despite your constant harping that she didn't know what she was doing and that it wouldn't work."

"She got lucky."

"Smart people don't need luck. I think it's time for me to bail out of this takeover."

"You can't!"

"No way!"

Rick and JoAnn spoke at the same time.

"Unless things change drastically I won't be able to get near Cassiopeia. Sorry you couldn't pull it off."

They were being dismissed. JoAnn couldn't believe how easily Jameson Miller waved them away. They left knowing Miller had dumped everything back in their laps. Rick and JoAnn would have to scramble hard if they wanted to be on his team. With the success of the Cassiopeia City, it appeared that Miller

would have to find another way to make his presence known
in the New York real estate market.

Every time JoAnn arrived at the salon she found the usual
mob. Rick liked working his way through the crowd; JoAnn did
not. She told him she'd meet him later and walked away from
the store entrance. With the success of the real life window
campaign maybe she didn't need Miller. At least not for money.
Maybe she needed him for something else.

She decided to go over to his house and see if Jameson Miller
was looking for a life partner. Rick had been pushing her away
since Leigh's accident. He must have thought she had done it.

When she arrived at Miller's hotel, she saw him coming out
of the building with a woman on his arm. They appeared to be
heading for the taxi at the curb. Miller turned the woman to
him and kissed her. He was saying good night so JoAnn waited.
She'd go in after the woman left. Then she got a good look at
the woman: it was Juliette Montgomery. JoAnn stayed in the
shadows as Miller pulled the woman around and kissed her
again.

JoAnn couldn't wait to get back to Rick. They had an ally.
She was positive that Caesar didn't know his mother was spending time with his arch enemy. She and Rick could stop worrying
about the process. Cassiopeia would be Miller's and they would
be the winners.

She hailed a cab and headed home. She made only one stop
at a liquor store to buy Rick's favorite champagne. Tonight they
had something to celebrate.

When she got to Rick's, he wasn't as enthusiastic. "What if
she's his foil rather than his betrayal?"

"Caesar would never do that."

"Doesn't matter what you think his character will do, I say
he's desperate. If he can't continue the success of the window
deal, he could be in the red. Maybe he's desperate enough to
ask his mother for a favor."

"Doesn't matter. If we find a way to bring the salon down, he'll be right back in the game."

Jameson Miller sat on the sofa. He'd stretched out and put his feet up on the coffee table. He was grateful the servants were off tonight. His housekeeper would have glared at him until he sat up and put his feet on the floor where they belonged. Men quaked at the mention of his name but not his tiny housekeeper. She knew he was more bluff than bite.

Juliette Montgomery had a similar power over him. The woman got to his core and he found himself backing away from the salon property. He even dared to use the word "love" when he thought of her. He was only fighting Caesar and Leigh Montgomery halfheartedly. If he ever got a chance to talk to them, he wanted them to know that their downfall would not be at his hands but the other members of the board. He could only string Rick and JoAnn along for a few more days before they realized he wasn't interested.

THIRTY TWO

When Caesar brought Leigh home from the hospital, he was still guilt—ridden about Stephanie. He waited until that night when Leigh seemed to be most comfortable. Despite her tumble, she had only suffered a badly sprained ankle and trauma to the body that would take a few weeks to go away.

"Can we talk?"

Leigh looked up to see Caesar balancing a tray of fruit. He put it down on the bed and then began taking off his shoes and socks. She didn't say anything as he threw his jacket on the chair.

He sat on the bed and swung his legs up so he was stretched out next to her. She was under the bed covers, he on top.

"We have to talk. I'll tell you everything about Stephanie and me. If you want a divorce, I won't stand in your way."

Leigh's heart was in her throat. If he was offering a divorce then they must have been lovers. Her mind warred with her heart in the minute he took to compose himself.

"When Stephanie and I met, she and Paul were having trouble," he said. "Marriage didn't prevent Paul from taking his pick of groupies every now and then. Helene was so afraid that if they broke up, she'd be poor again."

"I always knew my aunt to have money. She took trips. She lived a glamorous life."

"I don't know. That's what she kept telling me. She didn't want to be poor again. You know Jim and the others tried the restaurant business before deciding on the salon. They lost everything. I think they felt Cassiopeia was their last chance to be happy."

"And because Paul played around, you and Stephanie did the same thing?"

"No way. How could you think I'd get involved with a married woman?"

"But . . ."

"No. Stephanie and I became friends. She needed someone to talk to."

"And you let her use your shoulder?"

"Right. I should have known she'd changed from friendship to infatuation but I didn't."

"You were never lovers?"

"Never." Caesar lifted the tray and put it on the hope chest at the foot of the bed. He returned and pulled her closer to him.

"The night they were . . . murdered, Stephanie was at my house. She told me she wanted us to be more than friends. I said it couldn't happen. Then she said she was going to divorce him and she didn't care about the salon. It wasn't hers anyway. I sent her home to rethink her life with Paul. I was so afraid of what could happen if I got involved with her I sent her to her death."

Caesar was shaking as if he was reliving that night and making the same decision.

Leigh wrapped her arms around him. She could still feel his body tremors. All this time she had been speculating about Caesar being in love with Stephanie. She wanted to laugh and cry at the same time.

"It wasn't your fault."

"I can't help feeling it was. If I'd only let her stay with me. We didn't have to make love. We were just friends."

"You wanted her to know what she was doing was wrong."

"I wanted her out of my place before I took her up on her offer. Now I wish I had. She'd be alive."

"You don't know that. And if Paul had been killed, Stephanie would have been destroyed anyway."

"What makes you think that?"

"When we were still talking to each other, she told me how much she loved him."

"But you hadn't seen her for a while . . ."

"I know my sister. She knew about his affairs but she loved him, and while I would have walked out when I found out about the first one, she stayed because she wanted to."

"Sometimes I want to believe that and other times I . . ."

"Get off the guilt trip. You couldn't have saved either one."

He tightened his arms around her and she let a small gasp slip through her lips. She was sore from the fall.

"Sorry. When you get well we'll have to have another of these little talks. Then I can make love to you."

"I'll remind you when I'm stronger."

"Good. I look forward to it . . . "

THIRTY THREE

After a few days in bed, and Caesar following her around like a mother hen, Leigh was glad to be at work. She wore flat shoes that made walking easier and she took extra precautions on the spiral staircase. She hid a flashlight in her desk and carried a small one in her handbag. No matter what anyone thought, she knew someone had pushed her. She didn't dare tell anyone. Leigh wasn't sure anyone would believe her.

Leigh thumbed through the clippings notebook that Gayla prepared. She was grateful the woman had preserved it in date order. The salon was booked for the next two months. People were even calling up to be put on a waiting list in case of cancellations.

Leigh knew that they were still trying to get the woman who was suing them to agree to a settlement. The person most helpful had been Caesar. Now Leigh understood why Caesar was so determined to save the salon. He felt he owed it to everyone but especially to Leigh.

They were starting over again. It seemed that was what they always did. Leigh hoped that this time Caesar had told her the truth. She couldn't stand another lie. No matter what she felt for the man, Leigh swore to herself that she would walk away from everything—the man, the money, the salon—but especially the man.

"Penny for your thoughts." Caesar's voice broke through her reverie. "Although from that frown on your face, I think I'd pay a lot more than a penny."

"I was thinking what I'd do if all this fell apart again."

"It won't." He crossed the room and pulled her into his arms. His kiss was light and feathery at first but became more demanding. He couldn't break off the kiss. Somehow Leigh always managed to throw his mind into a tangled mess that only wanted the sensation to continue. Other women never made him forget reason. But Leigh had only to look at him and he was undressing her and tumbling into their bed.

She melted against his body and groaned as his hands ran up and down her ribcage. The tenderness of the night before had only increased her need.

They broke apart simultaneously as if each knew that control was slipping away and they might be willing to take a chance on not being discovered.

"Tonight?" his husky voice whispered.

"Tonight!" she answered back.

She was still in his arms when Juliette came into the office. "Aha, my son has finally learned that love is more important than business."

"If that were the case, I dare not describe what you might have been witness to, Mother dear," Caesar teased.

Leigh felt the heat rush over her face. How could he even joke that way with his mother? How could she have lost all her senses and forgotten about business? Even with her ex-fiance she never allowed her feelings to be overshadowed by her duty. Maybe that's why she didn't regret that that relationship ended.

She watched Caesar kiss his mother's forehead and stroll out the door. She couldn't bring her eyes to meet Juliette's.

"Don't be embarrassed. It's good to see young people lose some of their business demeanor," Juliette said. "I never thought I'd see Sarito so much in love."

"Surely you've seen him in love before."

"I have seen him infatuated, desperate and determined in his conquests, but I have never seen him in love."

Leigh wasn't sure if Juliette was seeing what they both wanted rather than the truth. Caesar could still turn off his emotions faster than anyone she knew. Maybe it was still an act, even though she didn't want it to be one.

"Juliette, I've noticed a twinkle in your eyes lately—could that be love?"

"Yes, I think so, but this is not good."

"Why not?"

"Well . . . he's younger."

"It's the way things are now. How much younger?"

"Just a little older than Sarito."

Leigh tried but failed to suppress the giggles. "Is it serious?"

"Quite. But I hate it."

"No, you don't. You're just afraid of your son." Leigh didn't even try to hide her glee this time. She was excited about the mystery man and she was happy that Juliette felt she could talk about this with her. Having lost her own mother early in her life, Leigh wanted marriage, children,and all the trappings.

"It is no laughing matter. Caesar will be furious."

"So what! You're entitled to happiness. Your son will just have to accept that."

"I want you to be there when I introduce them."

"Sure. When?"

"I'm not sure. I'll let you know."

"If you really think Caesar won't be able to handle it, I suggest a very public place."

"And you think that will keep him from making a scene?"

"No, but it will only be a small scene."

The two women sat on the sofa in Leigh's office and just talked. Leigh updated Juliette on the Cassiopeia City. An hour later, Leigh walked Juliette to the door. She used the cane Caesar had given her. It looked more like a fancy walking stick, with its jewel-encrusted top. She glanced down at her nails. The one good thing about owning a salon was that you got to pamper yourself. She arranged an appointment for that day.

JoAnn watched them and waited. She fell into step alongside Leigh. "So you and the mother-in-law getting along?"

"Yes, we are."

"Well history says she should be your worst enemy."

"That's not always true."

"I wouldn't count on it. Mothers are notorious for not believing that another woman could take *their* places."

"Juliette would never be that clingy."

"Suit yourself. But when you find out the salon business makes less money and has to be sold, just think who might have been whispering sweet nothings in your ear." JoAnn turned toward the manicure salon.

Leigh knew that it was JoAnn's way of needling her and she tried not to give any more credence to what the woman was saying. Things were different now. Before, Leigh's insecurities would have had her crying, but not now. She loved the fact she was finally stepping out on her own. She couldn't wait to tell Mark that she wasn't coming back to the law firm. Her new life was with Caesar and Cassiopeia, and that was where she wanted to be.

THIRTY-FOUR

Leigh was just about to leave the office when Helene stopped in to tell her that the lawsuit had been settled out of court. One of the stipulations was that she could not talk about what had happened or what the settlement was or she would risk being the defendant in any more litigations.

"I know you were insistent about having the man fired, but I think this is a much better way."

The stylist had been keeping a low profile since the lawsuit and that was fine with Leigh. She'd made it clear to him that he had no future with Cassiopeia so she expected him to shop around for a new job. She hoped his search wouldn't last too long.

"How is the search for the white knight coming?"

"We have a few offers."

"Well, don't take just any offer. We'll get one of those venture capitalists in here and never be able to breathe again."

"Don't I know it? I haven't even considered the offers from any of those people."

Leigh watched as Helene smoothed her hair back. The tiny woman was still beautiful. She wondered why Helene was so against marriage. Ever since she could remember there had been no man in Helene's life.

Not that her aunt was unfulfilled. She had plenty of activity with her clubs and business organizations.

"Are you going out?"

"Yes, the Friends of Theatre are having a dinner. I should still be in tomorrow."

After Helene left, Leigh had intended to do more work, but Juliette called.

"I want you and Sarito to join me for dinner."

"I don't know. There's a lot of work to be done . . ."

"You are too young to ever put business before an entertaining evening."

"Oh? And why is it going to be entertaining?"

Juliette laughed, a throaty laugh that said she had a secret. "I have someone I want you to meet."

"Ah hah! So tonight is the night we all meet."

"I think you will be a little bit shocked."

"Juliette, I don't think we could stand the shock. Who is it?"

Leigh felt a chill run down her spine. If Juliette embarrassed Caesar in front of Leigh while he was trying to save the salon, there would be more damage done. But Juliette wouldn't budge. The only way to see her escort for the night would be to meet them for dinner.

"I don't think Caesar is in the mood for surprises."

"My son has become stodgy and too intense about the salon."

"It's very important to us."

"More important than you are to each other?"

No matter how she tried, Juliette was not to be denied. She would not talk about her secret admirer. Maybe wedding bells were ringing for Juliette and she didn't want to make that mistake with her last chance.

Leigh hesitated and formed her answer carefully. "Sometimes if things don't go well in a career, it affects the relationship."

"Only if the two people are not meant to be together. You are a smart woman. You had a career before Cassiopeia and you can have another if it goes away."

But would she have Caesar if she didn't have the salon? "I was getting tired of my other career."

"You must know the value of your brains the same way I knew the value of my beauty. I knew it wouldn't last forever. I did other things with my life. I lived in Europe because I knew it would make me more 'interesting' when I came back to America. I knew interesting would beat out beauty in the long run."

"I don't know. Caesar has a lot tied up in the salon."

"Ah! If you insist, I will help you. I will find a way to convince your competitor to leave you alone. How is that?"

"If only you could."

They talked about clothes for a few minutes then said their goodbyes.

Leigh left the building and hailed a cab in front of the salon. The short trip home was not long enough to make the worry leave her face. Caesar was lounging on the sofa and looked up when Leigh came in.

"Your mother has invited us to have dinner at Le Cirque."

"Sounds as if she has someone she wants us to meet."

"Exactly."

"Then who?"

"Honestly, she wouldn't tell me."

"I can't let her get involved. As soon as I have a name, I'll have someone check him out."

"Your mother's an adult for Heaven's sake," Leigh said.

"I don't think you should be trying to play cupid when Miller's talking as if he can take the salon away tomorrow. I called my brother last night. Esteban said he'd help. I'm not sure I want to take his offer."

Leigh turned and looked at Caesar. His eyes said he was telling the truth. He would risk losing the salon to Miller rather than seek help from his brother.

"How can you say that? This may be our only chance. Cassiopeia is cash poor and we don't have too many offers to choose from."

Caesar dropped his suit jacket over the back of the sofa. "For you, it's so easy. You want the salon. So whatever it takes, you will do. Isn't that how it works?"

"I'm not the only one who wanted the salon."

"No, just the only one who would marry me to get it."

Caesar stormed from the room. Leigh slowly walked to her bedroom and closed the door. Why was he so upset? He was the one who suggested marriage. The one who had wouldn't be her partner unless they were legally wed. Now he was acting as if it was her idea. He'd made it very clear that if they shared a bed, he still wanted to be free to walk away at any time. She and Caesar had entered into a silent agreement that said there was no reason they shouldn't sleep together as long as neither of them got too possessive. She didn't want to admit in her heart that his machismo was being tested and he had to fight back and fight alone. And she would have to walk away from this relationship. She could not live with someone that closed in spirit.

She gathered her lingerie bag and went into the bathroom. Leigh stripped and stepped into the shower. The water beat down on her body for ten minutes. She couldn't take any more of Caesar's mood swings. She thought he and his brother had come to an understanding. Esteban was only repaying a favor.

She toweled herself dry and reached over and picked up her body lotion. As she rubbed it into her skin, she turned off the shower. Then she slipped into her lingerie, put on her stockings, and padded back into the bedroom.

Earlier she'd selected a black off the shoulder, ruffled dress. The crepe material adhered to her curves and provided enough cleavage to be slightly dangerous. It wasn't a dress for anyone with bad posture. She stepped into black sling-backs with a two inch heel.

Leigh wrapped her make-up cape around her and applied her foundation with slow, even strokes. After putting a light dusting of powder over her face, she chose a deep plum lipstick to complete her look.

She viewed herself in the full-length mirror and was pleased with the results. Lately, when she'd had to dress for some cocktail party or business dinner, she hadn't paid much attention to what she was wearing. Tonight she wanted to look and feel special.

Caesar couldn't believe how he'd reacted with Leigh. Why was he angry with her? She'd kept her end of the bargain. She hadn't tried to push him into declaring an undying love, although some days that's what he wanted. He should have just explained that all his life he'd been independent. Never had he needed anyone to get him out of situations. His mother made sure of that. Juliette was an iron butterfly. The facade was a fragile woman who needed to be cared for but the reality was that she could take care of herself if necessary.

He'd seen that same toughness in Leigh. She knew what she wanted and how to get it. Marrying him had given her the control she needed. But Caesar admitted the marriage had been his idea. He thought it would be easy to have a pretense of marriage that gave him more power to do the things Cassiopeia needed. Instead he found that he loved working with Leigh. They were kindred souls—and not only in business.

He wanted to be the one to get them out of trouble. He wanted her to have her dream. He showered and shaved and began to dress. He paired his black Canali suit with a white shirt with thin black stripes and added a Ralph Lauren tie and matching pocket handkerchief.

He waited in the living room for Leigh. Failure was not a word that Caesar Montgomery was accustomed to. However, if he continued to be so rigid that was what would happen—he would fail. He couldn't stand that. He wanted Cassiopeia and he wanted Leigh. From all her signals he could not have one without the other. He needed both of them and if all it took was a call to his brother, then so be it. He reached for the phone and dialed.

After a few minutes of haggling for an ironclad contract, he was satisfied. He was just putting the phone down when he heard Leigh's bedroom door close. He went to the tiny refrigerator that housed Leigh's favorite white wines and selected a California Sauvignon Blanc.

He poured two glasses and as Leigh came into the livingroom he handed her a glass. His raised eyebrow was all he dared as he looked at her provocative neckline. If their marriage was real, he'd never have let her out of the house in this dress.

"What's the occasion?" Leigh sat on the love seat, and Caesar chose the lounge chair.

"I just spoke with my brother. We've found a mutual ground we can both live with and he will be our white knight."

Leigh's reaction was not what he expected. Instead of jumping for joy she was subdued.

"That's wonderful."

"You don't sound as if it's 'wonderful'."

"I don't want you do to do something that you'll regret."

"I won't regret it. I just had to ask myself if my pride was standing in the way of my success. It was."

"No."

"Yes. I wanted to do it all. At first I thought you were in the way and I tried to keep you from interfering with what I thought was my job. Helene convinced me that if you came on board we would lose everything."

"She's never wanted me around. I don't know why. When she took Stephanie she said it was because she needed someone who was self-sufficient."

Caesar could only shake his head. He sipped the last of his wine and set the glass down in the sink. He couldn't imagine someone saying that to a child. His mother had dragged him from coast to coast, continent to continent. He supposed she could have left him with any number of relatives, but she didn't. Self-sufficiency was something he learned along the way.

"Come on, Juliette's waiting."

"Why do you always call her Juliette?"

"And not mom, Mother, ma, whatever?" he said and laughed.

"Exactly."

"I didn't grow up around many children. The adults around called her by her first name and somehow I picked that up."

"Did you call your father by his first name?"

"Not him. He would not tolerate such insubordination. I called him Papa."

Leigh marveled at the similar conditions she and Caesar had grown up in. A single parent who gave them each more love than some two-parent households.

She had to include Esteban when she thought about the lack of warmth. Groomed to take over from his father, he didn't have the choice Caesar had. Leigh felt that tension between them also came from Esteban wanting to make incorrect choices and learn from them. In his life, he'd never had the chance. Each of his choices had to be carefully planned.

She knew what it took to ask that favor but Caesar had made that phone call for both of them. She only hoped she made it worth his while.

Leigh wanted to ask more but it was time to meet his mother at the restaurant.

THIRTY-FIVE

The walls of the restaurant were covered with copies of French Impressionist paintings. Soft piano music played in the background—live music, not the canned variety. Any other time this would have been a wonderful dinner to be shared with her husband. Unfortunately he was so worried about the man his mother had been seeing that Leigh was afraid if he didn't like him the evening would be ruined.

After waiting at the bar for fifteen minutes, their table was finally ready. Once they were seated, they decided to look over the menu but not order until Juliette and her companion arrived.

Juliette wore a purple beaded dress by Lagerfeld. She and Leigh had laughed about their shared favorite designer. It wasn't his mother's attire that made Leigh gasp and Caesar shake his head—it was her escort . . . Jameson Miller.

Caesar watched as the maitre d' led Juliette and Miller to his table.

"Hello, darlings," Juliette said as she kissed Caesar's cheek and then Leigh's. "I think you've met my escort."

Caesar mumbled a greeting. How could she expect him to be civil to this man?

"Jameson, this is my son Sarito and his wife, Leigh," Juliette announced. "He calls himself Caesar, but I named him Sarito and that's what I call him."

"We've met," Jameson said.

"I think it's time you men became friends."

"Mother, that's not going to happen."

"Juliette, I'm glad you chose a public place for this attempt." Leigh had become a willing participant in this little scheme.

There was something in the way Jameson Miller looked at Juliette. Leigh had found him cold when Mark had pointed him out. Tonight, his blue eyes had a twinkle and Juliette had put it there.

The waiter brought two more menus and Juliette acted as if everything was normal. They ordered, and while they were waiting for the food, Jameson broke the silence.

"Montgomery, I like a good fight. That's what you and your wife gave me. I like to win. I didn't this time, but I believe there will be a next time."

"No, there won't," Leigh said. "You can't have my company."

"Don't get bent out of shape, Leigh," Jameson said. "I didn't say I liked the same fight. I've got a few more irons in the fire."

When the waiter asked about the wine, Jameson immediately turned to Juliette. "I would think that someone who's lived in Paris for so many years would be the one to ask about wine."

He handed the menu to Juliette. She browsed through it for a few minutes then ordered a Chateau Rothschild Bordeaux.

They relaxed and by the time the food arrived, they'd found several other subjects they could talk about without creating a scene. It was during dessert that Miller's conversation came back to the salon.

Throughout the meal, Leigh had watched another side of Miller. He laughed at Juliette's jokes, allowed her to make fun of his business ventures, but what she noticed most was the look in his eyes when he spoke to her. Leigh had seen that same look in Caesar's.

How was he going to react if Miller became his stepfather?

"I don't want this to sound like sour grapes but your company's still in trouble."

"Someone else wants it?" Caesar asked.

"No. Your trouble is more pressing than a takeover attempt."

"Well, don't just dangle the carrot," Juliette ordered. "Talk."

"Your mother is the only one who can push me around," he said. "I think something shady went down with another venture. I haven't gotten all the facts, but believe me, 110% of nothing is still nothing. These guys aren't your friends."

They left the restaurant but Miller and Juliette declined Leigh's offer to go to her condo for drinks.

"I'll see you around," Caesar said.

"Just remember to watch your back."

With those final words, Miller slipped his arm around Juliette's waist and guided her to his limousine.

As soon as his mother and Miller were out of sight, Caesar turned to Leigh.

"Don't say it."

Leigh affected a wide-eyed look. "Say what?"

"That they make a cute couple. That I should let my mother live her own life. Anything that pertains to my mother and Jameson Miller."

"Why? You two hit it off as soon as you realized you didn't have a choice."

"Exactly. We didn't have a choice."

"He didn't have to tell you that something's going on that not part of."

"No, but it's what you've been saying all along."

"So, where do we go from here?"

"I think the answer's in the brownstone."

A shiver of cold ran through Leigh's body. She'd only been to the brownstone once since she'd inherited it.

"If you'd rather go home, I can handle this."

"No. It's time I put the past behind me."

Caesar signaled for a taxi. When they arrived at the brownstone, Leigh took a deep breath as Caesar opened the door.

She went through the double outside doors and stood in the foyer. The first time she'd tried not to notice anything, but now she saw the care that had been put into the upkeep. The mahogany banister threw off little beams of lights when the overhead source hit it. From the panel by the door they turned on all the lights in the lower-level hallways.

The stairway led to the bedrooms. It would probably be a section she would never enter. How could she ever be comfortable here, despite its beauty?

"Did you ever wonder where they got the money to open Cassiopeia?"

"Are you kidding? That last concert tour sold out all over the world."

"Right. But he'd had three albums that flopped and a video he made couldn't be shown on TV."

"I didn't think about that. Most record companies will charge you for the expenses and take the money away from future profits."

"Not to mention the restaurant that failed."

"Somewhere in this house is the answer." Leigh walked down the hall and opened the door to the room Stephanie had called her office. Caesar was right behind her.

"If you'd rather look in Paul's office, I'll take this one."

"No. I can handle this."

She slid her hand along the panel until she found the switch and the room was suddenly bathed in light. She turned and nodded to Caesar, reassuring him that she was ready to face this.

Leigh sat at the desk and started going through the drawers methodically. Scrutinizing each slip of paper, studying each photograph, somewhere there was a clue to a money trail.

The desk was much like the one her grandfather had had. She remembered they found a secret drawer by pulling the drawers completely free from the desk. Leigh's heart pounded frantically as she did this with each drawer and to her complete dismay found nothing.

Caesar wasn't having any luck either. Paul's filing system was a tax man's nightmare. He kept all the necessary papers but they were packed in drawers, boxes, accordion files. It seemed he spent his life trying to get organized and failed.

It was now past midnight and all he'd found was a copy of the plans for Cassiopeia, a faded, yellowing term paper by Leigh Barrington. He put it on top of the desk. Leigh might want to hold onto it, in case their children wanted to know about their legacy. Children! He didn't even know if Leigh wanted to stay married. Both of them seemed to be avoiding the subject. He made up his mind to talk to her when they finished here.

He had to know, because he was in love with her. It was something he hadn't been able to tell her. He'd had women declare their love, and when he couldn't reciprocate, he'd seen the despair in their eyes. He didn't want Leigh to pity him.

Then he'd better find some answers, because if it was over between them, he wanted her to have her dream: Cassiopeia.

He pulled himself back to the job at hand. Tossing anything that wasn't business related in one pile and the items he needed to take a second look at in another. The answer was there and something Jameson Miller said struck a nerve. Something about 110%.

Leigh had only found papers for the brownstone, a condo for Helene, and a car for Helene. It was 12:30 A.M. and she was starting to feel it was hopeless. The next big move for the salon was the dispensation of the money from Paul's account. She'd finally decided what she wanted to do with the money after the visit from the tax man. She'd even scheduled a board meeting to make the announcement.

Her eyes started to droop and she started yawning. She left the room and made her way to the kitchen. After washing the dust from the coffee maker and rummaging through the cabinets until she found regular coffee instead of the fancy blends Stephanie preferred, she made a huge pot. After drinking a cup, she found a thermos, washed that, and filled it with coffee. She took it and a cup down the hall to Caesar.

He was hunched over the desk, so caught up in what he was doing that he didn't hear her come in. It was the aroma of freshly made coffee that made him look up.

"For a moment I thought I was hallucinating," he said and smiled.

"I hope you're doing better than I am." She poured him a cup of coffee.

"Sorry. I can't get over how these records are thrown haphazardly around this place. This is probably why the lawyer asked them to do a living will." He sipped the coffee slowly.

"We do have a board meeting to attend in a few hours."

"I know. But Miller's right. The money from Cassiopeia had to come from somewhere."

"I guess people just assume rock stars are rich and no one ever asked."

"Why don't you go home and get some rest? I'll make the board meeting."

She wanted to say no, she'd stay with him, but she was just too tired to argue. She got her coat, and Caesar waited until she was in a taxi before he leaned in and kissed her.

"We have a lot to talk about after this is over," he said.

She nodded. They would talk about the future. The one they would share. Leigh settled back and relaxed. She had a tough day ahead of her.

About three in the morning he stopped and took a nap. At six he was back at the task, and at ten he hit pay dirt. He gathered all his papers and called Detective Carver, the man who had shot the burglar. The man who felt there was still a piece of the puzzle missing. Carver agreed to talk to him. Caesar was in his office an hour later after he stopped by the condo for a quick shower and shave.

Leigh had already left for the salon and he felt a twinge of regret he'd missed her.

"So you think you have some revolutionary evidence that will make me take a second look at the Lambert case?" Carver leaned back in his chair and folded his arms across his chest.

"Did you ever see that old movie, *The Producers?*"

"I don't remember it."

"Gene Wilder and Zero Mostel?"

Carver shook his head.

"Here's the plot. They want to find the worst play in the world and produce it. The plan is to sell 50% to ten or twenty people. The play will flop and no one will expect to get any money. Since they've oversold, they make a bundle."

"Right. You only get money from hits."

"In the movie, that's how they get caught. The play's a hit and all these people expect big returns."

"Someone's going to prison. Okay, I can see that."

"I always wondered where Paul and Stephanie got the money for the salon. I wasn't part of the original group. Then I remembered Jimmy laughing about a previous venture that bombed."

"And you think the Lamberts pulled something like the movie deal?"

"I know they did. Here's the proof."

"I guess you did have something revolutionary. The other two names on this bankbook must be part of the scam."

"They might have gotten too greedy. They didn't know that Paul and Stephanie had new living wills."

"I think I'd better get a few arrest warrants and a team."

THIRTY-SIX

"Well, are we going to have a meeting or not?" Helene tapped her fingers on the table.

"I'm trying to wait for Sarito," Leigh explained.

"That may be all well and good, but some of us have a life outside the boardroom." JoAnn was glancing down at her watch as if she had an appointment.

"Let's get on with it. We'll hold the vote until he gets here," Rick said.

Outnumbered and with the restless behavior beginning to annoy her, Leigh called the meeting to order.

"We need to talk about Jameson Miller."

"What about him? He wants Cassiopeia, but he can't get it," Rick said.

"That's what I thought until last night. Sarito and I ran into him at a restaurant. He said something about being very close to the final jewel in his crown."

"So, what's the deal? Someone making plans without a vote?"

"I warned you that we weren't strong enough to fight off a takeover, Kevin," Rick yelled.

"Calm down," Leigh told him. "He can't take over because we have enough money to fight him off. And if necessary, we can use a white knight."

"Who'd be willing to take on this white elephant?"

"Esteban Valerian."

"Sarito's brother?"

"The same," she told them.

"That's great," said Rick.

They were congratulating each other on still owning Cassiopeia, when Sarito arrived with Detective Carver and two uniformed officers, one a policewoman. Dean Roman stopped in the middle of his tirade about too much time spent planning and not doing.

"Forgive the interruption," Sarito said. "Detective Carver has something to say."

"We've come across some new evidence that links Rick Adams and JoAnn Desmond to the murders."

Gasps came from all directions. As board members looked around in horror, the police carried out their mission. Carver walked over to Rick Adams. "Eric Adams, you're under arrest for conspiracy in the murder of Paul and Stephanie Lambert."

Rick's face blanched under his dark complexion. "I didn't do it. I was at the party," he screamed. "You know that." He waved his arms as the detective continued to read him his rights. Then he was handcuffed and led from the room.

"I can't believe this," Dean said. "Rick, a murderer? Nah."

The policewoman placed her hand on JoAnn's shoulder and Mirandized JoAnn. She tossed her head and glared at Leigh. "This is your fault. You just wouldn't leave things alone. You just had to know everything. I didn't kill anyone and I'm not going to prison for something I didn't do."

After the police left, Angela called for an explanation. "We seem to be completely in the dark about the activities of some of our colleagues."

Sarito explained how he'd been wondering about the numbers in the back of Stephanie's diary.

"Diary! She kept a diary?" Bob tugged at his collar.

"Don't worry, the police only have the pages I tore out that had the numbers on them. They aren't interested in anything else."

Leigh glanced around the room and saw relief spread across the faces of Bob and Kevin. When did they conduct business? No wonder they were ripe for a takeover if they were so busy with clandestine affairs. Helene's reaction was a surprise. She had a slight smile on her face, as if she were happy about the turn of events—as if she thought if Stephanie couldn't have it, she didn't care.

"Well, ladies and gentlemen," Jimmy said. "I think it's time to circle the wagons."

He was right. They were coming closer and closer to losing everything.

"Why would they do it?" Angela demanded.

Sarito had taken his chair next to Leigh. "Paul, Stephanie, Rick, and JoAnn met in Hollywood. They decided to open up a restaurant."

"I lost my shirt in that one," Kevin said.

"Me, too," added Jimmy.

"Exactly." Sarito looked at the puzzled faces. "Last night I had a conversation with Jameson Miller."

"Why even talk to that snake?" Helene finally reacted.

"He said something very interesting. One hundred and ten percent of nothing is still nothing. How much did you invest in the restaurant?"

"Thirty percent," came Jimmy's soft reply.

"That's what I invested," Kevin said.

"Me, too." The responses from Angela and Dean proved Sarito's point.

"Wait a minute," Leigh cut in. "You all couldn't have invested 30% each."

"But that's exactly what they did, darling," Sarito explained. "When the restaurant folded, none of you expected to see any of the money. You just wrote it off as a bad business debt."

"Stephanie would never have done that," Helene said as she jumped to her feet. "Don't start trying to destroy her memory. She wouldn't do it."

"Maybe not," Sarito said. "It doesn't matter. What they did was collect all the money from you and deposited it somewhere. They used a very small amount to rent a property, try to run a restaurant, and when it failed you'd all just go away."

"The numbers in the back of the diary were a code. It led to a bank account in Delaware that was just earning interest." Caesar remembered that his mother had changed her age, which would change the year of birth. He'd used Helene's quoted age and done the same thing.

"Ha," Jimmy yelped. "And we call ourselves businessmen."

"What about me?" Helene wept softly. "They were my family."

"It was about to happen again. They promised you a chance to recoup. Buy in for less, make a profit. It looked good on paper. Rick and JoAnn took a smaller portion so they wouldn't stand out. Unfortunately the thieves had a falling out. Paul and Stephanie moved the money. Rick and JoAnn couldn't say anything. But what they wanted was another failure. When that didn't happen, they saw that it was a candidate for a takeover."

"So what do we do?" asked Angela.

"We let Miller make us rich by taking the money and running, or by doing as Jimmy suggested, circling the wagons."

Leigh stood up. "I know that I want to fight for this place but I'm not going to force the rest of you to do that. If you want to take Miller's offer and we walk away with the money, it's only fair."

Sarito slipped his arm around Leigh. "My vote is your vote."

Silence. It lasted twenty seconds and then a cacophony of voices throwing out ideas.

"No way," said Dean. "I like a good fight."

"Me, too," added Jimmy.

The others seem to feel the same way. It looked as if Jameson Miller was in for the fight of his life. The publicity might even help. Despite Leigh's aversion, business did pick up whenever the salon made news. She just wished it had been for their service rather than their notoriety.

Leigh knew that Helene had amassed enough money to live comfortably for the rest of her life. She'd tried to get Stephanie to do the same. If the salon faltered, she would still be all right. Leigh was cognizant that the weak link in the Board was Helene. She would be happy to sell to Miller but she couldn't—not without Board approval, and Leigh was smart enough to know that it only took one weak link to break a chain.

Leigh and Sarito met with Mark to see how they would fare against a takeover. "He's not just going away," Mark explained. "He's going to hit at the weakest members, and while they're all ready for a fight now, that could change. What happens to JoAnn's and Rick's shares?"

"There's a morals clause that means they revert back to the Board," Leigh said.

"Umm. Maybe that's what they thought would happen if Stephanie and Paul were out of the way."

"I think everyone assumed Helene would have a larger share of the pie," Sarito said. "They felt since she was the one with the plan and the research they would be in safe hands."

"Humph. Her plan."

"I know, Mark. Leigh told me everything."

Mark looked over at Leigh and raised an eyebrow, then turned back to Sarito. "You should have seen the research. Of course she didn't plan on something directly on Fifth. But she'd even scouted locations." Pride filled his voice. She'd been like a daughter to him.

"Why didn't you fight them?"

"Oh I thought about it for about an hour. It was a no win

situation. If Stephanie had said they gave Leigh their plans to help her in school, who would the public believe? Sister against sister would not have been a pretty sight. Of course I really wanted to go after Helene. I'm sure she was the one who gave them the research. But God don't like ugly. Leigh got what she deserved. I'm going to help her keep it."

Leigh felt as if nothing she did could keep her out of the way of the paparazzi. Every time she thought her life was in control, something else happened to spread her name all over the front page. She wondered how Mark and Sarito could be so sure she'd made the right choice when she decided to take on the salon.

Sarito and Leigh were at her condo waiting for the news. All day long there had been sound-bites previewing JoAnn's and Rick's lawyers. They had decided not to fight as a team but for each to have a lawyer. The men representing them were already dropping hints of a plea bargain. So far they had admitted they wanted some papers from Paul and they hired the burglar. But both denied they knew he would take a gun or that he had a history of violence.

"They were wrong in seeking to obtain these documents by force," the lawyer said. "But neither my client, Ms. Desmond, nor Mr. Adams are guilty of murder."

"Can you believe that?" Leigh grabbed the remote and switched off the television. "Are they going to get away with it?"

"I don't know. But they've started the ball rolling."

"I'm going to call a press conference. I'm going to . . ."

"Leigh." Sarito caught her hand and took the remote away. She hadn't realized how tightly she was holding it. "I know this is a painful time but you can't let your emotions rule your life."

He stroked her arm then embraced her. "We haven't even heard from the District Attorney. By tomorrow they may be singing a different tune."

"It just gets to me. They're just as responsible for Stephanie's death as if they'd pulled the trigger."

"Absolutely."

Leigh curled her body into Sarito's. He took her hand and led her into the bedroom. Why did even speaking of death make people want to find a way to reaffirm life?

He placed her on the bed and began unbuttoning his shirt. He deftly pulled out the cufflinks and dropped them on Leigh's vanity table. The tiny clink of metal against glass spurred her into action. She'd taken off her suit jacket earlier and now began to unbutton her blouse. Sarito made a small noise as she slipped it from her shoulders, revealing a lacy white bra. He'd had a head start on her but she caught up quickly. Soon they were naked and in each other's arms.

Her dark skin against the pale-blue of the sheets forced another groan from Sarito as he covered her face with kisses.

"I knew we were meant to end up this way," he said, "the first time I saw you."

"The first time you saw me, you were just trying to figure out a way to seduce me."

"I know, but a man can't force himself to make love unless there's some feeling for the other person already there."

Leigh shivered as Sarito's lips found the sensitive place behind her ear. The raw sensual power that permeated the room made Leigh confess, "I love you."

"I'm glad. For a while I thought that I was the only one in love in this relationship."

She lifted her face and inhaled his intoxicating male scent. He was her man. They had come from a pretense of a relationship to the honest emotion of love. "I'm not an easy man to live with, and I don't expect our lives will be overly sweet."

"Absolutely not. But that's why we want to be together. We know that no day will be like the previous one."

"It's not why we want to be together. It's why we need to be together."

"Your mother warned me."

"About?"

"About men who were accustomed to being the center of attraction. That they needed to be taken down a peg or two."

"Don't take everything my mother says to heart. She hasn't always been right."

Passion and independence battled, and passion won. His tongue lightly grazed her nipples and she arched her back absorbing all the pleasure she could. She knew that he was past the point of no return as he shifted his frame and let her feel the pounding of his heart.

Sarito knew they had gone beyond the pretense to something more solid than anything he could ever have imagined. He heard her passionate whisper and wondered if she'd read his mind. He wanted to take everything she was willing to give.

"Mi vida," he breathed as he lay beside her. My life. Never before had a woman caused him to feel love so deeply. He'd walked away from other women as if what they'd shared had been no more than a cup of coffee. Women had done the same with him. They'd wanted Sarito Valerian—the image, not the man—and he'd allowed them to have him. Not once had a woman tapped into the soul of Caesar Montgomery, until now.

"You make me crazy," Sarito whispered later. "I think about you all the time. I could hardly concentrate on what Carver was saying. My mind kept flashing pictures of last night."

"Before or after you threatened your mother's date?" Leigh giggled as she remembered how angry he'd been.

"Oh, most definitely about after. Now that you brought up my mother's extremely poor taste in men, what do you think I should do?"

Leigh stroked his chest absently. "Nothing. Your mother knows exactly what she's doing and so do I."

"And what's that?"

"Looking for a man who isn't afraid of her."

"There aren't any."

"I think Jameson will be very much her equal."

"Well, I don't want to think about my mother and Jameson anymore."

"What do you want to think about?"

"Nothing. I don't want to think. I want to act."

He set the pace as if they had all the time in the world. At this moment he was sure of himself, sure of his wife, and especially sure of their love.

THIRTY-SEVEN

Late that night, Caesar and Leigh made some popcorn, slipped in a video tape of a newly released movie that they both had missed, and curled up on the sofa.

When the movie ended, Leigh felt a little sleepy and opted out of watching the horror movie Caesar had purchased. By the time she took her shower and climbed into bed she wasn't as sleepy as she originally thought.

She pulled out Stephanie's diary. It was two years old and she couldn't imagine why Aunt Helene had given it to her. She thumbed through the pages until the passage about the Grammy awards caught her eye. As Stephanie described the gown she'd selected—a gray and turquoise beaded top with an ankle length straight skirt—she described finding it "with Sarito's help." She wrote about the way people stared at her during the event and how many news columns and TV commentators talked about her sexy look—especially about her hair styled by Sarito Valerian. She wrote that she wanted to go on more shopping expeditions with him. How he really knew what a woman wanted and needed. A twinge of jealousy ran through Leigh—her husband and her sister shopping together seemed like such an intimate action. Was it one of the reasons Stephanie had thought about divorce? Leigh was sorry she'd been so determined not to read any articles about Stephanie and Paul after they'd stopped speaking. She'd closed herself off from anything that happened to them. Helene had hinted that Paul was a philanderer. The next page was a complete blur. Someone had spilled coffee or tea on the diary and the page was illegible. It seemed to be a continuation of her shopping spree. There was something about more shopping, lunch and then going to a hotel.

An icy shiver shot up her spine as the next paragraph described in explicit details an afternoon of lovemaking. Stephanie wrote about the way his fingers traveled over her body. The way the callused fingers thrilled and excited her.

Leigh closed her eyes. Helene knew about this and wanted Leigh to know—by letting Leigh read in her sister's own writing of her relationship with Sarito Valerian.

He'd told her that he had lived a full life and made no excuses about it. He'd said that as long as the stories were before he met Leigh, they should be ignored. But how can you ignore your sister's lover?

Leigh wrapped herself in a robe. She suddenly felt cold. She padded to the living-room, planning to confront Caesar.

Caesar was deep into the picture and didn't realize Leigh was there until she spoke. The angry look on her face puzzled him.

"What's wrong?"

She didn't say anything. She just handed him the book, leaving it open to the pages she wanted him to read. He took the book and perused the pages for a few minutes. His brows knitted together as he started to give the book back to her. She wouldn't take it.

"Leigh, sometimes women include fantasies in their diaries."

"Are you saying none of this is true?"

"I'm saying that not all of it is true. I did take her shopping for a dress. It was time she changed her image. I styled her hair for her. I took her shopping a few more times, but I didn't have an affair with her."

"What was different? Is that how you treat all the women in your life?"

"I can't explain her diary. I did not have an affair with your sister."

Leigh wanted to believe him and yet everything they'd done was chronicled in her sister's diary.

"It comes down to you accepting my explanation over believing your sister's diary. I'm not going to call a dead woman a liar. I'm just going to say that I never slept with your sister."

Caesar knew that a war was going on inside her brain. He didn't think it would help to tell her that JoAnn was the one who suggested the shopping spree and staying in a hotel rather than either of their houses. He'd taken it as advice from a friend, now he wondered if he'd just fallen into her little trap. None of the Board had made it a secret that they didn't believe in 'love at first sight' or any of the 'whirlwind romance' that the papers said happened to Leigh and himself.

"I think I'll stay at the St. Regis. Call me when you're ready to go to the salon and I'll pick you up."

"I'm perfectly capable of getting to the salon by myself."

"Let's try to keep up the appearance that we're still a happy couple until the takeover business is out of the way."

"You're right. And then?"

"And then, who knows? We get a divorce and I go back to owning ten percent of Cassiopeia. I think I've earned it."

Leigh gasped.

Too hurt to say any more, Leigh watched as Caesar went into the bedroom and a few minutes later returned with just a garment bag and his shaving gear.

"Let's not take this any further tonight. Call me in the morning. I can't explain what she wrote or why she did it."

Leigh nodded and he left.

That was not what she wanted. She'd wanted him to somehow explain away the diary's words, but he couldn't. How could part of them be true and the other part a fantasy? She'd stopped keeping a diary, or a journal, as her friends liked to called theirs, when she was seventeen. She only remembered that she'd never written anything that was a fantasy. There were wishes and dreams of a young girl. But never creative writing of an incident that never happened. If she couldn't do that as a young woman, how could her sister who was past thirty do that? If everything else was true, why would the hotel tryst be the only lie?

Leigh went to bed confused about her circumstances. Could she really be in love with someone from her sister's past?

At the St. Regis, Caesar picked up his key at the desk. His suite no longer held the welcome he once felt when he came home. Thanks to that diary. He couldn't understand it. Why would Stephanie tell half a truth?

The salon was doing brisk business the next morning when Leigh and Caesar arrived. Angela was coming back from getting her morning coffee at the same time.

"You won't believe this. Vogue has asked me to do a spread for them."

"A spread?" Leigh asked.

They were through the revolving doors and on the way to the corporate offices. "I know it's because of all the publicity we've been getting, but it's going to be called Models in Business,' and I'm representing the models who stayed in a section of the beauty business."

"Sounds great," Caesar told her. "Congratulations."

Angela was so bubbly about getting back in front of the camera she didn't notice how little Leigh and Caesar said to each other.

When they parted to go to their separate offices, Caesar placed a perfunctory kiss on Leigh's forehead. "See you later."

No sooner than she'd removed her coat, Helene appeared. She wore a navy pinstriped suit and a navy cloche hat. "I thought we'd have a little chat, the way Stephanie and I used to do."

"Chat?"

"Yes. We'd meet for breakfast in her office and just talk for a few minutes. Unless you and Caesar have already eaten."

"No, we haven't. Okay, I'll order breakfast."

Leigh rummaged through her desk drawer and found a menu from a deli a few blocks away. She scanned it quickly and handed it to Helene. She made her selection then crossed to the table for two by the window. As Leigh was about to pick up the phone, she called, "Are you going to see if Sarito wants something?"

"Of course." Pressing the receiver button down she dialed the interoffice connection to Caesar's office. He answered gruffly.

"Darling, Helene and I are going to order breakfast, do you want anything?"

"I had breakfast at the hotel," he began. "Order me a coffee and blueberry danish. I'll come over to make a happy couple picture for the old witch."

Despite her feelings about her relationship, Caesar's remark brought a smile to her face—one she couldn't hide from her aunt.

"Does he mind that I'm here?"

"No, Aunt Helene, he doesn't mind."

Twenty minutes later, they were gathered in Leigh's office, she at her desk and Helene and Caesar at the table.

"I have a confession to make, "Helene said. "I really didn't think you two could run things together."

"We still have our differences," Leigh said.

"But nothing we can't work out if we're both willing," Caesar added.

"Then you haven't opened my little gift?"

"No" Leigh exclaimed. "I'm sorry, I left it in Connecticut."

"I see."

"Don't feel bad, Aunt Helene. I promise the next time we're there I'll read it."

"Well maybe you shouldn't. I was feeling a little annoyed that you hadn't taken any of my advice. Forget it. I'll buy something else."

After Helene left, Caesar turned to Leigh. "Why did you lie?"

"My aunt knows that if I'd read it . . ."

"You would have reacted just as you did. That we wouldn't have a marriage."

"Exactly."

"How can I convince you that nothing happened between me and your sister?"

"I don't want to think about it right now." Leigh got up and walked to the window.

"Fine. Believe whatever but let's keep the sham going until we've got the salon back where it belongs."

"That's all I've ever wanted." As she spoke the words she realized the implication and turned to Caesar. "I didn't mean it . . ."

"Yes, you did mean it, and I hope you can live with whatever happens." He left quietly.

As he walked back to his office, Angela intercepted him. "I just got off the phone with Vogue. I told them that you had to do my hair."

"Angela, I don't. . . ."

"Please, please, please," she begged. "I need you. Make me glamorous."

"I'll think about it." He continued down the hall.

"You'll do more than think about it," Angela said aloud, "We were good together once. We could be again."

She took the stairs down to the salon level in search of Rick. "I heard them having a little spat," she told him.

"Over what?"

"I don't know. I didn't hear the words as much as the raised voices. All is not well in that little household. If we keep them distracted enough our plan will work."

"I don't trust Jameson Miller."

"We don't have to trust him. We just have to deliver Cassiopeia to him and walk away with the money."

THIRTY-EIGHT

Leigh sat in her office planning new strategies for the salon. In some ways she was hurt that Caesar would not be part of it. They hadn't said the word but the only way out was a divorce. She knew that added publicity would bring more spectators, but that would soon go away. She wanted people to come to the salon because the stylists did a good job, not because they wanted to gawk. The salon needed to regain its credibility. Leigh was determined to find a way out of this quagmire of notoriety.

Caesar had agreed she was the one to do the restructuring. As per the agreement, the shares that Rick and JoAnn owned were transferred to Paul and therefore to Leigh. She no longer needed Caesar's ten percent. He hadn't said a word when Helene had shouted at her. He seemed at peace with the fact that he would never own or control Cassiopeia. They had called an emergency meeting of the Board and worked out a statement. Since the money could not be traced to anyone but Paul, Leigh suggested giving it to charity.

Rick and JoAnn were beginning to crack, each accusing the other of being the mastermind. The one item they both clung to was that they only wanted to destroy the will. No one was supposed to die.

Leigh wanted the Board to stand as a united front as she made the announcement. It was not going to be easy to do this. Most of them had not been given enough time to put on business attire. Caesar still had on his black jeans and black bulky sweater. She looked at him affectionately and vowed to get him away from black. His old clothes had too much color but every now and then she wished he knew another color besides black. His coloring suggested burgundies, blues, anything would be a triumph. Then she remembered they were not going to be a couple much longer. She had to stop thinking of them as a couple.

The members filed in one by one. Jimmy Gilbert was wearing one of his favorite cowboy hats. It resembled the one that country singer Garth Brooks wore, big and black and slightly asymmetrical on his head. Bob, Dean, Kevin, and Angela followed quickly on his heels.

Only Helene arrived wearing something corporate for the meeting. Her brown dress with its gold buttons and her dark brown pumps gave her an air of elegance compared to the others.

Leigh didn't care, but she noticed Angela fidgeting with her denim dress as she checked out Helene's outfit.

Helene was content to sit at the other end of the table as she toyed with her gold hoop earrings.

"I hope this won't take long," Angela said. "I've had a couple of offers to be interviewed on talk-shows. I have to decide which ones to do. And I have to go home and decide what to wear." She turned to Kevin.

"What do you think I should wear? Something dark with severe lines that makes me look businesslike? Or maybe something wild that gets me attention."

"How about something like duct tape over your mouth to keep you from telling everything you know," came Dean Roman's answer.

"I'm not the one who leaked that stuff about hidden funds to the press. You can't say that to me."

"Ladies and gentlemen," Leigh said. "I think it's time to put our personal differences aside and do what's best for the salon."

"And what's that dear?" Helene asked.

"Give the money to charity."

Gayla was taking notes but even she had a look on her face that said Leigh's suggestion was incredulous. "I've decided that we should take the money Rick and JoAnn put in our California account and give it to charity."

There were gasps and everyone started trying to talk at once before Kevin managed to wrest the floor from the others.

"Four million dollars is a lot of money for charity," Kevin had said.

"It's money that was gotten illegally," Sarito added.

"But no one knows that," Bob threw in. "They can't prove it was illegal, just that it wasn't declared on our tax forms."

Leigh shook her head. "Let's not start any creative bookkeeping. That can only get us in more trouble. You forget I worked for a lawyer and I know what can happen if you do."

"Come on," Kevin coached. "There must be some way for us to get a little money for ourselves. I've had my eye on a neat little cabin cruiser."

"Yeah, but if we use it, people will think the whole Board was in cahoots with the other four," Jimmy Gilbert drawled.

"I understand that," Bob said. "But how's it gonna look if we give away all this money and the salon folds?"

"If the police don't know where it came from, why should we give it away?" Helene shouted. "People know that Rick and JoAnn were the crooks. Why can't we use the money to keep Cassiopeia running?"

For the next hour they haggled, Bob, Angela, and Dean jumping from one side to the other. Finally Caesar had had enough.

"Look, all of you. Leigh and I want this to be unanimous," he told them. "But it doesn't have to be that way."

"Sarito, you can't expect us to feel good about giving money away when we could use it," Angela said. "It isn't natural."

"No," Leigh agreed. "It isn't, but if we don't, I'm sure that a lot of people out there are wondering what kind of people we are. JoAnn and Rick are in jail for goodness sake. Do you want people thinking the rest of us should be there also?"

The somber faces around the table told the story. They didn't like it but they would agree. Looking like a criminal could be as detrimental to the business as being a criminal.

After the meeting they all went their separate ways to prepare for the announcement. Leigh and Caesar were alone in the boardroom.

"Think they understand why I have to do this?"

Caesar took a deep breath before answering. "We all understand. We just don't know if we're still going to have the salon when our creditors come calling."

"I can't use that money."

He walked over and stood behind her chair. "I know, but it's still a risk." He kissed the top of her head. "I've got a few errands to take care of. I'll see you later."

"I've got to go over to Stacey's. She and your mother are planning a reception for us."

"Are you going to tell them the truth?"

"I can't let them think that . . ."

"Can't you talk to them? Explain this is for the best."

"That's why I'm going over there. But I don't think I'm going to succeed. Call me at Stacey's in about an hour."

After he left the room, Leigh read over the speech Mark had recommended. Then she went down the hall to her office. As she put the speech away, a flash from the past jolted her. She remembered playing with Stephanie. They were running around their grandfather's den. They loved the big oak table he called a desk. Stephanie had hidden under the desk and Leigh was trying to find her. As Leigh leaned on the desk she pulled out a drawer for leverage and it had come out of the desk completely. They had marveled at the hidden compartment. Stephanie had found a paper. She wouldn't let Leigh see it, but the look on her face said it was important. A month later Aunt Helene had arrived and announced she was taking Stephanie with her. She told Leigh she was too young to travel. Being five to Stephanie's fifteen, Leigh understood but hated to see her sister leave.

* * *

Caesar had hailed a cab immediately upon leaving the salon and was quietly letting himself into the brownstone. Leigh had avoided the house and he understood why. Even he felt as if he were an unwelcome guest. But there were answers here that Leigh would need one day. If he could give them to her then something good would come from their brief married life. He didn't know how he could stay on the Board and see her and wonder if they could have made it. How could he call her deceased sister a liar, though?

He started searching the room Paul used as an office—the one where the will was filmed. There was more to the story about skimmed money. Rick and JoAnn had admitted to hiring the burglar, but claimed he was only after the papers that would tell them where the safe deposit box was located. They had to know where the money was hidden because they were afraid Stephanie or Paul would take the money and run. Especially when it looked as if they were breaking up.

Although she was supposed to be away for several days, when they learned that Stephanie was in the house with Paul everyone had assumed it meant they were reconciled. He, along with the others, believed that if Stephanie and Paul had gotten back together, the salons were fine. They'd had other blowups. There had been other times when they'd seemed on the verge of ending it and the next week they were acting like honeymooners.

By the time he'd gone through the office, he was frustrated because he was still in the dark. He went into the media room. As he scanned the huge array of videos he noticed there was a pattern as to how the videos were placed. He climbed on the footstool next to the shelves and ran his hand along the top shelf until he found a tape dated Halloween 1996. That would have been the first party thrown for the Board—before he became a member. Before anyone else was invited to the soirees. He pulled it down and popped it into the VCR.

It was obviously a home video. The camera shot and missed some faces as it panned the room. Then the only members had been Stephanie, Paul, Jimmy, JoAnn, Rick, and Helene. They'd called themselves the sensational six. Helene had been the one urging them to find something that set them apart. They'd had several business ventures fail but when they decided on the salon they were right on target—a fancy salon on Fifth Avenue. While the clientele had been the spectrum of the rainbow, the fact that blacks owned it made more people of color come there. They loved the fact that it wasn't just for hair and nails. It was designed to make people feel pampered and that's what set them apart from other places that seemed to intimidate average people.

He watched them cavort in silly costumes. Stephanie and Paul were vampires, JoAnn was a harem girl and probably had on a lot less than anyone who lived in a harem. They were telling why they selected their outfits.

Suddenly the screen filled with someone dressed in white face, a white outfit trimmed in black. "I chose a harlequin, to show off my figure," Helene said. "I chose the gun to show I'm dead serious."

Caesar leaned forward. Harlequin. Clown. Hadn't Stephanie said she'd been shot by a clown?

The night after the murders Gayla had complained about having to do Helene's hair that morning. She said that somehow Helene had forgotten to put on a shower cap and destroyed the style. Helene had said she was so upset about the deaths. But what if she hadn't gotten wet in the shower? What if she'd gotten wet escaping from the brownstone after she'd murdered Paul and Stephanie? Greed. She'd wanted the salon so badly she'd killed her own niece. He knew that Leigh was in trouble. Helene wanted to use that money for renovation. She might feel that with Leigh out of the way she could do just that.

Caesar's hands felt cold and clammy as he pulled out his cell phone and his address book. He found Stacey's number and dialed.

"Hello, Stacey, it's Caesar."

"And just where are you and my best friend? Forgot all about us," she said, then called to Juliette. "They forgot about us."

"Stacey, isn't Leigh there yet?"

"No. I just assumed you were coming over together."

He didn't want to alarm them. "I think we got our signals

crossed. I'm at the brownstone. She was supposed to meet me here." He didn't mention she was meeting him after she'd gone to Stacey's.

"Well the two of you better get it together. Or you'll just have to take what Juliette and I decide to give you."

He said good-bye and hoped he'd kept the alarm out of his voice. Then he dialed the salon. The phone just rang.

Leigh went into her office and began pulling drawers out of the desk. Nothing. She wasn't afraid of being alone in the salon. It was protected by more than one alarm system. Besides, with the rumors of having to file bankruptcy after JoAnn and Rick were arrested, who would even try to break in?

Something had been bouncing around in her brain. Something in the diary. She just couldn't remember what it was.

A flash of memory: Caesar's smooth fingers caressing her scalp the night he washed her hair. "My God!" she said aloud. That was it! Caesar's fingers were smooth. The diary talked about callouses on the man's fingertips. Guitarists developed callouses as they plucked the strings. A gentle man who uses his hands to make a living was what the diary said. Rick. Stephanie and Rick were having an affair, not Stephanie and Caesar.

She couldn't wait to tell him. It was probably too late she thought. He'd asked for trust but she'd waited for evidence. She'd make him believe her. She'd find a way so they could have another chance.

Another flash of memory—this time about her childhood and her grandfather's desk again. She pulled the chair back and got down on her hands and knees as she surveyed the underside of the desk. She stood up and pulled the middle drawer all the way out, then she tapped on the thin wooden sheet the drawer sat on. It sounded hollow. Using a letter opener, she lifted the piece of wood and saw a very flat oblong box. She pulled it out and began to go through it. The first was a yellowed strip of newspaper. The heading read: "Actor killed in freak accident." Leigh read the rest of it. It seemed that in Los Angeles an acclaimed black actor named Jeremy Broadman was driving home from the studio and had been killed when an earth tremor had caused him to spin into a telephone pole. The pole shattered and the debris fell on him. He died the next day of head injuries. He was survived by his wife Lucinda and son Jeremy, Jr.

That seemed strange. Why would Stephanie hide it or even have it? The next item she picked from the box was another yellowed piece of paper, and as she opened it she found the answer to her question. It was a birth certificate. Stephanie's birth certificate—Stephanie Barrington. Father: Jeremy Broadman. Mother: Helene Barrington. Somewhere in the distance, she heard the phone ring but she couldn't move. Let her voicemail take it. Parts of her life were scattered over the floor like a jigsaw puzzle and she had to put it back together before she could talk to anyone.

Sarito tried a few other numbers at the salon, including his. Everyone must have left. He tried Leigh's condo, cell phone, and beeper. Where the hell was she? Could he find her before . . . he didn't even know why he was afraid. Something told him that he had to find Leigh and warn her about Helene.

For Leigh the pieces of her life fell into place. No wonder Stephanie had gone with Helene. She knew. That day they were playing around their grandfather's desk, that's when she found out who she was. That's why Helene was always saying you can't trust men. She'd been betrayed and had never recovered.

Stephanie was not her sister. She was her cousin.

THIRTY-NINE

Leigh folded the crumbling piece of paper and put it back in the shoe box. All these years. She'd asked her grandmother why Aunt Helene chose Stephanie to raise and not her. Leigh thought it was because Stephanie was tiny and truly beautiful. Grandma had just said it was because Stephanie was older.

Now she knew the truth. When Leigh's parents died, Helene could finally claim her daughter. While Stephanie was beautiful, she didn't have the cunning of Helene nor the intelligence of Leigh. That's why she was such a follower.

What had Valerian's mother said: "I knew the value of my beauty." As cold as that may have sounded, she was right. Everyone has something of value, but most don't know how to cultivate it.

Leigh picked up the phone to dial Caesar. Just as he answered Leigh heard a noise and turned around.

"Don't do that."

Leigh found herself face to face with her aunt, who was holding a gun. She dropped the phone down but not quite in the cradle.

Blocks away, Caesar heard the click and then faint voices. Then more clearly he heard Leigh say: "Are you going to kill me the way you did Stephanie and Paul?"

Fear caused him to break out in a cold sweat. Leigh was alone with a murderer. But where? She was supposed to meet him at the brownstone but she hadn't arrived. Now he knew why. He just didn't know where or who. He could only listen and pray. The constant static on his cell phone reminded him that he hadn't charged it.

"Aunt Helene, why didn't you tell me?"

"Your parents stole her from me. They said I was too young, that I was too much of a Gypsy. I wouldn't know how to raise a child."

Helene! My God, he thought, Stephanie was Helene's daughter. Caesar held his cell phone between his ear and shoulder while he picked up the phone in the media room of the brownstone. He dialed the precinct and asked for Detective Carver. It would be useless to dial 911 when he couldn't tell them where Helene and Leigh were.

Detective Carver picked up and Caesar quickly filled him in. "Try to get a location," Carver told him. "I'm going to send a car for you."

Leigh, please tell me where you are before the phone goes dead, Caesar silently pleaded.

"You don't deserve this office," Helene was saying. "My daughter had decorated it so well."

Cassiopeia! They were at Cassiopeia. Caesar relayed the news to Detective Carver then hung up. He didn't have time to wait for the police car to pick him up. Instead he ran from the brownstone and hailed a cab. A few minutes became an eternity. As the cab drove he couldn't help noticing the sea of red lights in front of them. Why were the streets so crowded when he needed them to be empty?

"I've got to get away from here," Helene said. She waved the gun around as she indicated she meant the salon.

"It's over. You can't kill me the way you did Stephanie and Paul."

"I don't have to kill you. I can make it look as if you took off with the money. And I didn't mean to kill Stephanie. She wasn't supposed to be there. You women. You just let men run your lives."

"Caesar isn't going to believe that. Neither is Mark."

"You're just like Stephanie, depending on men. I told you before—they only let you down. Like Stephanie's father. He was going to be the next Sidney Poitier. I worked while he studied acting. Then as soon as he got that role in the TV series he forgot about me."

"Just because you made a mistake with Jeremy Broadman, don't think all men are bad."

"Aren't you the clever little one? I told Stephanie when she was fifteen that men were to be used and thrown away. That we had to do to them before they could do anything to us. But she loved Paul and she just had to come back early. She wasn't supposed to be there."

Leigh walked around in front of the desk. She would simply have to stall and pray that Caesar could hear her. Something in her demeanor must have alerted Helene. She waved the gun at Leigh motioning for her to back up. Then she came over to the desk and saw the phone. She spotted the phone slightly askew and pushed it into the cradle, severing the connection.

The steady dial tone shocked Caesar. If Helene had found it, would she turn the gun on Leigh? This can't happen, he thought. We just got our lives together. I can't lose her now. They had so many plans. The cab made a sudden turn off Fifth Avenue.

"Hey! What's going on?"

"Calm down. I just think we'd make better time if I took another street downtown."

"Okay, sorry." Caesar found himself staring at another group of red taillights but the driver was right—there were fewer than on the other street. It was only a few more blocks.

The brisk January night forced Leigh to pull her coat tightly around her neck as they walked out of the salon. New York streets seemed never to be empty and tonight was no exception.

A scattering of people walked along Fifth Avenue. None were close enough for her to even try to signal for help. But she had to do something. Leigh knew she wasn't going to get into a taxi with Helene. She would pretend to twist her ankle or stumble. Somehow she would get space between them and Helene wouldn't shoot her. It wouldn't serve any purpose. Helene wanted Cassiopeia and killing Leigh in full view of people wouldn't achieve that goal. That was one thing Leigh considered in her favor. However, she still felt at this point Helene might be completely over the edge, and innocent people on the street could get hurt. Leigh ran through several scenarios and still came back to her first thought. Put distance between them any way that she could. She surveyed the street and saw several yellow cabs waiting for the green light at 57th Street.

"Call a taxi," Helene hissed.

"We have to get closer to the curb." Leigh moved and her height made her stride longer than Helene's. It caused the older woman to stumble and she squeezed Leigh's arm tighter to keep up.

"Watch it."

"Sorry, Helene. I think the light is, about to change. We'll have more of a chance if we're by the curb."

As Helene lifted her head toward 57th Street, Leigh took two long strides that threw Helene completely off balance. She caught the heel of her shoe in the webbed mat she'd insisted on having in front of the store—the one Stephanie had selected. The one Leigh warned her about. As Helene fell, she instinctively pulled her arm from Leigh's and put her hands out in front of her.

Leigh took advantage of the situation, bent down, pulled the gun from Helene's hand, and slipped it into her coat pocket. People rushed over to help the fallen woman.

"Don't move her," Leigh shouted. "We need an ambulance."

"No, I don't." Helene gasped as she struggled to get up.

"Ma'am," said a man kneeling at her side. "Don't move. You don't know how badly you might be hurt. And I suggest you see your lawyer on this." He pressed his hand on her back and she sank to the ground.

Leigh heard a woman say, "I don't know why a classy store on Fifth Avenue would have a mat like that."

A hysterical bubble of laughter welled inside Leigh. She fought it down. The people standing around wouldn't understand a woman laughing at her aunt. Helene had been caught by the one item she insisted on keeping because of Stephanie. It was as if from the grave, Stephanie denied her mother twice—first when she wrote the will and now the webbed welcome mat.

Leigh didn't look up as she heard the sirens. She assumed someone had called 911 for assistance. It wasn't until Caesar roughly pulled her into his arms that Leigh realized he was there.

"Oh God, I was so scared," he told her. "I was listening to your voice and afraid the next thing I heard would be a gunshot."

"Why were you at the brownstone?"

"Something clicked when JoAnn mentioned the previous salon. The one that failed. We'll talk about it later."

He pulled Leigh to the side of the building and poured quick kisses all over her face. He'd come so close to losing Leigh that he couldn't let her go for several long minutes. As they watched the police help Helene to her feet and Detective Carver escorted her to the patrol car, the people were a little puzzled. Murmurs from the gathering crowd had people wondering why she was getting into a police car and not an ambulance.

After securing Helene in the patrol car, the detective came over to Caesar and Leigh.

"I'm sure there's quite a story to go along with all this and I'd be interested in hearing it."

Leigh reached in her pocket and pulled out the gun. "it's Helene's. I think it's the one she used to kill Stephanie and Paul."

"Now I know I want to hear this story. When can we meet?"

"I want to take her home now, but I'll call you in the morning and tell you when we can come in."

"Good enough."

Caesar led Leigh to the cab, who had been waiting patiently

for payment. They got in and Caesar noticed that the cabby hadn't turned off the meter while he waited. It didn't matter. He gave Leigh's address and they were off.

"I know you're upset," Leigh began. "I know you told me to meet you at the brownstone."

"So why didn't you?" His words were harsh but he still had his arms wrapped around her.

"I remembered something. I remembered Stephanie and I used to love to play under my granddad's desk. It had a secret drawer. I just figured she would have the same thing in a desk she designed."

"But instead of telling me or the police you just decided to investigate yourself."

"I didn't know what I would find. Suppose it was nothing. Then you and the police would have just laughed."

"Okay. Maybe you're right. But don't ever do anything like that again."

Ten minutes later they were walking through the front door of Leigh's condo. She realized that Caesar had not let go of her hand since he'd pushed his way through the crowd and found her by Helene's side. She knew he was angry. She knew it was because he was afraid. And if he was afraid, he loved her. She waited for the eruption. It happened after they'd changed into some casual clothes and he'd poured her a brandy. As she took the glass from his hand, he exploded.

"What were you thinking of?"

Leigh took a sip of brandy and let him rave a few more minutes. Before she smiled up at him and asked, "Are you going to give me a chance to answer or are you just going to hurl questions all night long?"

"Leigh, do you realize what you almost got into? The woman killed two people."

She stood up, walked over to him, and put her arms around him. "I wasn't afraid of her. The minute I dialed that number and you answered I knew you wouldn't let anything happen to me. Deep in my heart I knew it."

He kissed her first gently, then more urgently. "Don't ever do that again." He picked her up and carried her to the bedroom. He laid her down and started tearing off his clothes. She sat up and pulled off her robe and dropped it on the floor. He sat on the bed and removed his shoes then the rest of his clothes. He said nothing. He just wanted to be inside her. It was a way to confirm to himself that she was still his. Over and over again throughout the night he made love to her. By morning they slept.

He awakened first and showered and dressed. Leigh was surprised to find him in the kitchen preparing breakfast. He placed a cup of tea in front of her and two slices of toast.

Leigh told him what she'd learned about Stephanie being her cousin and not her sister.

"I heard that part. The static prevented me from hearing everything. I had to admit that I needed help. I couldn't take the chance that Helene would panic and shoot you."

"She didn't mean to kill Stephanie."

"I know."

Leigh talked about Helene's affair with the television star, a man who denied his child and married another.

"When Stephanie learned about her heritage, she hid all the information she could about the man. Aunt Helene must have been furious. Then she learned about the will."

"Yes. Why did Stephanie taunt her with the changes?"

"She didn't mean it as harassment. She wanted to make things right and Aunt Helene didn't want to have to explain how she got my business proposal."

Caesar explained the other part that Leigh didn't know, the project that failed and the money she used for charity was the money they expected to divide up one day. Rick, JoAnn, and Helene planned to do the same thing with Cassiopeia. Leigh's choice for the money was the better idea.

"We have a busy day," she told him. "We have to find a lawyer for Aunt Helene. And I want to start cleaning out the brownstone. I'm going to sell it."

"My, we've been busy thinking this morning."

"I'm serious. I've got to do it while I have the strength. I'm going to pack everything in boxes and label them today. Then I put the house on the market. I've had several real estate people calling me since I inherited the place."

"Helene won't want your help."

"I know, but I don't care."

He added soft scrambled eggs to her plate, then fixed a plate for himself and sat down across from her. "I guess I'd better help with this. In case you change your mind in the middle and I have to explain to the movers. That you really didn't mean it."

"That won't happen. Do you think I should sell this place also." She waved her hand around indicating the condo.

"Where will you live?"

"With you. Forever."

He looked in her eyes and knew she was telling the truth. She was putting the past in perspective and carving a future. She was doing it her way. Quickly.

"I think we should keep it. We'll need it when we're too tired to go to Connecticut. My brother is home and he sends his regards."

"I'm glad you two worked things out. I'd hate to think that our family could be divided by anger as well as by geography."

"He suggests I bring you home for the wedding."

"I'd love that."

Leigh decided not to tell him her plans for the salon until later, when they were finished with the more pressing issues.

Cassiopeia - she'd named the salon well. Everyone on the Board had defied the gods in some way. She guessed her punishment was in finding out that she'd wanted the impossible. She'd wanted Helene to have taken her along on the journey she chose for Stephanie. Perhaps then they'd have been a family. But Helene had chosen the path for all of them. Now it was time for Leigh to forget about the nights she spent wishing she was Stephanie. The life of a rock star's wife wasn't glamorous. It wasn't exciting. It wasn't happy.

FORTY

The brownstone was filled with boxes. Leigh had started packing the morning after Helene's arraignment, and still there was so much to do. Everything was being put away and labeled. One day she might have the inner strength to go through the boxes and learn more about her cousin. It was still hard for Leigh to think of Stephanie as her cousin. Why hadn't her grandmother told her? Why hadn't Helene or Stephanie?

All these years, she'd thought that Stephanie had been selected because she was beautiful. It must have bothered her all the time. Perhaps that was the real meaning of the will.

Leigh walked over to the China closet, opened it, and began wrapping the porcelain pieces in paper and putting them in a box. She'd refused to allow the company hired to pack up the house to touch the China closet. Stephanie and Helene had shared a passion for collecting these delicate pieces. Leigh wanted to exert extra care that these were packed and marked.

"Are you really sure you want to put the house on the market?"

Caesar's voice startled her for a moment and she almost dropped the crystal frog she'd been wrapping. She turned and found him leaning against the door jamb.

"I'm sure."

"Have you decided on a real estate agent?"

"Uh-huh. I'm going to give it to the firm I bought my condo from."

"They weren't among the bidders."

"I know, but I'd still rather give it to them."

Caesar crossed the room to Leigh and pulled her into his arms. The tight grip made her feel breathless and protected.

"You don't have to sell the house nor do you have to live in it. You could do something else with it."

"I couldn't. I've really thought about this. I have to let it go."

He knew when his wife had made up her mind, and he could understand her reasons. He just wanted her to know that he would be at her side no matter what she chose to do.

The police still wanted to question Leigh, but Caesar had stepped in and the police deferred. Late in the afternoon she sat down with Detective Carver. She had to absorb so much. All the secrets of the past had come out and the newspapers would have a field day. She felt she was back to the time Stephanie and Paul had been murdered and the police and newspapers were all over her. Would there ever be a time in her life that she would not cringe when she walked by a newsstand?

This time she wasn't alone. This time she had someone who loved her at her side. Mark had offered to help, but Caesar had explained this was something they had to do together.

She lay staring up at the ceiling, half sprawled across Caesar's body. Nothing had felt so right for them. She ran her fingers slowly down his chest to his waist and back again.

"I've decided to step down from the Board."

"You can't be serious, darling." Caesar shook his head. "Give this up?" Leigh stared into the fireplace as if she hadn't heard his question. She'd come full circle with him. The first day they met, she'd been waffling about running the salon or letting the Board do it. Now after three months she'd decided to walk away. As she let the idea flow through her mind, she suddenly felt a comfort she hadn't felt since the day she left the law firm.

They'd answered questions and found a lawyer for Helene. It would be up to the justice system to decide her fate. They knew the lawyer would try for a "diminished capacity" plea. All Helene's clawing her way to the top had ended with her daughter's death. Was breaking the glass ceiling worth it for a woman?

They'd hardly spoken on the drive back to Connecticut. Helene had refused to see Leigh. That wasn't unexpected. Still, Leigh wanted to make sure she was in good hands and Caesar had suggested the lawyer. Once home, they'd taken hot showers in separate bathrooms. Leigh had changed into a navy satin nightgown and climbed into bed. The white sheets were soft and inviting. She was about to doze when Caesar appeared, his hair still wet from the shower—now that he was letting it grow, it formed little ringlets. He wore only his pyjama bottoms. He was pushing the hostess cart loaded with pastries, steaming coffee, and hot tea that had been warmed in the microwave.

"Umm, that smells heavenly," Leigh said.

"I thought we could use a snack before we settle down for the night."

She knew what he was really saying. Neither of them had appetites after all they'd been through that day. The police had been as kind as possible under the circumstances.

He pulled the cart next to the bed on Leigh's side then walked around and got in next to her. He'd bought the house because of the fireplace in the bedroom. Now the flames brought warmth to the room the way Leigh brought warmth to his heart.

In so many ways, he was similar to Helene. He, too, had grown up wanting something of his own. He, too, was surrounded by wealth and not permitted to touch any of it. He'd found a way out. Helene hadn't. Now she would pay in the winter of her life for choices she'd made in the summer of that life. He could almost forgive her. He couldn't forget she'd stolen a young woman's dream. It was up to him to make it up to her. To give her as much power with the salon and let her enjoy the good times and ride through the bad.

"I'm going to resign from the Board," she repeated again as she lay against him.

"Why?" He was still waiting for an answer about her intentions of leaving the salon when she sat up and turned to face him.

"I'm very serious. I know now that I should have let the Board run things for a year. I picked the correct name: Cassiopeia. In a way I defied the gods because I thought I was so smart."

"You are smart. You're responsible for uncovering the truth."

"I know, but . . ."

"But it wasn't the truth you wanted. You were fine when the others were suspected of engineering Paul and Stephanie's deaths. Now you know it was your aunt. So you want to run because the truth left a bitter taste in your mouth?"

Leigh heard the sarcasm in his voice. "It's not only that. Sure I'd rather think that JoAnn and Rick were murderers. But, to hear Helene so . . . so desperate."

"She'd lived through her daughter. Actually she'd created a life for her. It was all Helene wanted. No one knew what Stephanie wanted. The guilt she lived with when they stole your idea. Yes, I feel sorry for her. But I'm not going to pretend I don't want her to get what's coming to her."

There was no bitterness in his voice. "No matter what life throws you there's no reason to resort to murder."

"I agree. I just can't get over the fact she never had any dreams of her own. She only had mine."

"Do you know why Stephanie would have you as her heir and not her mother?"

"I think so. Remember I told you we lived with my grand-mother?"

"Yeah?" He slipped his arm around her and pulled her across his chest.

"You know how grandmothers drag you to church and tell you about sinning and forgiveness?"

"Now I understand." He laughed as he remembered his own grandmother shaking her finger at him and warning him that the Lord knew everything he did. She told him often about Judgment Day. How he would be held accountable for his sins. "She wanted her last act on earth to be the right thing," he said. "Cassiopeia was your brainchild."

Leigh twisted to a more comfortable position but never left

Caesar's arms. She'd found happiness. She loved her husband. She could go back to handling sports superstars and would-be superstars.

"I don't need it anymore. I am perfectly content with being the wife of a board member."

"I don't believe that and I know someone who can help you with this."

"I don't need any help."

Keeping one arm around Leigh, Caesar reached for the phone and brought it to the bed next to him.

"Who are you calling?"

"Don't be so impatient." He dialed a number. Then he leaned down and kissed Leigh. What was meant to be light, teasing kisses became something more and he almost missed hearing the voice that answered.

"Hello . . . Hello," came a whispery voice.

"Hello, Mother," Caesar said. He twisted the phone so Leigh could hear.

Leigh poked him in his ribcage. But his arms were around her and she was forced to listen. She couldn't believe he'd called his mother.

"It's quite late so it must be important," Juliette said.

"Of course. Leigh is thinking of giving up the salon and letting me run it."

"Leigh, I'm sure you're listening."

"Yes, Juliette, I'm here."

"Do you really want to turn over all that power to my son? After all that's what he's always wanted."

"I know. I guess I was thinking out loud and he pounced on it."

"Remember what I told you. Know your value. The salon needs you more because you're different from the rest of the vultures. That includes you, Sarito."

"Thanks, Mother. I think Leigh's eyes are telling me she's changed her mind. Goodnight." He hung up the phone before Leigh could say good-bye.

"You have a lot of nerve, Caesar Sarito Valerian Montgomery."

"I know I'm in trouble when you suddenly remember all the names I've ever used."

"How could you sic your mother on me?"

"You wouldn't listen to me. I knew you'd listen to her."

"Well that could backfire. After all, your mother said you were a vulture."

"My mother exaggerated."

Leigh turned so her body was anchored against his. "Do I have the power to tame a vulture?"

He leaned down and kissed her. "You have the power to tame me. You've had it since the first time we met."

"I never told you this, but I thought you were a reporter."

"Wait a minute. You told me a lot about yourself."

"I told you everything I wanted you to know and report. I thought I'd give you the facts, and you'd print them. I wanted to look defenseless."

"Why would you want to look defenseless?"

"So if anyone tried to take the salon I'd rip his heart out."

"So how did you know it was Adams, that Stephanie had the affair with and not me? Women's intuition?"

"That and when she wrote about Rick she mentioned his hands."

"And?"

"She said she loved the way his roughened hands caressed her skin."

"And?"

"Stop saying 'and.' Your hands are not rough. They're smooth."

"I wanted Jameson Miller to be the bad guy. I still think he's capable of anything."

"You only say that because he's seeing your mother. In fact, he might have been there when you called. You might have interrupted something important."

"My mother would not have answered the phone if she'd been otherwise engaged. Not that I want to even entertain the idea of them being serious. I don't know what a woman of her age would see in him."

"Oh, come on. So he's a few years younger." She had seen the reaction between Jameson and Juliette. She even thought their names made them sound like a couple.

"A few . . . he's only a couple of years older than I am," Caesar shook his head. "Can you imagine him as my stepfather?"

"Get over it. Besides, that would be a good way to make him keep his hands off Cassiopeia."

Caesar laughed. He should be thanking the man. If he hadn't mentioned how easy it would be to sell 110% of a venture that failed and pocket the money, Caesar might not have remembered the book with the numbers that seemed slightly off. That had led him to the brownstone and Rick and JoAnn's little scheme that had failed.

"You're right," he said. "We should be busy planning the future."

"The future?"

Leigh found herself being pulled under the covers as Caesar's fingers traced her body, leaving behind spasms of pleasure. His kisses, light and teasing, were powerful enough to elicit deep sighs that she couldn't hold back. She'd fought the demons of deception. All the false glitter of the past had now been revealed and they could build a relationship of honesty for eternity.

About the author

Viveca Carlisle was born Marsha-Anne Tanksley in Detroit, Michigan. She grew up in New York City. Her love for reading is a gift from her mother, who started reading to her from the day they came home from the hospital. She is Vice-President of Romance Writers of America's NYC chapter. She belongs to Women Writers of Color. Currently she is a customer service supervisor with New York City Transit.

COMING IN FEBRUARY . . .

ONE OF A KIND, by Bette Ford   (1-58314-000-X, $4.99/$6.50)
Legal secretary Anthia Jenkins and Dexter Washington, director of a Detroit community center, were good friends. But Anthia wanted more than friendship. Once unjustly convicted of his wife's suicide, Dexter didn't want to love again. But he couldn't control the passion between them and now he needs to convince Anthia to believe in him and in love.

TRUE BLUE, by Robyn Amos   (1-58314-001-8, $4.99/$6.50)
When her sister announces they've won the lottery, Toni Rivers is off to the Florida coast and a new life. Blue Cooper is ready to sweep Toni off her feet when she walks into his nightclub. But the powerful feelings between them frighten Toni. She holds back more so when a dangerous past surfaces. Now he must find a way to prove that his love is true.

PICTURE PERFECT, by Shirley Harrison   (1-58314-002-6, $4.99/$6.50)
Davina Spenser found out that her father was actually the brilliant painter Maceo James, who had gone into hiding for a murder he didn't commit. She was determined to clear his name and take his paintings from Hardy Enterprises. But the handsome new CEO Justin Hardy was a tempting obstacle that could bring her delicious disaster or perfect love.

AND OUR VALENTINE'S DAY COLLECTION . . .

WINE AND ROSES   (1-58314-003-4, $4.99/$6.50)
by Carmen Green, Geri Guillaume, Kayla Perrin
February is for Valentine's Day, but it can also be a time of sweet surprises for those who aren't even looking for love. Delight in the joys of unexpected romance with reignited passion in Carmen Green's "Sweet Sensation," with the eternal gift of love in Geri Guillaume's "Cupid's Day Off" and renewed hope in Kayla Perrin's "A Perfect Fantasy."

Available wherever paperbacks are sold, or order direct from the Publisher. Send cover price plus 50¢ per copy for mailing and handling to Kensington Publishing Corp., Consumer Orders, or call (toll free) 888-345-BOOK, to place your order using Mastercard or Visa. Residents of New York and Tennessee must include sales tax. DO NOT SEND CASH.